Iris Before the Storm

S.L. Vaden

ISBN-13: 978-1-7336254-0-1

Contents

Chapter 1 6

Chapter 2 17

Chapter 3 24

Chapter 4 35

Chapter 5 47

Chapter 6 54

Chapter 7 63

Chapter 8 76

Chapter 9 101

Chapter 10 107

Chapter 11 136

Chapter 12 145

Chapter 13 163

Chapter 14 180

Chapter 15 213

Chapter 16 241

Chapter 17 253

Chapter 18 270

Chapter 19 298

Chapter 20 314

Chapter 21 336

Chapter 22 347

Chapter 23 357

Chapter 24 370

Chapter 25 379

Chapter 26 394

Chapter 27 406

Chapter 28 420

Chapter 29 431

Chapter 30 440

Indicators for change of scene and change of character

Iris

Garrett

Cole

Isabelle

Alvera

Scene Change

Chapter 1

Iris found herself walking down a dirt path that led to the middle of the town she would be calling home for a few weeks to a month. She hoped getting away from the hustle and bustles of city life would give her the rest her mind and body needed. Looking around at her scenery, she smiled at the lushness of it all. Iris had never seen such deep green before, and the air was so clean and clear. This mountain town was quite different than the valley below. It was almost a desert where cattle were farmed, which seemed to be the main revenue for this area.

Spinning around, her long black hair caught in the wind. Bags in hand, Iris started back down the path. Reaching the small township of Valden by mid-morning, she noticed a slight fog still had a hold on the sleepy community. Continuing toward the center of town, a few people were walking here and there, the wood buildings laid out in an X pattern. The main street was a mix of dirt and gravel. The one building not built of wood was the large red-brick building in the center of town, the courthouse. Alongside it was the jail and sheriff's office. The only person who knew she was here had only known her by a letter, and for now, it had to stay that way. The fewer people knew of her and her mission, the better.

It was to the bigger of the two brick-buildings that she made her way, kicking up loose dirt and gravel along the way. A lady across the street stared at her. She smiled and waved at the lady who startled at the notice and soon rushed off as if scared.

Iris knew the reason the lady had been staring at her. It wasn't the first time, nor would it be the last. The way she dressed always turned heads. Of course, she wore a dress, but it wasn't a normal one. It was cinched in the front, showing off a pair of pants the same color as the dress. She had gotten lectured on how women should conduct themselves ever since she was able to dress herself, so it didn't bother her anymore. She wore this attire because of functionality. It was quite difficult to run in a skirt. And for style, Iris liked how the dress part still showed off her femininity.

Iris turned the corner and had to sidestep to miss from running right smack into a very tall man. Without missing a step, she continued forward after excusing herself. He tipped his head in return. Iris looked back at the tall man's figure as he continued walking down the street. She smiled to herself as she reached the door to the courthouse, meaning to inquire about an apartment to rent.

The next day started without incident, boring. It was a long day of work, consisting of watching the pub and street from her window while not being seen by townsfolk and trying to not get muscle cramps. Afterward, she headed to the saloon to grab a warm meal like she had been doing since she arrived in town. Iris sat down in the back of the saloon near a small fire that was barely ablaze. Taking out her pencil and notebook, she tried to push herself into the shadows, not wanting to grab anyone's attention. The saloon was bustling, which reminded her that it must be Friday. Payday.

Iris hunkered down and watched her surroundings, occasionally writing down a note here and there. She ate the soup of the day and was about to get up and leave when a drunk man approached her table. He reached for her notebook, which laid open. Within a few seconds, he was flipping through the pages. She leaned back in her chair, staring at the back of the man's head, who had turned away from her. A sly grin came to her face.

The man turned around, red-faced and sweaty. "You're a witch…" he said shakily, his voice raspy. He then turned around to the people crowded into the confines of the building. And in a loud voice, he repeated, "She's a witch! Look! Look at this strange wording!"

He held the book up for all to see. Everyone now stopped talking and looked at the sweaty, fear-stricken man. People started to whisper, then a voice rang out among the crowd. "And look at how she dresses!"

Another one chimed in, "To lure men in to kill them!"

Iris sat, watching, listening, all the while trying not to grin as things unfolded. This wasn't her first rodeo and probably wouldn't be her last. Whispers became more frantic, but as she stood up, the room went silent. One thing Iris regretted above all else in that moment was wearing red. She laughed at herself as the man who held the book stared at her, his hand shaking. As she looked from his hands to his panicked expression, she smiled at him, making him take a step back. Iris held in another laugh.

"The weird wording is a language called Latin," she said calmly. "It's an old language that a lot of people don't know." She paused, taking in the people's faces who were all eyeing her. "People who study a lot in schools may know it. Well off families teach it to their children. I am neither of those. I learned it for the fun of it." She looked down and then back up at the man who still looked scared. "Is the school teacher in here tonight?"

Everyone waited a moment, scanning the room. An older man shakily stood up. He shook not from fear but from old age. "I'm afraid I don't know any Latin. Not to say that it's not a language, it surely is, but alas, I don't know it," he said wearily, looking down.

Silence once again fell across the mass of people. "Is a doctor present?" Iris asked, scaring the young man who still stood near her with the notebook in his hands.

The crowd again hushed. She scanned the room and spotted a figure with a large coat and hat near the door. He took off his hat and coat and put them on hangers near the entrance. The bag in hand told her he was a doctor, but had he heard her? As he stepped from the shadows, Iris got a good look at him. He was quite young for a doctor, about her age. His broad shoulders made him appear even taller than he already was, his black hair was cut short, and his tan skin made her grin deviously as her pulse quickened. Then his voice reached her, making her let out a sigh just at the sound of it.

"Yes, I know Latin. What of it?"

"This girl says she's reading Latin, but we're not certain. We're thinking she might be a witch," someone from the crowd said, a lanky man from the back.

Nodding his head in understanding, he made his way to the stairs and placed his bag on the last step, then he waved his hand for the man with the notebook to come forward. He looked at it, then at Iris, and, with a smirk, started flipping through the pages.

"This indeed is Latin."

He was about to hand the book back to the sweating man, but someone screamed, "What's it say?"

The doctor looked at Iris who nodded. With a shrug, he opened the book back up and studied a page. Clearing his throat, he read aloud, "I've come to a town with lush forests and gentle breezes, but will the calmness that lays within the land seep into the people who inhabit it? Will the land stay forever in peace, or will it scream out in pain as it does among the cities?" He eyed Iris then handed the notebook back to the man. Picking up his bag, he started up the stairs.

Iris and the doctor's eyes locked as he ascended the stairs. She took in his golden-brown eyes that seemed to pierce right through her. The veins outlining his muscles made her pulse quicken. The moment slowed and for an instant, it seemed to be only the two of them in the room. Iris had never felt such magnetism before. It wasn't just his sun-kissed skin, but his whole being pulled her toward him, as if he were a dream catcher and she the dream.

The man shoved the notebook back at her, abruptly bringing her out of her daze. Taking it, she grabbed her bag and started from the saloon. She was almost to the door when someone grabbed her wrist, forcing her to turn around to face them. It was a tall man with blonde hair.

"I know what you are. You won't fool me," he said, leaning in. His breath was rank with the smell of whiskey.

She glared at him, but her eyes drifted to the doctor on the second-floor landing. His eyes fixed on her and the man who held her wrist. The doctor's knuckles were almost pale from gripping the railing. And he was staring and almost looked angry, but at her? Iris was again brought back by the man's rank breath.

"I won't let you kill us all, you witch."

Looking from the doctor to the man who stood in front of her, she smiled. "Witches were over two hundred years ago. I am not, nor have I ever been a witch, good sir. Now if you will excuse me." She roughly pulled her arm away from him and made for the door. After closing the saloon door behind her, she let out a breath she didn't realize she had been holding in.

Had she made a mistake by coming to this town? Would it be her downfall? She thought about this as she made her way to a small room above a shop across the street from the saloon, which she was renting. Climbing the stairs, a shiver raced the length of her spine, though it wasn't cold out.

After bolting the door, she sank down on her bed. Was the way she dressed too much? Was that why she always stood out? She was hoping to be ignored. And liked being ignored. In her case, being ignored was far better than being noticed. Because being noticed always led to the bad kind. Like what happened tonight and so many nights before in different towns with different faces.

But she knew she would leave this world like she was brought into it. Unwanted and barely noticed. If someone hadn't happened upon her near a stream and brought her to a nunnery, she would not be alive. She would not care what these people thought of her. This was not her town, not her people.

Come to think of it, she didn't have a town or people. And she liked it that way. Easier to move on. No connections, no worries.

The morning brought rain, and with the thought of the weather, she pulled out her dark brown dress, designed just like the one she wore yesterday. She was worried about what the day may bring. But she would face it like all the days before in her life, with determination and courage. Stepping outside, Iris made her way toward the jail and the sheriff's office in the rain.

Only one person in town knew the true reason behind her appearance, and it had to stay that way for her to pull off what she was sent there to do. To play her game, she had to be patient and observant. But she also had to be low key and not bring too much unwanted attention, but she had already drawn a lot last night. So, to combat that, she headed to talk to the sheriff.

Right before she was about to enter the office, someone caught her attention out of the corner of her eye. Turning, Iris saw the doctor opening his clinic. The pull she felt toward him still remained, but it was best for both of them to fight it. So, she let herself smile at the sight of him and entered to see the sheriff.

"Sir, I hope you received the information you need for my arrival." She studied the sheriff who sat in an old leather chair cracked with age. The man had white wavy hair, and his tan, wrinkled skin showed his age.

He stood, showing he was far from old. He was strong and sure, and his eyes showed kindness. In that second, a thought crossed Iris's mind. *In all the times I imagined my own father, this man far outshines those images.*

"Ah, yes. I received it just a few days ago. Come, sit." He pulled over a small chair and took his own seat again. "So, I hear we are in need of your special talents in our town." He eyed her over a letter he was looking at. She presumed it was the information on why she was there, so she only nodded and waited for him to speak again. "I've heard of you, but you're not quite what I was expecting. From the rumors and the letter, I expected…"

She grinned. "A man."

He blushed as he looked back down at the letter. Clearing his throat, he went on. "Oh, where are my manner?" He stood and extended his hand, and she took it. "My name is Micah. Nice to meet you, Miss Iris." He sat back down.

"The pleasure is mine."

"So, what is it that you need from me? The letter only stated why you are here."

Iris smiled. "I need a cover. A reason that explains my presence here, besides just passing through. I need something that will help me blend in. It seems I may be here longer than first expected. And with the events that occurred last night, I no longer can pass as just a visitor."

Leaning back in his chair, he rubbed his chin, which had more than a five o'clock shadow of growth on it. "Well, I've only ever talked of my niece to the townspeople here. And knowing her, she won't ever come to visit. So, why don't you use that? You are my niece who is well-read and well-schooled." He sat back up.

Iris nodded, liking the idea. "That might just work."

"I heard about last night and the language that scared everyone." Micah laughed. "That's the funniest thing. I do have to admit, people in small towns seem to be scared of anything new or different. And you are both, my dear."

She returned his smile, and they talked further on collaborating stories and answers to questions people might ask. Micah told her about his past along with some of his niece's. It was well into the afternoon when they paused for a break. He decided to take her to the only restaurant in town and introduce her to a few of the townsfolk.

Chapter 2

The two of them walked into a quaint one-room restaurant that held no more than twenty people. With barely any room to move, people still turned to see who entered, bringing a hush to everyone inside. Only a few whispers could be heard as they took their seats at a table almost squished up against someone else's. They ordered one pot pie to split between them and began to talk, knowing all ears were listening.

"I'm so glad you finally came to visit me, my dear niece," Micah said in a voice loud enough to be heard but not too loud that it was obvious.

"Thank you, Uncle. I'm glad to see you again. It's been way too long since our last reunion."

"I do wish you would have given me more of warning. To come in and wait a day to come see me. Quite rude, I must say. I thought my sister taught you better."

She smiled. "Yes, I am sorry. I didn't want to come see you when I was a mess from traveling. Since I haven't seen you in years, I wanted to make a good impression."

"Oh, you made an impression all right. People think you're a witch now because of the different languages you use. Seems like there is a downside to an education like yours."

"Very true. I didn't realize the differences between the city and a small town. I will try my best to change people's view of me, Uncle. I owe you so much. I don't want to bring you any trouble."

They talked throughout their meal and during tea. As they made their way back to the Sherriff's office, Iris put her arm through his, showing affection. Walking toward the jail, something caught Iris' eye.

Nudging Micah, she leaned in to whisper, "I think the good doctor might suspect something."

The tall, black-haired, bronze-skinned doctor was watching the two of them from the porch of his office. Leaning against the post, arms crossed, the sight of him made Iris take in a breath. *This doctor might end up being trouble if I have to keep seeing him, much less meeting him.*

"Oh, dear. That is something I quite forgot. He met my niece when he went to the city for some kind of meetings. We best take care of this now. Come, I will introduce the two of you and we will have to let him in our secret."

"Some of our secret..." Iris stated, not wanting the good doctor to know the full story. Her stomach sank, her heart starting to race.

"The only person who knows the whole truth is you, my dear." He winked at her and guided her toward the doctor's office. As they got closer Micah waved, saying, "Garrett! Good to see you on this lovely afternoon. Can we come inside and speak with you?"

The doctor didn't say a word, only nodded and opened the door to let them in. They all sat down in his office, which had lush chairs. Iris tried not to smile at the softness of them. The whole room reminded her of a great library she had once visited, not a doctor's office. Books on seers, dreams, plants, and more. There were two large book cases that were carved in ornate patterns. And a grand globe in the corner. This was far more than just a new age doctor's office.

Micah leaned forward. "Garrett, you've met my niece while you were in the city, did you not?"

"Yes, I met her briefly."

"Did you ever speak of meeting her to anyone besides to me?"

"No, you are the only one I mentioned it to. Well, and my sister, of course."

"Of course." Micah nodded and then looked from the doctor to Iris. "Then I assume you realize that this is not my niece."

"Quite. When I heard two ladies talking about the sheriff's niece being the strange girl from the pub, I knew something was off."

Iris only smiled sweetly but all the while, she was thinking, *Why does being in his presence send my heart racing? This is ridiculous. I need to get this under control.*

Micah looked back at Garrett. "Yes, in truth, she is not my niece, but this must stay between the three of us. Her life," he nodded to Iris, "is at risk. I trust you will keep this secret."

Garrett seemed to be thinking about it, which made Iris almost mad. Who would not keep a secret for someone's safety? "Why is it for her safety and why are you in on it?"

Micah wasn't expecting questions and cleared his throat in surprise. "Well…"

Iris interrupted. "The reason is because I am on business here and it's the kind that has to do with an outlaw. The less you know, the better. Just know it's a matter that needs to be dealt with in secret. I can show you the letter from the governor to the sheriff if you like."

Micah looked at Iris in question, then to Garrett for his answer. "They sent a girl to deal with outlaws?" He almost laughed.

Iris sat up straighter. "What do you mean, deal with? All I could be doing here is to track them and send word on their whereabouts. A girl is less of a threat and wouldn't worry the outlaws as much as a gun-wielding man." She glared at him, thinking that he, like most men, must view women as the weaker sex. The words she just spoke were lies.

How could I have been attracted to this ignorant man?

Nodding, Garrett smiled. "I do see what you mean."

Iris caught herself admiring his looks once more and was mad at herself for it. Blinking, she said, "Good, so will you help me and Micah out by keeping our secret?"

Garrett looked at Iris then to Micah and nodded. "I will, but do the townspeople know your niece's name, Micah?"

He grinned. "No, I don't believe they do. I've only ever really talked about her as my niece."

"Good." The doctor looked from the sheriff to Iris. "And what is your name? I don't think we've been properly introduced."

"Oh, forgive me." She extended her hand for him to take. "I am Iris. Nice to meet you, mister…"

"Just call me Garrett. Everyone does."

"Well, either that or doc or doctor," Micah chimed in.

Garrett nodded at Micah and then gazed back at Iris. "And you are living above the shop?"

She nodded but before answering, the sound of an inner door opening stopped her. A petite, blonde girl entered with a large grin on her face. Garrett's eyes dilated in surprise.

"Garrett!" The girl almost floated toward the doctor who sat back in his chair, staring at the blonde woman. "Above the shops? No, no. We can't have that. If we're supposed to help with this ruse... I am Isabelle, by the way. Garrett's half-sister. Even though I may be younger of the two, I act like the older sibling."

Garrett moved to the end of his seat, his eyes narrowing. "Were you eavesdropping, sister?"

She held out her hand to him, stopping him. The brother and sister looked like quite the opposites, like the shadows of the moon and the rays of the sun.

With hands on hips, Isabelle turned to Iris, giving her a big smile. "You will stay with us. My brother and I have more than enough room in our house. We do live a mile outside of town but if one of our acquaintances comes into town, I wouldn't put them up in that drab room. You will stay with us." She nodded as if she was agreeing to her own decision.

"I really appreciate that, but it's best I stay in town, more apt to see who I'm looking for that way. But I'm grateful for your hospitality." Iris smiled at the young beautiful woman.

It was as if she was taken from a fantasy, perfect in every way from the button nose to her petite stature, curves and pale skin. Almost fairy-like. But there was depth to her and great kindness. It radiated from her, filling the room with a presence of ease, whereas her brother was like a majestic bear staring at you from a high mountain. He emitted protectiveness and profound wisdom. But as with a bear, only family may enter their den.

The girl frowned. "If you say so. But the offer will always stand." She winked at Iris.

After the four of them went their separate ways to fulfill their daily duties, none of them knew that the quiet lazy days would not last. Iris had brought change to this sleepy village that would reshape its very core.

Chapter 3

The next several days passed without event. The man Iris was hunting was a no-show, and this worried her. If she did not find him soon, there was no telling what he might do. The only thing that stood out to her was whispers she had heard on the street. The rumors were of the witch and spell book. *So much for laying low.*

When she woke one day after being in the small town for over a week, everything seemed like every day before, dull.

After eating some cornbread Isabelle had given her, Iris headed out for the day and took her usual walk around town before stopping at the sheriff's office for lunch.

As they sat and talked, loud noises and screams echoed from the street. On her way to the door, she reached inside her half-skirt and pulled out a pistol. Micah saw and raised an eyebrow, to which Iris only shrugged. Hiding the pistol behind her back, she opened the door and stepped out, followed by Micah.

A mass of people ran out of the saloon. Just as Iris and Micah reached the street, a man rushed through the swinging doors. A horse satchel swung from his shoulder, and from the sound of it, the bag was filled with coins. Dragging the sweaty,

24

terrified saloon owner, the man brandished a pistol, making it clear he wasn't playing around.

As the gunman lifted his head, he stopped in his tracks just as Iris and Micah did. At the sight of the man, Iris' eyes narrowed, her grip on her gun growing tighter. The man she had been looking for had shown himself in outlaw fashion. She had a feeling he would get an itch to rob but hoped with his pals not around, he wouldn't have been so keen on doing so.

The man pointed the gun at the barkeeper's head. "Don't come any closer, or I'll shoot him! I'll do it!"

Micah was about to respond when she flicked her fingers, a signal for him not to speak, such a slight movement the gunman didn't notice. Micah let her speak in his stead. "Yes, of course. How can we help? What is it you need to free the man you hold?" She made her voice soft and feminine, something she could do but tried not to make a habit of.

His eyes blinked rapidly, shocked at the softness and phrasing of it. "Umm... I need for you to leave me alone. To... to get away," he stuttered.

She smiled slightly, trying to ease his nerves. "I understand. You stole money and..."

The man shook his gun at her, making Micah start forward, but Iris held him back by extending her arm.

"I… Let me through, or I'll shoot him!" the man shouted shakily.

"I understand. You needed the money, didn't you? It's hard to find work nowadays with all the mines closing. It must be so hard." Iris made her voice sound like honey, soothing the tense air that lay between them. "I have an idea…" She took two steps forward, keeping their eyes locked with her timid expression. "Why don't I take his place? Him for me? I would be a lot easier to handle, don't you think? A strong man like yourself would be able to handle me quite easily."

"What are you doing? Are you insane?" Micah whispered.

Iris shook her head with a quick motion so the armed man would not see.

"What do you think of that idea?" She sweetly smiled at him, trying to look as sincere as possible. He stared at her. His confusion let her take a few more steps forward without the man noticing. "I would like that very much, sir." Iris kept her voice as smooth and soft as she could.

Just when Iris thought she had him compliant, a noise came from her left. Loud, heavy footsteps on dirt and gravel came through the air. "Drop your gun right now!" a raspy, deep voice shouted.

A middle-aged man carrying a shotgun ran toward them. The new man on the scene pointed the end of the gun at the robber and the barkeeper. If he shot one, he would shoot them both. She had to think of something quickly before either man fired.

Without taking another breath, she whipped the gun out from behind her back, aimed and fired. The bullet hit the robber's arm that held the gun, lodging itself in the bone. The man's hand went limp, dropping the pistol. The barkeeper pulled away and ran toward the sheriff.

In another swift movement, Iris sidestepped to her left, toward the good-intentioned shopkeeper with the shotgun. Using her momentum, she fell to her knees, gliding on the dirt and stones to position herself under the man's gun. She struck his hand hard with the palm of her left hand. Then with the right, she grabbed the barrel of the shotgun, pulling it away from him.

The man stumbled back, shocked and angry. Before she could even stand, he'd balled his hand into a fist, clearly intending to get his gun back with force. Before he could make contact with her, Micah grabbed his arm and pulled the shopkeeper to the sidewalk. Micah whispered to him, trying to explain what had just happened.

Iris turned to look at the robber who was lying on the porch of the saloon. In the corner of her eye, she saw a dark figure move from the far-right buildings. Turning, she saw the dark-skinned, dark-haired doctor. He stared at her as he moved toward the injured man.

Iris couldn't read his face; was it anger, or something else? But if anger, then why? What was there to be angry at? She saved two men's lives; surely, it wasn't because she was a girl and did what she did.

Shaking her head, she walked up on the porch and knelt beside the bleeding man. He tilted his head toward her, eyes almost glazed over, and whispered, "Who... Who shot me?"

Iris brushed some hair out of his face. "I think it was the sheriff. You'll be all right. You won't die."

The doctor was now there and knelt on the other side of the man, looking at his arm. The man groaned in pain. "You might lose your hand, though. Whoever made the shot is a great marksman." For a split second, the doctor's eyes shifted to her and then back to his patient.

The streets filled with people, making Iris force her way back to the sheriff's office across the street. Before she went in, Iris whispered something to Micah. "Uncle, dear." He grinned. "Let's tell everyone you shot the outlaw, shall we? I was just a bystander. And with the shopkeeper..."

"You tripped as you were running after I fired my gun." Micah winked at her and Iris felt that feeling again.

If I ever had a father… She shook the thought from her head, not letting herself have wishful ideas. Iris nodded in approval to the sheriff and went into his office.

Sighing, she sat down in the chair across from the desk. Iris hoped when Micah questioned the residents, no one saw her shoot the man. The fewer people knew about her, the better, and besides, who would even believe she was the one who had made that kind of shot?

But she still felt uneasy. Something was still stirring in the air. It was nearing dark and Micah still had not returned, so Iris headed back to her room to rest for the night.

As she drew closer to the shop, she saw people on the landing to her room on the second floor throwing everything to the ground below. It didn't matter if it was hers or not. Other people then picked up the items and threw them into a nearby fire that blazed with heat. Iris was taken aback by these people's actions. Granted, it wasn't the whole town, but it was a good number of them.

Just as she was about to back away, someone saw her, and before she knew it, several men had grabbed her and started dragging her toward the fire.

"Witch! Burn the witch!" one of the speculators screamed.

"She is the reason the robber came to us. She cursed us all. She cursed our town!" another yelled.

All she could think of was, *Oh, shit, this is real. This is how I die.* No matter how much she struggled, none of her training did any good against a mob of angry, crazy townspeople. Iris had flashbacks of tortured filled days. Those memories she buried deep inside rose to the surface. Now she wished for the fire, so the memories of the past would not come and haunt her. Iris was caught between dread of the present and the terror of the past.

Then she thought maybe she could reach her gun. She had put it back in its hiding place before she had disarmed the merchant.

As they grew closer to the fire, so many thoughts raced through her mind. Was this truly her end? Then a loud booming voice rang above all others, shadowing the crowd's chants. "Put her down. *Now!*"

The men froze, and Iris followed their gaze toward the street, craning her neck to see. The dark figure of a tall mountain of a man came toward them. The men holding her stiffened at the sight of him. The firelight's glow only made him look even larger than he already was. She had never been so happy to see anyone in her life. But the look on his face almost made her retract that thought. Iris had never seen someone so angry in all her life, and she had been around a lot of angry people.

But this, this was different.

"I said drop her!" Garrett's voice had become deeper, his gaze more intense as if he were trying to pierce their hearts.

They froze and then dropped her to the ground with a thud. She groaned as her butt hit the ground, hard. Before she could even sit up to look around, he was right in front of her, leaning over to pick her up in his arms. She wrapped her arms around his neck, surprising herself.

The closeness of his body made her own heat up. Her thoughts ran in several different directions, primarily focusing on how amazing he felt against her, but his voice soon halted those thoughts. The deep timbre of his voice echoed through her like waves, sending even more sensations through her body.

"Are you all mad?" he asked, rounding on the townspeople with a thunderous look. "What gave any of you the right to destroy not just her property but that of the storekeeper? And I know for a fact that no law under heaven gave you any damn right to burn a person alive! No matter what imaginings ran through your skulls. That's right, skulls, because right now, as a doctor, I don't think any of you have a brain to toss among you, and if you do, you have completely forgotten how to use it." He paused and glared around.

"But — she — she —" one of the onlookers stammered.

"She what?" Garrett snapped. "Reads a language you don't comprehend? You should all be ashamed. What will the preacher say to you all when he hears about this? Or Micah? You all tried to burn his own niece alive. Witches indeed. The only villains in this town are the lot of you. Every single one of you better pray for forgiveness from the heavens above, because if any of you fall ill in the following weeks, I'm tempted to let you meet your maker early." He laughed at the anger on some of the people's faces. "Oh, don't give me that look. What you were trying to do was far worse. I would just be letting nature take its due course. And good luck getting another doctor. The closest one isn't for 60 miles."

Looking disgusted, Garrett turned to go. Isabelle was holding balled up clothes. The sheriff had folded arms and a stern look. Next to him stood a small fellow who looked almost ill. As the doctor neared the two men and his sister, Micah was the first to speak.

"You should have given them a lot more. And I must say, I've never seen you so fired up before—"

"Or talk so much," Isabelle said, interrupting the sheriff without paying any mind to what he was saying. "I've never heard you go on a rant before. I'm proud." She was grinning from ear to ear. The clothes she was holding almost swallowed her.

The preacher just stood there. If he had words, they would not come past his lips. Iris was about to protest and to ask to be let down, but Isabelle shook her head, subtly telling her to stay put. As Garrett walked down the street followed by Isabelle, Micah addressed the crowd.

Clearing his throat, he told them seriously, "I know each of your faces and I'm taking names. If any of you make a move, and I mean the smallest of moves, look at my niece the wrong way, and I will put you behind bars and throw away the key."

Iris couldn't make out the rest of his words as they increased their distance. Soon, they reached two tied up horses. It was dark, and Iris couldn't make out the color of the coats when Garrett placed her on her feet.

Looking at him, she smiled and said, "Thank you. I really—"

He held up his hand for her to stop speaking and, without a word, lifted her onto his horse. Anger emitted from him. Despite that, she couldn't get past the thought of how her being in his arms had pushed all her memories back into the depths where they belonged.

His sister followed suit and mounted her own mare. Garrett then took both reigns and walked them to their home a mile away. Isabelle smiled at Iris reassuringly.

This doctor was quite the puzzle. One minute he saved her from crazed townspeople and their fire, the next he stops her from speaking to him. Iris was starting to wonder about the good doctor's sanity as well.

Chapter 4

Isabelle set Iris up with one of the two bedrooms on the second floor of their farmhouse. She explained to Iris about how she had to tear away the dresses from two older town ladies who were wanting to keep them for themselves, but with her feistiness, she had come out the victor. Imagining this small fairy-like girl taking on two old hags made her laugh. Iris wanted to ask Isabelle about Garrett, but it was late and thought it best to wait until the next day to venture into that domain.

The next day was met with heavy rain. Everyone in town, including the three of them, would most likely be staying inside. The thought of the three of them alone, having to talk, made her nerves stand on end. And the thought of even trying to speak to Garrett again made her even more nervous, which was rare for her. She hardly ever got nervous about anything, much less speaking to a man, especially one who may think less of her because of her gender or career choice. But there was something about him that pulled her towards him. That pull scared and intrigued her at the same time.

She had to remind herself that it wasn't safe for anyone with her around.

Iris knew she had to go face her troubles head-on and work through them. That was the only way things would work out, and her mind would then give her some peace.

She tossed and turned all night, thinking not of the fire but of Garrett and the many confusing sides of him and how to even try to approach him. Was he even approachable? Would he let her speak to him? Or would it be like when she was a child, where children, especially a girl child, were to be seen and not heard?

Pushing those thoughts away, she got dressed and headed down to the kitchen where the two siblings were waiting. Isabelle saw Iris come down the stairs and in her sweet perky, bordering-on-hyper voice, said, "Good morning, Iris! I hope you slept well! It was quite an adventure last night. Come, sit." She pulled out a chair for Iris to sit in. "We have a good meal today since it's all rainy. I thought why not treat ourselves."

Isabelle sat down next to her and filled Iris's plate with everything that lay spread out on the table. Garrett sat there quietly reading. "You didn't even ask what she likes to eat," he told Isabelle, gazing at her over his book.

"Who doesn't like bacon, eggs, with biscuits and gravy?" she answered with a mischievous grin. "No one is the answer to that." She laughed at herself, finished filling up Iris plate and handed it to her.

Isabelle then filled up her own plate. Garrett had apparently already eaten. His plate sat dirty and empty in front of him. As the two of them ate, he went back to reading his book. His sister kept things lively, speaking of this and that, filling up almost every silent pause with her words. Iris was just happy that Garrett didn't seem to be in an odd mood, but the day was still young.

After they ate, Iris helped Isabelle clean up the dishes. When she reached for Garrett's plate, he placed his hand on it. Looking over the cover of his book, his eyes were almost a golden color today, like that of gold shining in the sun.

She found herself staring and reached for the plate again. And again, Garrett wouldn't allow her to take it. Closing his book, he placed it on the table. "Sit, Isabelle can handle the dishes this time. She was the one who insisted on cooking all of this. I have some questions I would like to be answered. Sit." He tilted his head toward the chair she had sat in before.

Iris sat back down and folded her hands in her lap, trying not to stare at him. She was surprised Isabelle hadn't said a word, but it seemed she knew when not to bother her brother. Garrett sat back in his chair and crossed his arms, gazing at her. Her body temperature rose under his stare, but she willed herself to calm down. This was quite unlike her. This doctor seemed to make her act beside herself.

"So, was the man you shot the one you had been looking for?" the interrogation had begun.

She nodded. "One of them."

"One of them? How many are you looking for? From what you had told me before, it sounded like you were only looking out for one person." His stare never wavered.

"This one was in the area, so I knew I would find him first. He is part of a bigger group. The other members are far more dangerous than this one man is. To the people I work for, he was the easiest to find, therefore the first. He will lead us to the others." She wanted to stare right back at him, but her thoughts strayed onto things far too inappropriate. It far surpassed how nicely she fit into his arms last night. She breathed deep, trying to steady her pulse. *I have got to get away from this man.*

"Who is this us? Will someone else be finding the others in this group?" The expression on his face twisted for a slight second, but most people wouldn't have even noticed. Iris was not most people.

Clearing her throat, she glared at him, willing her thoughts to stay on topic. "Us is an organization that operates under the control of the government. The name and its members are not something I can disclose. The ones who will be going after the group is me and another person who is working on finding some of their hideouts in hopes it will lead us to them. I can't tell you more about the mission at this point."

He nodded. "All right. Can you explain how you did what you did yesterday? It's as if you calculated the moment and went into action before most people could even comprehend what was happening. And your marksmanship, I've never seen such an accurate hit before. I'm assuming you only wanted to injure him, not kill him. You also wanted to make sure the barkeep was unharmed. So, you needed to get the gun from him somehow. So, you shot the arm that held the gun, but you knew that if you didn't hit the bone, the bullet would have gone through and may have hit one of his vital organs. And you couldn't let the shopkeeper fire because he would have killed both the gunman and the barkeeper. Does that pretty much sum it up?"

She nodded at his words, almost surprised he had seen and understood everything. "Yes."

"So, how are you able to do that? Is it pure talent? Self-taught? Or were you trained?"

Iris grinned, noticing his interest and how hard he tried to hide it. "I guess it would be all three. Talent, some self-taught and some trained."

The interest that she had seen seemed to turn to worry, but his expressions were well controlled, and most people would never notice his changes. "And they chose you and one other to go after this group of people who are insane criminals. All on your own?"

"Sometimes fewer is better. Several people would be more apt to be seen coming. As you've seen, I have skills a lot of others don't have, despite my gender. But my gender can also help at times. Others see me as less of a threat when it's quite the opposite." Iris was interested in seeing what his reply would be.

Garrett's eyes narrowed even more as if he was trying to see into her depths. "I see…"

That's it? That's all he has to say? After all of that, that's it? She was confused and thought he was odd. And right when she thought she could read him, he turned into stone. Isabelle turned from the dishes and Iris could tell that she was about to speak, but Iris wanted to know something.

Leaning forward, elbows on the table, she locked eyes with Garrett and smiled. "I never got to thank you for last night." He held up his hand again, just like the night before, but she wouldn't abide this time. "I really am thankful. I had a question, though; last night it seemed as if you might be angry at me. If I did something to offend…"

This time he interrupted her with a voice that was far different from what she had heard last night. His voice was now sweet and soft, as if it was a breeze and she was a leaf touching her slightly as it passed. "No, no. I wasn't mad at you…" He looked down, his expression clearly sad this time.

Isabelle went up behind him and placed her hands on his shoulders, as if saying go on, you're not alone. Sighing, he went on. "Last night, seeing them about to throw you into the fire brought back memories I have tried hard to forget."

His sister took the seat next to him, taking his hands in hers. Looking at them side by side was like looking at two polar opposites. Him with his dark tan skin, black straight hair and sharp facial features. Her with her long blonde wavy hair, porcelain-like skin and soft features.

"You see, his mother was burned…" Isabelle said haltingly.

It was even hard for her to say and she seemed to be a person who was always on the sunny side of things. As she went on, Iris could tell Isabelle had inner strength, stronger than most, hidden under her sunny disposition.

"Our father and his mother were living on a small farmstead, far away from people, trying to avoid others because of her heritage. You see, back then people were hunted based on their skin tone. Our father is white, and you know how the masses are about interracial relationships. Somehow, people stumbled upon the three of them one day. Long story short, our father got badly beaten while his mother was burned to death.

41

The only reason Garrett escaped the same fate was by hiding under the house. It didn't keep him from seeing it all, but it saved his life."

Garrett nodded, sadness written all over him. Still looking down, he said, "Sadly, some still hunt others based on skin tones… And yesterday brought all that back. Seeing you almost burned to death… I was barely controlling my anger. I wanted to kill every last one of them. I have a hard time speaking of it. Many people today are still prejudice. Bringing up the past is painful, but at times necessary. So, I don't mind when Isabelle tells my story for me. To change the future, sometimes one must revisit the past."

Isabelle leaned over and hugged her brother, resting her head on his shoulder. The story took Iris aback. She stared at the two of them from across the table. She was about to speak when someone knocked on the front door and then came barging in a second later. They all jumped to their feet and saw a soaked Micah with mud up to his knees.

He stormed inside, a trail of mud following him. Gasping for breath, he tried to speak, but no sound emerged.

"Do you need some water, Micah?" Isabelle asked, her face scrunched in concern.

He shook his head. "No… Thank you…" He paused, still trying to catch his breath. "He… got away…"

"The gunman?" Isabelle asked.

"Yes… His buddies…"

Iris interrupted him by slamming her palm on the table. "Shit… Cole had one job… One job. To trail the others and warn me. I'm going to wring his neck when I see him next."

Garrett eyed her. "The other person working with you? Cole? Are you sure they didn't kill him and that's not why he didn't warn you?"

Iris laughed, seeming to surprise the others. "No, he wouldn't die that easy. He knows I'd kill him first."

The two men just stared at Iris for a moment, not certain how to take her words. But Isabelle didn't miss a beat.

"What are you going to do?" Isabelle asked.

"They shouldn't have gotten far, and they will be easy to track because of the rain. I'm surprised they even planned the escape today."

"I'll come with you." Garrett started to go for his boots, but Iris stopped him.

"I mean no offense by this, but I think it's best you stay behind. For one thing, who's going to patch us up if we get hurt? And second, I try not to fight alongside people I haven't fought with before. It could end up worse than it would be if I were alone. Thank you, though." She smiled at him. "Micah, did you see which direction they headed?"

He nodded. "They headed southeast, I think. I'll come."

Iris smiled again and shook her head. "I think it's best you not."

"But you need help. I know this area."

She nodded. "True, you know the area more than I do, but would you be able to keep up on foot?"

The other three stared at her and in unison asked, "On foot?"

Nodded again. "Yes, they didn't come or leave on horseback, did they?"

Micah shook his head, confused. "No."

"It's easier to hide with no horses and that's how I will follow." She looked down at her dress and was thankful she had changed to her brown dress and high boots. Looking at Isabelle and then to Garrett, she said, "If Cole knows what is best for him, he will seek out the local sheriff. He will follow Micah's trail here where you will then tell him which direction I followed the crew." She smiled devilishly. "And tell him if he doesn't get his act together, he'll wish the crew had killed him."

"So, I'm staying here? Waiting for this Cole fellow?" Micah asked, not quite following.

"Yes. He's a tad shorter than me with brown hair, cut short. Sharp blue eyes and very sarcastic. He'll have a tattoo of a raven's claw on his inner wrist." Iris looked down at herself again.

And as the others stood there watching her in bewilderment, she pulled a string and the skirt part of her outfit fell to the floor, leaving her in pants and a top. Reaching down, she pulled out her gun from its hiding spot in the skirt and handed the skirt part to Isabelle, who held out her arms to take it.

Turning to Micah, she eyed his waist. "My holster was burned in that lovely fire last night. Would you mind?" He shook his head no and gave it to her. She wasn't a skinny girl. She had muscles and a tall frame, which made her taller than Micah, who seemed to be five-six and almost as wide as she was but his was not all muscles like hers. Tightening the holster and putting her gun in its place, she turned to Garrett. "Do you have any cutting knives, anything sharp?"

While Garrett ran to the other room to find a knife, Iris asked Isabelle for some hairpins and Iris put her long black hair up in a bun.

"You are just going to track them down, that's all, right?" Isabelle asked.

Iris lifted her eyes to the sweet girl in front of her. "Yes, to track them."

The doctor returned from the other room carrying three short knives. Taking them, she put one in her boot, one in a hidden pocket in her pants and one on her belt.

Isabelle looked Iris up and down, grinning from ear to ear. "Well, aren't you a sight. I've never seen a girl like you."

"A rare breed indeed," Micah chimed in.

Garrett just stared at Iris, his face unreadable. Iris smiled at each of them, thanking them. She then turned to the doctor. "Thank you again for last night."

He smiled slightly. "Don't just throw it away today to catch these guys, all right?"

"I don't intend to." With that, she headed out the door and into the woods, traveling southeast.

Chapter 5

After a while, she was able to pick up the group's trail despite the pouring rain. They were moving slowly due to the injured robber, which was good for her. Thinking back to her childhood, one thing she was thankful for was the orphanage she had been placed in. It was a two-story house with a leaky roof where children slept on mats on the floor with the rats.

Most of the children there were Native American who were taken away from their families to live a religious life, which meant sitting in a small church on Sundays and nightly prayers. During the day, during free time played outside, and they taught her the tracking skills they'd learned before being wrongfully taken away from their parents.

Iris never agreed with what they did to all of them, taking them away from their own families, denying them the love of a mother and father. Some of the so-called teachers would pick on the small ones, and she always stood up for them. In the end, she got a beating for it, but in her mind, it was better her than the other children. She took it better than the smaller kids, the ones who wouldn't eat because they missed their parents. Iris ate, and she didn't miss anyone. There was no one to miss, no family. Her parents had given her up. For what reason, she didn't know. She never knew them, never remembered them.

It was past midday when the tracks became fresh. They were nearby and slowing down. One good thing, they had no idea she was coming. By counting their tracks, it seemed to be about five of them, not counting the injured one. Their footprints were deep in the soft earth, but it was hard to tell how big they were because four of them carried the robber. The leader walked in front, not carrying the other man. His footing showed he had a wide stance but light footprints. He could be a smaller man or someone who knew how to distribute his weight.

Iris pushed her nerves down like she did every time she faced danger. She thought back to what her captain had told her if this situation were to occur. *If you do encounter all of them at once, don't hesitate to take their lives because they will not falter in takin' yours. They have killed many. Don't let them add to their numbers.* He knew there was a risk, only sending Cole and herself and in separate directions at that. But he also knew it was the most likely way to entrap the outlaws.

She slowed her pace and softened her footsteps, knowing she neared the group. The rain had slowed to a drizzle, and the sun had started to set. As she came upon them, Iris noticed the injured man stretched out next to the fire. There were three men in sight of where she stood, keeping an eye out. The other two could not be seen, which made it hard for her to scope out the area. And with the fading light, she had to act fast. Iris hoped the other two men were far enough away that she could take these three out before those two came upon her.

Iris would have a clean shot at one, but once the shot was heard, she'd lose the element of surprise. She should be able to immobilize another man, which would then leave three: the one near the fire and the two out of sight. After formulating her plan, Iris had to get closer than she would have liked to see through the encroaching darkness. The fire gave off some light, but she needed clean shots to make her strategy a success. Steadying her breathing, she unlatched her gun and took aim at the closest of the three.

After Iris squeezed out the first shot, everything moved fast.

One bullet to the head. One down. She aimed again, hitting the closest one in the stomach, sending him to the ground. Seconds later, she shot the third guy in the leg. As he stumbled toward her, she shot again, hitting him in the head. She had been able to take out more than she had first anticipated.

Because she had been so focused on the three in front of her, she had not seen the other two flanking her. Hearing a twig snap, she quickly turned to face off with another man, but he was closer than she had realized.

He knocked the gun out of her hand, and it flew into the darkness of the woods. Iris reached for her knife, but she wasn't quick enough. He stabbed her in the stomach with a knife she had not seen. He was right against her, pinning her right arm against her chest. Thinking quickly, she reached into her left-side pocket for the other knife, but instead of stabbing the man up against her, she looked to her left and saw the other man taking out a gun.

Without another thought, she threw the knife, hitting him in his right shoulder, making him drop the gun. The man still against her pulled out his knife to stab her again, but she took the opportunity to move from him. Both men then started toward her. She stepped back toward the fire.

Iris pulled out the knife at her belt and held it in her hand, readying herself for a knife fight. She loathed knives. Give her a gun fight any day. Throwing them would only give them more weapons. Instead of trying to find the gun the man had dropped, all of them now held knives.

As they advanced, she edged back, trying to maintain her distance. Turning her head slightly, she saw the man she had shot in the stomach moving, the darkness masking his movement. Thinking he might have a gun, she waited to see his arm move. When he did, she flung herself out of the way, missing the bullet meant for her heart. The man was quick and fired again, hitting her left arm.

Pain blasted through her, but it wasn't the first time she'd been shot. She fell to her knees as more bullets popped, but it wasn't the men around her. In a split second, the one who had shot her stopped moving.

"Go! Run to Rune!" one of the two men in front of her yelled to the other one. He took off into the woods as the other man started toward her. Before he got to her, Cole was kneeling next to her, causing the man to hesitate in his weakened state. It seemed as if he was thinking of running as well. Why didn't he run?

"Oh, shit, Iris, you should have waited…"

"Dammit, Cole, now is not the time. You ran out of bullets, didn't you?"

"Yup," he said grimly.

"I've scolded you about not bringing extra. Go run after the other one. Don't let him get away. That's an order. I'll be here waiting when you get back. Go, now." She looked at him, daring him to say no. He didn't argue and ran after the man who went further into the woods.

Now it was just her and the shorter man, the leader. She stood, making sure not to show her intention. The two of them glared at each other, daring the other one to make the first move. Iris let him move closer. She stood unmoving, feeling her life's blood leaving her body. But something unexpected happened.

Instead of lunging for her, he sprinted to his right toward the fire. The gun. Her heart skipped a beat. She ran to the fire as well, not wanting him to get it. But the man rushed to the robber's side and, in a swift movement, cut the man's throat. He had laid asleep this whole time due to the drugs the doctor had given him.

Iris found where all the guns were. They had stupidly laid them all together. Picking up one, she aimed. He quickly threw his knife, barely missing, cutting her on the side of the stomach. They locked eyes as she pulled the trigger. The bullet hit its mark, and the man fell back to the ground. Sighing, Iris dropped the gun and fell to her knees, knowing she may never find out why he had killed his own man.

Shaking her head, she forced herself to stand and made her way back to the farmhouse from which she had come. She wouldn't last long, but she needed to help Cole out by getting closer to the doctor's house. Because he wouldn't leave her to the wolves. They were like brother and sister and would do anything for one another. Iris pushed past the searing pain just like she had been trained to do. Her body protested every movement, her mind not comprehending the severity of her own wounds.

Her vision blurred around the edges, and her breath became ragged as her pulse slowed. *Damn stab wound must be worse than I thought… If I make it back, the good doctor is going to be pissed…* She had slowed now and leaned against a tree.

Iris was about to black out. She recognized the signs. And just before she lost full consciousness, she felt warm strong arms picking her up and then the feeling of, what was that, flying? No, running…

Iris heard the voice of someone very familiar to her. "Dammit, Iris, you should have waited for me. Look what's happened. This is all my fault. I should have trailed them better. I should have been faster. I'm sorry. I'm so sorry. You hang in there. You're not allowed to leave me. You hear me? Hang on…"

Chapter 6

Cole had run as fast as he could, her blood soaking not just her but him as well. The rain only made things worse. He lost his footing a few times and cursed himself for it, knowing Iris would have as well.

He didn't think he had ever felt so worried before. He couldn't lose her. She was his sister, his teammate, his partner in crime. Iris had always been there for him ever since he was a kid, making sure he didn't end up in jail. He owed everything to her, and now she might die and it was all his fault for always being one step behind.

Iris had always said it was a good thing because if they were both moving at the same speed, they would end up running into each other during missions, but now that he thought back on it, she was just trying to make him feel better.

Cole felt like a lifetime had passed. It was dark and raining, making things harder than they should have been. Thankfully, he had no trouble finding his way back. That was one thing Iris said he was better at: tracking and always knowing his direction. It was all the iron in his nose she had said. But he had not tracked well enough, not this time. This time he had been too late, always one step behind. He cursed himself again. He saw lights in a distance and ran even harder.

After Cole had come and gone, Garrett, Isabelle and Micah sat at the table, waiting. Not a word passed between them. Not even Isabelle spoke. So many thoughts ran through Garrett's mind as he sat there in silence.

Iris was in the forefront. He had never been so captivated by someone before. She wasn't like any woman he had ever met. Yes, he had met independent women before, but she was more than that. It was in the way she acted under pressure and how she controlled situations. She reminded Garrett of himself. As a doctor, situations sometimes called for a calm mind but, at the same time, one who could analyze situations on a deep level. The faster, the better when a life was on the line. She was also a mystery to him, which captivated him even more.

And the way she dressed. Everything about her was so diverse that it made his heart race. Garrett tried to think back to when he had felt like this before. It had been so long ago it was almost too hard to recall. It was when he was seventeen, just starting his medical studies. His mother being Native American made it hard to get admitted, but his father had become a judge, which meant he was able to pull some strings for his admittance.

His father's station and money brought some attention from young ladies to Garrett.

This girl had been walking the campus on a rainy day when he saw her. He offered his umbrella, starting a friendship. She didn't care about money, who his mother was or what station his father held. She herself was a daughter of an aristocrat and knew how it felt to be only wanted for money and status. He remembered sharing his first kiss with her, and the butterflies he had in seeing her.

But one day, he saw her walking with someone else, a well-dressed handsome fellow. She started ignoring him, and when he finally got to ask her why, she told him she had met someone she cared for and who her father approved of. That was that.

Ever since then, he had kept his distance from relationships. He had a few girls try and pursue him, but he would have no part of it, knowing most were either seeking him for his father's money and position or their families would not approve of him. Now in his mid-thirties, he had not given love a second thought. Not until he had seen Iris, but would she return the sentiments? But then again, he still hardly knew anything about her. This could turn out to be something completely different than what he was hoping.

Time passed, and thoughts shifted and ran circles in his mind. Eventually, he heard someone yelling from the front yard of the house. By the pain and fearfulness of the tone, Garrett knew something was wrong. Jumping to his feet, he ran out to meet who it was. His heart raced in his chest but soon almost stopped at the sight in front of him.

Cole had Iris in his arms, who was limp and unresponsive. On impulse, he grabbed her from Cole's now shaking arms and ran her inside. Clearing the dining table with one careless swipe of his arm, he laid her out on it. Isabelle cut off Iris's clothes and fetched water, her nursing skills kicking in just like his.

Cole watched from the side with Micah. "This is all my fault," Cole said, fear plain in his voice. "If I had tracked them like I should have. If I had been faster. I can't lose her, not like this..."

The words *I can't lose her* stuck in Garrett's mind as he looked over her wounds. The injury that took precedence was the deep knife wound in her stomach. He could tell someone had been up close when they had stabbed her. The other two—a graze from a bullet on her left arm and a long cut on the side of her stomach—were just flesh wounds.

"What happened? Wasn't she just to track them?" Isabelle asked Cole anxiously.

"We... I mean, her orders were different than mine. She was to get information from the one who had broken off from the group. But her orders were to take matters into her own hands if she had all of them in her sight."

"That sounds like suicide," Micah voiced.

"If it had been me, probably. I wouldn't have killed but maybe one before they killed me. But that's not Iris. By the time I got there, she pretty much killed all but two. If it hadn't been dark and raining, she would have been able to kill them all, no probably to it. But the darkness and the sound from the rain hindered her ability. She could have waited for daylight, but she wouldn't take the chance of them finding her and making the first move. She takes action instead of waiting. She told me that waiting brings doubt and fear to the front, best to act before they come to the forefront of one's mind." Cole murmured a quiet thank-you when Micah handed him a tumbler of whiskey.

Garrett had stopped listening after that and concentrated on Iris. She was lucky. Despite the wound being deep, the knife had missed any organs. Once he had sewn the injuries shut, he cleaned the rest of her up and put her in a robe. The loss of blood worried him most. Iris had lost a lot and had gone several hours without treatment.

The sun had started to rise when he finished. Looking around, he saw everyone else dozing off, their work done. He gently picked Iris up and walked to his room on the first floor. He placed her in his bed and pulled the covers over her. After, he sat on the end of the bed, staring at her pale face.

Why she would confront the group of known killers by herself, and who had given her such insane orders? The next twenty-four hours would tell if she pulled through. She was strong. He knew that from the short time they had spent together. But she had lost so much blood, and he still worried.

Even when she woke up, she wouldn't be able to move around a lot, not until the wound had healed enough, which could take some time. The thought of that made him smile. Somehow, he doubted that Iris would be pleased about bedrest and would probably try to defy his orders.

After watching her for a while longer, he took his leave and went back to the kitchen. He saw Cole and Isabelle talking over some coffee and oatmeal. Micah must have gone home because he was no longer there.

"Come get some coffee. It's freshly made." Isabelle held out a cup for him, which he took and sat down next to her He listened in on their conversation.

"Iris and I have known each other for years…" Cole paused. "I believe it's been about ten years or so. She found me wandering the streets when I was ten or eleven. I'm not quite sure. I think Iris was about seventeen when we met. When she was twelve, she had to leave the orphanage she had grown up in. She has always had a smart head on her shoulders and started doing some work for an investigator and then the police. Iris could go into places they couldn't and spy on who they

59

wanted more information on. She made herself invaluable by tracking down criminals that had evaded them for so long. As she got older, an agency that I will not name got wind of her and her improving gun skills."

Cole smiled. "When they came to her and offered her a position, she told them that the only way she would accept was if she could bring me along and I would work for them as well. They didn't see that as a problem because she was the one they wanted. I was just a bonus. With their training, she had only gotten better at honing her skills. I look up to Iris so much…" He looked down. Isabelle reached over the table and took his hand in hers, squeezing it for comfort.

Garrett had been staring into his coffee as he listened, consumed with his own thoughts. He thought back at all the scars he had seen on Iris, how much she had been through, a past he hardly knew anything about, but a voice in the back of his mind kept whispering, *I want to be in her future.* He pushed those thoughts away, not wanting to get his hopes up.

The three of them took turns looking over Iris. First watch was Isabelle. She sat next to Iris on the bed, reading a book out loud to her while Cole and Garrett slept. During the afternoon, Cole watched over her while Isabelle fixed them all something to eat.

"She's awake!" Cole called out. Immediately, Garrett rushed to her bedside where Cole and Isabelle already were.

Her eyes were still closed, and she was moaning. Garrett leaned in close, barely making out three words in between her groans. "It... Rune... Leader..."

"Oh, shit..." Cole said.

"What do you mean? What or who is Rune?" Isabelle questioned.

"Long story... Short version, he's a really bad guy she has crossed paths with several times. And if he really is the leader, then we're in deeper shit than any of us, including our boss, realized." He shook his head.

Garrett looked over Iris's wounds and redressed and cleaned them, not wanting them to get infected. He took over Cole's turn while he and Isabelle ate. The doctor wiped the sweat off Iris's forehead with a damp cloth, not wanting her to get a chill. He let his thoughts take him.

He thought of his lips on hers, the feeling of her soft body against his, how she would fit perfectly in his arms. As his thoughts started to explore what he would do to every inch of her if she would let him, he was brought back to reality with a start when Isabelle came into the room with a plate of food for him. He quickly moved the towel he had dried Iris with over his lap in an attempt to hide what his thoughts had brought to the surface.

Clearing his throat, Garrett said, "How are you doing? You haven't slept yet. Aren't you dead on your feet?" His voice still held a rasp, despite his best efforts to get rid of it.

She smiled at him sweetly. "I am perfectly fine. I'd rather go to bed early tonight and sleep the whole night. That way my sleep pattern won't be messed up. Do you want me to take over for a while?"

He shook his head as she handed him his plate of food. "No, thank you. I am all right."

After Isabelle left the room, he let his shoulders droop. Garrett was so ashamed of himself and his thoughts. She was lying there, helpless, and his thoughts had turned to dangerous territory he had no business exploring. It's not like he hadn't seen naked women before. He had, tons, and didn't have one thought about them, not in that way. But this, her, it was all different. Garrett didn't know what had come over him. To fight off the thoughts that continued to creep into his mind, he took out his flute, something he hadn't played in quite a long time. One of the only gifts his mother had given him.

He started to play; to push away the feelings of the present, he would bring out the pain of the past.

Chapter 7

Cole sat at the table, still eating the food Isabelle had made. *Damn, she's a good cook.*

"Why the smile?" Isabelle asked.

Cole looked up at Isabelle. Her beauty took his breath away. It took a moment for him to answer. Clearing his throat, he said, "I was just thinking about how good this food is."

The sound of music suddenly echoed from the room Iris was in. A bright smile came across Isabelle's face. "Why the smile?"

She turned to him, still smiling. "A girl can't reveal her thoughts."

"Oh, really? Come on. Out with it," he said, eyeing her with a grin.

Isabelle giggled and sat down across from him. "Well, you see, my brother rarely plays his flute. Reminds him of his mother." She paused, thinking. "Seems like he wants to get something or someone off his mind."

Cole was taken aback by her wink. "So, you're saying that he wants to get... Iris off his mind? Is that where your thoughts were going?"

Isabelle leaned forward, putting her chin on her folded hands, and slightly nodded. "Maybe."

He frowned. "Wait! Wait! Didn't they just meet?"

"Yes, that is true, but sometimes people can't help how they feel or how fast those feelings come about." She stared at him.

"So... He's in love with her? No... That can't be..."

"But it is quite possible." Isabelle smiled at him.

"No..." He looked at her. "Yes?" She nodded again. "No... It can't be. They can't! She would tell him so... Not with Rune about..."

"Wait, what do you mean? Tell him what? And what does it have to do with this Rune fellow?" She eyed him, daring him to hold his tongue.

He looked away from her. "I can't... It's not my place to tell."

Isabelle glared at him. "I suggest you tell me."

He turned to glared back just as fiercely. "And what if I don't?"

She sat back in her chair like she had already won this argument. "I will stop feeding you. And all you will have is bread and water." Her eyes dared him to accept that fate.

Swallowing, his mouth had become dry at the thought of stale bread. Isabelle laughed at him, still waiting for his answer. Turning his head, looking at the ground, moping, he whispered, "Fine..."

She leaned forward. "What was that? I didn't hear you..."

"I'll tell you." He looked back at her with a look of defeat on his face. Isabelle smiled. "You see, there's this guy... Rune. He has this thing for Iris. Every time he thinks someone likes her, they end up dead or injured. We don't know how he finds out. It's like he has spies in the woodwork. But because of that, she pushes everyone away, not that she had ever had real feelings for much of anyone. The only reason I'm safe is because we both make it clear we think of each other like siblings."

"I see... So, she has never been in love?"

Cole shook his head. "Not to my knowledge. She tries to keep most people at a distance. I'm the only one she has let in. And I still don't know her that well. She keeps a lot to herself and tries to keep topics of conversation on other people. The only reason I know about her past is because of our boss. He says she is that way because of growing up the way she did. Deep down she'd rather not know love, instead of knowing of it and losing it in the end."

Isabelle nodded, a mischievous grin coming to her face. "I see."

"What? What is it?"

Her eyes sparkled with delight. "You see, that sounds very similar to my brother. I think we should try to push them together."

Cole found himself nodding along with her, but he then realized and shook his head. "Wait. No. We can't do that. Why would we?"

"Because they're meant to be, that's why." He was about to object, but she leaned over the table, putting her finger on his lips. "Ssshhh… Listen to my plan."

He blinked at her in surprise as a grin spread across her face.

After playing the flute for a while, Garrett felt a little more at ease, despite the images from the past that came to mind. Once he checked on Iris and her wounds, he took his plate into the kitchen. When he stepped into the room, he saw Isabelle and Cole sitting side by side. Cole whispering and Isabelle giggling. The sight made him smile but also confused him. Shaking his

Iris Before the Storm

head, he went to wash his dish. As he had his back turned to the others, he heard more whispers and then a chair slide back.

"I'll go sit with Iris now," Cole said and then his footsteps echoed out of the room.

Turning, he saw Isabelle staring at him. "What? Why the stare?" Garrett asked, taking a seat across from her.

"Dear brother." She reached over the table, motioning for him to do the same. When he did, she took his hands in hers. Her eyes showed concern. "You haven't played your flute in so long. Do you want to talk about what's on your mind?" He looked away. "Is it still the memory of your mother and the fire a few days ago that is bothering you?"

Garrett shook his head. "I'm not even certain of what's happening myself."

She sighed and squeezed his hands. "Could it have something to do with Iris?" He looked up at her in surprise. "Tell me what's going through your mind. If you can't talk to me, who can you talk to?" Isabelle sweetly smiled at him, squeezing his hands reassuringly.

He sighed heavily. "I'm quite confused by all that is going on in my mind. Thoughts I hadn't thought in a long time or at all have come to the forefront. And the feelings I've started to feel have no explanation."

"The explanation couldn't be that you're falling in love? Don't give me that look. Listen, love can come like a crashing wave. One you didn't see coming. And this one I've seen coming. You've fancied her ever since she came to town a month ago. I've seen the way you watch her from your office as she takes her daily strolls. The times you accidently crossed paths on the streets. There's no point in denying it."

"But I've only truly known her for a couple weeks. We've hardly talked. How could I be falling in love in such a short span of time with someone I hardly know?" He shook his head in disbelief.

"Love can be that way. It's rare, but it happens. Wasn't it like that with your mother and our father?"

"Yes," Garrett admitted grudgingly.

"When she wakes up, get to know her and let her get to know you. You always have a wall up. Take a chance by letting her see you for you."

Nodding, he stood. "I'm going to tend to the horses. Let me know if she wakes up or her condition changes."

Isabelle stood as well, and with a smile and a small salute, she said, "Aye, aye, doctor."

He tilted his head in confusion but then smiled and walked out into the yard toward the barn.

Iris felt as if she were floating through a dark heavy fog that seemed to be crushing her with its pressure. Muffled voices could be heard within the fog that surrounded her. After the voices came mind-numbing silence. She tried to swim through the darkness, but her body felt too heavy, too weak. Then after what seemed like years in the quietness came the sound of lovely music, but what instrument and who was the musician?

As the music played, the dark heavy fog slowly lifted along with the heaviness that seemed to hold her down.

After tending to the horses, Garrett sat outside, still trying to clear his mind from all the thoughts that were trying to drive him mad. He was so confused. How could he feel this way and so fast at that? None of what he thought or felt made any sense to him, and he hated to admit to himself, but it somewhat scared him. It felt as if all of his thoughts and emotions were out of his control, and Garrett didn't like being out of control, even in the slightest. If he could, he would control every situation to his liking.

Another thought crept into his mind, one that surprised him. *That's why you like Iris. She seems to control every situation she's in.*

Shaking his head, he heard Isabelle's voice. "Garrett, she's waking up!"

He jumped to his feet before his mind even comprehended what his sister had said. Within a few large steps, he was in the house and headed to his room where Iris lay. As he opened the door, he saw her trying to sit up.

Pushing past Cole, he gently laid her back down. "No moving. You'll pull your stitches."

Iris looked up at him. Her weak smile made his heart race even more than it already was, and when she spoke, he felt like he was going to go insane. "Doctor's orders?"

He returned her smile. "Yes, doctors' orders. And this doctor doesn't play nice when his orders are defied." Garrett winked at her and was rewarded with a brighter smile. He then turned to Isabelle who was watching their exchange. "Sister, would you mind making some broth for our patient?"

"Of course." Isabelle left and headed to the kitchen.

Then he turned to Cole. "Would you get her some water please?"

Cole headed to the nearby pitcher and put some water into a mug that sat next to it. He then handed it to Garrett, who helped lift Iris' head to sip some water.

"I'm going to go see if Isabelle needs any help," Cole murmured. "I'll be right back, Iris."

Iris nodded and smiled reassuringly at him.

Garrett pulled up a chair and sat next to her. She turned her head and studied him with those captivating eyes. "Seems like you've saved my life twice now." When she laughed, she started coughing. Garrett gave her a little more water.

Sitting back down, he said, "Don't push yourself. The knife wound was pretty deep, and you lost a lot of blood. It does seem like trouble follows you."

She laughed lightly. "You have no idea..." But then looked away as if she were thinking of a memory that had come back to haunt her. "How long will I have to be bedridden?"

"In a hurry to move on?" Garrett eyed her, trying to figure her out as she warily looked back up.

"In some ways. Like you said, trouble follows me. And it's not done stalking me yet. The last thing I want is for my trouble to extend to you and Isabelle. Even this town doesn't deserve what shadows me." She looked away again and whispered, "Yes... A shadow... Always there, never far behind."

Garrett took her smaller hand in his, making her turn to glance at him. "What if we want to fight this shadow with you?" The expression that came across her face shocked him. He didn't think anything scared her, but his words seemed to hit a deep nerve.

She tried to smile. "Garrett, I appreciate what you and your sister have done for me, but I cannot bring either of you into what haunts me. To do so would be very selfish of me. Neither of you deserve what is to come."

He gripped her hand harder. "And you deserve it? You deserve to be alone and face all of it by yourself?"

The surprised look on her face didn't fade. Her eyes grew wider, making the purple in them shine. "There is a lot you don't know, don't understand. You wouldn't be saying all of this if you knew."

Garrett leaned closer, his hair falling in his eyes. She reached up and brushed the loose strand to the side. He impulsively grabbed her other hand and kissed her palm then inner wrist. His actions stunned not only himself but Iris as well.

His face darkened, returning to its stone-like features, showing no emotions. He left the room without another word, knowing he had to get away from her before he did something even stupider.

Iris laid there, her heart racing, her mind muddled. The warmth from his lips still lingered on her hand, making her pale face flush. Blinking, she looked around the room and saw a flute lying on top of the dresser drawers. Seeing this made her hold her breath. *It was him… It was Garrett who cleared the dark fog from my mind.*

Iris knew she liked Garrett, but all of this — the flute, him kissing her hand and wanting to take on her troubles — scared her. She had to get out of there as soon as she could. To stay would only bring suffering to innocent and kind people who were not able to defend themselves from the onslaught that was to come if she were to stay.

Isabelle came in a while later and fed her broth. And as if she knew eating would stop Iris from talking, Isabelle ventured toward topics she knew Iris would not speak on. "So… Garrett seems to have shined up to you, which is rare for him. I've never known him to really take interest in anyone. He told me once there were two types of girls he's met. The first is the ones who only like him for his father's money and status. The other may like him for him, but in the end, her family will not allow it, and most girls won't go against their families. But you, my dear Iris, are quite different, aren't you?"

Isabelle kept feeding her as if to keep her mouth too busy to talk. Iris almost choked a few times because of her rapid feeding. She didn't allow Iris to swallow the first before taking another spoon full.

"Now you're wondering what all Cole has told us, aren't you? He hasn't told us much at all, but as for myself and my brother, we could tell from the start that you are your own breed of woman, much like myself. Cole was saying that someone may try to find you? Or something. He was so vague that I was left confused. Anyway, now that you've found yourself here, why not let us help you? Because we want to help you, Iris. We have become friends, haven't we?"

Isabelle didn't give Iris time to answer. She continued to speak. It seemed as if she didn't need to take a breath. Just one word after another. It stunned Iris, so all she did was stare at Isabelle, listening as she went on. After all the broth was gone, Isabelle left Iris to rest.

As she laid there, thinking, Iris knew she would have to try harder to push them all away. It was for their own good. But why did it seem so hard to do so? This was going to turn out to be her hardest mission yet, to keep all of them at bay. She hadn't connected with people so much or so fast before. Not since Cole had it happened.

But Iris had to keep reminding herself it was for their safety that she did what needed to be done. She would turn her heart to stone to keep them all safe.

Chapter 8

Iris slept throughout the night and woke to the rising sunlight shining in from the window to her left. She was relieved when Cole brought her broth this morning. Iris wasn't sure if she could stand seeing either of the brother-sister duo at the moment. It only made what she had to do harder.

Garrett didn't want her to feed herself yet because she didn't have the strength to hold the bowl yet. But before Cole could start feeding her, she looked up at him. "Listen, Cole. No, listen. I need your help."

"Uh, all right, but if you need to pee, I should get..."

"Ugh, no... I need your help getting out of here." She eyed him, trying to read him.

"Wait, what? No. You need to rest. You almost died. You can threaten to kill me, but I'm not helping you move an inch. No way, no how, no."

"Cole, listen. If Rune is behind all of this, it's best to keep Garrett and Isabelle out of it. You know what will happen to them if Rune finds me here." Iris pushed down the memories that tried to rise to the surface and the fear and anger that came along with them. She had to focus to save innocent people from the clutches of a madman.

"But we're here to protect them. Are you going to run all your life? Never stopping long enough to love and be loved in return?" Cole stared at her. He had never been this up front with her before, and it shocked her. "They want to help you. Why not let them?"

Iris glared back. "Because — they — will — die," she whispered, enunciating every word. She paused to judge his reaction and then went on. "They will die gruesome deaths because of my presence here, Cole. Don't you understand that? The only reason you aren't dead yet is because of the agencies help and Rune knowing you are like a brother to me. That is why you are still alive right now. If he finds out I'm still alive, he will come down on this town with an army and nothing can stop him. Do you hear me? Nothing." Cole tried to speak but what came out only sounded like a squeak. "Do you want to endanger Isabelle's life and that of her dear brother's? Are you willing to risk them for the sole reason of me to feel loved? I don't see that as a valid excuse, Cole." She stared at him, daring him to tell her that it was worth the risk, knowing he knew it wasn't.

He sank back into the chair, looking down at the untouched bowl of broth. "All right, but we have to at least wait till you're well. If you still want to leave then, I will help you leave." He looked defeated, as if his whole world was crashing around him.

"Cole…" she said softly, touching his hand. He looked at her. "If you want to stay here, if you want to settle down, you are allowed to. My lifestyle doesn't have to be yours."

"But what will you do without me?" His eyes widened as if he were a begging pup.

"I will come and visit you from time to time. The reason I've kept you around so long was for your safety. But I see that was a selfish decision on my part, and I am sorry for that. So, if you would like to stay, I am more than happy for you, Cole." She smiled at him sweetly, trying to ease the worry she knew was starting to creep into his mind. "You start living your life the way you want to. And don't worry about me. You know I'm a fighter and can take anything thrown at me, all right?"

He nodded and was about to speak but couldn't. He sat the bowl on the side table and left the room. Closing her eyes, Iris sighed, knowing she had hurt him and more than she probably even knew. He wouldn't be the last one she would end up hurting, but she would rather have hurt feelings and have them be alive than the alternative.

There were so many mixed emotions floating around inside him. He never knew he could feel all of them at once. Cole had never had a home before. He was always on the move, just like Iris.

But on cold winter nights as a child, he would sneak into town from whatever hole he had been hiding and watch families through windows. On the other side was a warm caring world he had never known. Meeting Iris gave him a piece of that world, someone to call family.

Then, coming here, walking into this world and being welcomed into to the warmth of it all. And Isabelle, Cole had never felt such pure kindness radiate from someone before. She was like rays of light, casting away all the loneliness he had felt throughout his life. Cole gravitated toward Isabelle as if she were the sun and he the earth, forever in her orbit.

Frustrated at these feelings and thoughts, he went out to the barn, up to the loft. Iris' words rang through his mind. She had seen that he wanted to stay, to have a home. But for the longest time, she had been his home. She had looked out for him when no one else would, given him a safe place, fed him.

Cole had almost lost her, and now he might lose her again at his own choice. Could he really do such a thing? Choose between the love of a sister and love of someone he had just met, that he hardly knew anything about?

Punching the wall in frustration, he heard the floor boards creak behind him. Turning, he saw the blonde fairy-like creature that caused so much joy within his heart, it hurt.

"Cole, are you all right? Let me see your hand." Before he could even protest, she had taken his hand within the two of hers, looking it over.

"How did you become a nurse?" All the thoughts he had been thinking before seemed to wash away at her touch. *Shit, I really am under her spell.*

"That's a long story. I mostly picked it up from following Garrett and watching him. Reading what books he has laying around. I've also helped out on small battlefields when skirmishes happen."

"Wait, battle, around here?" He couldn't even imagine Isabelle in the middle of such a scene. Blood-stained cheeks, mud-drenched clothes.

"You would be surprised at what people fight over. Now, would you like to tell me what brought this on?"

All he could do was stare at this ray of sunshine that stood before him. Thinking of leaving behind Iris made him feel sick to his stomach, making him say words he didn't even feel. "I can't feel love, Isabelle. I'm unable to love like normal people."

"Don't say such things, Cole." She wrapped her arms around him, making his body responded in ways he didn't think possible.

"Isabelle, we just met. You shouldn't…"

"You know as well as I that we both feel something, something undeniable. Can you really say otherwise?" Her blue eyes looked up at him, pleading.

"I… I have to keep Iris safe…" It took everything he had to not lean down and kiss her. "I'm sorry…" He pushed her from his arms.

"My feelings remain the same, no matter your actions." Her voice faded as he left the loft and barn.

Cole had never felt so much unlike himself more than in that moment. His words and actions felt so unnatural that his own skin crawled. But he knew, when he was in her orbit again, the façade he just had would come crashing down.

Isabelle came in later and saw she hadn't eaten. "This won't do at all. I will go make more. Don't you go anywhere." She laughed and winked at Iris then left the room to make more broth. She figured Cole and Garrett would not return the rest of the day, and she thought it best that way.

Better to push them away now rather than later. When Isabelle returned, she wasn't her usual talkative self. Iris wondered what was bothering her but thought it best not to ask.

Once Isabelle left, Iris was alone with her thoughts, which waged a war.

Half of her wanted to stay, to be with them all like a family. The other half knew better and wanted to leave as soon as she was well enough. She slowly drifted back into the dark fog that held her before, her thoughts continuing to gather strength. But this time, it felt as if she were in a raging storm. In this chaotic storm, she heard someone groan in pain, one after the other. Surely that wasn't her? It hurt to think...

She let herself drift deeper into the dark waves.

"Garrett! Get in here!" Isabelle voice rang through the house, making his heart skip a beat.

He ran from the kitchen into his room in the matter of a few long steps. As Isabelle moved aside, he saw Iris soaked in sweat, her body shaking. Her eyes were slightly open but only showed the whites of her eyes. All he could say was, "No... No, no, no." He pulled back the covers and saw the wound on her stomach had gotten infected. White puss oozed from the wound. He tried to steady his breath when he heard Cole's footsteps behind him.

"What's happened?" He didn't have to see Cole's face to know he was worried. He could hear it in his voice.

Garrett immediately spouted off herbs he needed, already formulating the best treatment plan.

Isabelle merely looked at both of them in confusion. "I don't know what any of those are."

"I know what you need. I'm certain I can find some. Keep her with us while I go look."

Garrett looked up at him in surprise but just nodded to the determined looking Cole who promptly ran out of the room. Garrett untied the stitches and started to clean her wound. Isabelle boiled water and gathered clean cloths. Using his tools, he cut her infected flesh away and stitched the area once more. Isabelle wiped Iris' forehead with a cool damp rag.

"How bad is it, Garrett?" Isabelle asked with a worried expression.

He shook his head. "It's deep. If we're not able to pull her out of the fever within a few hours, we may lose her." Garrett almost choked on his own words. His hands shook as he washed her wound. He had never been so shaken before. Not even his first year at medical school made him react this way.

Isabelle placed her small hand on top of his and smiled sweetly at him. "You know what you're doing. She couldn't be in better hands, Garrett. I believe in you. Believe in yourself." Her nodding her head made him nod. It was strange how she did that.

Smiling back, he sighed and reached out his free hand to grab Iris'. "Hold on, Iris. We're all here, waiting for you."

"Garrett?" Isabelle almost whispered.

"Yes?"

"You wouldn't tell me earlier, but will you tell me now? What made you storm out of here yesterday?" Her eyes begged him to tell her, urged him to confide in her.

Sighing, he looked from his sister, then to Iris. "I was telling her to let us help her with her troubles. Trying to convince her to stay…" Sighing again, he shook his head in disbelief at what he was about to say. "I leaned toward her. Some hair fell in my face and she brushed it away. And before I knew what I was doing, I kissed her hand."

Isabelle burst out laughing. "What? That's it? You kissed her hand and that sent you into a tizzy?"

He nodded, embarrassed. "I know. It wasn't something to get worked up over. But…"

"But you scared yourself," she finished for him, trying to mimic his voice and manner. "And you have never acted in such a way before."

Garrett let out a little laugh. She had eased his nerves. Isabelle always surprised him like that, always finding ways to comfort him without making it obvious she was doing so. The two of them sat next to Iris' side, waiting for Cole's return. The night dragged on minute by minute.

"Do you think he'll find what you need?" Isabelle asked. "It's quite dark out."

Before he could answer, they heard a distant door open and close, footsteps and then the door to the room they were in opened. A panting Cole stood in the doorway, holding out herbs for Garrett to take. The doctor rushed to take them, his heart leaping at the sight of them.

"Thank you!" Garrett immediately went in the kitchen to prepare what he needed.

Cole sat down in the seat the doctor had just vacated, still panting. All the sudden, Isabelle wrapped her arms around him, squeezing him tight. "What was that for?" he asked with a laugh.

"For you finding what was needed. Even in the darkness of night, you were able to find small plants no one else could even find, much less see. Cole, you are a true wonder." His cheeks burned. The heat must have been visible because Isabelle smiled even wider.

Clearing his throat, he said, "How is she doing?"

Isabelle released Cole and leaned over to Iris to wipe her brow with a damp cloth again. Sighing, she sank back in her chair. Cole was worried not just for Iris but for Isabelle as well.

"What's troubling you? I miss your smile," he asked, hoping his smile would rise another one out of her.

Those words brought a small spark of a grin to her face, which lit up his heart. "I'm worried for her and my brother. He really is falling head over heels for her, it seems. And then she was talking about needing to leave? That would break his heart…"

Iris suddenly moaned, and when Cole glanced over, her body was trembling.

"Garrett!" Isabelle called out.

He rushed in carrying several bowls. He pushed past Cole and Isabelle, sunk to his knees, and put the bowls on the floor next to him. Isabelle and Cole moved themselves and the chairs out of the way.

Garrett lifted the covers again to put some herbal salve onto her deep stab wound, but she was moving too much. Seeing her in pain, all he wanted to do was take it all away. All the scars that riddled her body he couldn't even begin to imagine the mental trauma. Thinking of how much pain she must have had to endure in the past made him feel sick. Pushing the feeling down, he focused on his patient.

"I'm going to need you to hold her," Garrett said grimly, hating the thought of forcibly restraining her but knowing it was for her own good.

Both of them looked at him reluctantly but still did as requested. Isabelle held her legs while Cole kept her upper half still. He quickly applied the salve, wincing when she moaned. After he finished, he placed a cloth over it to keep it in place.

"Thank you," he told them, and they released her.

The doctor then did the same thing to all the other wounds, but they were far less severe. It was very late into the evening when he finished.

He glanced over and saw Isabelle staring into the distance, a clear sign she was past exhaustion. Cole looked dead on his feet, almost falling over where he stood. "Go get some rest," he told them. "Doctor's orders."

They both needed sleep, and he didn't want to leave Iris' side until her fever had passed.

Isabelle hesitated. "Are you positive?"

"Yes, little sister."

"Aye, Aye brother." She tried to be her hyper self, but there wasn't much hype left. "Promise you'll come and get me if you need me." He agreed and waved goodnight.

After the two of them left, Garrett sat next to Iris on the bed and wiped the sweat from her to keep her dry, trying to keep her from catching cold. But whatever he did, nothing seemed to keep her from shivering.

He knew the best way to combat the cold, but did he dare? He hesitated, reason fighting again feeling. It might be a stupid idea considering how he felt toward her, but it was the only thing he could think of. He decided to lay next to her. As he wrapped his arm around her, he felt his own body heat rise. There shouldn't be a problem using his body heat to warm her. Looking down at her pale face made him sad and wistful. But those thoughts shifted when Garrett placed his face against her raven colored hair, smiling at the softness of it. It took all his will power to push the sensual thoughts from his mind.

And as he felt her forehead against his lips, his concern for her grew. Now all he could think of was how he wanted to protect her, to heal all her wounds, even the scars.

Why does it have to feel so good to be this close? he thought as he closed his eyes.

Unable to sleep due to worry over Iris, Isabelle made her way down to the kitchen. She was still upset at what Cole had said earlier, talking about not being able to love, needing to stay with Iris to keep her safe. She took to washing the dishes with feverish motion, trying to busy her mind more than her hands. It wasn't that she questioned her feelings. She knew they were true. What upset her was that Cole was trying to push her away. Yes, it was happening fast, but that was how some things worked out. It wasn't that either had seen little of the world and fell for the first fancy face they saw. No, this was much deeper.

Slamming a plate down into the water, she closed her eyes, trying to ease the rushing of blood that filled her ears. Isabelle was a smart girl and knew the reason behind Cole's actions and words. Iris was like a sister to him. He was worried about her and had reason to be. She also knew he couldn't deny his own feelings. They would eat away at him, just like hers would as well.

She left the dirty dishes behind in search for Cole but didn't have to look long. She was walking toward the barn when she spotted him coming from the other side, a determined look on his face. It was quite unlike him and made her giggle.

Before she could say anything, he rushed to her and tugged her into the barn where they were hidden from view. Cole released her but backed her against the wall of the building. This wasn't like Cole, but Isabelle didn't want to stop him. She wanted to see what he was playing at.

Cole leaned down to her ear and whispered, "I'm sorry." And in a flash, the Cole she knew and adored was standing before her. "I've never been in love, uh, I mean, in like before." He blushed, confused at his own words. "I've never felt like this. And then almost losing Iris. My feelings are raw and I got scared."

"Thank you for telling me. And I understand. It's hard seeing family sick." She wrapped her arm around his neck. "I've never felt this strongly for anyone else as well. But I know these feelings are true, and I won't push them away or bury them. We can be in like until you feel ready to be in love. As for me, I feel you are the missing piece of my heart. And now that I have you, I feel whole." Isabelle was always confident in her decisions, rarely giving into doubt and fears.

Isabelle stood on her tiptoes to meet Cole as he leaned down for a kiss. But the once soft kiss turned passionate. Unable to quench the flames of desire that rose in both of them, Cole lifted Isabelle up and she wrapped her legs around his waist.

Garrett woke with a start.

He hadn't meant to fall asleep. Sitting up, he looked Iris over. She had thankfully stopped shivering. He kissed her forehead, feeling her temperature. It too had gone down. He sighed in relief and checked her wounds. They were doing all right, but he reapplied the herbs just to be safe.

The sun had started to rise when he decided to play his flute for her. The notes floated through the air, filling the house with its sweet melody. As he played, he gazed at Iris' sleeping form. How could he be so taken in by someone so fast? If felt as if every fiber of his being was being pulled toward her. He didn't understand how one person could hold his whole heart and not even know it.

After a while, he started to get concerned that Iris had not woken up yet. Garrett heard a noise in the kitchen and decide to get some coffee. First thing he saw when entering the room was Isabelle's beaming smile. It seemed even brighter than normal.

"What's got you in such a cheery mood? More than normal, I mean." He stared at her as he poured him a cup.

Isabelle brightened, her cheeks flushed. "Well... I kissed Cole."

"What! You just met."

She laughed at him. "When you know, you know, brother." She winked at him and went back to cooking, turning her back to him.

"Just make sure it's only a kiss. I don't think I can handle helping you give birth anytime soon." Garrett knew Isabelle had a good head on her shoulders, and the two of them didn't shy away from most topics. He just hoped she didn't move things too fast. If there's one thing he knew about his sister, it was that she was impulsive.

Isabelle spun on her heels, pointing a wooden spoon at him. "Don't say such things! I'm not ready for children. Don't worry, I know how they come about and that's not happening till our wedding night."

"Wait... Wait... Don't tell me you're already planning on marriage this early." He almost spat out his coffee but put it down before he did.

She only laughed at him and turned back to cooking. He shook his head, hoping she wasn't really thinking that far, not with someone she just met and hardly knew. But then again, who was he to pass judgement? And this was Isabelle, after all.

Garrett went back and sat in the chair next to the bed, reading but keeping one eye on Iris. Her breathing was steady, she no longer had a fever, and had stopped shivering. But why wasn't she waking up yet? His concern grew as morning gave way to noon.

Cole came in and put his hand on Garrett's shoulder. "Let me take over for a while. You need your rest as well. She won't be running off anywhere."

Garrett sighed and ran a hand down his face. He was tired. "All right but come get me straight away if something changes or if she wakes up."

"Absolutely," Cole easily agreed and ushered him out of the room to get some rest.

Garrett had a fitful sleep filled with nightmares. He found himself lost in a dark deep forest with twisted trees that loomed over him like giants. Every time he tried to find his way out, he only got more lost.

Then it shifted, and he found himself in a dark fog, but it wasn't fog at all but deep dark waters. With each movement he made, his body grew heavier with the weight of the water atop him.

How was he going to escape? He couldn't see or hear anything. Garrett continued to swim, but he could hardly move through the darkness. Knowing he was indeed dreaming, he decided to see if he could wake himself. When he yelled, his voice went through the water like ripples atop a pond. Yelling again, he found he could swim forward through the ripples.

Garrett kept moving forward but everything looked the same. Why couldn't he wake up? After repeating it a while, he got discouraged, but his ripples then hit something, sending echoes of waves back to him. His heart pounded in excitement. He moved faster toward it to see what else would be in this dark place. Soon, Garrett saw a faint outline in the shape of a woman, which made his chest tighten.

Reaching the figure, he could hardly see to make out their features, but somehow, he knew who it was. Iris. But how was she here, in his dream? And why couldn't he wake up?

He hugged her limp body to him. She felt so lifeless. They needed to wake up. He needed to wake up to make sure she was all right. He ran his fingers through her hair and brushed his thumb across her lips. He leaned in and kissed her, hoping in some way that this would wake him up like in those fairytales all the girls went crazy for.

But to his surprise, her lips moved under his, kissing him back. Her arms wrapped around him, and her lips parted for his. His tongue explored her mouth as she pressed her body against him. If this was a dream, the feelings were all too real.

When he pulled away from her, he found that their scenery had changed. They were in his bed, the one she now laid in. But this room had no door, only the window from which the moonlight shone in.

He then noticed he was lying on top of her. Garrett rushed to move off, but she gripped him, not letting him move. She leaned up and kissed his lips, pulling him closer. Her lips felt warm and lush, sending warmth all throughout his body.

Trying to pull away, he said, "This can't be real… Iris…"

"What if this is real, Garrett?" she asked, surprising him. "What if you saved me again? But this time it was on a much deeper level?"

He shook his head. "I don't understand what you mean. This can't be…. It's all a dream."

She smiled at him. "All right then, if it is a dream as you say it is, why not show me how you really feel?"

He swallowed hard. "I have to wake up, to get back…"

She put her finger on his lips, silencing him. "Ssshhh, everything will still be there when you wake. Right now, focus on this moment. What if this is our only chance to be together?"

Her words took him by surprise. He didn't know how to respond. Her purple colored eyes drew him in. He had never seen such a lush hue. Seeing his hesitation, she pushed him off and rolled on top of him instead.

Garrett looked up at her, shocked at where this dream was headed. She sat atop him, and he could feel her warmth. She leaned in again, kissing him. He kissed her back, cupping the back of her head and pulling her even closer. When she moved her hips, rubbing against him, he froze, surprised at her actions.

"If this is really a dream, why are you holding back? This is your mind, is it not? Or is it mine?" she whispered into his ear before he could say a word.

But her health was more important than having his fantasies play out in his dreams. "I need to wake up…" He needed to check on her, to see if she was awake.

"I hope we connect again, Garrett." She leaned back, and the room went dark.

Garrett woke with a start; he was sweaty and breathing hard. He couldn't believe how vivid the dream was. How real she felt, the kisses, how she straddled him in his bed. Just thinking about it made him desire her so much, he thought he might go mad. He took a longer time to calm himself so he could go down and check on his patient. After trying to push the thoughts of the dream out of his mind for the time being, he headed downstairs.

At the bottom landing, he ran into Cole. "I was just about to come get you. She just woke up."

Without even giving his brain time to process the words, his feet practically ran to her. Isabelle was already there at her bedside.

Rubbing her eyes, she looked around at each face in turn. "Why are you all staring at me as if I'm on my death bed?"

Cole snorted out a laugh. Isabelle elbowed him, still sweetly smiling down at Iris.

"That's because it almost was... Again..." Garrett looked over her wounds, his doctor side taking over, stone wall up.

"So, I guess that means I owe you three times for saving my life then?" She stared at him as he peeled back the cloth that held the herbs.

"I'll clean your injuries again and then put more salve on them." Before anyone could say anything, he left the room to gather what he needed.

Cole looked at Isabelle. "What is going on with him?"

She answered by shaking her head. "We're all glad you are better," she told Iris. "You gave us another scare."

"I even had to go out in the dark cold night to find the herbs Garrett needed. When you get injured, you get injured, don't you?" Cole smiled, making Isabelle nudge him again. He elbowed her back, making the two of them laugh and smile.

Iris watched them being playful with each other. "Seems this has happened fast." They turned to her in surprise.

While Isabelle hid her reddening face in Cole's shoulder, he just smiled brightly. "Maybe."

Then Iris turned serious. "Cole, you haven't sent word back to base, have you?"

He shook his head. "No."

"Good. Let's wait a while to inform them. It's best if people think me dead for the time being, at least."

Cole nodded in understanding as Garrett returned with the herbal paste. Isabelle nudged Cole, a secret sign for the two of them to leave the room.

"We're just going to step out for a minute so you can examine her wounds," Isabelle said sweetly. As they left, Isabelle caught Iris' eye and winked.

Iris lay still as the doctor did his work, neither of them saying a word, not knowing what to say. But then, Iris wasn't one to be embarrassed. Once he was done, she looked out the window. "Were you able to sleep any?"

He only nodded stiffly.

Why did she yearn to hear his voice, to have him near? Even though he was in the same room as her, he had never felt more distant.

"I saw the flute on the drawers. Do you play?"

"Yes," Garrett replied curtly.

She sighed, which made him turn and look at her. "You really are a hard one to read. It's like you turn to stone. It's easier that way, though, isn't it?" Iris closed her eyes. "To not feel, to not connect. I completely understand." She paused, and he waited for her to speak more. "It's better that way, easier to let go when a person leaves your life. The pain is still there though, even though we turn our feelings off and push them away..."

Her words trailed off when she felt his warm hand on her arm. Opening her eyes, she saw him staring at her, his golden eyes sparklingly with the new day's light. The shadows played with his features, making them seem even sharper. And his skin, it was as if the sun's rays wanted to touch every part of him. As her gaze drifted over him, their eyes locked, neither of them knowing what to say.

But it felt as if they were being pulled to one other. She reached up and touched his cheek. Her breath caught in her chest as he drew his face closer. *Is he going to kiss me?* she thought and hoped, but his eyes shifted as he pulled away as if a dark curtain was pulled, blocking the connection they had. She questioned why she even wanted to kiss him. It would only make leaving harder.

When he stood up, he gathered his things to leave. "I'll get Isabelle to bring you more broth."

She smiled at him, but he did not see with his back turned to her. "Thank you again, Garrett."

He froze as he reached for the door handle. Clearing his throat, he said, "Just doing my job."

And with that, the good doctor left the room, leaving Iris questioning why she longed for him more than she thought possible, even when she knew her mere presences would bring them closer to the clutches of a madman. Only she knew firsthand the lengths he went to and the brutality he inflicted.

Thinking of these things made her heart feel like it was breaking in two. One half being weighed down by the past and all the pain it held, the other wanting nothing more than to be hopeful for a future she might have to run away from before it had a chance to even start.

Chapter 9

The next few days followed the same routine. Iris woke up, ate some oatmeal and Garrett checked her wounds; Isabelle would come in at lunch and talk with her while feeding her broth. Then in the evening, Cole would come in with some more broth with a little bit of chicken bits mixed in.

She remained very isolated, but Iris kept reminding herself that it was a good thing. Better for her to be able to leave, no attachments. From time to time, she could hear Cole and Isabelle's laughter through the door. It seemed the two of them were growing closer and closer. She was happy for them and knew that to keep them safe, to help them continue to live their happy life, she would have to leave. And soon. The longer she stayed, the more danger all of them would be in. If you love someone, you have to let them go, right? So, they could have the best chance at happiness, even if it meant not being with them.

One night, she had an interesting dream. She was in a forest surrounded by fire, but when she reached out to feel the heat, there was none. When she placed her hand directly over the flames, her skin did not burn. This dream world she found herself in didn't feel like her own. One of the children in the orphanage told her we could connect with past ancestors and spirit guides through dreams and on rare occasion, you could connect with someone else's dream, but to do that, you have to be bonded. He couldn't explain how this bonding worked or how it happened.

Iris was never sure if what he was saying was true but always thought it was interesting. But being in this dream, something felt different. Just like a dream she had a few nights ago before she had woken up after the fever. Iris had thought that dream was something brought on from the feverish haze, but she was starting to think otherwise.

As she continued to walk, the fire grew in intensity. Her instinct pushed her toward the center, where the fire was billowing as high as the trees that stood around her. As Iris neared the center of the fiery storm, she saw a young boy with long jet-black hair who sat hugging his knees. He was surrounded by a ring of fire that was about the height of her.

Iris neared the wall of flames. The boy jumped to his feet. "Don't! You'll burn! Please don't!"

He had been crying. Tears streaked his dirt-caked face. Looking below him, she saw a little dug out area. He must have been trying to dig a hole for him to cover himself with. To protect himself from the heat. But Iris didn't feel the heat because this was his dream. And because of that, he was the only one who could control all of this.

She had to help him calm down. So, stepping forward, she reached the fire's edge.

The boy screamed in pain and fear for her. "No! Don't!"

She gave him a small smile. "Trust me. I won't be hurt."

She moved forward, all the while the young boy cried out to stop her but dared not move, hiding his face in his hands. Iris moved through the high flames. She felt no heat, and she wasn't burned.

Kneeling, she took his small hands in hers. He looked up. Iris wiped his tears away sweetly smiling, trying to ease his worried heart. "It's all right now. I'm here."

"Who...who are you?" he asked between sobs.

"You can call me Iris. What should I call you?"

He weakly smiled. "My mom calls me little bear."

"That's a nice name. Why don't I call you bear? Because you're not so little anymore. You're strong like a bear."

Her words brightened his expression, making his small smile grow. "How can we leave here?"

"What I'm going to need you to do is to not think about what is scaring you. Think of a happy, recent memory. Can you do that for me?"

"I... I don't know how."

She hugged him tightly. "You are strong like a bear. Close your eyes. Think of what has made you happy."

He did as she said, closing his eyes. Iris held him, waiting and hoping it would work. After a few long moments, the scenery started to change. The fire faded, leaving a bright open forest. She blinked. The young boy disappeared, and she found herself in the kitchen of Garrett's home.

She looked around in confusion. It was exactly like it looked now, but how? Little bear was... Whose dream was she in....?

Garrett's door opened, and he stepped out. His warm, tanned chest showed through his loose shirt, which hung about him. As her eyes guided down, she saw he was in his undergarments. She frantically looked somewhere else, not knowing what to do. This was his dream. Why was she still here? She should have been pushed out when the dream shifted, right?

Iris stood there, stiff, unmoving. Before she knew it, he was in front of her.

"Why can't I escape you? Every waking second my thoughts are consumed by you, and even in my dreams, you find me. The harder I fight these feelings, the more you are on my mind." He grabbed her tightly and wrapped his arms around her, nuzzling his face in her hair.

"Garrett..."

"Say it again," he rasped, his voice washing over her like a chocolate treat. "Say my name."

She looked up at him. "Garrett..." she said breathlessly.

His eyes shifted as if a lever had been turned, breaking the stone exterior he held so tightly in place. He placed his lips on hers, bringing her closer to him. Iris returned the kiss without even thinking. He lifted her, and she instinctively wrapped her legs around his waist. Garrett pushed her against the wall for support as his kisses grew more intense.

He moved his hands to her butt, squeezing while holding her in place. She let out a moan as a wave of pleasure crashed over her. Breaking away from her mouth, he moved to her neck. It was only then that she noticed her dress had turned into an almost see-through nightgown.

Iris looked at him in surprise, but he didn't notice. He was too focused on what his lips were doing. He had let go of his wall, and for now, there was no putting it back up; and she didn't want to. At this moment, she didn't want to leave him, Rune and his hellfire be damned.

If this really was his dream, if this really was him and his true feelings, she wanted him all the more.

Garrett cupped her breast, the other arms still easily supporting her weight against the kitchen wall. She gasped as he squeezed and rubbed a nipple.

"Garrett..." Iris said in between moans.

He returned to kissing her lips, keeping his hands where they were. She lifted his nightshirt, digging her fingers into his back. His skin was hot to the touch as if he were a kettle about to blow. Her actions had pulled him closer to her, letting her feel his hard erection.

Chapter 10

Garrett woke with his heart pounding, his bed soaked with sweat and other bodily fluids. That dream was all too real. He could hardly face Iris before. How could he face her now after what he had dreamed? He knew his mind was going to think back on that dream so many times. Garrett had never seen or even felt such vividness within a dream before. He started to get a rise again just at the mere thought. *She felt… Her body was so… Dammit… I can't be near her… Not right now.*

Knowing Iris was well enough, he decided to go to his clinic in town. He changed his sheets, cleaned off, and got dressed. After gathering his things, he headed downstairs.

As soon as his feet hit the kitchen floor, he heard a bird-like greeting. "Morning, brother! Are you off to see patients today? Shall I come along?"

He shook his head at Isabelle. "No, I will be fine on my own. Why don't you stay here and make sure Iris doesn't move too much? Please." Before his sister could respond, he headed toward the door.

"No breakfast?" she yelled out.

"No, thank you!" He sighed in relief as he mounted his horse. Incredibly, even that made him think of the dream. As he hardened in his saddle, he muttered to himself, "This is going to be a long day."

Iris was panting when she woke. *These dreams are getting out of hand.*

She'd thought the previous dream, the one from the night when she had a fever, had been just that, a dream, but not anymore. These dreams were connected somehow. This was going to make things harder for her to leave. With what happened last night, she was thankful it was only in a dream. If that had been in person... She shook her head, not wanting to think of it.

Deciding she couldn't stay in the bed any longer, she sat up and as her feet hit the floor, the bedroom door swung open, ushering in a smiling Isabelle. This pretty, fairy-like girl almost made Iris have a toothache due to her sweet nature, but it faded with the knowledge that Isabelle had the best intentions behind her smile.

"Get up slowly now. After you eat, I will get a bath set up for you. I'm sure you feel ghastly." She laughed, placing the bowl of oatmeal on a small table in front of the window. "Come, sit here."

Iris did as Isabelle ordered. It was a beautiful day, and she couldn't believe that spring had finally come to full bloom. More time had passed since arriving than she first realized. Isabelle came back into the room after Iris had eaten, hands on hips.

"Cole! I could carry that faster than you. You're like a snail on a rainy day," Isabelle yelled out the bedroom door. "Shake a leg. We don't have all year."

"I'm coming. Hold your horses." Cole yelled back.

"That is not the proper thing to say to a lady, Cole. Ladies do not hold horses." Isabelle smiled at Iris who knew she was just playing with Cole, trying to make him flustered, which was quite easy.

He finally arrived with the large tin barrel for Iris to wash in. It took about thirty minutes to fill it with enough warm water. Isabelle laid out a thin spring dress for Iris. "It's loose, so it won't pull on your stitches. Take your time. Just yell if you need anything."

Iris nodded and undressed once Isabelle left. She had to admit, the bath was refreshing. It was good to be clean and soak in warm water. As she sat there, her thoughts drifted to the dream from earlier. Closing her eyes, she tried to push those thoughts out of her mind and just rest. But as she washed, her thoughts began to wonder, thinking of Garrett and how he let himself go last night.

She bit her lip, thinking of all the things he had done to her, and how much better it would have been in person. But as she looked down at her naked body, she saw all the scars. The reminders of why Iris didn't let anyone get close. Because they would end up being another one of her many scars. And that was not a collection she wanted to be adding to. Pushing away the thoughts of Garrett, she finished the bath.

When Iris was getting dressed, she heard a high-pitched voice coming from the kitchen. It wasn't Isabelle's voice. It wasn't as musical like hers. This sound was like someone raking their nails across a chalkboard. After braiding her hair, Iris reluctantly went into the kitchen to see who this voice belonged to.

She was hardly in the room when the newcomer said, "And who is this creature? What a drab thing. Is she your maid?" Iris was about to say something but the lady went on. "And you have a new beau, but why is he living with you?"

Iris hoped Isabelle would not tell this mouthy lady the real reasons, but what reason could Isabelle come up with? She stood there, watching, not wanting to get involved. But what happened next almost sent her to the floor in shock.

Isabelle smiled mischievously. "Well, you see Iris here," Isabelle waved her hand at Iris who was cautiously watching, "is Garrett's fiancée." The other girl looked more shocked at this than Iris did.

She looked from Iris to Isabelle in disbelief. "No, that can't be. When did this happen? How?"

Isabelle seemed to be enjoying this immensely, her grin never wavering. But then Cole jumped in. "Yes, you see, me and my sister were traveling here when she fell ill. That's how they met, and because she is still recovering, we are staying here. Our uncle is the sheriff, which is why we came to town. Lucky that the good doctor was around."

The girl just sat there, dumbfounded. As Iris stared at Isabelle and Cole, almost laughing at how excited they both were at their well-formed idea, she had to admit they worked well together.

"Where… where is Garrett? I have to hear this from him." The well-dressed lady with golden hair stood.

"Flora, you can't just up and leave to town. You just got here. Cole will go and get Garrett. I'm certain he will be surprised to see you. Why don't you come and rest in my room?" Isabelle escorted Flora up the stairs to rest.

Cole went over to Iris. "I don't think Garrett will like going along with this plan. But it's too late now, isn't it?" He winked at her and headed outside to get a horse to go and fetch the good doctor.

Iris gathered her some bread and cheese. She ate slowly, hoping not to be disturbed. Iris knew Garrett would definitely not be happy about the story Isabelle and Cole came up with. Especially with the dream from last night. Iris knew it was real, that they had a connection and could somehow get into one another's dreams. But he didn't seem to know that, and she couldn't tell him. That would make leaving harder. She still had to leave, to keep them all safe. And now, she had to play along with their false engagement, too.

After she was done eating, she went into the back of the house and for the first time noticed there was a garden. Or what used to be a garden. Garrett and Isabelle must not know how to tend to it. So, she decided to pick the weeds and see what vegetables might still be growing. Iris wasn't sure how long she had been kneeling, pulling weeds. But she heard of Garrett's return by the shrill voice of Flora. She didn't know the lady, so Iris tried hard not to judge, but that voice physically hurt her ears; so much so she was tempted to stick some roots into her ears to block the sound.

She blocked out the sound of Flora's voice by busying herself, not wanting to be subject of it. Iris had found a brown sack and decided to kneel on that to pull the weeds, so not to mess Isabelle's dress. She was surprised the dress fit her. It must not have been Isabelle's at all. Their bodies were completely different, and no dress of Isabelle's would fit Iris, much less be loose on her.

But what voice she heard next sent chills down her spine. "You aren't well enough. Who told you, you could do that kind of work?" Iris raised her head to see Garrett's face darken more than its natural shade. "Am I going to have to keep an eye on you every minute of the day?" His voice was full of concern, but his stare was full of anger. But was the anger toward her or someone else?

This man is so hard to read... Iris thought. As she stood, she winced, forgetting about the cut on her leg. Before she could look up, strong arms wrapped around her, lifting her up. Looking around, she saw Flora's pale face. *Poor girl. Wait, why did Isabelle have to say engaged? There could have been other stories that would have worked.*

Garrett carried her back to his room and put her on the bed. He left the room without a word, and just before he closed the door, she saw a glimpse of a grief-stricken Flora. Iris wished she hadn't gotten so injured. If she hadn't, she would have long been gone.

To her surprise, Garrett came back in with changes of bandages for her. "Let me take a look at your wounds. I'm afraid you might have pulled out my stitches."

Because he had already seen her many times, she didn't mind getting undress in front of him, but he turned away nonetheless. Once she was robed, she laid down for him to change her bandages. As Garrett got close to her, she whispered, "Garrett, I'm sorry. I wasn't thinking about pulling the stitches." He didn't answer, so she lowered her voice more. "I'm also sorry for the story Isabelle and Cole came up with. I had no idea. I could have come up with something different given time."

She thought she saw Garrett smile slightly, but it was gone before it even fully appeared. "I understand the reason behind Isabelle's idea. You see, Flora has been chasing me for years. No matter how many times I've told her that I'm not interested in her, to move on, she never listens. So, this all might turn out all right. Maybe Flora will be able to move on now. Doesn't make me comfortable doing this, but I want her to move on." He cleared his throat. "It also seems that Isabelle has bunked us together."

Iris laughed slightly. "Of course, she did."

He was soon done with changing the cloths and checking her wounds. "You look to be healing nicely now. But just because you are feeling better doesn't mean you can start moving around like you use to. Not yet at least. Do I make myself clear? These are deep wounds and aren't just small cuts."

Iris nodded. "Yes, doctor. I understand." He smiled at her, making her heart flutter.

"I'll let you rest and will come in to get you for dinner." Before she could say a word, he was out the door.

As Garrett closed the door behind him, he saw Isabelle and Flora staring at him. *If it isn't one woman, it's another.* He contemplated going back into the room with Iris. At least he didn't have to worry about her wanting to fill the air with her voice. Gritting his teeth, he walked toward the two ladies who seemed to be preparing dinner. And not to his surprise, Flora was the first to speak.

"Why isn't your lady out here, cooking for you?" She eyed him, trying to find flaws in his choice of bride.

Sighing, he said, "They didn't tell you? She had a bad fall off a horse at a high rate of speed and was stabbed by a sharp tree limb in the process." He surprised himself. He was almost as good as Isabelle at telling lies. It kind of scared him.

"Oh, dear, that must have been quite bad, then," Flora said, her concern inauthentic.

"It was. We were scared we were going to lose her the first few days after her accident. She is just now getting better," Isabelle chimed in.

"Is that so?" Floras eyes flashed, making Garrett and Isabelle stare at each other. They'd seen that look on Flora before. They'd known her since they were all children. That look usually meant she was planning something, and her plans tended to have bad outcomes for others to make things more favorable for herself. One major reason Garrett didn't care for her much.

Garrett left the two ladies and went to tend the horses, but Cole was already tending to them. He sighed in relief at the sight of him. "Good. I'm glad you're here."

"Where else would I be? If I could, I would stay in town for the time being. One can only take so much of idle chatter and such."

The doctor nodded in agreement "I wanted to let you know Flora isn't as innocent as she makes herself out to be. She might try to find a way to hurt Iris. Can you take extra care to watch them around each other?"

Cole laughed. "You think Flora will get something past Iris and hurt her? Like a loose floorboard? Or a rake hidden in leaves? I wouldn't worry so much about Iris. But I will keep a look out nonetheless." He winked at Garrett. "So... You two are almost newlyweds. Any plans for tonight?"

The doctor rolled his eyes. "How can you talk about your own sister in such a way?" Garrett feigned degust. Cole burst out laughing again. He liked Cole. He seemed like a good fit for Isabelle, both with their cheery disposition and playfulness. Then he thought about how his life would be if he had married Flora like she wanted. Those thoughts didn't last long and were overtaken by the vivid dream featuring Iris.

"Garrett? Garrett?" Cole waved his hand in front of the doctor's face.

"Yes?" He blinked, looking at Cole questioningly.

"Were you daydreaming of something good or bad? I couldn't tell." Cole lightly laughed. "Iris was right. You can be really hard to read. It's like you turn to stone in an instant."

"She said that?"

"I thought she would have told you. She's quite open with her thoughts. Don't worry. If she hasn't, she will. Iris is probably trying to be nice, which means holding her tongue. She can be very blunt at times, but she has the best intentions behind her words, even if they sting a little."

"What makes her so blunt?" Garrett asked curiously, wanting to know more about what made her tick.

Cole grinned at Garrett, his eyes beaming. "She's always said what was on her mind for the most part. The only thing she doesn't talk about is her past or hopes for the future. She's more live day by day kind of person. She probably does have hopes and dreams but doesn't want to voice them, thinking if she does, they will be lost on the wind, never to be made true." Cole's cheeriness shifted to more of a solemn, sad look. Looking down at his feet, he scuffed them against the dirt. "If by chance you reach her, if she confesses her fears, her hopes to you, don't let her go. Because if you do, she will be lost to all of us." He paused and swallowed hard. "She will even be lost to herself. So, if she shows you her innermost thoughts, hold onto her with all the strength you possess."

Garrett stared at Cole in confusion. "Why are you telling all of this to me?"

"Because I've tried to reach her for years, and in some ways, I have. She's never let people in, not truly, not deeply. But I think you might have a chance for whatever reason. Call it fate or what have you. If she lets you in, don't let go." The stable fell silent. Garrett wasn't sure how to reply. All of this was too much, too sudden.

He started to walk out of the stables but turned to look at Cole. "Tell the ladies I'll be back in time for dinner. I'm going for a walk. I would suggest holding off on going back in as long as you can." Garrett smiled at Cole and made his way into the woods.

Garrett had never had so many conflicting thoughts running through his head. On one side, he did feel a connection with Iris, one he couldn't explain. Then, on the other hand, it all happened so fast and so strong that he could hardly even believe it was all real. Not just lust or loneliness? But if it were one or both of those things, he would have felt them for other women. It wasn't like he lived his life as a monk.

All of it scared him, but the real reason whispered in the depths of his mind. *What if these feelings are all real? And you truly care for her? That you are afraid of loving and losing. Just like she probably is…*

He sighed and leaned against a large oak tree. Garrett had always admired the strong oak tree. How well rooted they were, how they stood up to the strongest of winds and if they were to fall, their seeds took their place. As he leaned against the strong tree, another small voice whispered his mind, *You are scared that what you are feeling isn't real.*

Shaking his head, he stood from the oak, taking deep breaths to ease his racing heart. Garrett wanted to tell his inner voices to shut the hell up. They only made his overthinking worse. The sun was starting to make its descent when he made his way back to the house. Dragging his feet, he pushed through the door, finding all but Iris at the table talking.

Flora saw him come in and ran to him. "Where were you? I've wanted to talk to you all day. I just got here, you know. And you go off, busying yourself. Now, after dinner, you are mine for the rest of the evening. We will play cards and drink some mulberry wine I brought. No, if, ands, or buts. I will hear none of it from you." She flicked his nose.

All he was thinking was how he hated cards and preferred stronger drink. He would definitely need a stronger drink. "If you say so. I will go get Iris for dinner."

He was about to walk off when Flora grabbed his arm. "Why doesn't Cole take her in a plate? That way she can rest some more? Wouldn't that be best?"

This wasn't the first time Garrett was thankful for his stone expression, because if the young girl in front of him could read his thoughts, she would run screaming. "I think it will be good for her to get up and move some." He pulled his arm from her light grip and went into his room. Iris was up, sitting at the small table in front of the window.

"How are you feeling?"

She continued to stare out the window and, without turning, said, "I'm fine. Been trying to block the sound from the kitchen. It's as if she makes her voice extra loud and cheerful, like she was trying to bother me." Iris turned and looked up at Garrett. "But why would she want to do that?"

Garrett wasn't sure, but he thought he had seen a small grin appear on her lips, those lips... His mind started to wander to dangerous places such as the delighted sounds she'd made in the dream. He shook his head to clear away such thoughts.

"Would you like to come join us for dinner? Or have your meal here?"

"What would be best for all involved?" She was truly sincere in her question, leaving Garrett speechless.

Taking a moment, he thought through which would be best, for her to stay here or join them. Iris stared at him as he mulled it over.

"Why don't you join us? You have my permission to speak your mind. I would rather you do so in front of Flora. I warn you, she has always tried to hurt or mess with others to make herself look good. So, she will probably do or say something to you."

The look Iris gave him made him step back. "Other women don't intimidate me," she said easily.

Another reason why she was exceptional. "All right, then."

They left the room and ventured out into the kitchen. Isabelle had already laid out plates and put the food in the middle for everyone to grab. Flora seized Garrett and guided him to a chair next to hers across from Cole. Iris took a seat at the end. Better to watch everyone from.

They all gathered food on their plates. Flora and Isabelle controlled the conversation. Flora only spoke to Garrett or

Isabelle and looked at Cole a few times with a nod but seemed to try her best to completely ignore Iris.

Toward the end of dinner, when most were done eating, Flora turned her attention to Iris. "So, where are your father and mother? What do they think of this quick union?" She glared at her.

Iris' expression stayed calm. "Well, you see, our parents died a while back. My uncle helped put me through school to become a school teacher. I was top of my class. He helped my brother Cole as well. But you see, Cole has a different mom, which doesn't make Micah uncle by blood. But that doesn't matter to Micah. He's so kind-hearted. He sees people for who they are and their actions. Not by what they have and don't have. Or who their parents were." Iris smiled sweetly at Flora who kept glaring.

"It's always good to know where one comes from. To form a better family unit. I know my family tree dates back to the medieval ages." Flora puffed up her chest in pride. Cole held back a snort of laughter and busied himself with his drink.

Iris kept her smile plastered to her face. "Indeed, that's something to be proud of." She paused, probably to see how Flora would respond. "I've always thought that it's not someone's past that defines a person. Because how can one person look at someone's grandparent and judge their grandchild the same way when they are not the same person and didn't grow up the same? I see the past as a learning experience, something someone can learn from. But not something to be judged by. Someone should only be judged by their actions here and now. That doesn't mean the whispers of others because if someone is having to whisper about someone, what they are saying probably holds no truth to it."

Game, set, match, Garrett thought.

It was Flora's turn. Sitting up straighter, she said, "But if someone doesn't know their past, how can they build a future?"

"The past can greatly affect one's future, but our ancestors have taken their paths, made their choices. Future generations should honor them by keeping their stories alive and learning from them. Everyone today seems to judge too harshly, not even taking time to sit down and talk because of a skin tone, missing out on knowing a person true nature." Iris still held the sweet smile. Garrett's was in awe of Iris at this moment. He wanted to just stare at her, take her in. But the sound of a chair being pushed back and a voice made him look away.

Flora was now standing. "Garrett, you promised me a game of cards. Shall we?" She started walking toward the small sitting room, which they never used. It laid next to Garrett's, now Iris', room on the first floor. As Flora opened the door, a puff of dust hit her face, making her stumble back, coughing. He heard Cole trying to hold back a laugh as Isabelle elbowed him, causing him to cough instead.

Garrett snuck a peek at Iris once more before he walked reluctantly past Flora. He had to return to the kitchen to grab a damp rag to wash the tables and chairs.

"I'll bring in the wine she brought," Isabelle whispered, out of ear shot of Flora, who stood waiting in the doorway of the parlor. "And for you, my dear brother, whiskey." She winked at him. He just shrugged, knowing not even whiskey would do much good with all the thoughts that ran rampant in his mind.

He could feel Iris from where she sat at the table, just the mere presence of her. And now he had to sleep in the same bed? All he could do now was hope that Flora with her cards and gossip would give him the distraction he needed. Taking the washrag with him to clean the room, he once again walked toward Flora who took his arm, making sure everyone they were leaving behind saw. She shut the door behind them with a smug grin on her face and her giggles could be heard through the door. The long night had begun...

Flora held Garrett until late in the evening, past midnight. He bid her goodnight and when she leaned in for a kiss, he backed up, making her stumble forward. She frowned, but he already had his back to her and went into his room before Flora could catch him. He closed the door carefully, hoping not to wake Iris who seemed to be asleep already. What he had hoped would become a distraction ended up being anything but. It had only made his mind wander more. The whole time his thoughts kept creeping to Iris and the dreams he's had.

And now, Garrett couldn't believe he had to bunk with her. It was better than Flora. But lying next to Iris, he wasn't sure if he would be able to control himself. And if he had a dream, that would be so much worse.

He slowly lowered himself in bed and pulled the covers over him.

"Did you have fun?" a soft voice murmured next to him, sending chills through his body.

Laughing lightly, he said, "As much fun as one can when one hates cards and gossip." Garrett sighed. His body was already reacting to her closeness.

"How good of a shot are you?" she asked, and Garrett could almost hear her smile.

He turned his head, surprised at her question. "Um, I'm all right, I guess. Haven't really done much in the way of shooting targets or animals or anything really. Why do you ask?"

Iris turned to him and sighed heavily. Garrett's breath caught in his throat. What was she thinking? Did the nearness affect her as much as it affected him?

"I was hoping once Flora leaves, I could teach you how to shoot," she said after a few moments. "Cole has already asked to show Isabelle. She's quite excited."

All Garrett could do was stare at her mouth, her full lips. He nodded, unable to speak. *Oh, shit, this isn't good*, he thought as her mouth formed a smile.

"Garrett," she whispered.

The sound of her whispering his name set him on fire, more than he knew he could be. It was just his name, something he'd heard hundreds of times from hundreds of different mouths. But it was from her lips. And the softness of it…

Fuck it.

He reached for her, putting his hand on the back of her head to pull her in closer. He softly took her lips with his. They were so much softer than he had thought. The sensation sent yet another rush through his already burning body. Much to Garrett's surprise, she didn't push him away. She leaned forward, kissing him back. He almost stopped at the realization of how much she wanted this. But he couldn't stop, not now.

Iris wrapped her arms around him. When he lowered his other hand to the small of her back, she threw one leg over his, bringing them ever closer. She moaned lightly, making him kiss her more passionately. He tried his hardest to hold back, but if this was holding back…

"You set me on fire…" Garrett whispered in her ear and was rewarded with a shiver.

"My sentiments exactly," she whispered back. He captured her lips once more, dominating her mouth.

"I think… we should… stop…" Garrett said breathlessly after the fire had almost grown out of control.

"Before… we go… too far…" she finished his sentence for him. He nodded in agreement. They slowly and reluctantly pushed away from each other. His body throbbed for her touch, only hers. Only Iris.

"I think I best sleep on the floor…" Garrett said.

She cleared her throat. "That might be best."

It took him a while to settle his emotions enough to try and sleep. It was at least an hour before he heard her breathing even out as she finally slipped away.

Garrett woke from a dreamless sleep the next morning to see the sun had already fully risen. Sitting up, he saw Iris had already left the room. He sighed, thankful for a moment to calm himself.

After brushing his hair and flattening his clothes, Garrett headed into the kitchen. He saw Iris sitting alone, eating oatmeal. "Where are the others?"

She looked up and smiled at him, dark circles under her eyes. "I think Isabelle and Cole are out back and... Flora is out front. She told me not to disturb her."

Garrett first saw Flora in her pink dress that made him want to puke at the unnatural hue of it. Looking past her, he saw a small fire going. Fire? Picking up his pace, he saw a dark red gown being burned.

He glared at Flora. "I didn't even know you knew how to start a fire. Much less burn someone else's clothing!"

Flora stood tall and looked at Iris who now stood next to Garrett. "Oh, dear. Was this your dress? I saw it in the wardrobe in my room and assumed it must be from one of the old servants and set to burn it." She glared at Iris, who only gazed back at her unflinchingly.

His jaw ticked and his hands balled into fists as a rush of near-overwhelming anger surged through his entire body. Iris stepped back. As if he'd ever hurt a hair on her precious head, no matter how angry he was.

Flora, who was not as perceptive as Iris, grabbed his arm. Looking up at him with the best pouty face he'd ever seen, Flora said, "I was just trying to help. That's what good friends do."

He turned on her like a snake to a mouse. "You think burning someone's things is being a good friend? You think belittling someone is being good friends?" His voice grew progressively louder. "You think being a good friend is pushing yourself on someone who doesn't want you?"

She stepped back, letting him go. Tears fell down her pale cheeks.

Garrett still glared at Flora. "Do you think your tears will work on me? I've seen your fake tears before and know the difference."

Flora glared right back at him, all tears gone. "I will tell my father!" Flora yelled as if she were a child.

"Oh, do tell. I've told him many times that I will never marry you. And I know I've made it crystal clear to you. I thought with the knowledge of my betrothal..."

Flora cut him off, screaming at the top of her lungs. "Don't say it! It's not true! You can't marry a thing like her! She's probably not even a woman under there!" Flora reached for Garrett's hand, but he pulled back, unable to stand the thought of her touch.

"I think you should head home. I will have Isabelle take you to town." He was about to turn when she stomped her foot.

"No!" she screamed. Her screams had brought Isabelle and Cole from around the back. They stood, stunned, watching everything unfold.

"What did you say?" he asked quietly, convinced he heard her incorrectly. She thought she had a choice in the matter? How wrong she was.

"I said, no! No! No! I won't go, and you can't make me!" she screamed, stomping both feet, her hands balled into fists.

He sighed. "How old are you Flora?" he asked calmly.

"W — what?" Her voice shook with anger.

"How old are you?" He still glared at her, daring her to not answer.

She looked down and whispered, "Twenty."

"That's right. You are a young lady, therefore, should act accordingly. Do you think you are acting your age right now?" She shook her head. "I think you need to go home and find someone more suitable for you to marry. I am not the one for you. Never have been. Never will be. I am sorry if all this hurt you. But you need to realize this before the right person passes you by when you were too busy looking at me to notice him."

Her eyes widened, and it seemed like for the first time, the words reached her in a way they hadn't before.

Flora left that night in a stagecoach and headed back to her home in the city. As they all lay asleep in their own separate beds, the noise of someone knocking on the front door woke Iris.

Jumping to her feet, she hurriedly put her boots on and headed for the door. Seemed like everyone else were deep sleepers, which meant she was the first one to the door. Micah stood on the doorstep with several other men behind him on horseback.

He held a light to their faces. "Looks like I'll be needing your help, Iris."

"What's happened?" The others, having finally roused themselves from bed, lined up behind her.

Micah's eyes shifted from her to Garrett. "Looks like the coach Flora was on was highjacked. They are holding hostages."

Iris put out her arm, stopping Garrett from stepping forward. Without looking at him, she said, "We will follow you. Garrett will stay behind with you and your men on the road, while Cole and I flank their camp. Any objections?"

No one said a word as they mounted their horses. Micah had brought extra. Garrett rode behind Iris. She could feel his gaze on her and it took every ounce of effort to push away the thoughts of their passionate kiss from the night before and what it sparked inside her. She focused on the mission and made a plan of attack with Cole as best they could without knowing the facts or the lay of the land.

But as they rode, the searing heat that continued to build inside her would not wean.

Iris and Cole made their way to where the camp was. This wasn't their first time dealing with a hostage situation, probably the only reason the sheriff and his men let them to go ahead with their plan. Cole would go in, seemingly unarmed, counting the number of guns as they tied him up. Iris would watch from a nearby tree. She was thankful for the sun starting to show its rays. The light would help her line of sight.

Cole entered the camp. Kneeling and holding his hands above his head, he fingered a number to Iris. The men were surprised at the newcomer and scrambled to subdue him. Cole was then tied up and put with the others. The look on Flora's face was priceless. The poor girl was shocked, relieved and smitten all at the same time. Iris was determined not to show herself. To let Rune and his men think she was dead. For as long as she could, that is. They would eventually find out she wasn't, but until then, she was worm food to the rest of the world.

Iris was glad these men seemed to be amateurs. They only had five guns among six men, and several hands shook while holding them. The shaky ones were more apt to kill a hostage by accident. Iris knew she had to move fast.

She took both of her guns out; the pistols Micah had given her. One in each hand, she took aim. Iris had never shown anyone but her captain that she could shoot two at a time. Cole didn't even know. Iris didn't like for all her talents to be well known. If they were, she wouldn't have the upper hand. There were even a few things her boss didn't know.

Focusing on which hand would shoot who, Iris readied her muscles and steadied her breath. Once the first shot was fired, everything moved fast. But to her eyes, everything almost moved in slow motion for her.

First two were bullets in the head, second two were hit in the chest, the last two were hit in the shoulder, and then the other shoulder. No one would be picking up a gun this time. She thought back to when she faced off the group she had been hunting for so long. Taking them on should have been as easy as this was. But some things were out of her control.

Iris sat there as she watched Cole untie the others and then signaled for others who were meeting with two of the bandits to draw up terms. After his signal, Iris heard two, no, three shots fired. She hoped only the bandits were hurt. Bead of sweat dripped down her forehead despite the cool morning air.

Images of Garrett, Cole and Micah injured flashed through her mind, reminding her once again why she couldn't stay...

She sat there, watching, as the group came into the woods. Iris sighed at seeing everyone safe. When Flora saw Garrett, she went running toward him teary-eyed. She doubted Flora would let go of Garrett, but she did after a moment surprisingly.

This would be a good time to leave for everyone's safety, but Cole knew which tree she was in and shook his head as if he read her mind. She grudgingly admitted he was right. She was still too weak. So, Iris slowly climbed down from the tree and went to the horse she'd tied up, not wanting to say any goodbyes or meet any new faces. The fewer people saw her, the less likely Rune would find her. For all she knew, all of this could have been planned to lure her out. She shivered at the thought, but then thought it strange that she was still sweating and cold...

She rode almost in a daze. As she neared the doctor's farmhouse, Iris heard a horse behind her, following her, but didn't look to see who it was. Not until she put her horse in the barn did she make out the rider. Quite unlike her. It was Garrett, his horse moving slowly down the hill.

Iris blinked, not sure if she saw him correctly, her vision blurring. He had a look of determination on his face. Her breath caught in her throat. What inspired such a look?

Her body responded with a wave of heat building in her. Garrett jumped off his horse, moving fast toward her. Iris was so taken aback by his manners that she unconsciously backed up to a large haystack. Looking behind her, then at him again only made her freeze. The smile he gave her made every thought disappear from her mind.

Chapter 11

Garrett had no idea what had come over him. All he knew was that he couldn't wait. He had fallen in love with her. He could deny it no longer. Her being so determined and so willing to save others at the risk of her own life made his heart thunder in his ears.

As he reached out to her, he noticed her eyes had become vacant. The look of determination vanished as he took her in his arms. He palmed her forehead to find her burning up.

"Fever?" she whispered.

Her voice was so soft he barely heard her. Picking her up, he rushed her inside. In their room, Garrett quickly undressed her.

"In a rush?" she asked.

He knew she had no idea what she was saying in her feverishness, but that didn't stop his heart from racing.

He looked at each wound and found no sign of infection, but what was causing her change in health? She had been doing well. Looking her all over, he finally took her hands in his. "Dammit, Iris…"

"So feisty." She laughed wearily, barely conscious.

"I told you not to pull weeds…" She had cut her hand while pulling weeds. The area was now swollen, puss oozing from it. How could he had not seen it? How could she not tell him? He body had already been so weak from her other injuries, making this one come on strong since it was unattended, causing her fever. "When it rains, it pours for you, doesn't it?"

"Don't be silly. I don't like rain," Iris whispered.

He couldn't help but smile at her child-like behavior. Garrett was able to clean the area and cut away the infected flesh then bandage her hand. "Seems we are starting from the beginning again. Bed rest for you. No gardening, no gunning." The doctor thought on how Iris holding the reigns of the horse and the guns tonight, probably didn't help her infected hand. And yet, she hadn't complained about any of her wounds since she got them. Which made him think again on the scars that marked her body.

Noticing she hadn't said a word, that Iris had fallen asleep. He wouldn't risk her getting up and doing too much again, so he crawled in bed with her. Stroking her cheek with the back of his hand and playing with her dark hair, he couldn't get over how beautiful she was. Garrett couldn't wait until the day when he didn't have to worry about someone dying from a small fever. And it seemed like Iris kept wanting to play with death.

Iris found herself in a cave. Sitting up straight, she looked around, heart pounding. How did she get here? *No...* She looked down at herself, shaking. *This isn't real.*

Her mind didn't listen to her own words and continued to panic. She hugged her knees and rocked back and forth. Hearing a noise near her, she squeezed her eyes shut. Iris tried to calm herself down but couldn't. It was as if she wasn't in control.

Someone knelt next to her and put a warm hand on her shoulder. She looked up and what came out of her mouth did not match her thoughts. "Who are you?" Iris asked, but her heart already knew. *Garrett.*

He gave her a warm smile. "I'm Garrett. What are you doing in this cave?" His demeanor was as if he were speaking to a frightened child. Garrett lowered himself to her level, making himself as small as possible.

She looked in front of her at the small fire she had made. "I'm hiding. Why are you here?"

"I'm here to find a friend of mine. Maybe we can wait here together. Who or what are you hiding from?"

Iris rubbed her eyes. "A bad man. He keeps chasing me. I've been running for so long. I'm so tired." All the while she was screaming in her head, *What are you doing? Who the hell told you to tell him this? Stop! Stop speaking!* No matter how much she screamed, whoever was in control, ignored her commands.

"Now that I'm here, you don't have to worry. You can rest for a while."

She studied him suspiciously. "How do I know I can trust you?"

A grin stretched across his face. "Because I'm a doctor and I care for people. I wouldn't hurt you."

She mirrored his smile, which made her scream even more. Why was this dream so different? Why couldn't she control what was going on? This wasn't like her dreams before.

Her exterior-self continued to talk, expressing feelings and fears she had never told anyone. "I'm scared I will end up with this madman who chases me. That I will never find someone to truly love or feel that love back. But I'm tired of running, and giving in would be easier."

Garrett put his arm around her, and his warmth enveloped her, comforting her. "But you know just because something seems easy doesn't mean you will get what will make you happy. You have to work toward what you really want. You can't give up, right?"

She felt herself nodded, the tension inside her core easing.

Iris woke to the sound of birds. Glancing to her left, she saw a sleeping Garrett. The last thing she recalled was him coming toward her with a determined look. Looking down, she saw she was in her nightgown, but he was still fully clothed, so nothing had happened? Did she dream? She couldn't remember but felt like she had. But if she had dreamed, all she could do now was hope Garrett still didn't realize they were connected.

She stared at Garrett, taking in his sharp nose and cheekbones. His bronze skin, his raven-colored hair. His caramel toned lips, which she lightly traced with her finger. But as she raised her hand, she saw the bandage. As she looked at her hand, a big, strong hand wrapped around her own.

"Morning," Garrett said smiling, sleepiness coating his voice, made it deeper than usual.

Smiling back, she replied, "Morning. I don't quite remember…"

"You had yet another fever. This one was caused by a cut you neglected to tell me about that got infected because you are still weak from your previous fevers. So, when I tell you not to garden, I mean it." He pulled her hand closer to his chest and kissed it.

Her heart thundered in her chest. She found herself staring at his long lashes, so she looked back down at her hand. "Did you sleep well? Have any dreams?"

"I slept fine." He removed the covers. "Rest some more. I'll have Isabelle bring you oatmeal."

Before she could say anything else, he was already out of the room. She didn't like that he didn't answer about dreaming. Had he figured it out, as she had? She laid there, trying to remember if she had dreamed, and if so, what happened? Slipping out of bed, she went and looked out at the window, frustrated at herself. Iris felt like she had forgotten something important, and it was going to bother her to no end.

Isabelle came in, bringing her oatmeal. As she ate, Isabelle sat on the bed. "I'm concerned about Garrett."

Iris stopped mid-bite. "How so?"

"You see, when he came into the kitchen, he seemed fine. Asked me to fix you something. But when he thought I wasn't looking, his exterior changed. It was like a dark figure is haunting him."

Iris' eyes widened. Before Isabelle could go on, Iris was on her feet. "Where is he?"

Isabelle looked worriedly at Iris. "He is out at the horses, I think."

Iris dressed quickly and headed to the barn, thankful Isabelle only followed her to the door and no further. Looking around, she hoped Garrett was still there. She went all around the stable and then looked around the area.

Seeing a trail behind the house, she followed it, her heart pounding faster. She didn't know how long she had walked or ran but in front of her now as a small creek. It had a wide area that looked like a nice-sized swimming hole.

Someone grabbed her arm, turning her around. Garrett held her wrist tightly in his grip, his eyes burning. As she looked down, she noticed he was only in his undergarments, shirtless. Her heart pounded even harder.

"Why are you here? You're supposed to be resting! Why don't you ever listen!" He stared at her, waiting for her answer.

"Did you have a dream?"

He shook her arm. "I told you to rest. You run all the way out here after having several fevers to ask about a dream?"

"Did I talk in my sleep?"

He gave her an incredulous look. "Iris, really? You look dead on your feet and you want to know about a dream or if you talked in your sleep?"

"Garrett..." She looked down, not wanting to meet his stone-like gaze. "You can't fight my battles for me. No matter how much you want to, no matter..."

He pushed her hard against a tree, pinning her with his body. "No matter? Finish what you were saying!"

"Dammit, stop trying to save me!" she yelled at him, tears springing to her eyes.

In the next instant, he pressed his lips hard against hers. Letting go of her arm, he wrapped both around her, bringing her in close. "Push me away all you like. I will never let go. Not now," he whispered into her ear, sending shivers down her spine.

She pushed against him, gaining some inches of space between them. "Not now? What do you mean? What happened?"

"I know how hard you push others away, scared to love and be loved. Wanting to give into the darkness that chases you..." She froze in his arms, sure she heard him incorrectly. "I want to give you a home, a safe place."

He has no fucking clue on what he's wanting to get into. No fucking idea... And safe place, there was no such thing, from her past, and the one chasing her.

Iris hit her fists against his naked chest. "You can't give me a safe place! There is no safe place! I told you, the only safe place for you and the ones you love is far from me. The devil is after me and he won't stop until he has me. I'm not going to bring you, Isabelle or Cole down to hell with me!"

Garrett held her tighter as she pushed hard to get away. "We want to help you. We want to fight with you. Dammit, Iris. Let us."

Pushing with all her weak strength, she staggered back away from him. Leaning one hand on her knee to catch her breath, she pointed at him and said, "Don't! Don't you dare! I told you I have to leave. Don't act like a knight in shining armor! If I can't take on this man, what the hell makes you think you can?"

Why couldn't she breathe? She felt like a mountain came crashing down on her chest. Iris fell to her knees, and a blurry figure rushed to her.

"Shit…"

Chapter 12

Garrett scooped some water from the creek and wet Iris' forehead and chest, making the dress cling to her breasts. He tried to focus on his doctor training and for some reason, he thought of breathing his breath into her. So, leaning down, he put his mouth on hers, making sure hers was open and breathed deep into her until he saw her chest rise. He repeated this several times until she regained consciousness, her eyes fluttering open.

He lifted her into his lap, cradling her. "I'm here and there's no getting rid of my love for you," he whispered.

Leaning against a tree, he couldn't believe he had just said those words. Even more surprising was the fact that he accepted those words as his true feelings. And no way in hell would he let her push him away. He would hunt her down, just like this crazy Rune seemed to always do. Garrett would do so because he knew deep down that she loved him as well but was too scared. And in her own way, she was also trying to protect all of them.

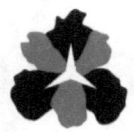

Iris opened her eyes to a lush green forest. Her eyes widened as they landed on Garrett, his shirtless chest up against her. *He is gorgeous...*

He opened his eyes and smiled down at her. "Sleeping beauty awakens. You gave me a scare there. That's what happens when you hold everything in."

She glared at him. "Is that so? This coming from the stone wall."

He grinned at her. "Are you still going to push me away?"

"Yes," she said firmly. "With every fiber of my being. To protect you from the shadows that follow me. Don't tell me you can handle them because you have no idea what you are up against."

"All right then. Why don't you teach me? Show me how to protect myself and mine." He smiled at her again, sending her heart racing. She stood up and moved a few feet away from him, putting some distance between them.

She stared at him, questioning herself. *How can I feel so attracted to someone yet be so angry with them at the same time?* And in response, a small voice came from the back of her mind that whispered, *You love him.*

"Shit..." she muttered under her breath, avoiding his questioning gaze.

This can't be happening. I'm a loner. I can't bring others into the shit storm that is my life. Iris looked back up at him and as their eyes met, all her tension fell away. Gritting her teeth, trying to push away unwanted feeling, she said, "All right... I was wanting to teach you how to shoot either way. But we," she motioned between the two of them, "can't do this. We can't get closer."

Garrett grabbed her wrist and, with a few large steps, pushed her against a large tree. Still holding her, he leaned in, whispering, "Can you really deny this? Can you really say you aren't feeling the same exact feelings I am? Tell me you've felt this before. Tell me that what we have isn't rare. That it happens all the time."

His eyes dared her to say that the two of them had nothing. That his feelings were all one-sided. The words rested on the tip of her tongue, but she couldn't force them out, no matter how hard she tried.

Leaning further down, he put his lips gently against hers. For a split second, Iris resisted — but only for a second. As he slightly pushed his tongue inside her mouth, she moaned. He groaned low in his throat and pressed his body against hers, his heat radiating into her.

Her hands explored his bare chest and then reached around him, feeling his skin against her bare arms. And as she lightly scraped his back with her nails, he gasped, pushing his pelvis against hers, letting her feel how much he desired her. Her body responded with a flood of warmth, needing him closer, so much closer.

Oh, she desired him just as much as he desired her, but images of what might or would happen to him if she stayed made her push him away. They stared at each other, both wanting to move forward. Both wanting more, but Iris knew she couldn't, no... *wouldn't* let him get hurt.

"I can't... Garrett..." Sighing, almost panting, she turned from him. "I'll set up some targets out back. I'll meet you there after lunch." She could tell he wanted to rush after her, to take her, all of her. But he stood rigid, staring at her back as she walked up the path back to the house.

Iris wouldn't let the thoughts of his naked chest haunt her. Or how incredible he felt pressed so tightly against her, his erection pressing into her hip. How safe she felt... *Stop... Remember, for his safety, push him away now, before the feelings grow to something more.*

She replaced those images with darker ones. Ones she knew would happen if she didn't leave soon. She made herself busy by finding things they could use as targets. Such as tins, glass jars and bottles, along with several other items. Cole saw what she was doing and found some old wooden boards and nailed them together to make a stand for all the targets to sit on.

Isabelle and Garrett watched from afar. Gritting her teeth, she pushed her emotions away and focused on the task at hand.

"I understand why you don't let others in," Cole said, "but are you always going to live your life like that? Never having a connection?"

She glared sideways at him. "I'd rather live a life of solitude than have others die because I was fucking lonely," she hissed. He stepped back, clearly not expecting to be met with hostility. Iris stepped closer. "This isn't a game, Cole. I will not play with other people's lives. What right do I have to put them in danger? Just because you haven't seen Rune in years doesn't mean he hasn't been watching. I will push away as many people as I can to save them. No one deserves the pain and death that comes by being around me. Do you understand?"

Cole solemnly nodded and turned to join the others in the house. She sighed, letting go some of her tension. Iris hated to be so frank, but the sting of her words was nothing compared to the wrath Rune would bring. He caused terrible things to happen, beyond most could imagine.

Her scars ached at the thought, him being the root cause of each one. Some were quick. Most were drawn out, torturously so. The devil himself hardly compared to this man. For all she knew, he could be working for the prince of evil.

After she was done, Iris went into the house to grab a small meal, having no appetite after filling her mind of all the painful things of her past. When she stepped into the kitchen, the conversation came to a halt. This wasn't new to her. It seemed to happen to her a lot where her mere presence brought a room to a hush. Iris cut herself a piece of bread and cheese and went back outside. And just as her foot hit the dirt ground, the voices started up once more.

Her heart ache at the thought at how lively and happier they already seemed without her. *No, no. This is a good thing. This is what I wanted…*

Garrett sat with the others, eating a light lunch. He was hurt by Iris, but he wouldn't give up easily. Not after all that she had revealed in the dream. Even though it had been a dream, deep down, he knew what he heard was real. Their dreams were connected, and she had revealed a lot that she had been through and seen. He knew her actions were out of fear, not just for herself but for others as well.

"Are you all right?" Isabelle asked Cole. "You look shaken."

He nodded, looking down at his food. "It's just that I have never seen Iris try so hard to push people away before. She's even pushing me away, and Iris has never done that before. I'm scared I might lose her this time." His shoulders sank, almost in defeat.

Isabelle grabbed his hand, squeezing it. "We're here with you. And we will help hold on to Iris as well. With all three of us, we won't lose her. If she pushes us away, we just have to hold tighter, right?"

When Iris came in for food, Garrett stared at her, despite her not noticing. He imagined himself jumping across the table, going up behind her and wrapping his arms around her. Holding her tight, he would kiss her neck. Lifting her skirt, his fingers would follow the outline of her leg. Up, up. All the way up...

Isabelle laughed at something Cole said, bringing Garrett back to reality. Blinking, he noticed Iris had gone back outside. He sighed, feeling strained, more physically than mentally.

After eating, they all headed out to the back garden. Iris showed him how to properly hold a gun and what happened when you did hold it wrong. Not only did you miss your target, but you ended up hurting yourself. She went on to how to aim and how your breathing can affect that along with your environment. There was a lot more to it than just pointing the gun and pulling the trigger.

"And a moment of hesitation could mean your life. The longer you think, the quicker you die. Let your body take over, and your mind will follow."

"It seems your mind is several steps ahead of anyone else's, that you can see their moves before they do," Garrett asked.

"She's amazing like that," Cole chimed in before she could answer. "Our boss says he's never seen anyone who can see the outcome of a situation before it even happens. Let's show them, Iris!"

"I've spared with you so many times that I already know your moves."

"So, you're saying that I bore you?" Cole crossed his arms.

"Why don't you spar with me?" Garrett suggested with a shrug. "I used to wrestle in college."

Iris looked Garrett up and down. "And how long ago was that?"

"Wait, you weigh so much more than Iris," Isabelle said with a frown. "Wouldn't that be an advantage?"

Iris laughed. "Weight can be used against someone. Being heavier than someone isn't always better. It can depend on skill and movement."

Garrett grinned. "All right then, what do you say? Spar with me?" He knew neither of them should be doing this. She should be resting, but he couldn't pass up an opportunity to touch her.

Isabelle folded her arms. "Weren't we supposed to be training with guns today?"

"It will be fun! I haven't seen you spar in so long," Cole said, unable to mask his enthusiasm.

Iris nodded. "All right, a little. I still have healing wounds and such. I need to get something. One moment…" She ran into the house. Making them all wait. Questioning each other on what she could be doing.

A few moments later, Iris returned in men's pants and a shirt. Garrett's mouth opened as he took her in, appreciation clear in his eyes.

"Wait, aren't those mine?" Cole asked, smirking.

"Why are you dressing like a man, Iris?" Isabelle asked.

Iris smiled. "Since all of my clothes were burned... I can't move well in a dress, which would then give Garrett the upper hand."

"And that wouldn't be fair." Garrett smiled. He had to admit he liked what he saw.

So, the two of them took their stance. Whoever got the other one in a hold, on the ground, would be the winner. They circled one another, taking in each other's movements.

He moved his foot as if he were going to strike but didn't, trying to trick her. She kept her eyes fixed on him with unwavering intensity. When he went to actually strike, she easily dodged his foot and lunged.

He somehow managed to grab her, wrapping his arms around her and bringing her back against his chest. "I've got you now, and I'm never letting go," he whispered into her ear. A shiver raced the length of her spine.

She placed her feet wide and then went weak in the knees, making him go forward. Using his momentum, she lifted his weight and pushed forward, flipping him over her. This move knocked the wind out of him, giving her another opportunity. She sat on him, pulling his arms over his chest and locking her hands around them.

He looked up at her and she could feel, from where she sat, that he was enjoying this too much.

He then flipped her and now straddled her, holding her arms against her chest. In an instant, she had lifted her legs, wrapped them around his neck, and pulled him off her. She now had him in a lock, holding his arm in between her legs.

Isabelle and Cole clapped and laughed. Iris let go of Garrett and stood. "Now, back to the lesson at hand. How to shoot a gun."

They spent several hours practicing, aiming, shooting, moving and shooting.

"Why don't you show them how it's done, Iris? Please? I've always liked to watch you shoot." Cole said when it was near nightfall.

She nodded and reloaded her pistol. Iris walked away from the targets that were reset. Isabelle and Garrett gave Cole a questioning look. "You'll see," he said loud enough for Iris to hear, grinning from ear to ear.

"Surely no one can make that shot from such a distance," Garrett said skeptically.

Cole's grin only widened. "Wait and see."

She turned and took aim. There were five targets fifty yards away. The sun was to her back, helping her see. With very little movement, hardly blinking an eye, Iris shot each target, one after the other. To her, shooting was second nature, almost as easy as breathing.

When she rejoined the others, Garrett was staring at her with a peculiar look on his face. "What?" she asked, despite over hearing Cole and Garrett talk.

He shook his head. "Nothing. Just thinking that most men are probably intimidated by you, but it just makes me want you even more."

The words made her heart ache…

Iris was so exhausted by the day, she went to bed after dinner, and when her head hit the pillow, she fell fast asleep. But with sleep came dreams. Iris found herself in a large empty room. Above her were vaulted ceilings carved out of stone. The walls were intricately designed with stained glass windows every few feet that stood almost the height of the two-story walls themselves. The floor was made of inner lacing wood panels that shined as if they were made of marble.

She spun in a circle, taking it all in. She had never seen such majesty before. It was as if she had stepped into a fairy tale where knights, dragons and princesses lived.

Iris had only read of such things when she had snuck into a library but hadn't seen anything like this in the storybooks. So, she doubted this was her mind, but was it Garrett's? All of this seemed to be far more than she had ever imagined. She stood, looking at the artistry around her when she heard a voice.

Turning, she saw Garrett in an outfit fit for a king. His caramel skin and black hair made the gold and red of his royal attire stand out all the more. "I remember you saying something about not being a knight in shining armor. But I think it's you who is the true knight, and I am your prince in need of saving…"

He looked her up and down, prompting her to look at herself. She was in white armor that fit her body perfectly and held a sword that shone in the low light.

"You look stunning. I much rather see you in this though," he motioned to her outfit and went on, "than a dress. It suits you." Garrett half smiled and winked as he stepped closer to her.

"What are you playing at? What is all this?" She almost glared at him, thinking he was making things hard for her. That he was making letting go of him harder than it should be.

"I wasn't aware we were playing any sort of game." Garrett smiled at her, the curve of his lips holding a hint of mischievousness.

Looking down again, she noticed this time she wore a silk see-through nightgown that hugged every curve. The thin straps attaching the gown were more like threads. The top of the gown was low cut, barely covering the pinkish hue of her nipples, putting her breasts on full display.

She glared at him all the more. "Really? It seems to me that we are playing a game where only you know the rules and I am just a pawn to play with."

He laughed. "No, we are not playing any kind of game. And you have just as much control here as I do. Why not try and imagine me wearing something different?"

Iris stood there, trying to think of what he should be wearing. Closing her eyes, she imagined Garrett in different clothing. Opening her eyes, she looked him up and down, finding him shirtless and wearing only a loincloth, like cavemen would have worn. She averted her eyes, looking at the intertwining wood instead.

"How did you imagine all of this? It's all so ornate." Iris tried to think of Garrett dressed in something else, anything else. As Iris turned to look in the other direction, he came up behind her, wrapping his arms around her waist, pulling her in close.

She felt his bare skin against hers. His warmth through the silk. Her body responded by sending chills down her spine. Every dream felt so real, so instance.

He lifted his hand and moved her hair from her shoulders, revealing her neck. Leaning down, he lightly kissed it while brushing his fingertips down her bare arm.

"I loved sparring with you earlier," he whispered into her ear, and she bit her lip, her body responding to his touch by demanding more. Garrett went back to her neck as he wrapped his other arm around her once more.

"I could tell..." She sighed as he licked her neck.

"I want you in real life, Iris. I want all of you." Garrett sighed in between his ravishing kisses. He moved his hand under her silk gown, creeping ever upward.

His touch set her aflame. She moaned at his touch and kisses, all the resistance in her melting away.

She swallowed hard. "We can't... I can't..." Iris gasped as both of his hands explored her body.

"Let me prove myself. Let me show you that I can protect myself. I can't lose you. Not to an unseen threat." Her body unconsciously tensed, and his hold on her tightened, grabbing her hips with his hands, roughly, making her let out an unheeded moan.

"Just because something is unseen doesn't make it less real, less of a threat. The hidden ones do more damage than the ones you see right in front of you." Iris grudgingly pulled away from his embrace, mourning the loss of his closeness almost instantly.

Closing her eyes, she focused. Opening them again, she saw him in his regular clothes. She sighed, still feeling his touch even when his hands hung at his side. Locking eyes, she sighed again at the sight of his. The deep pools of gold held her in their depths.

She shook her head. "Garrett, I've told you. I can't be with you. That would only bring trouble to you and Isabelle. And I admit I can be heartless at times, but I won't drag the two of you into this. Please, try and understand."

He took two steps, closing the distance between them. Putting his hands on her shoulders, he gripped hard. "What I understand is that you want to handle everything by yourself. You push away anyone who shows any affections because you fear loss, you fear feeling loved. Love is what you fear more than anything else, Iris." His eyes seemed to look right through her, making her catch her breath. "I admit that I, too, was... no, still am afraid of love as well. But then I met you, and I couldn't be afraid anymore. I knew being able to love you meant more to me than my fear of losing love. And now that I have you, I will fight to keep you." Garrett leaned in, kissing her lightly on the lips, whispering in between kisses, "I can't let you go. Please, tell me that you feel the same for me." Garrett pulled back, searching for an answer.

Iris felt as if she was being pulled in two. One side wanted to follow her heart. To be with him, love him and be loved in return. The other half wanted to run as fast and as far as she could, knowing it would save his life but kill her heart in the process.

So, she had two choices. Be with him while they both still lived, which wouldn't be long once Rune found them. Or leave and let him live his life out, to have another chance at love and have a longer life. Tears she didn't realize she had been holding in ran down her cheeks.

Garrett wiped them away while holding her face in his hands. He moved her to look at him. "Iris," his eyes showed pure hope and determination, "I love you."

The words he spoke were true. Knowing that made her tears flow even more. The ache in her heart grew. "If I care for you, I have to let you go. I can't let Rune hurt you because I know he will. You have to understand," she whispered.

He wrapped his arms around her. "We can defeat him together."

She shook her head, pushing him away. "I'm sorry, Garrett."

As soon as the words left her lips, the dream shifted, and everything faded to black.

Chapter 13

Iris woke up to a dark room. Her heart felt as if it were going to pound out of her chest. She rubbed her cheek, feeling the wetness from her tears. She tried to think back to the last time she had cried but couldn't recall it. Her body throbbed with the want and need of Garrett. She wished for nothing more than to storm upstairs, kick in his door and let him take her, just as he had in the dreams. To have his strong, warm hands cupping her breasts... *Shit... I can't believe this is happening... I've gone my whole life without feeling this kind of passion, this kind of love... Shit...*

Frustrated with herself, she dressed, went out into the garden toward the edge of the woods and gathered twigs. Once she got what she needed, Iris headed back into the room Garrett had let her stay in. He had moved back upstairs once Flora had left.

Sitting at the desk, she wove the twigs together with the help of the moonlight. She was done soon. Holding it in front of her, she spun the circler sphere in front of her with its interweaving pattern of twigs and twine. She sat there, staring out into the woods, waiting for the sun to rise.

Once the sun was up, Iris put the dream catcher under her pillow and got ready for the day. All she knew was that she had to leave and soon. The morning started off like any other. She helped Isabelle with the grits and eggs. Cole came into the kitchen early to watch Isabelle cook. And Iris watched Cole watch Isabelle, knowing he was truly head over heels in love, which brought a smile to Iris' face.

Garrett didn't come down for breakfast, and the three of them went different ways after. Isabelle and Cole went out back to practice sparing, and Iris went out front to tend to the horses. As she was leaving the barn after feeding the animals, she heard horses approaching. Looking up the road, she saw Micah headed for her at high speed. He stopped his horse in front of her, sending gravel and dirt flying.

Jumping off, Micah almost ran to her. "Is Garrett in? There's been an accident during the cattle run. We need his help."

Without saying a word, Iris headed toward the house, yelling, "Garrett, Isabelle! There's been an accident and you are needed." Iris heard heavy steps and loud thuds as Garrett jumped down the stairs, bag in hand. Isabelle came through the back door in a rush, Cole following close behind.

After gathering some things, she followed Garrett to the stable. He turned to Cole. "You and Isabelle ride on one horse. Iris and I will go on the other."

Iris looked at Garrett in confusion. Without a word, he grabbed her arm and lifted her up on the horse. He then threw his bag to Micah while Isabelle and Cole mounted. As they rode for the cattle farm, Garrett leaned in closer. "I'm not letting you out of my sight."

A million butterflies filled her stomach. Iris sighed. He was scared to lose her just as she was scared to lose him, but the loss would come in different forms. They made their way through town and toward the farm. He would see in time that her leaving was for the best.

"When, how did you know of the dreams?" Iris whispered.

"I guessed until last night," he replied in a raspy tone that made her wish she hadn't asked. "You confirmed it for me. Because our dreams are connected, it only shows how deep our love is, Iris. You know how I feel and how I want to take care of you. I don't want to control you. I don't want to harm you. I just want the chance to love you and to protect that love."

Micah brought his horse next to Garrett, speaking of what had occurred, what to expect when they arrived, putting Iris and Garrett's dream conversation on hold.

Once they got there, they all jumped off their horses and went to tend to the wounded.

Iris went up to the farmer. The man was distressed, his body trembling. "What happened to your cattle?"

"We were putting them in a smaller area, trying to get ready for the cattle run when something spooked them. And… and…" He waved his arm toward his men, who lie hurt or dead nearby.

"So, all the cattle ran off? Do you have men out gathering them?"

His eyes were fixed on the ground as he shook his head. "No, ma'am."

It seemed all his men were either hurt or too shaken to go after the cows. "Which way did the majority go?"

He slightly pointed to the west.

She walked over to Micah who was mostly watching the others help the wounded. "Micah, want to help me wrangle some cattle?"

He looked at her in confusion. "Wrangle some cows?"

"He's already lost some of his men. Let's at least get some of his livestock back."

Micah shrugged. "That's kind of you, Iris. I'll come."

She could see that the scene of death before him was a rare sight for him. Despite being a local sheriff, there was little in the way of outlaws and large numbers of deaths in this area. Not until she had gotten there, that is… The knowledge gouged a pit in her stomach.

When Iris mounted Garrett's horse, he looked her way. Their eyes locked, and after a moment, he glared. She nodded in response, knowing the meaning behind the look. She and Micah roamed the nearby fields and woods, trying to find some of the missing cattle. They were hopeful they would find most of the cows. Daylight was on their side with several hours to search.

They came upon a lot of the cattle at a small creek in the woods. Taking a few at a time, they would go back to the farm and put them into a small field. As they headed back to the creek, Cole joined them in their efforts.

It was dusk when they stopped their search and ate some soup neighbors had brought to the farm. Several families had gathered to help the wounded and their families. Iris sat off from the group, not wanting them to recognize her from before and blame her for the accident. She watched Isabelle and Garrett still tending to others. How giving and hardworking they both were made her heart warm.

Someone sat next to her, and even before the person spoke or she saw them, her nerves sent warning signals, making her reach for her gun. "I wouldn't do that, dear Iris."

Iris looked to her right, at the man who still wore his hat, despite it being nightfall. "What do you want?" she asked calmly, keeping an eye on the others, making sure no one was making a move toward them. All the while, she kept her guard up toward this unwanted visitor.

"I've come with a message. Rune sees you but also sees them." The man nodded his head toward the group where Garrett, Cole, Isabelle and Micah were. "He's tired of waiting. He's been hunting you for so long with no reward of capture. And now that he sees something to bargain with…" The man paused, letting his words sink in. "The longer you linger here, the more pain he will bring to them. But, if you leave within two days' time, he will pardon them and look at them no more. There will be a distraction in town. Take that time to leave."

Iris gritted her teeth. "And is that an order?"

"Are you willing to pay the price if you stay?" And with that, the man stood and faded into the shadows as if he had never been there.

She sighed. Her heart beat so hard and fast, it actually ached. Iris gripped her shirt, her breath becoming ragged. Now there was no choice but to leave. Rune knew she was alive, knew to threaten the ones she had come to care for. She was fooling herself, thinking she could have a different life, despite the cards she'd been dealt. No, there was no other life for her, and she wouldn't let anyone get hurt because of her and her foolishness.

But visions of a life she could have with Garrett flashed across her mind. Them waking up to a new day together, wrapped in each other's arms. Her cleaning her guns as he cleaned his surgical tools. Cole and Isabelle coming over with their children and Micah acting like a grandfather to them.

Then another outcome came to mind, Rune's consequence. Cole screaming in pain as he held Isabelle's lifeless body in the front yard of Garrett's house. And in front of her lay Micah at her feet. Rune dragging Garrett's unmoving form towards her, his body covered in all the scars he had put on her and then some.

Iris knew this tightness in her chest would continue to be there. She would have to return to how she was before, unfeeling, uncaring, or she wouldn't make it out of this alive, and neither would they.

Coming to this conclusion, she stood and brushed her dress off. But before she could walk away, Garrett had made his way to her. "Who was the man with the hat? I hadn't seen him around before."

Iris stared at him, trying to push down the feelings he brought to the surface. She let the image of his bloody body come to mind. "He was just a passerby asking what the chaos was all about."

"That's an odd time to be passing by." Garrett still stared at her as if she would disappear.

"Quite." Iris didn't know what to say and thought that the less she said, the better. He was already a part of something she never wanted him to be a part of. And now she had to leave, or they wouldn't live until the end of the week. That was her life, to go from place to place. Never calling anywhere home.

"Micah told me you are going to look for some of the cows again at first light," Garrett commented.

Iris nodded. "Yes, I'll try and get a few more." She was trying to keep her answers short, trying not to elongate the conversation, and they both knew it.

The night dragged on. Iris slept little due to the thoughts running through her mind. Garrett slept little as well, due to tending to the wounded and keeping an eye on her. She could feel his gaze, which didn't help her situation.

The next day several people, along with Iris and Micah, went to herd more of the cows back to the ranch. Afterward, Iris made her way back with Isabelle and Cole. Garrett would stay a little longer at the cattle ranch.

Iris knew she didn't have much longer and spent the rest of the afternoon with Cole and Isabelle, watching them laugh and talk. She enjoyed this, enjoyed watching them love each other. Tomorrow, she would have to turn her feelings off, just like she had before. That was the only way to live going forward.

Garrett didn't like having to let Iris go while he stayed and tended to his patients, but it had to be done. All the while, he had this nagging feeling that something wasn't right. Something was coming. He couldn't see what it was, and it made him worry for Iris all the more. He stayed until nightfall then he made his way back to his homestead, hoping to see Iris before bedtime. Seeing her face would reassure him that she was real and tangible, not just a dream.

He put his horse in the barn and surprisingly found Iris sitting next to the house, looking at the stars. Smiling, he went up to her and sat down next to her. Neither of them said a word for quite a while. Just enjoyed the moment together.

Garrett leaned toward her. "I meant what I said. I want to spend my life with you, Iris." Before he could go on, she stood. He shot to his feet, grabbing her hand in his and turning her around to face him. He put his other arm around her, pulling her in tight.

Garrett leaned in and kissed her passionately. She returned the kiss with just as much fervor. Both pulled away breathlessly. He wanted to tell her how much he wanted her, loved her. She seemed to pull away for other reasons.

"Please listen to me, Iris. We're connected on a level I don't understand. And I want to be with you, no matter what that might bring. We will face it together." He looked down at her, the teary-eyed girl he had seen a few nights ago no longer there. In her place stood a determined, cold-blooded, strong woman. The face she wore was far more impassive than his stone exterior. He had decided to put away that façade to show and accept his true feelings, despite the outcome.

The change in her made his heart leap, making him love her all the more. Garrett felt as if he were going to go crazy with desire for her. It took everything he had to not take her against the house right then and there. He pulled her closer to him, even when she was trying to back away. "I love you, Iris. Please, tell me how you feel."

She didn't speak for a long moment. "It's late," she said finally, glancing away. "You've hardly slept in the last twenty-four hours. Why don't you go rest? We can talk more tomorrow."

He was reluctant to let her go but did agree that he needed sleep and he had to return to check on his patients in the morning. But Garrett hoped he would see Iris in his dreams.

Sadly, no dreams came to him. He was up with the sun and left bright and early so he could get back in time for breakfast to see Iris. He rushed through his checkups and took the back way through the woods to his house. Rushing off his horse, he almost ran to the front door, but he took a moment to gather himself, to steady his breathing.

Garrett opened the door to see the three of them eating. Isabelle stood when she spotted him. "Welcome back. That was fast. Hope you don't get any complaints later on for that. Come, food is waiting for you." She guided him to a chair and put a plate full of food in front of him.

He watched Iris as he ate. She seemed to be watching Isabelle and Cole, who were talking and laughing. Not too long after, a yell sounded from the front yard. Iris was the first one to her feet, rushing to greet Micah at the door. The whole scene made Garrett flashback to when the prisoner escaped and Iris had gotten hurt. He didn't like the sinking feeling in his stomach. He didn't like it at all.

"What's going on?" Iris asked in concern.

"This crazy man showed up in town, saying he'll start shooting up the town if the best gunman didn't come and duel him. He has several townspeople as hostages. Several men have already tried to have a fast draw with him, but both of them are now dead. And I dare not."

Garrett stepped forward. "And you came to see if Iris is willing to risk her life? Again?" Garrett glared at him, and Micah almost stepped back.

Iris put her hand on Garrett's shoulder, gently squeezing. "He was right to come."

"I could try and do it," Cole said.

"I don't think so," Isabelle immediately said, her tone firm. "I won't let you do that." She narrowed her eyes at him, making him bow his head in defeat. "Micah, I'm glad you came to get me. It's not worth risking more lives. But I'm going to need something." She looked to each man, landing on Cole, eyeing him.

"What? What is it? Do I have food on my face?" He wiped his face in confusion.

"No. I need your extra change of clothes."

Cole's confusion turned into utter shock. "What? Why?"

"I'm not going out there in a dress. That won't look intimidating at all. And I can't fit in Garrett's or Micah's clothes."

Cole realized what she was saying and nodded. "Give me a moment." He turned to go get his clothes with Iris following. "Why are you following me?"

"I have to change somewhere. I'm not changing in front of everyone. Why not change where your clothes are?"

Cole smiled. "Smart thinking." He put his finger to his head and then lifted it away as if lighting a flame. She followed him into the room and shut the door. He looked back questioningly.

"Cole, listen. I was visited by one of Rune's goons. He said if I don't leave, you will all pay for my selfishness. I have to leave today. I can't stay. If I do, that will mean the death of all of you. I won't be responsible for the loss of your lives. I care for all of you too much to stay. Please, don't ask me to stay." Her eyes begged him. "Don't tell the others. I have to leave for your safety."

Cole laid out his clothes and turned to her. "I understand. I don't want you to go. I want you to stay with us and fight against Rune. But I won't ask you to do that." He went over and hugged her. "I love you, Iris. I just wish you could have a chance at happiness. Like I've finally found. I was hoping we would all be one big happy family." He pulled away and looked at her. "I will always, I mean always, be here for you. No matter what your need, I will help you, any way I can. Always…" She hugged him back, and to her own surprise, she had to hold back tears. "Keep in touch, Iris. Don't just disappear. Come and visit if you can ever find a chance to do so. Let me know how to contact you."

"I will keep in touch. And let me know of all the events that happen here. When you ask her to marry you, let me know. I won't miss the wedding." He reddened at her words, clearly embarrassed at the thought of marriage. "You are my brother, Cole. Blood doesn't matter. We've been through more than most other siblings have. I will always look out for you. And I'm so happy you have found a family and a safe place." They hugged again, and she once again made him promise not to tell the others.

He left the room, and she changed into his clothes. Her hands shook as she picked up the shirt. *No... No... Now is not the time to give in to weakness. Be like stone. You have no feelings.*

She changed into his shirt, vest and pants, putting her boots on, along with a wide-rimed hat. Iris then put a gun holster on each side of a loose belt. Sighing, she looked herself up and down in a small mirror and tucked her long black hair under the hat.

Iris opened the bedroom door and headed down to the kitchen. When she stepped into the room, she felt all eyes on her. She could see Garrett's worry-filled look turn to a slight smile. Isabelle went up to Iris with her big bright smile.

"Amazing! You can almost pass for a man." Isabelle studied her. "Almost." Isabelle winked and hugged her. "Be careful, will you?"

Iris nodded. "Always." They all then turned to Garrett, whose smile had vanished from his face.

"Are you sure you can get this guy on the quick draw? That you will be faster than him? I really don't want to have to dig a bullet out of your chest." He crossed his arm.

Isabelle smacked his arm. "Don't say things like that. You know she can do it." The sister-brother had their own stare off.

Micah stepped in. "Now, now. We don't have time for this. We better head there before anyone else tries to take a shot and ends up dead." Everyone agreed and followed Micah on horseback. Iris and Garrett on one horse, Isabelle and Cole on another.

When they arrived in town, it seemed like every resident was watching to see who would come to face off with this madman. They tied up their horses, and Iris turned to them.

"All right, you four get to a safe place to watch. I'll walk in from the main street. Might as well give the people a show since that's what they're here for." She smiled slightly. Her heart sank at the sight of Garrett. She wanted nothing more to leap into his arms and run off together, but that would be a death sentence for them all.

"Just don't die. I don't know how many times I can bring you back from the brink of death."

She smiled at him, which changed his annoyed look to one of confusion. "Go on. I'll see you all soon." Iris shooed them away and went from a side building to the main street. She adjusted her hat to better hide her face and walked toward the crowd. She had to give it to Rune. When he made a distraction, he went all out.

When she neared the back of the crowd, a man passed her. "Kill the man with one shot, or your man dies." The man tilted his hat and continued to walk the other way.

Iris had stopped walking and looked for Garrett and the others. Garrett was always easy to find in a crowd with his height and build. Her heart was racing, her eyes searching.

The four of them stood on a landing in front of the post office, which rose higher than the rest of the crowd. Iris narrowed her eyes and focused on the people around them. A man leaned against a post, hiding his face with his hat. He looked up as if to see Iris staring. He responded with a nod and opened his jacket to show the hilt of his gun. Iris' eyes went back to Garrett, Micah, Cole and Isabelle.

She swore. "Dammit, Cole... You become a love-sick puppy and lose all the skills I taught you."

Iris was pissed, not just at Cole for not seeing the treat. At Rune for being the bastard that he was, but mostly at herself. For getting so close to someone, for caring so deeply and passionately. She had let herself fall in love, and this was the result of that. She wouldn't be the only one who would end up hurt. Iris took in the sight of Garrett one more time. He would hurt as well. But being hurt was far better than being dead.

She started toward the center of the group where the gunman awaited once again. The crowd soon saw her and parted to let her through, whispers surrounding her. In this moment, Iris knew she had to become the thing she promised herself she would never become. A monster. An unfeeling, unyielding killer. Once she started down this path, would she ever be able to come back from it? Sucking in a sharp breath, Iris moved forward.

Toward an oncoming storm she wasn't sure she would live through.

Chapter 14

Garrett watched Iris move through the crowd. He had been holding his breath but not because of his nerves. But because she took his breath away. No matter what she wore, she was a force to be reckoned with, and he loved that.

He turned his attention to the man who had been threatening the townspeople. The man was tall and broad with a messy beard and messy hair as if he hadn't washed in weeks.

"So, you're the one the town has chosen to face me?" the man asked. He laughed and staggered back. Garrett then realized this man was drunk, yet he had already killed two people? He must be a good shot indeed to be able to do that while on the sauce.

Iris merely tipped her hat to the man.

"Great! I'm tired and just want to go eat. So, let's get this over with."

Iris nodded yes in response, not wanting the townspeople to hear her voice, hoping they would be too excited to see a duel to notice she was a woman.

They stepped apart as a man counted in a loud voice, trying to be overheard above the whispers that grew with every step. Iris sucked in a breath as they turned to face each other. *This is it. This is the calm before the storm. There's no turning back after this. I have to become what is trying to destroy me, so I, in turn, can destroy it.* She let out her breath as the man ended his counting...

This time Garrett did hold his breath in fear, not wanting to blink in anxiety of missing who would shoot first. Those ten seconds were the longest ten seconds Garrett had ever felt. The crowd's whispers drowned out the sound, so the man counting had to yell to be heard. But as he neared the lower numbers, a hush came across the masses.

Garrett's eyes were plastered on Iris, watching her every movement. The intake of her breath as she turned and letting it out as she faced the man. The sheer focus that came across her very being stunned him.

But when he heard "One...," everyone stood still, not daring to blink as he sucked in his own breath.

He saw everything as if in slow motion. Iris reached her gun in what seemed like a half a second before the man did. She lifted the pistol, and the bang roared over the sound of the crowd. The gunman, who had also pulled out his pistol but had yet to raise it all the way, jerked and fell to the ground. Garrett was brought back to the moment when everyone rushed toward the shot man to see if he were still alive.

Women tried to pull their children away from the grewsome scene as a pool of blood grew under the man. Someone put a rag over the man's face to hide the now gaping hole in his head. All the while pieces of clothing and other things were being taken as souvenirs of the event. The men and children showed great interest in it all despite the blood, even some women.

Garrett looked over the crowd, trying to catch sight of Iris, but he didn't see her.

"She's gone... She really did it," Cole murmured in a low, sad voice.

The doctor turned and looked at Cole, anger building in him. "What do you mean she did it? What did she do? I know you're not talking about the duel." He was hoping Cole wasn't saying what Garrett already knew to be true, deep down.

Cole looked down. "She left us. Like she said she would. She made me keep it a secret."

Isabelle gasped. "Why did she leave? What would make her...?"

"To keep us all safe," Cole interrupted. "She knew if she stayed, Rune would come and possibly kill us."

"So, she left you as well, then?" Isabelle asked, hugging Cole's arm. All he could do was nod his head.

"Which way did she go, Cole?" Garrett was steaming now, his body shaking with the anger that was rising. He pushed down the fear that rose alongside it.

"She didn't tell me."

"You know her best. Which way would she have gone? Tell me." He tried not to yell, to keep a level head, but with every second she got further away from him and the thought shook him to the core.

"West, I think," Cole said in an unsteady voice. Garrett could see that her leaving affected him as well but had no time to think more on the subject.

"Garrett, what are you —?" Isabelle started but he was already running for his horse.

Mounting it, he steered his mare west as fast as she could carry him. He felt like his heart was going to beat out of his chest. After all they had been through together, after he had exposed himself and his feelings, she still planned to leave him? No way in hell was he going to let that happen, not now, not ever. She didn't get to make this choice for him. How dare she?

Garrett had opened his heart to her. Something he had never done before. If--no, when he caught up to her and she still left him, he knew his heart would be crushed. Could he forgive her? Would he be able to go after her, like he said he would? Garrett felt as if his heart were breaking at just the thought of it. His anger built rapidly as he pushed his horse further and faster.

Iris hated to leave them, but she kept thinking of ways they would be killed, all because of her. That knowledge kept her feet moving. The last thing she expected was to fall in love, but fall in love she had. Iris hadn't told Garrett that when he had confessed. It would only make leaving harder. But now that she knew she really did love him, she couldn't risk his life. She wouldn't let him die because of her.

And if the only way to save his life was for her to break both of their hearts, she would.

She sighed in relief when she got further into the forest, knowing she probably wouldn't be followed.

But her hopes were dashed when she heard a voice yell louder than the horses' hooves. "Iris!"

She turned, seeing Garrett dismount his horse in one swift movement, and almost as fast, he was standing in front of her, grabbing her arms. His intense stare and strong grip stole her breath.

"How dare you!" Garrett said in a low angry voice before she could speak. "How dare you leave us, leave me. And without a word. What gave you the right to make such a decision for me? Are you my master to tell me who or what I die for? I will be the one to decide how I die, not you!" He shook her, his anger starting to boil over.

Iris didn't know what to say. Her mind was in a tizzy, her emotions on high alert. "I..." She hadn't expected this, yet her heart had yearned for it all the more.

"Dammit, Iris." His voice had become soft. "I will not let you leave me. Not now, not when I've found you. I'll never let you go, Iris."

Garrett leaned down, kissing her. It started out as a soft, light kiss that rapidly turned into something much more. With every second, every movement, his kisses grew more impassioned. He pulled her closer, placing a hand on the small of her back, the other on the back of her head, pushing her toward him.

It was clear that all the desire he had been holding inside had finally broken through his iron gates, and there was no stopping him.

Iris could stop him, but she didn't want to. In the depths of her heart and soul, she wanted him just as much as he wanted her. She kissed him back just as hard and just as passionately, and that only encouraged him all the more. He lowered his bottom hand, pushing her pelvis into his, letting her feel how much he wanted her. She wanted him just as much because of it.

When Garrett pulled back, Iris gasped for air, but soon her breath was taken away when he lifted her shirt, revealing the scar from the wound he had stitched up. Leaning down, he softly kissed her stomach. But then his kisses turned into licks, lighting her body on fire. He moved up her stomach and gripped her butt, pulling her toward him again, and she groaned in pleasure.

Before she knew it, he had ripped the vest and pulled her shirt over her head, undershirt and all, revealing her top half to him. He looked her over. In his eyes shone pure desire and adoration, and her heart skipped a beat at seeing such strong emotions.

He pulled her in for a long kiss. Garrett all the while kept one hand on her bottom and cupped her right breast with his free hand. Iris moaned in between kisses. He lowered his head, taking her nipple in his mouth, sucking it. He hardened against her even more, making her throb with desire.

Her moans grew louder as he held her in that position, sucking her breast while the other hand cupped and squeezed the other nipple; his other hand moved lower down her butt.

In one swift movement, he laid her down on the ground. His eyes were dazzling in the afternoon light, setting off the gold in them.

"I… I want you so much, Iris," he said breathlessly. "If I don't stop now, I don't think I'll be able to later."

She smiled at him. "Is that your way of asking for permission?"

The question seemed to surprise him. "Maybe."

Iris laughed and then in a soft almost gasping voice said, "Garrett, I love you."

The words just slipped out, but she didn't care anymore. She wanted him. He leaned down, kissing her hard. He cupped her breast again, but this time she was at a better angle. With her right hand, she reached over, lightly brushing the bulge of his pants with her fingertips.

He stopped kissing her and looked into her eyes. "Are you positive?" he asked tightly.

She nodded and reached for the hem of his shirt, tugging it off him to reveal tone muscles. His skin was soft but hard to the touch. His caramel skin made her mouth water. Gently, ever so gently, he tugged her pants down, and the moment she had been longing for ever since she had laid eyes on him was inching closer. Her body throbbed with anticipation and yearning. He stood before her, as she watched him lowering his own pants. At the sight of Garrets erection, Iris knew, that the bliss she was about to feel would make her body crave him every waking moment.

Leaning back down, he trailed his fingers from her ankle up to her hips. She stiffened at his touch when his fingers moved closer to the tuff of hair there.

He lowered his fingers, finding the perfect spot that made her groan more. She saw him bite his own lip as he watched her reaction. He then flicked his fingers, making her back arch in pleasure. Garrett leaned down to capture hers lips for a few soul-shattering kisses and then moved down to her breast once again.

Their passion grew with every touch, every kiss, every sigh.

Iris wanted to please him as well, but her body was too overloaded with such delicious sensations. He moved atop her, rubbing his erection on her inner thigh. Reaching down, she guided him to her entrance, desperately needing him to be inside her, for them to be one at long last.

When he pushed into her, they both moaned. He paused halfway to let her get used to the new sensations of being stretched, of being full. She arched up when he pushed all of him in.

Kissing her, he moved slowly, stroking all the right places. Iris never thought she'd be a vocal lover, but she couldn't contain her moans and gasps as he took her to new places. She had never felt such pleasure before. Soon, his thrusts became more rapid, harder, making her wrap her legs around him, hugging him closer to her.

"Iris…" he gasped.

"Yes?" she breathed.

"I've wanted you for so long."

She smiled. "You have me. I'm yours, Garrett."

She moved in sync with him, their movements becoming more rhythmic. Her nails dug into his back as she arched into him. But then he grabbed her arms and pinned them above her head. As one hand held her wrists, the other played with her nipple. She screamed and he swallowed the sound, thrusting his tongue into her mouth, mimicking the movements his hips made.

So good. So close. The coil in her pulled tighter and tighter until a toe-curling, full-body orgasm washed over her in waves, captivating over everything in its wake. But her body wanted more, and desire rushed through her once again.

He let go of her wrist and leaned up to look at her, both of them panting for breath. He slid his sweat-drenched body atop her, wanting to feel her skin against his own, loving the closeness of their bodies. The feeling of her breast touching his chest made him harden more.

Iris smiled up at him. "I'm not sure you're done."

He couldn't deny it, and he wanted more. He didn't think he would ever be able to have enough of her. She arched as he pushed into her hard. Seeing her like this was maddening. The warmth of her and how wet and open she was only made him want her even more.

In one swift movement, he flipped them so she was on top, letting her ride him.

Her eyes widened, and a slow smile spread across her face. "I think I like this."

"Is that so?" He groaned in pleasure as she rode him. *Shit, I'll never be able to get this image out of my head.* Iris' black hair draped over her shoulders, playing with her swinging breast. Her purple hued eyes shined bright despite the shadows around them. He moved his own eyes lower, to watch her moving hips, to watch her pelvis grind against his own. She was truly going to drive him insane. If she left him after all this, she might break him.

"Mhm." Iris moaned.

Garrett loved the way she looked, her facial expressions, how her body swayed and her breasts bounced. Putting his hands on her hips, he helped her move, making her gasp in delight. Reaching up, he massaged her breasts. He could feel how wet she had become, her shudders increasing.

He would come soon, but he wanted more, needed more. Garrett didn't want this to end. He didn't think he could ever get enough, not with her, not like this. The feel of her, how wet he had made her and how well she took him into her made him want to never leave, wanted him to give them endless pleasure. The thought of such pleasure, such excitement that he had never felt, only made him crave more. But the throbbing increased and there was no stopping the wave of pleasure that crashed toward him.

With another swift movement, he was on top again. With just a few hard thrusts, Iris cried out and arched against him, holding him inside her. He finally met his own release, the strongest orgasm of his life making him see stars.

Garrett laid atop her, tip still inside, while they both tried to catch their breath and ease their racing hearts. He moved to hold Iris in his arms, not wanting to let her go. Having her mind, body and soul made him feel free but fucking scared at the same time. Their dreams were connected, and he had only read about that in extreme cases. Most were believed to be just make-believe, fantasy. But what they had between them was definitely real and unique. Now that Garrett had felt her completely, fully, he knew he had fallen in deep.

He had fallen, no, plunged so deep into the ocean of love that is Iris, no light could reach him but hers. And if she were to leave, would that leave him alone in the dark love he had dove into? He didn't want to think about this. He wanted their love to shine bright. Because that's what love was supposed to do, right?

Garrett had fallen asleep with Iris in his arms. She looked up at him, not wanting to wake him. Iris couldn't believe she'd given in. How much more would leaving hurt him now? Hurt her? She stared at his bare chest, taking in every inch of him, wanting to remember this moment forever. It wouldn't happen again. For his safety, she had to leave. Her selfishness would not be the end of him. She wouldn't let it.

Iris slipped from Garrett without waking him. As she dressed back into Cole's clothes, she stared at the sleeping form of the man she loved. Her heart was breaking. She didn't want to leave him. Her body and heart ached for her to warp herself in his arms. But if she truly loved him, then leaving was the only answer, no matter how hard it was.

Iris had never hated what her life had become, and what she had become in living it. But leaving him like this made her loathe herself. She couldn't entirely blame Rune, even though he was the torturous demon that shadowed her, and she was the monster's sustenance. Now was time to dispense with both.

With that thought, she lightly walked away, trying not to wake him. Even though she left him physically, her heart remained with him and always would.

The noise of rustling leaves woke Garrett. Looking to his left, he saw his horse looking for something green to eat. Turning his head to his right, he looked to where Iris should have been to find only flattened leaves in her place. He sat up, looking around. Her clothes were gone, and the sun was starting to set.

He balled his fist and hit the ground. "Dammit. Dammit all!"

After screaming into the evening air, he stood and dressed as fast as humanly possible, wanting to search for Iris, hoping she hadn't gotten far. Garrett grabbed his horse and mounted it. Nudging his heels against the side of his mare, they started forward. He hoped he could catch up to Iris. Surely, she hadn't gotten far on foot.

After traveling for miles, there was no sign of her. He stayed out well past sunset, and finding her in the dark would be nearly impossible for him. So, he reluctantly made his way back home.

Dragging himself through the front door around dawn, he went through the kitchen and heard Isabelle ask, "Where have you been? Were you able to find Iris?" She slowly walked up to him and lightly put her hand on his arm.

He shook his head. "Do you have any idea where she would have gone?" he asked Cole.

Cole frowned. "I don't. All I know is when she doesn't want to be found, she won't be. Even by me." He sighed, as if giving into something unseen. "Look, with Iris, there is no place she calls home, nowhere she regularly visits. She has always been on the move, trying hard to not stay in one place for too long. If you do go in search for her, know this: The agency we work for, I worked for," he corrected, "has tried to keep tabs on her, and very few have succeeded. I am here if you are in need of a tracker."

He exhaled, just fully realizing how long Iris had been living this life, how long she had been running and hiding. What chance did he really have in finding her? And it was clear in the way she left him, naked in the woods, that maybe she didn't really feel the way she had said. Maybe she didn't feel the same way he felt for her after all.

Without another word, he went to his room and to the bed Iris had been sleeping in. He just stood there, staring at the empty sheets. He acutely felt the loss of her presence. It was as if he were drowning in an ocean of despair. That he had willingly fallen in love and gotten so hurt in return made his heart turn cold. Grinding his teeth, Garrett pondered the two options left open to him.

Either go after Iris, an experienced hunter of outlaws and, from what he's heard and seen, someone able to best any of them, which also meant she could probably hide from an amateur like himself. It would be like a mouse casing a cat. Or, he could stay and continue his work in Valden. They were still in need of a good doctor, and there were a lot of new research studies he had yet to read.

After a long, hard debate, he decided to continue his life work, something he had labored over for more than ten years. He studied for his doctorate before he had entered college and then opening his practice here after graduating. To set off on a wild goose chase and lose all that... his heart grew heavy with frigidness, then he felt a lightness to it as he thought, *No, I will wait. If we're truly meant to be, then we'll find our way back to one another.*

This was going to be an inner warfare between his heart and mind, and it was only just beginning.

The good doctor went back to his office in town, spending most of his days and nights there in between making his rounds to the sick. He was rarely home. It all reminded him too much of Iris and the loss of her. And seeing Isabelle and Cole fall ever more in love made him hurt all the more. It wasn't their fault, but he just wanted to stop from feeling because that way, he could stop his hurting.

One day bled into the next. He was never certain what day it was or how much time had passed. He merely blocked out all feelings, numbing himself to the world around him. It was the only way he could keep living. If what he was doing could even be called that. It was more like existing. If he didn't have patients or rounds, he would stay locked away. Trying to busy his mind during the day did very little do push away the thoughts of Iris that crept in. At night it only worsened, his dreams overflowing with images of her. He felt as if he, too, had become haunted. She with Rune, and he with her.

Garrett was sitting in his office, trying to go over some paperwork when he heard a tap at the door. "Come in, it's open," he answered without looking up.

"Aren't you a sight for sore eyes?" a feminine voice asked. He looked up to see a ravishing woman standing before him. "Oh, my. I think I retract my statement. You aren't looking quite yourself. I've never seen you with such dark circles under your eyes, even when we were both studying for our final exams." The young woman who took the seat across from him had long flowing red hair. When he had first met her, she reminded him of a mythical phoenix. She had poise and grace, and though her temper rare, once sparked, it was a fiery rage that was not easily subdued.

After she was seated, a thought, one he tried to quell, came to mind, *That was where Iris had sat. During our first meeting.* He sighed. "It's nice to see you, Abelia. What brings you to this part of the country?"

She stared at him with her cool eyes, not like Iris' that were amethyst shining in the sun. He shook his head.

"I came on behalf of your dear father." She lifted one eyebrow, awaiting his reaction.

He leaned back in his chair, folding his hands in his lap. "Oh, is that so?" he asked, cocking his brow in imitation of her. "And what does my dear father want? It must be something special for you to come all the way here."

Abelia solemnly nodded, her red curls swaying. "Your father has become ill and wants you to come and visit him."

"And to take over his business?" As he stared at her, he could only see Iris in her place, shadows of the past haunting him.

"Side business. Yes."

"I will go to see him because he's my father and I am a doctor, but I will never take over his *side* business. It's like he lost all morals when my mother died." He sighed, looking up at the ceiling, a vision of Iris' smile haunting him.

Leaning forward, Abelia put her chin in her hands. "It looks like someone is lovelorn. Do tell." She smiled.

His eyes shifted from the ceiling to Abelia. "It doesn't matter…"

Garrett turned back to his papers, trying not to think of Iris, but no matter how hard he tried, his thoughts always wandered back to her. Some days, he thought he would go insane, and even though he dreamed about her, it was not like before when they visited each other's dreams. Iris had somehow severed the connection when she left.

"Garrett. We've known each other for so long. Why not confide in me? You know I'm always here for you. And I don't want to marry you." She tried to comfort him with another smile. "Keeping things in will only make them fester even more. You might find relief talking about it all. I won't tell your father."

He sighed and closed his eyes, trying to push all his feelings away, something he had been trying to do for…. How long had it been now?

Iris didn't stop running until nightfall. Her muscles screamed in protest. She hadn't been as active as she had been before being injured. She was deep into the forest. No towns should be near her; at least that's what the map she had stuck in her pocket before leaving told her. She fell to her knees, panting. Visions of Garrett floated into her mind. The memories of his body on hers made her yearn for more.

She screamed into the darkness, trying to let out her pain. Her broken heart made her feel like she would die. The only way she would be able to live on would be to rip out her heart, to never think of Garret, to close off all feelings and thoughts of him and their time together. Tears flowed down her cheeks as she beat her forearms and fists against the ground. Her sobs filled the air around her, making her feel even more alone. After beating the earth, she laid on her side, hugging her legs to her. Iris had never felt such heartache.

After she pulled herself together, as much as she could. Iris promised herself she would never cry like this again. But somewhere deep in her mind, she knew that was a promise she wouldn't be keeping. And no matter how much she let herself cry, the pain in her heart would not ease.

When she opened her eyes, the morning sun nearly blinded her. She hadn't meant to fall asleep in the woods. It was unlike her to let her guard down. It seemed like Cole wasn't the only one who let his feelings cloud his judgement.

She traveled for several days, stopping only once in a small town to gather some food but kept moving, eventually traveling through a larger town to get to an even bigger one. Before going to buy a ticket for a stagecoach, Iris decided it best to change into a dress.

She bought a dress that wasn't too homely but also not too fancy. It had a full skirt that flared at the bottom, just like all ladies wore. The color was a dark blue with small white flowers. Quarter-length selves with laces on the end and even the collar had lace. Iris fought the urge to pull the lace off. She hated the stuff, saw no use for it. Trying to blend in was harder than most people would think. She had also put her hair in a bun. Her long black hair always got her in trouble. If she let it flow like she had been doing, it would stand out even more. Now she would head to the larger city of Smithington.

There was no better place to hide than a place with a large number of people. The coach pulled up to the crowded streets. Strangers hardly nodded to one another if they knocked into the other. Yes, this was the place for her. Looking up, she saw most buildings stood three stories tall. They all linked together, as if one big building, but the styling of brink and iron work changed with each housing unit. The sidewalks and even some of the roads were made of the same red and brown brinks, showing this city had money with probable stakes in the railroad business.

Remembering all the cities she had been in, this one was nearing the largest. She coughed and instantly missed the clean air of Valden, which brought memoires flooding back.

Iris had nowhere to go. She had never owned a place of her own or rented a flat, not wanting to have something or someone could use against her. And everything she had owned had been burned several months back by the townspeople Garrett had saved her from.

Dammit... She promised herself not to think of him anymore. Shaking her head, she headed to a bank to withdraw some money for new clothes and a hotel to stay in. After her dresses were made the way she liked with pants, she would go to her captain's office to get some work. One of the reasons she picked this town was because the main office was here. And there was nothing better to forget one's past than doing busywork.

Iris went to a dress shop after the bank and told the confused prim seamstress what she wanted and in what color. She went as far as to draw out a pattern for the poor lady. And the dressmaker was getting all flustered. Her loose ringlets seemed to be tightening as she tried to explain to Iris that women do not wear such things. But she explained she would pay extra. Iris wouldn't mind sowing it herself, but she didn't have the time or the machine to do it with.

Once she had spent over an hour explaining what she wanted, she left to find a hotel. She contemplated between a hole in the wall type hotel or a nicer one. Which one would someone be less likely to find her at?

After deciding to stay in the largest hotel she could find within the city, Iris went to find something to eat. She had hardly had anything to eat since she left. Shaking her head, trying not to think of the past, she headed down the street in one of the new dresses.

After eating a lovely lunch, which just consisted of a ham sandwich, from a sidewalk vender, Iris went and checked into the hotel under a false name.

The room was luxurious. In front of a huge four post bed with fluffy covers was a large fireplace with seating for two. Then there was another sitting area next to bay windows that lead to a small balcony. Iris hadn't realized how tired she was.

She just planned on lying down for a second, but once her eyes were closed, she fell fast asleep.

Dreams came to her, but none were connected to Garrett. These dreams were reflections of her fears. The first images showed herself as a child in a rundown plantation home turned into the orphanage she had grown up in. It was quite large, four rooms in the attic, and six in the second floor. The first floor was mostly for the staff, a study, lounge, kitchen and three bedrooms. Then, there was the cellar, cold, dark and damp. That's where they sent the children when they misbehaved, to set beside the bones of the ones before them…

Finding herself in a shadow-cast room, a faint humming noise radiated, growing progressively louder. She took in the sight of the two dark figures standing in front of her. Her body froze in fear at the sight of their mouths opening wide to let out large bugs and worms that flew and crawled straight for her. When the horde of insects swarmed toward her, she slammed her eyes closed but felt no tearing of her flesh as expected. Opening them, she saw her surroundings had shifted to another nightmare.

Another shadow came toward her, and even though she couldn't see their face, she knew it was Rune. He held a knife in his hand and was bringing it down toward her. Again, closing her eyes brought another shift in scenery.

This time, she saw Garrett, or what looked like him. The expression he wore was not his own; it was twisted and devious. It was that of Rune. He tore at her clothes, his hands claws that cut her tender skin.

Iris cried out, sitting straight up in bed.

She was panting and sweating. It took a moment to get her racing heart under control. She was still in the hotel, but it had grown dark out. Iris put her face in her hands, trying not to shake or cry, but it stopped neither from happening.

How have I become so weak? she thought.

It's not weakness to let down your walls, a small voice in the back of her mind responded. *To open up to someone, to let someone in. To depend on others.*

"I don't want these feelings. I don't want to love. I don't want to hurt," she cried.

She hugged her knees, trying to stop her cries. Because there was a chill to the air, Iris started a fire in the hearth, and instead of going back to bed, she sat near the fire, staring into the flames. Iris just stared, trying not to think of anything at all, trying to go numb.

Once the sun had risen, she went down to the bakery and bought a small pastry that she ate on the way to the office deeper into the city of Smithington to see her boss. It had been years since they had seen one another, and he had greatly changed. The once young, determined man she once knew had been replaced with one who looked worn with worry. His brown hair, dusted with gray, only reminded her that she too had aged along with him.

The captain eyed her, lifting his bushy dark brows as he sighed. "Are you sure you're up for this? You've only just recovered, and this guy isn't someone to take lightly. He has already taken out two of our men. Remember Robertson?"

"Of course, I do." Thinking back, he had been dubbed the name ton. Because they said he weighed a ton and couldn't be knocked off his feet by even their best. She had only seen him in the training yard in passing many years ago but believed the stories. He seemed sturdy.

"He was one of our biggest men. He's now in the hospital with a broken leg and ribs. I won't stop you, but are you sure you're up to this level? You know your body better than anyone. I don't want you to take this just to prove yourself. You sure as hell don't need to prove anything to me." He leaned forward, putting his elbows on his desk. "Are you doing this to prove something to yourself?"

The words stabbed into her. Knowing the truth of them only made them sting all the more.

"Just give me the information." Iris held out her hand, eyeing him.

Nodding, he took a file from a pile on his desk and handed it to her. As she reached for it, he held the other side, meeting her gaze. "Be careful, Iris. This isn't your normal bounty."

"I understand, captain." She stood.

He released the file and sat back, still eyeing her with his gray eyes. "Good luck, Iris."

She went back to her hotel room and sat near the open window for better light. Flipping through the file, she came upon a fading picture. The man had several scars on his face, one long one on his forehead and two deep ones on his cheek and chin. His eyes shone with an evil glint that could even pierce through a photo. An involuntary shudder went through her body as she stared at the menacing eyes of the man who was wanted for unthinkable crimes.

The man was nicknamed Hector the Dissector, which didn't seem menacing enough to her. According to his records, the last sighting of him was two states away in the mountains. Where she was headed, no woman would dare go alone. Bear country was no place for a lady. Because of this, she went to the seamstress to buy more men clothes and told the woman to send her dresses to the address all the agents used when they didn't want to use their own, or had none of their own to use.

Knowing they would hold her clothes for quite a time, she went to buy a horse. Because of the duration she would need it, she thought buying one would be better than leasing one out. The agency didn't provide transportation. The less paperwork showing their existence, the better. It took several days for Iris to gather everything she needed to travel. It took longer than usual because of how long she might have to travel and the changing of seasons; winter freeze would be coming sooner than she realized.

Traveling as a man would help her along the way. She sat in front of the mirror in her hotel room on the last night. Taking a knife to her long black hair, she chopped it off to just above her shoulders. Iris sat there, staring at her new look, not quite sure what to think. It would be harder for someone to grab her by the hair now at least.

Needing a good night's sleep, she went to bed early, but tossed and turned all night, her thoughts not letting her rest. And when sleep came, so did dreams. She dreamed of a life she could have had with Garrett. The image of him sitting at his desk, mulling over books while waiting for a client, her cleaning a gun next to a small fire. It would have been simple but theirs. Forgetting Garrett might be the hardest thing she had ever done.

She got up from her soft bed, knowing it would be the last time she would have such a nice place to sleep for quite some time. After changing into the men's clothes she had bought and arming herself, she gathered her things and left the hotel. The seasons were amidst change as she made her way through forests and mountain terrain. When she had first gone to the sleepy town of Valden, it had been spring, but autumn was now upon them all. With the mixtures of white and yellow from the birches, the red orange and brown from the sugar maple and oaks, Iris felt as if she were in a painting. But moving further into the mountains, the only trees to hold any color were pine and fir.

Heading north meant winter would be coming earlier to that area, which didn't make her feel at ease in the least. Iris traveled for weeks, trying to pick up any lead on this Hector fellow. For such a big man, he knew how to hide. Finally reaching the last known place he was seen, she went into the town's saloon, which reminded her of the first time she had seen Garrett with his strong muscular form and tan skin. The thoughts sent a deep need through her body. Shaking her head, she tipped her hat to hide her face and reminded herself to think of the mission and nothing else. If she didn't focus, it could — no, would be the end of her.

She watched the townspeople come and go, knowing if they were regulars by how the barkeep greeted them. Reading the man's file, she knew he was a fan of drink. Seemed like a lot of men were fans of spirits nowadays. Whiskey on a cold day did warm her up, so she saw the appeal somewhat. Iris continued to scan the crowd for any sign of a newcomer. She was thankful for the outfit she wore. Wearing baggy men's clothes helped her blend in and not have to worry about standing out.

Iris sat there until evening when she had dinner and some more whiskey afterward. Late into the night, she gave up her search and headed to the nearby inn. When she stepped through the doorway, the broad shoulders of a tall man blocked her path. Her heart skipped a beat at the thought of the broad shoulders she so desperately missed. But she was brought back to reality by the gruff voice of the man.

"Look where you're going, would you?" he grunted, glaring at her.

Iris bowed her head and moved aside, eyeing the man from under the lip of her hat. By pure luck, she had found Hector.

He was headed out the door, which meant so was she. After checking in with the innkeeper, she headed back outside. The time it took her to check in gave her enough space from Hector to follow without being noticed. He was definitely a large man; he stood taller than Garrett, which meant he must be well over six feet tall. And there she went, thinking of Garrett again. *What am I going to do with myself?*

Iris assumed the man was going to a job or maybe a meeting to find a new job, which meant he would be going to kill someone or find out who he was to kill. Hector was always on the job, his thirst for blood never quenched. Knowing this gave her an upper hand. It was the perfect time to follow. Now all she had to do was keep out of sight and find out who the target was. She kept an extensive distance between them as he walked to a shack that lay hidden in the woods. Once he was inside, Iris crept close enough to hear, putting herself up against the siding of the poorly built shed.

Inside were two male voices. "Good to see you, Hector. I trust you know why you're here."

"Why him?" Hector's voice rang out, deep and gruff.

"I assumed you had heard of the pest, just like the rest of us. This man has won the affection of our boss's love. He must be eliminated." Some movement could be heard inside. Iris pressed herself closer to the building. "I'll be glad for it once it's done."

"You mean the boss's toy?" Hector grumbled.

"Don't let him hear you say that. Just do your job and everything will be fine."

Hector fell silent, as if hesitating. But why the reluctances?

Without awaiting a response, the other man said sharply, "Just get it done, will you?"

"It will take me a while to get to where he lives…"

"Why do I get the feeling this hit bothers you?"

"No…"

"Good, you have a week. And Hector, I don't have to remind you of what will happen if you don't succeed?"

"No…"

"I look forward of hearing about the pest's death from the smiling face of our boss. Am I clear?"

The man grunted in response, and their movements increased, indicating they would depart soon.

Iris had an eerie feeling about all of this and dashed into the trees as the two men came out.

"Good job on your other assignment. Do this one and maybe you will earn your choice of killing next."

Hector only shrugged his large shoulders and headed back to town. Iris again followed at a safe distance. She didn't like the feelings she was having. Something was different with this hit. Then, in an instant, she froze, realization hitting her like a train. The boss, the pest that has his love's affection…

Rune. Rune was the boss. Of course, he was, and the pest… The pest must be Garrett. So, Rune was going back on his word to not touch them if she stayed away. Well, two can play that game. Because she knew she wasn't his love but was really his plaything, his toy. She would never be fooled by him, never again…

Anger built inside her. Not just at Rune and his back-stabbing ways but at herself for not seeing it. For not understand what she had just heard sooner. Her hands balled into fists, staring at the men as they went their separate ways. Everything seemed to lead back to Rune. All the thugs she had chased down probably had ties to him. And now this…

No way would she let any of Rune's goons touch Garrett. This would be the end of all that. Her new mission was to take down everyone she could find with a link to Rune.

Her new mission in life was to end Rune's organization no matter the cost.

Chapter 15

Garrett and Abelia slowly walked back to his house, talking of events that had happened since they had last seen each other. Such as, her engagement to a wealthy party boy. "We have an agreement. He can keep going out and doing as he pleases as long as I can do the same. But if either of us gets caught by our families, we have to stop and play house."

"I see… But will you truly be happy that way? Having to live your true life in the shadows?" Garrett eyed her under his lashes.

"Even if it is in the shadows, at least I get to live the life I want. I think it's better than not at all. Don't you?"

"I suppose so."

"What about you? Are you truly happy living your life without the woman of your dreams? I mean literally, your dreams…"

They both fell silent.

She nudged him, trying to banter. "You really aren't going to go after her?"

He looked down, kicking the dirt and loose rocks. "I wouldn't even know where to start. And now father wants me to visit. It's all too much."

Grabbing his hands, his friend turned him to face her. "Is that really the case, Garrett? We know secrets about each other that most friends don't. Who else would you have told about your connection with Iris? Have you even told your sister? Gare bear, what is really holding you back?"

Looking down at the friend he knew would tell him the truth, no matter how it might hurt, he remembered how she gave him the nickname Gare bare after hearing his mother had called him little bear. But could he really tell her why he wasn't going after Iris?

"She left for a reason. Right now, I have to trust her in that and wait… If I do go after her, who's to say any benefit will come from it?"

"So, you're going to stay away from her then?"

Taking her hands from his, he turned to his farmhouse, which was now in view. "Yes…"

Once inside, Isabelle excitedly introduced Abelia to Cole, who was his usual friendly self. Garrett watched the three of them talk, his mind wandering to Iris. That night, he tried to stay awake, not wanting to see his fears come to life in his dreams, but for the first time in quite a while, he slept soundly with no dreams or nightmares.

After breakfast the next morning, Cole pulled him aside and put his hand on Garrett's shoulder, his bright smile wavering. "I was wanting to help you hone your shooting skills."

Garrett sighed. "Isabelle and Abelia set you up to do this, didn't they?"

Cole shrugged. "It's possible."

Knowing his sister, she wouldn't stop until she got what she wanted. Garrett sighed again. "I guess I will take you up on the offer. It won't hurt to be a better aim, would it?"

Cole smiled. "Right! Let's get to it, shall we? I already have everything set up."

The two of them headed out back to where they had practiced before. Garrett pushed away the memories of Iris and tried to focus on aiming. Isabelle and Abelia stood nearby watching and talking. Garrett assumed the two of them were probably talking about him and how he should find Iris.

After shooting for a bit, Cole showed him how to throw knives. "This is probably the only thing I'm better at than Iris," he said with a laugh, obviously proud of the skill. "You should do well because you work with your hands as a doctor."

He did catch on better with the knives than the gun. "That's right. Hold the knife at the point, then throw. Having the heavier end lead gives the tip more thrust in the air to stab your opponent," Cole instructed further.

But Garrett's mind started to think of Iris, her purple eyes and how they were even more vivid in the fading light of the day. What was she doing right now? Did he make the right choice in not going after her? *Shit, I have to stop this… Focus…*

"What's happening? Are you all right?" Cole asked, concern written on his face.

"Yes, I'm fine. Why do you…"

Garrett was cut short when Cole turned from him to dig a knife out from the siding of the house. "I'm getting hungry, aren't you? I think my stomach is about to eat itself." He laughed. The doctor knew why he did that, to cut the tension that had started to build. Cole wasn't quite as good as Isabelle in reading people and situations, but he was getting there.

They took a break for lunch and afterward, Cole trained Isabelle more on shooting. He was going to show Abelia as well, but she showed them she needed no help in that area. She coyly walked over, as if bashful. But then she took a stance similar to one he had seen Iris use. With fluid motions, she hit each target, almost in a blink of an eye. Turning back to them, she wore a large smile on her face, proud of what she had once been shy to show.

"Where did you learn to shoot?" Garrett asked in surprise.

She smiled at him. "I am a woman with many talents. Many are frowned upon by men, so I tend to keep those hidden." Abelia winked at him, aimed and hit her target again.

They all practiced until the sun had fully set. Garrett was too tired to eat much and went straight to bed, falling asleep fast. He hoped for a night without dreams, but what came was something he never expected.

He found himself on a mountain terrain. To his left was a mountain peak covered in snow with clouds hovering overhead. To his right was a vast landscape with small cedar trees, grass and large stones. Garrett looked around. He felt something nearing him. He turned to see a large black bear on the trail next to him.

And as Garrett stared at the animal, it shifted into an old man who stared back at him. The man's long white hair shone like the snow on the mountain peak, and his skin was tan like the bark of the cedar trees. Both just stood there, taking each other in. The man wore clothing similar to tribal clothing he had once scene long ago in his travels when he had tried to find out more about his mother.

The man then spoke, his voice sounding as if it were echoing around them, yet close to his ear at the same time. "It's been a long time. I've kept an eye on you for quite some time."

Garrett frowned, confused about what was going on. Who was this man? "You've been watching me?"

"As a raven would a mouse in a field. I see many paths, and those who walk them. I do not reach out to all. But you, I feel I need to speak with before your path wavers. You have connected with someone who in turn has awaken a deeper level of yourself. The reason I am showing myself to you now is because of this connection."

Garrett eagerly leaped at the topic. "What about Iris? Do you know where she is?"

"No." The old man shook his head solemnly. "I am merely here to tell you this: You have two paths before you. One leads to her, and one leads to others. If you choose her, you will be faced with hardship you would not know otherwise. Heartbreak awaits you down this path, but so does the potential for great joy. You could be the light in her darkness."

"I'd suffer anything for her," he responded immediately, accepting this as his fate.

"Perhaps. But if you choose another path, you will never know the love that could absorb your world and the pain that awaits you down this path. No matter what trail you walk, know that you have the inner and exterior strength of a bear. Use this throughout your life, but remember to lean on others when you feel weak. Those you hold close to your heart are not your weakness. They will make you strong again. And if you are ever in need of guidance, I am but a thought away."

Before Garrett could even breathe a sigh, the vision vanished, sending him into dreamless sleep.

Iris' mind shifted, turning all emotions off expect one. Hate. It would fuel her vengeance.

She had to attack while he was on the road, away from any town and witnesses. She didn't like that because he could use the big open space to his advantage. So, that night, she thought of a way to trap him, finding the route he would take; she would wait and lay a trap. Reminding herself the reasons she was doing this, she settled in position to wait for Hector the Dissector.

She sat next to the road. Hidden by bushes, Iris watched for him to come by. It was nearing dusk when she heard horse hooves on the road. She was thankful there was still some light to see by, and as the horsemen neared, Iris took aim. But this time it was with a bow and arrow, not her pistol, another trick hidden up her sleeve.

It would be more efficient to shoot with a bow first, knowing she wouldn't kill him in one shot because he was a moving target, and her placement made it difficult.

As he drew closer, she waited to make sure the man on the horse was the man she wanted to take down. And in a split second, she let loose the arrow, hitting the man in the back shoulder. He fell off his horse and hit the ground. He yelled and quickly got to his feet, pulling his gun out, looking for the person who shot him.

With a grunt, he broke the arrow sticking out of his back, still looking for her. She took aim again, hitting him in the upper leg, and just as fast, he broke that arrow as well, yelling in pain and anger all the while. Aiming again, she hit his other shoulder, making him drop the pistol he was holding. He had seen where the arrows were coming from and slowly walked toward the bush she was using for cover.

Throwing the bow down, she saw he had drawn a knife. Of course, it had to be a knife. She'd much rather he still held his gun. He would have trouble aiming due to the arrows in his shoulders.

"Who the fuck do you think you are?" he growled.

She studied the big man who slowly moved toward her, almost dragging his leg behind him. He was quite formidable. Even shooting him three times with arrows didn't slow him down much. She patted her side where the gun should have been. The belt she had borrowed that held the gun was gone. Iris knew it hadn't fit well in the first place and now regretted not buying a proper one. She didn't have time to look for it, though. Hector lunged for her with his knife.

Why does it always have to be knives? Iris thought, dodging the swipe of his knife. Reaching down to her boot, she pulled out a long dagger. *Fucking knives.*

"You're going to regret doing this. I will make your death slow and very painful."

"I'm certain you will. Just like you have done with so many others. But I fear this will be your last bout." She swiftly moved to the side, out of the way of his knife. His arm shook, making him change hands.

He thrust the knife at her again, and she moved back into a tree. The sun had fully set now, making seeing difficult. Staggering back, the heel of her foot hit a root, making her fall on her backside, knocking the wind from her.

Hector took this opportunity and fell to his knees, plunging the blade toward her chest. She rolled to her right side and hit the bush she had been hiding behind. Reaching behind her to stand, she felt the missing belt and then the gun. Pulling the pistol out, Iris pointed it at the man who was now crawling toward her. Despite it being dark, the man was close enough where she could aim. Pulling the trigger, a loud bang filled the air, and Hector's lifeless body hit the ground.

It was a good thing she had poisoned the arrow tips. Because of the man's blood pumping harder, the poison acted faster, making him far less a threat then he would have been if he hadn't been shot three times. Despite all that, she was cutting it close. He laid a few feet away from where she found her gun, just in the nick of time. She was one of the few within the agency who would go to such great lengths and use things like poison.

Iris looked down and noticed a few new cuts on her arms and sides, but nothing deep enough to go seek a doctor. She really didn't want to see any doctors. She grabbed her belt and gun and started toward where she had stored her belongings. After disposing of Hector body in a shallow grave she dug earlier, Iris went to find the horse he had been riding. Searching in the evening haze, she finally found the mare. She took the saddle and everything from the horse to let it roam free in the hopes that no one would recognize it.

Then it was time to go through the murder's things to search for any known whereabouts of his comrades. While doing so, Iris came across a note that explained why Hector was so hesitant. The words she read tore at her heart, filling the gaping wound with hate.

Doc,

I cannot change my ways. You saved me so long ago. A

stranger on a dark road. I could have killed you. And you

should have killed me. I am sending this letter ahead of me. I

can only warn you of my coming. Rune is a bastard who has

set eyes on you. I am now sent to kill you because of a girl. A

girl he fancies his own. If I do not kill you, someone else will.

And if I do not follow through, the family I left behind die in

your stead. I am coming. I advise you run. I am sorry...

Hector

Iris built a small fire and watched as the fires burned the man's things, including the letter. Despite the heat from the flames, Iris felt cold. Rune had gone beyond destroying her life. He sought to crush all that she held dear and didn't care who he hurt along the way. And now she had a few names to add to her list to bring her closer to Rune's down fall. First, she would go find the man Hector spoke to and try to get information from him. Iris needed to know who would now be appointed to go after Garrett and the others.

Then, she'd destroy Rune's forces, one person at a time. She would break him and his organization.

This would be her life now. Nothing but her new goal and basic human needs mattered. She rested several miles away from where she had fought Hector, only halfway sleeping, never letting her guard down. This had been her habit for quite some time and would continue to be so.

As the first rays of light lit the sky, she gathered her things once more and headed to small mountain town to see if she could trace the other man. He was older and moved around in a large carriage with several people attending to him, so this hunt would not be a long one.

Iris changed into new clothes, ones that weren't blood-spattered or cut. She wanted to buy an extra pair but didn't want to draw more attention to herself. So, she passed a laundress who had been working on cleaning her master's and mistress's clothes, which were now hanging to dry. The maid was busy with other duties, such as trying to ward off the master himself. After watching and waiting for a few moments, she took a pair of man's pants and a shirt. Feeling bad for the laundress, she left several coins, not knowing if her warden would fire her because of the missing clothes. Sticking the garments in her bag, she returned to the shadows.

She kept to the shadows, searching for the man who had spoken to Hector. She weaved in and out of the small wooden buildings that made up the cold mountain town. Someone as high in status and hedonistic as him would probably not be in too much of a hurry to be off, wanting to seek out every worldly pleasure and height of luxury he could find before moving on. Iris had seen him from a distance before and knew of him as the face of Rune's business. Hardly anyone had met Rune and that was how he liked it.

As she watched a fancy carriage outside the high-end hotel, Iris thought back to when she had first met Rune and how that moment had changed her life forever…

Iris had been in a bad part of a town on a cold rainy day at the age of fourteen. She had long worked with police to track people down but had yet to be sought out by the agency at that point in time. She was tracking down someone who had been smuggling illegal goods. All Iris had to do was find their location. Nothing more. She stepped near a large building located in the back of the streets near the docks and saw a man coming toward her.

If she had known who this man was and how he would haunt her for the rest of her life, she would have turned and ran the other way. But she had been a young naïve girl at the time. That was the first time she had met Rune and the first time he kidnapped her. After several days, she broke free. She escaped every time he captured her. It was all part of his sick twisted game of cat and mouse he liked to play with her.

Iris tried not to think much past the moment of their first meeting. She tried hard to bury the memories of the time with

Rune. Thinking of the past would not help her move toward the future.

Blinking, she found herself back in the present, watching the luxurious carriage now filled with its occupants. She was happy she had already packed her things onto her horse and tied it near the carriage. Once it started down the road, she mounted her horse to follow.

Garrett woke from his dream, confused about what the bear-turned-human had told him. Two paths to choose from, one that would lead to Iris but also pain. The other would hold no such love, no such pain...

Sighing at the thought, he shook his head, trying to dislodge the images of Iris that floated in his mind, regardless of his actions. The moment they shared in the woods fought to drive him insane with desire. Desire not just for her body but her very being. Emotions tore at him, and if it continued at this rate, he would have to be admitted to a madhouse in the near future. He imagined himself sitting against a white wall, drooling, the only coherent thought of Iris.

Sitting up in bed, he looked around. When he lifted his hand, he hit something underneath his pillow. Dragging it out, he looked down at a dreamcatcher made of twigs and red twine.

Garrett stared at it, unmoving, as if his very breath would blow it away like dust. Garrett slowly, lightly, curled his fingers around the object he held so preciously as if it were a link to Iris that could be easily broken.

Garrett's feelings were a mix of anger and sadness. So many emotions bombarded him. When he accepted his feelings for her, he never knew it would be this hard. He was angry she left him and right after their intimate moment at that. Didn't that mean something to her? It meant everything to him. Yet, she left anyway. Without a word or even a goodbye. Was there such a thing as a goodbye?

He tried not to curl his hand and crush the dreamcatcher. So, he took a deep breath and exhaled, calming himself. Her absence hit him like a brick wall. His chest felt heavy, making it hard to breathe.

Shaking his head harder, Garrett pushed the dreamcatcher back under his pillow. He had to try and occupy his mind to keep the thoughts of her at bay. So, he decided to be with the others. Walking into the kitchen, he saw his sister, Cole and Abelia sitting down to eat. He smiled at them and took a seat at the table, a plate of food already in front of him.

Cole, Isabelle and Abelia all exchanged subtle glances that Garrett ignored. Cole cleared his throat. "When are we going to go after Iris?"

Garrett glared at Cole. "I have to go see my father. He is not doing well. Will you come with us, Isabelle?"

She scoffed. "Over my dead body will I ever go see that madman. And I'm putting that nicely. I cut ties with him long ago when he tried to marry me off to a man twice my age just so he would sign with him." She leaned back in her chair, crossed her arms and stared back at Garrett. "He knows how I feel about him, and I am fine with that."

"He changed so much after my mother died, and even more so when he lost your mother, Isabelle. It broke him, and he turned his feelings off and jumped headlong into work and his new business. Despite all that he has done, he is still our father."

"I know that," Isabelle said, cutting him off, "but his business isn't right and you know it. And how he wanted to use us for his own gain." She paused and took a deep breath. Cole put his hand on her shoulder for comfort. "He will try it again, Garrett. Once he sees that you came, he will try to bend you to his will and use you. Be careful, brother."

"I will be on my guard," he said finally.

"And I will be there to watch out for him." Abelia smiled at them all. "Wait one moment... You two are going to be here. All alone. With no supervision." She glanced at Garrett to see if he had realized this.

He just stared back at her, leaning back in his chair with his arms crossed. She looked back at the couple.

"That isn't a problem, Abelia. We're engaged. That should help people and their wagging tongues," Isabelle said softly.

"Wait! When did this happen? Why are you just now telling me? Where's the ring? You should have told me first thing when you saw me."

Isabelle laughed. "So many questions!"

"Calm down," Cole said. "It wasn't that long ago. And as for a ring, I haven't been able to accrue one yet. But soon…" He placed his hand on Isabelle's. "When are you leaving to go to see you father?" Cole asked, looking at Garrett.

"We'll probably head out tomorrow morning when the stagecoach comes to town. Abelia isn't fond of horses." Smirking, he looked at Abelia who was pouting.

Her pout formed into a smile. "I expect an invite to this wedding of yours. No excuses. I will hunt you both down if I don't get to see your wedding."

As the day went on, Garrett left the three of them and went to his office in town. He knew of a few patients who needed more than just a check-up. One man who seemed to be as old as the town needed help with a fence. His pigs kept getting loose and running amuck. Listening to the man talk about his day, Garrett went about fixing the poles and railing, hoping the hogs would stay in this time.

Next stop was a house occupied by elderly twin sisters. They always baked him apple pies and asked if he had gotten married yet. He would always tease and ask who he would marry. They always responded with *Us!*

After seeing a few more patients, he went to see Micah. Stepping into the sheriff's office, he saw Micah reading a letter. Garrett cleared his throat, and the sheriff quickly looked up and put the letter away just as fast.

"Must be an interesting letter," Garrett commented. He sat down, eyeing Micah, taking in his aging features. He often forgot that Micah was almost twenty years older than himself.

He eyed Garrett, and then with a sigh said, "It was a letter from Iris."

The sound of her name made his heart race and hair stand on edge. "Iris? How is she?" he immediately asked, needing to know she was okay. Not wanting to show how eager he was to know news, he tried to hide how much he was about to jump out of his skin to get the letter, to see her hand writing. He had to clench his fists in anger to keep him from leaping across the desk.

The sheriff cleared his throat. "She's fine. Iris found out that Rune, the man after her, is now sending people to kill you." He paused and looked down at his hands and then back up at Garrett. "She's now hunting the hunters. Keeping them away from you and here. Iris only wrote me to tell me to be on the lookout for anyone new in town. To be on guard..." Micah looked down again.

Garrett just gaped at the letter. Thoughts swam in his head. *She left in the hopes that this Rune guy would leave me and my family alone. And then she found out he wasn't going to back down that easy. So, Iris is...*

As if reading his thoughts, Micah said, "She is trying to protect us all, especially you... the best way she knows how." Garrett looked up, locking eyes with Micah. "I have heard of her before all of this, Garrett. I didn't realize it was her until the day she stopped Harry the merchant from killing the gunman and Ned the barkeep. The stories I've heard are mostly of her marksmanship."

"To tell the truth, I hardly knew anything about outlaws and bounty hunters. Until I met Iris, I would block out chatter of such things. I really didn't know much..." After Iris had left, he had looked into outlaw and bounty hunters but had to stop. It had only made his worry for her grow.

"The thing is, because she is a woman and a bounty hunter, she not only hunts down killers, but she is also the hunted. For her safety, the people she works with try their best to keep her likeness out of the papers and so on. Garrett, I heard her be called The Storm. I'm guessing the agency she works for put that out there to try to keep from people knowing her. You have to understand that she is keeping away not because of herself but to keep you safe, to keep everyone she has grown fond of here, safe."

Before he could go on, Garrett murmured, "That's why she is always on the run because she is always being chased… She won't accept help…" Rage and sadness fought for dominance within his very being.

Leaning forward, Micah asked softly, "What move are you going to make?"

Garrett cocked an eyebrow. "What do you mean by that?"

"Are you going to get Cole to help find her? Are you going to go after her?" Micah asked, both men staring at one another.

"My next move is to go see my father who is ill. Iris made her choice, and I will not get in her way." Garrett stood, nodding to the sheriff. "I will see you when I return. Until then." He still felt, deep down, they would somehow cross paths, like falling stars crashing to earth.

Garrett left and went around to people in the town, taking care of those who needed his attention and telling others of his travels and when to expect him back.

The next morning, he headed out in the coach along with Abelia to the town of Smithington, where his father lived. After changing carriages a couple times, they made it to the city a day and a half after first leaving. Abelia went to her family's home a few blocks from Garrett's father's town house.

The brick townhome connected to other homes on each side. He glared at the dark oak stairs leading to the front door. After knocking, he was greeted by a doorman who showed him into a parlor just past the front door on the right from a small hall.

A small fire blazed in a fireplace surrounded by the same brick as the exterior. In front of the fire was one sofa and two high back chairs facing each other with a table in between. Sitting down on the sofa, back to one of the two windows, he surveyed the room. There was a large grandfather clock along with a large table near the other window, an area to have tea or play cards.

He had only been to this home a few times. It always seemed odd that there were no paintings or portraits. Most homes housed a family portrait or a landscape scene, but the room was all dull-colored, floral wallpaper. Garrett sat there, trying not to think of what always seemed to creep into his mind when he was still, Iris... He hoped his father would come greet him soon. He always had to wait for him to come from his study, rarely being allowed in his work area.

After waiting a while longer, the sliding doors that separated the parlor from his father's, the judge's study slid apart. Standing, he turned to see his father enter. As he took the older man in, he noticed that despite his white hair and wrinkles, the man looked to be in good health for his age. But a good doctor knew looks could be deceiving.

"Nice to see you, Father," Garrett said, stepping forward and extending his hand. "You look well."

The shorter man nodded to the doctor. "Yes, well, looks aren't everything. Come, sit." The judge shook his son's hand and then motioned for them to sit near the small fire. "I'm glad Abelia was able to persuade you to come and see me. It has been so long since we've come together like this. I'm sad Isabelle wasn't able to accompany you. I know she has her reasons. But I am glad to see you, son." His father slightly smiled at Garrett.

He returned his smile, leaning back in the sofa. "So, why have you called me here, Father? What has been ailing you?"

"I have been under stress for a while now and have spells where my heart races."

"How many cups of coffee are you having a day?" Garrett asked, leaning forward with his forearms on his legs.

"I would say about seven or eight throughout the day," he answered after a moment. "I don't see that as an unreasonable number."

"That is quite a high number, and I have spoken to you before about how coffee affects your heart, making it race. I suggest going down to three or four cups a day. Or switching to tea instead. Even then you still should only drink a few cups and more water through the day. I can examine you if you like. Are there any other symptoms?"

The judge was giving very little details in the way of his symptoms, as his son, the doctor tried his best to study him.

Father and son spoke more while having lunch. "Tell me, Garrett. How is your practice in that small town of yours?"

"It's nice. It gives me good work and variety, which is why I like it." He tried to keep his voice level and calm.

"But not much in the way of money, I suppose." His father was trying to get him to come back to the big city, where all the big spenders lived.

"It's not all about deep pockets, Father. We take care of one another in other ways."

"And how's your sister? Has she found herself a wealthy husband out in the sticks?"

"Father, do you remember you used to live in a place much more remote than Valden?" Again, he tried to keep his tone light, trying to not let his frustration show through his voice.

"That was many lifetimes ago. And you didn't answer the question." He eyed him over a cup of coffee.

"You should really drink more tea, Father."

After examining his father, one of the servants showed Garrett to a room where he could rest. He turned in early and fell asleep quite fast due to the long travel. But with deep sleep came deep dreams.

Garrett found himself in a deep forest, so thick with undergrowth he could hardly move. Branches and twigs intertwined with one another, making every movement almost impossible. Hardly any moonlight shone in from above the canopy. There was this intense feeling that he was being chased. It filled his very being. Why was it that he always found himself in a forest?

Looking down at his hands, he saw they were smaller and paler than normal. Garrett stopped in his tracks. Reaching up, he fingered his hair, but it was shorter than he remembered

Iris' being. Confused, he sought out anything that might give off a reflection. Running through the trees once more, he found a small creek. Following it, he soon stumbled upon what he was looking for. An area in the creek where water had pooled and stilled. With the help of a spot of moonlight from above, he looked into the water.

His breath caught in his chest. Staring back at him was Iris but not the Iris he remembered. Her hair was shorter, better to hide under a hat most likely. She had dark circles under sunken eyes and even paler features. The sight made his heart ache, but along with that ache came anger. Anger that she left, that she might be hurting herself, putting too much on her shoulders. It felt as if his heart was being pulled in two, warring between worry and anger.

As he stared into the water, a ripple went through the creek...

Iris stepped outside a farmhouse, blood dripping down her left arm, which hung limply at her side. Her eyes were vacant, looking but not seeing the world around her. She had spent the last few months going down a list of people connected to Rune. After reading Hector's letter, she went and moved his family, then hunted those who hunted them.

The only thing present in her mind was to destroy his organization one person at a time, keeping them away from Garrett and the others. This was her mission in life, to take Rune down, piece by piece. She would always be chased by one person or another and didn't want to bring anyone she cared for into her messed up life.

She shuffled into the nearby woods. Going person after person was taking a toll on her body. Her mind had a good way of shutting out the physical feeling of pain. The exhaustion was another matter. Her brain couldn't push away how heavy her body felt, how tired her eyes were. They could hardly stay open as she made her way between trees. Flashes of the faces she had killed came to mind. Knowing these people had families weighed on her. They had all worked for Rune and had taken lives themselves. They would have taken Garrett's and hers given the chances, which drove her on. But that didn't help the guilt she felt and carried with her. Iris knew she would never forget the lives she had cut short. One day, she would have to pay the price.

Sadness filled her heart and soul, making her numb to the bitter cold. It wasn't just from losing the one she loved but also losing herself in the madness of it all.

The cold winter air whipped around her. The white fluff caught her eye. Small snowflakes fell onto her outstretched hand. And as her eyes took in the pureness of the newly falling snow, tears she had been holding in for months flooded her well-built walls.

She had carefully built walls to hold back all the feelings that would hinder her revenge, and now they were starting to crumble. The pain that had been held at bay came rushing in like waves from a stormy sea. Falling to her knees, she hugged herself, her body shaking. Everything she had done and gone through seemed to be catching up to her. The loss, the guilt.

But she had to keep moving, finish what she had started. The list she had gathered was shortening, which meant fewer people to go after the ones she cared for. Now was not the time to let herself feel. It was time to push through, to move to the next step. Sitting up on her knees, Iris placed her hand higher on her shoulder. With quick movements, there was crack and a scream as her dislocated shoulder popped back into place.

Lying back on the snow-covered ground, she thought of her next move. She would go to the city, back to Smithington. That was where the list would lead her. To protect the ones she loved. Reaching into her pocket, she took out a list of names smudged with blood and dirt. The list had about thirty odd last names, twelve of which had been crossed out. One name at the very bottom separate from the others was circled, *Clarkson*. Iris rubbed her thumb across the name, admiring it fondly. That name was the fuel to her fire, feeding the flames. But she knew she couldn't think of him for too long or too often. Because right now, all she wanted to feel was physical pain and not think about what she had left behind.

No matter how her heart ached or her head throbbed, there was only one direction to take, and that was forward.

Chapter 16

Iris walked down the busy street, her mind full of thoughts and yet, again, she wasn't paying attention to her surroundings. It had become common in the last few weeks after she had let her emotions get the better of her in the mountains.

And she would soon regret it. When Iris looked up, the sight of Garrett and a well-dressed girl hugging his arm stopped her in her tracks. The girl was lovely with red hair and fine porcelain skin. The way the lady was dressed told Iris that she was in the same class as Garrett, which stabbed at her heart. *I didn't think he cared about station.* The stabbing pain was accompanied with a seizing of lungs, like someone had grasped them and squeezed all the air out.

Then her eyes caught the sight of an expensive-looking engagement ring adorned on the lovely lady's left ring finger. The way it glinted in the sun made Iris want to rip it off her finger and burn it with the flames of her jealousy. How could he move on so fast? Did he not think of her as she did of him? They stared at one another, neither of them moving, as if ghosts of the other's past. And then he looked her up and down with a worried expression on his face. Worried she would ruin things with his fiancé? And just like that, the flames of jealousy turned into a torrent of rage.

Iris moved her hands behind her, balling them into fists as she shook her head in one quick movement. His face showed relief.

The change in his features made her blood boil even more. She wanted to smack that chiseled face of his. She looked again at the ring on the lady's hand. Garrett started forward, but the lady gripped his arm, stopping him. Iris nodded goodbye and rapidly crossed the busy street before the anger she felt got the better of her.

She'd spent so many months of trying to push her feelings down, and now, seeing him with her nearly destroyed all that progress. These feelings of pure rage and jealousy were uncalled for. Iris had no right to him, and she knew that. She had let him go for his safety, because she loved him. Didn't he know that? Shaking her head, she pushed the thoughts deep down, trying her best to not dig them back up. He was happy with a lovely young lady.

A stray tear fell down her cheek. As she was about to brush it away, someone grabbed her arm and turned her around. Taken by surprise twice in one day?

I must have a death wish, she thought.

Garrett stood before her. His caramelized skin shone in the afternoon sun and set her ablaze.

"What is it, Garrett? How can I help you?" she asked angrily.

She couldn't look him in the eyes and kept looking at different places, his cheek, his neck, his hair. Would she grip his hair as she did in the woods? She shook her head again, trying to gather her thoughts.

"Iris, I wanted to explain. She thought I shouldn't, but I want to. Please, listen."

"No, Garrett, she was right. There is no reason for you to explain things to me." She sighed heavily. "I wish you all the best in the future. I am glad you are alive to have a future." Before he could say more, she ripped her arm from his tight grip and ran down the street.

Garrett stood there frozen. Someone touched him lightly on the shoulder. Turning, he looked down to see a white-haired man. The judge.

"Father, you crossed this busy street all on your own? You could have fallen. Come, let us get you into the house." He grabbed his father's arm lightly and guided him back across the street.

"Who was that girl? She was dressed quite odd." He looked up at his son.

"Father, you need to focus on getting well, not on my affairs."

The judge nodded and once they were back inside the house, he said to Garrett, "I have to make some inquiries if you will excuse me."

"Yes, of course, Father."

Garrett sighed, sitting down on a large sofa, closing his eyes. He shook his head, trying to get rid of the images of Iris' face floating in front of him. *I can't believe I thought for a split second she could have been pregnant. And I think she knew what I thought, too. I've finally found her and I've fucked it up… Dammit…*

"Having some trouble, are we?" He opened his eyes to see Abelia standing in the doorway. "I told you to grab her and kiss her, not to try and explain. How well did that turn out, by the way?"

Garrett leaned forward, putting his elbows on his knees and face in hands. "I'd rather not talk about it right now, Abe."

She sat down next to him and put her hand on his shoulder. "Does that mean you're moving on, then?"

"Who says I want to move on?" His voice was muffled by his hands. "Speaking of moving on, where is your fiancé?"

Abelia laughed lightly. "He is out with his band of men at the moment. I let him do his own thing, and he lets me have my life. You know our deal."

"Don't you wish for love and not just someone you can deal with?" He moved his head slightly to eye her.

She huffed and crossed her arms. "Not everyone gets a chance at love. Despite what others say, falling in love and being loved in return is quite rare. As I'm sure you know."

Garrett leaned back into the sofa, crossing his arms as well. "Let's not talk about this anymore for the moment, shall we?" He was too busy cursing at himself to have a discussion.

Iris didn't know how she made it back to her flat, but she did. This wasn't good at all. She had let her guard down way too many times today. And who knew what repercussions that may have later on. She laid on the small bed that took up most of the space. Iris didn't even want to call it a room, more like a closet. One single-pane window that was sealed shut with old paint didn't help the stuffiness of the closed-in space. And that old paint extended to the walls, which peeled and chipped, making her cough every time she opened the door.

She decided to rest until morning and start the day anew with a clear head would be best. As Iris lay on the mold-sodden bed, the image of Garrett and the lovely young lady on his arm kept floating in her mind. She grabbed the pillow, put it over her face, and screamed into it. The tears she fought so hard to keep in on the street streamed down her cheeks. And the yells became muffed cries. The pain that gripped her heart was far more painful than anything she had ever felt, just like the anger from earlier. All the stab and gun wounds her body had endured was nothing compared to what she was feeling now.

Then the thought of Garrett's warm skin, touching someone else… His golden eyes looking upon them and no longer on her. And his voluptuous lips enveloping hers. His strong arms lifting her, hugging her to him. Iris sobbed even more, gasping for air. No amount of tears or screams would ease the pain she felt. She had truly lost him, just as she had meant to…

Iris didn't remember falling asleep, but she soon found herself in a dream that was not her own. Surely, this wasn't Garrett's. She hadn't entered his dreams since she left. If this was his dream, she wasn't going to search him out. She would just stay in this spot until one of them woke up. Iris didn't think she could handle seeing him again.

The place was familiar. It was the woods near the farmhouse Garrett and Isabelle shared. What was it with him and woods? But after some thought, it was better than where her dreams would lead her.

Even though there was a chance of seeing Garrett here, she didn't have to deal with her inner demons in his dreams at least. Leaning back against a large tree, she rested, keeping her eyes open to any movement. Garrett must have forgotten they could connect through dreams. After all, they never fully spoke of it with one another or figured out how or why.

Hearing a sound behind her, Iris stood, pushing away from the tree. She turned to see a dark outline, but it wasn't the shape of Garrett.

She froze. "You shouldn't be here. This isn't my dream..."

Her dreams were the one place where her fear got the best of her, where she had the least control. Trying to move as far away as possible before fear rendered it impossible, she backed up slowly, panic setting in.

"You think you can hide from me?" the figure hissed. "I will always follow you until the day one of us dies."

Iris shook her head. "This can't be, not in his dream..."

She closed her eyes, focusing on anything but the figure closing in on her. Opening her eyes, the figure now stood in front of her. That's all he was, a dark outline. In her dreams, she never saw the face of Rune. Before Iris knew it, she was on her back, the dark figure on top of her. She tried to push and kick him off, but it was as if her arms and legs went right through him. But how could she feel his whole weight on her?

Closing her eyes again, she shook her head. "This isn't real. This isn't real."

The figure tugged at the hem of her shirt. She tried again to move, tears rolling down her cheeks. Iris wouldn't scream. If this was Garrett's dream, she didn't want him to see her like this.

The figure kissed her, making her try all the harder to get free but it was as if she wasn't moving. "This is a dream. This is only a dream."

His cold fingers moved up her thigh, and she gasped. Iris couldn't hold in her screams any longer. "This isn't real! You are not real!" The figures moved further up her leg. "Nnnoooo! This isn't real!" Her screams came out in sobs, her body shaking.

Iris kept her eyes closed, trying to remind herself that it was a nightmare, one she could wake up from. But there was nothing she could do, nothing to wake her, nothing to stop this. She hated feeling weak, not being able to help herself. Only in her dreams would her fears overcome her. When she tried to scream more, she couldn't. Her mouth had gone dry. Fear paralyzed her, making her feel as if a ton of bricks laid atop her.

No matter how much she wanted to move, her body couldn't listen to her commands.

Iris wished she could fall into a deep pit of nothingness where no feeling could find her, where pain and nightmares would never reach her. She wanted the pain and fear to end…

The terrifying dream continued. She tensed with each of his movement. Rune's breath filled her ear, heavily panting. Iris bit her lip to hold in the cries she desperately wanted to let out, but they would do no good. The figure was all over her as if it was a shadow, fill every pour. She let out a sob of pain.

And in the next instant, the weight of the figure lifted, and she was able to move. Opening her eyes, she saw… No, it couldn't be. Her heart ached at the sight of Garrett holding the dark figure by the throat. His eyes focused, and the figure burst into flames and then to ash that floated to the ground.

Iris pushed to her elbows, still shaking. She hated that her dreams had to feel so real, good or bad ones. Garrett knelt and picked her up in his arms. She tensed at his touch, but he only pulled her closer. He took her to his farmhouse, put her down in a seat near the fire, and covered her with a blanket.

Iris' feelings were still raw. She couldn't control the tears. "I'm so sorry," she sobbed. "I'm so, so, sorry. I didn't want to leave. I wanted to stay." She couldn't stop the words from flowing out of her. "I wanted to keep you safe. I wanted to see you happy." She buried her face in her hands, hoping he wasn't really here, that he didn't realize this was all real.

She felt movement beside her. Garrett had sat down on the floor next to her. Reaching up, he took her hands away from her face and covered them with his own. Iris didn't dare look at him, so she studied the wood floor instead.

"It seems your fears somehow drifted into my dream space. To do that, they must be strong in you. I must say, you keep your fears well hidden. I've done some research on dreams and connecting with others while you were away." She looked sideways at him in surprise. "One or both of us are dealing with strong emotions. It's interesting that I have been unable to enter yours as of late. Yet, you can enter mine and bring your nightmares with you."

Iris didn't say a word, not knowing what to say. He knew her fears, her weakness. Tears flowed down her cheeks, and she couldn't or wouldn't stop them. He sat there, still holding her hands in his.

"I'm glad you've found… someone…" she said in between sobs. His hands tightened. "I wanted you safe and happy… Even if it wasn't with me…" Iris wouldn't dare look at him. If her emotions were raw now, they would be even more so if she saw his face.

Before either of them could speak again, Iris felt something outside the dream. Something wasn't right. She had to wake up now. Her heart raced, her breath catching in her throat. It felt like she was being choked. Garrett, seeing her distress, tried to help, but he couldn't. She closed her eyes and focused on waking up, which was easier with the nightmare gone.

When she opened her eyes, a figure stood over her, their hands around her throat. She gripped the man's hands hard, digging her fingernails in. He screamed and let go. She immediately reached for her gun, but the man was gone, the door wide open.

Iris gasped hard, her lungs burning. Holding her throat, she looked around for any signs he might have left behind. Not giving the dream a second thought, she gathered her things and moved to a cheaper, more hole-in-the-wall hotel. She didn't sleep the rest of the night, staying alert to any threats.

Her attacker wasn't Rune's man. He wouldn't kill her. He would kill those she loved before harming her. Then who was trying to kill her? Who would have known where she was and taken such a risk at that? The only men she had killed were Rune's. Iris had made sure of that. Who had she pissed off so much to get a hit put out on her?

Only one way to find out, and that was to search. For the bounty she hunted and any word for the bounty on her.

251

She was out on the streets at sunrise, searching for her bounty. Iris decided to search the slums; he probably had turned back to his old lifestyle of drug use. Iris searched the darkest parts of the city she could find, where no one else would go. The plague ward, it was called that back when the plague was at its highest. The name remained and all those who had contagious illnesses were sent there. A good hiding place for someone not wanting to be found or for those wanting a quiet place to use illegal substances.

It was dark with no windows for light to come in or air to escape from. She gagged within the first few feet of the front door that led to deep rooms under the city. Many who take the long winding staircase down do not make it back up. Her heart sank at the sight of those being cranked down by levers. Unable to walk, this place only made their conditions worse.

Chapter 17

Several days had passed since Iris had entered his dream. He couldn't stop thinking about her and if she was all right. She hadn't been in a good state in the dream, and the nightmare plaguing her now haunted his every waking moment.

"What's on your mind? Still thinking of love lost? If so, does that mean someone is finally going to go find her?" Abelia smiled at him. They sat in the parlor reading.

He looked up from the newspaper. He had seen an article of a mass murderer being caught by an unknown hero, which made him think of Iris again. "Don't you have someone else to annoy? Say, your future husband perhaps?" Garrett eyed her.

Her laughter was interrupted by his father barging into the room. "I want to speak with you, son…" Abe stood to take her leave, but the judge stopped her. "No, stay, you need to hear this as well." The aging man went to sit in the high back chair, almost glaring at Garrett.

"Yes, Father, what is it?" He folded the newspaper and put it on a side table.

"I did some questioning on that girl you chased in the streets the other day. Did you know she is a rebel? Works for an unknown part of the government? She has no family ties, no friends, nothing to her name and no name at all it seems. It is as if she hardly exists. Yet you were trying to keep company with her?"

This was one reason he didn't want to come see his father, knowing he would never understand Iris or the life she led. "Father, it's not what you think."

"Don't tell me," he interrupted sharply. "I don't want to hear it. I don't care if it was a one-night fling. You are not to see her again. She is trouble and will only bring you pain. Stay away from this low-life before she drags you into the slums along with her."

Garrett gripped the side of his pants, something he had been wontedly doing since a child, to hold in his anger, "You act as if you know her, Father."

"I know more than you, I am sure. As I said, I had a slight investigation done, and she is not a good person. I don't care if she supposedly works for the law." His father's face turned red. "No matter, you will not see the likes of her again." And before Garrett could say another word on the matter, the judge had gone back into his study. The door slammed behind him, letting Garrett know that the conversation was over.

He sat there, dumbfounded. He never thought his father would be so interested in who he talked to, to go so far as investigate them. What did the files really say about her? Did they say more than he knew?

Abelia leaned forward. "All right, Gare bear," she whispered. "Now can we talk about how to find Iris? Or are you still wanting to stay away from her?"

He solemnly nodded, and they set about formulating a plan to search her out.

Iris had felt uneasy for days, ever since she let her guard down and that man tried to kill her in her sleep. She had been trying to find any lead on who had put a hit on her but had found nothing yet. Whoever this was, they had covered their tracks.

But the uneasiness she felt was worse today, and a few miles back, she noticed a large man trailing her. He followed her down dark paths. When she took abrupt turns into crowded streets, he still ended up behind her. She even ran into a textile mill where ladies screamed at her and threw things at him, making it clear he was following her.

The chase was on. She picked up her pace, headed to where she would have the advantage. The hotel she had been staying in for the last few nights was dark with uneven stairs and small walkways. This tag-turned-chase was about to become a fight. With this in mind, Iris weaved in and out of the streets, trying to get him to lag behind her by several yards. She reached the hotel and ran up the broken, uneven steps to her rented room.

Iris entered the small windowless room. Leaving the door ajar, she hid in the shadows. Not wanting to kill the man, not yet at least, she found a loose floorboard and pulled it up. Holding it in both hands, she waited.

Steadying her breath, she heard distance footsteps moving closer. She lifted the board, and as the man slowly entered the room, she hit him on the back, sending him face-first to the floor. She quickly and efficiently pinned his arms behind him and tied them with string. She then sat on him, holding a gun to his head.

"Who sent you?"

"Why in hell would I tell you?" he huffed.

"Is their life worth more than yours just because they have money?" She was guessing but most of the time, her guesses were correct.

He moaned. He tried to lift her off, but she would not budge. "Some old man."

Iris pressed the gun to the side of his head. "What is the name of this old man? Think carefully. His life for yours." This was her element. She could push all her fears away, all her feelings aside.

A few moments of silence filled the room before the man reluctantly told her, "Clarkson. That's all I know."

She thought of the name. Clarkson. Then it hit her. Garrett Clarkson. But he had said old man. Was it Garrett's father? Surely not. *Please, don't let it be...*

Iris stood to let him go. Her mind centered on thoughts of Garrett and what this might mean for him, for them. And before she could react, the man knocked her against the wall, and within seconds, he had his hands in front of him and a knife in between them.

It just had to be a damn knife. She dodged his attacks, but she needed to get close to hit him. Iris didn't want him dead. As she neared him, she hit him in the back of the head, hard, with her gun. She wasn't quick enough, and the man cut her side. She hissed as pain flared up her side, but she had no time to inspect her wound.

Shrugging it off, Iris lifted the man, holding him up from underneath his shoulder, half dragging him. She wasn't quite sure how she got him into a carriage. Everything started to become a blur. Her heart raced. What would she do if it was Garrett's father? Garrett Clarkson's father might have set a kill order out for her. How do you tell someone that? Not even remembering how, she got herself and her would-be killer in the carriage. She told the driver to take them to the Clarkson residence, the judge when he asked which one.

Iris wasn't sure why she was doing this. Maybe because she didn't take kindly to hits being put out on her, no matter who the person was. Maybe she wanted to see if it really was his father. Warm blood seeped down her dress. It must have been deeper than she had realized. Her vision blurred as they pulled up to the house.

Garrett and Abelia had been talking for hours when they heard a noise at the door. Several thuds, the maid's screams and then the sliding doors from the hall slid open. Standing at the threshold was Iris, who had a half-unconscious man under her arm. Then his eyes went straight to bright red blood from a wound on her side. Blood soaked her stomach area and ran down her skirt.

He stood, still staring. "What happened?" His heart leaped out of his chest, but his feet were like lead, keeping him in place.

Iris roughly shook the man she held. "Wake up. Tell them who sent you to kill me. Twice." She shook him again, but this time more forcefully. The man groaned.

"Clarkson," the man said in a low raspy voice.

Abelia gasped and covered her mouth, and Garrett's eyes went wide. Mr. Clarkson stepped into the room, obviously having heard the commotion.

Iris studied the elder Mr. Clarkson with a cold look on her face. "Right on cue, sir. This man here just told us who had hired him to try and kill me, not once but twice."

The judge groaned. "It seems you are a hard one to kill."

"Father! Do you know what you are saying?" He hadn't realized how far his father would go, how deep into corruption he had gotten. The woman he loved stood before him bleeding and his father was the one behind it. He had no words…

"I may be ill, my boy, but I still have my mind." Father and son glared at one another. He turned back to Iris. "Why couldn't you just die? It's not like you have anyone to miss you."

Garrett gaped at the man who was supposedly his father, not knowing what to believe anymore. "How could you? You don't know a damn thing about her! Just reading some papers doesn't give you insight into someone's true being. You have no right to take someone's life. No matter what some piece of paper says." He stepped toward his father, anger boiling up inside him. Abelia stopped him, placing a hand lightly on his wrist.

Mr. Clarkson just waved at his son, as if he were a fly buzzing by his ear.

Garrett wanted nothing more than to punch his father right then and there and rush over to Iris to treat her wounds. His heart sank and as Iris spoke the next words, his heart grew even heavier. "I choose when I die, and you and your money are not going to be my end."

"You have not just caused me grief but my clients as well. You and your agency. And now you have found your way to my doorstep." Mr. Clarkson groaned, as if annoyed.

"All thanks to you, sir."

"I wouldn't have minded so much if you had been a man, and then I find that my son fancies you. That was the last straw. You are going to leave this world just as you were brought in."

Iris cut him off, waving her hand. "All alone, yes, yes. I've heard that before, old man. Give me something new, will you?"

"Rune will not be pleased that I tried to have you killed, but no matter. I don't answer to him."

Iris laughed, and the sound held a cruel edge. "You think he answers to you? He answers to no one. Your money and title won't save you from him. And now you made things worse for your own son. He won't stop. He will kill your whole family because of your disobedience. No amount of money will save you now, you foolish old man. You have sentenced you and your family to death."

"Father, you were in with Rune! Are you fucking insane? She's right, we're all dead and it's your fault."

"How dare you speak to me in such a way! I am your father and this is my house! I will be spoken to with..."

"You don't deserve my respect at this moment. You don't deserve the title father. What you did to Isabelle so long ago, I tried to understand what you had gone through, losing two wives one right after the other. But this... Teaming up with a madman, someone who toys with people, uses a a's body as his own person cutting board... To be in with the likes of him... She left to save me... To save your children... And now, now you do this... Tried to kill my..." He couldn't wrap his head around all of this. Garrett was about to move toward his father once more, but the hired hitman moved faster.

Mr. Clarkson stood there, glaring, shaking with fury at his son's words and was turning to move toward Iris when her would-be assassin pushed her to the ground with great force. She landed with a thud and a groan. The man pulled a gun out and pointed it to the older of the two Clarksons. From the angle, only Garrett could see Iris. She reached into her hidden pocket in her skirt and pulled out her pistol. Quickly aiming it, she pulled the trigger, sending a lone bullet right into the man's temple.

Abelia screamed, the shrill sound, piercing, and terror-filled. But he heard Iris groan through Abelia's scream and saw her holding her side, blood starting to soak the floor. He didn't care to even glance at his father, almost wishing he were dead and not the gunman. Garrett watched as Iris stood. There was nothing more that he wanted than to rush to her side, but the look on her face told him to wait.

Standing with the help of the chair, she glared at the old man. "You have annoyed me to no end, which is quite hard to do. I try not to anger easily, but you, sir, have set the record. I'm more than tempted to kill you myself and save Rune a trip." She muttered something under her breath. "But I dare not make the lady faint with two deaths in front of her. Seeing one murder in one lifetime is one too many."

She laughed, which turned into a cough. "I've seen more deaths than I can count, and I tried so hard to keep your son from all this. Yet, here you are!" Iris waved her hand out to the old man. "Dragging him into it. You've made things worse for him, far worse than I ever had." *That's why she was so angry. She had left me to save me, and here was my own father, putting me back into it. And what made it worse was that he did it unbeknownst to him.* "Now that this is all cleared up, I shall take my leave."

When Iris turned to leave, she lost her footing. Garrett rushed to her, catching her before the floor did. "Iris? Iris, can you hear me? Please…"

There was no response. Her eyes were closed. Breath shallow, skin clammy. Blood everywhere. The only heart that was racing was his own…

Garrett didn't want to speak to his father. No matter how much he tried to speak to him, he would not reply. Abelia suggested they take Iris to her uncle's place, making sure the elder Clarkson didn't hear. They made their way there under the cover of night, switching carriages several times, hoping no one was trailing them.

Garrett and Abe cleaned and stitched Iris' wounds. "I understand why you like her so much," Abelia said. "She is quite different. I think you two suite each other well."

Garrett didn't respond. "Why did you scream at the shot? You've seen death before." She was a doctor, after all.

She smiled. "The loudness of the gun is what scared me. Now, stop talking and focus. This poor girl."

He was about to point out that she started talking first but left it alone, knowing she was right. Now was the time to focus on Iris. The wound was hard to stitch because of the knife used to make it. It had been jagged making the flesh uneven, which made the skin hard to sew it back together. And if you cut away any, then there won't be enough left to close the wound. He looked her over, finding new scars and fresh bruises all over her. Garrett wanted to kiss them all away. To take all her pain, physical and mental. He sighed, sitting down on the bed next to Iris.

"She will be fine, Garrett. Iris is strong and wouldn't let this be what kills her."

He nodded at Abelia's words, knowing she spoke the truth. Garrett laid his head down on the bed next to their intertwined hands.

Drifting into a dream, he was startled to find where he was at. Looking around, he saw a large empty room. In the center sat Iris holding a gun. He tried to reach her, but every movement he made only pushed him further away.

To his surprise, she looked at him and whispered, "Now you come to my dreams when I am hurt. Why is that?"

Garrett desperately tried to reach her, but no matter how much he tried, how fast he moved, he couldn't get close to her. "Please, Iris! I want to help you. I want to be with you. I'm sorry. I'm so sorry. I should have tried harder…"

She moved to look at him. "She is a lovely lady. I wish you both happiness. But I must go to keep you safe. I have run away from him for fourteen years, half of my life. I can run no longer. If I go, he will not come for you. Because I love you, Garrett, I must leave you. This is the only way I know to combat what has happened. I can't see you hurt." The smile she gave him made him feel as if his heart were being ripped out of his chest.

"No! Iris! Please!" He blinked, and she moved to stand in front of him.

"I want all of you to live happy lives for me. I was never meant to live such a life. I've known that since I was a child. And thinking that you, Isabelle and Cole are happy will give me some sort of peace." She wrapped her arms around his neck. "Thank you, Garrett, for saving me countless times. Let me now save you. And know I do this now out of love."

Tears rolled down his cheeks. He could not move or speak. She kissed him passionately, and Garrett realized Iris had made it where he could not move. She was saying goodbye… He had never felt so frustrated within a dream. Wanting to reach for someone, something and not being able to move. Iris wouldn't let him tell her how he felt. How he loved her with every fiber of his being. He had to tell her, but no matter how much he tried to scream, no words would come.

Garrett woke with a start. Sitting up straight, he looked around the room and then to the empty bed. He jumped to his feet and rushed around the house, looking in every room, until he came across Abelia who sat near a fire in the great room.

"Where is Iris?" he asked in concern.

Looking up at him, she smiled. "She was in bed right next to you, silly." When he didn't immediately agree, a look of dread crossed her face. "She wasn't in the bed next to you, was she?"

Garrett shook his head. "Did you see or hear anything? Anything at all?"

Sighing, Abelia looked down. "I'm afraid not. I'm sorry, Gare bear. If I had even thought she was well enough to move on her own, I would have stayed nearby. Seeing all she can do and all that you have told me, I think I might be in love with her as well."

He quickly hugged her. "I'm going to say goodbye to my father. Then I have to go see someone. Take care, Aby, and don't give up on love so easily. Fight for your dreams to make them a reality. You are the only one who can do that for you." Hugging her once again, he left her teary-eyed to go and face his father.

Standing, staring at the front door to his father house, made him see red. If he went in there, Garrett knew, he would probably not be able to restrain the anger that built inside him. Taking each step in stride, he went to knock on the door but froze inches away. How could he face his father, the one who sent a hitman to kill the love of his life? Resigning to his decision, he knocked, softly. *Please, don't be home. Please, don't be home.*

When the door opened, Garrett was expecting to see the butler or maid, but his eyes met none other than his own father's.

"Yes, that's right. I'm having to answer my own door. The staff is busy cleaning the mess your barbaric woman made last night." His father went into the house, still talking as he went, expecting Garrett to flow. He stood, waving his hands this way and that, showing him the blood stains that lined the carpets, walls, floor and furniture.

All Garrett did was stand there, smiling. *Good, this is the least you deserve after what you tried to have done to Iris.* "You have more to worry about with Rune, you arrogant ass."

The judge had been talking that whole time and stopped to turn an ugly gaze on his son. "Yes, Father. You heard correctly. You are an arrogant ass. Over the years, you have only learned to care about yourself, money and power. I know I should be upset about your impending demise, but, right now, I feel no affection for you. No warmth of a son toward his father. I see you as what you are, a piece of shit. Goodbye, Father."

Garrett turned his back on the father he had lost along with his mother so many years ago. The judge had never been the same after her death and had only worsened over the years. His son stayed by his side for Isabelle in the younger years and mostly out of loyalty later. And as Garrett left him with his staff, all of them gaping at the blood stains, Garrett realized he lost and mourned his father decades ago.

Iris had gotten a carriage and made her way out of town, knowing she had to reach Rune before he sent people to reach them. She wondered if his base was still located at the same place, but Iris knew it was. She switched stagecoaches several times, trying to make her way there as fast as possible. In her deliria, she couldn't tell how long she traveled. Everything came in and out of focus. It was midday when she reached what she thought was the place. The only way she knew the time was because of the heat of the day. Stumbling forward, she heard shouts and saw several guns pointed at her.

She fell to her knees, putting her hands on the back of her head, showing she was unarmed. Iris was too tired to care, so she let them drag her into what she thought was a large building. Looking up, she saw the figure that had haunted her every waking moment and shadowed her dreams for years. She almost laughed.

Her nightmare had finally come true. And she was the one to blame.

Chapter 18

Iris found herself hanging suspended in the air.

Thick ropes secured her arms to the beam overhead. Looking down, she saw all she had on was her thin undergarments. She was hanging there like a piece of meat. And was already regretting her decision, knowing full well she had done so in haste and in fever. But it was to save Garrett and Isabelle from their father's actions.

Looking around the room, she saw a large table full of maps and disorderly papers. She was hanging in his office… His office, like a painting to be viewed at his leisure. Iris was so angry at herself. She had turned into such a stupid girl. In the back of her mind, a small voice said, *That's what love will do to someone.*

She rolled her eyes at the thought and tried her best not to think of Garrett with his long eyelashes and beautiful lips… She shook her head just as the door leading to the damp room opened, revealing the infamous Rune. His hair was wavy and reminded her of the color of dry dirt. He was almost attractive, with soft features that kept him looking young despite being in his early forties. His gray eyes took in every inch of her. His tongue darted out to swipe across his lips as if he were about to devour her, and she repressed a shiver. Disgusting. He looked paler than she remembered. He must be keeping himself hidden.

If he wasn't the devil's spawn, he might be handsome. But Iris knew better. He was pure evil that loved to play with people and their lives. People were his toys to do with as he pleased.

Rune walked up to her and put his finger under her chin, lifting and moving her head from side to side, as if he were appraising her like cattle. A sly grin came across his face. Iris tensed. She knew that look never led to anything good.

"Aren't you a sight for sore eyes? I must say, I was quite surprised at you coming to me. I guess you got tired of the chase. Or did it have something to do with keeping that doctor alive?" He slowly trailed his finger down her chest in between her breasts. She fought the urge to squirm away from his touch, refusing to give him that satisfaction. "I think you made a good choice. If you hadn't come, I probably would have killed him and his family. But since you came like a good girl, I only killed his father." Iris glared at him, and he chuckled. "Don't give me that look. He should have never sent someone to try and kill you. His actions left a nasty mark." Rune ran his finger over her still-fresh wound, making Iris flinch. "He had it coming. And the one person who escaped you, he also died. After he told me you had killed all the rest in the woods and that you were badly hurt, I slit his throat. He was the only one left who had a part in hurting you, so again, he had to die as well. But that was quite a while back. Almost a year, now. That's when you met that doctor of yours… I really should have torture that boy more. You falling into that man's arms is truly his fault, is it not?"

Iris still glared at him as he slowly trailed his finger lower. He looked up at her, his gray eyes sparkling with amusement. His eyes were like storm clouds and it made her dislike them all the more. "I've always made it clear to everyone who works for me that you are off limits in every way. They are only to report back to me of your whereabouts and your actions. But they just had to go and cross that line. Therefore, I am not to blame for their outcomes. Like I've told you ever since we met so long ago, you are mine, and you will always be mine."

She spat in his face. "Go fuck yourself. You're a piece of shit who plays with people's lives because you have some unspoken issues that… Oh, I know, you can't get it…"

He cupped his hand around her mouth and jaw. "Now, now, Iris. If you play nice, I will play nice as well. You wouldn't want that good doctor to meet with an accident, would you?" A jolt of fear shot through her. Rune never bluffed. She quickly shook her head. "Good, I'm glad you understand. But that's not enough." His voice lowered. "I have to break that strong spirit of yours, just like any good master would do to a new bitch."

Not caring about the consequences, she swung her legs at him, taking Rune by surprise. Iris wrapped her thighs around at his neck and squeezed. "I am not your bitch!" He only laughed at her words.

He lifted his hand and pressed his thumb against her still-healing wound. Glaring, he pressed harder, daring her to keep going. Pain blasted up her side. As he pressed more, she screamed and let go, causing her to swing back and forth.

"Damn you…" She glared at him. Everything within her wanted to fight, but she wanted to keep Garrett safe, knowing she was too weak to kill Rune at the moment…

"Looks like I need to take extra measures. I had almost forgotten how strong you can be. But no matter, I will break you." He went over to a small table in the corner of the room. He blocked her view with his body, so she could not see what he was doing.

Rune turned and walked back to her, holding a damp cloth. She looked at it and then to him. She knew what that was. "You see, I found someone to this for me. It sells quite well on the open market. Your good doctor probably even uses it. But most don't realize how dangerous this stuff can be…" He pressed the cloth against her mouth while holding her head still with his other hand. "Too much and you can never wake again. Now." He smiled at her. "When you wake up, you will feel dizzy, but it will pass. Don't worry. Once I make you mine, you will be treated like a queen."

Her head swum unpleasantly, her vision blurring. Within a few moments, she blacked out.

After Garrett said a quick farewell to his father, he sent a letter to Cole and Isabelle and then bought the fastest horse he could find. Packing light, he headed off to his farmhouse as fast as his steed could take him. There was only one person he knew who could track well. Cole. All Garrett could think of was finding Iris. He couldn't believe she would willingly go into the arms of her nightmare. The source of all her fears, the reason she was always running. He felt as if he had been stabbed in the heart. Garrett had to find her and fast before she was lost to him forever.

It would take him about two days just to get from the big city of Smithington to the small town of Valden, where his farmhouse sat near. Those two days were torture for him. Thoughts of what Iris was probably being exposed to filled his every waking hour and even his dreams. He had seen the scars Rune had left on her body and her mind. Garrett was not going to leave Iris to this madman. Every night as he closed his eyes, he hoped to somehow find her in a dream, but he only suffered from his own nightmares.

The man who sold Garrett the horse was true to his word. The young steed helped him get back half a day early. After putting the horse in the stable, he ran to the house. Before he could reach for the doorknob, the door swung open, revealing a teary-eyed Isabelle.

She grabbed him, burying her face in his chest. "Garrett... I'm so, so, sorry," she said, his chest muffling her voice. "Poor Iris. Poor, poor Iris." Isabelle sobbed into his shirt, letting her tears flow. It was unusual to see her so upset, but he understood. She had come to love Iris, as well.

"We will find her. Where is Cole?" he whispered, patting her head comfortingly.

She shook her head. "When we got the letter a few hours ago, he ran off into the woods." Her sobs increased. "I don't know where he is. What if he doesn't come back?"

Garrett pushed her away from him so she could see his face. "He wouldn't leave you. Iris is like his sister, and he knows more than most what might be happening to her. Probably like me, he's mad and is blaming himself for not being able to protect her."

Isabelle hugged him tightly again. He hugged her back just as tight. She was so small compared to Iris. *Dammit, Iris.*

They sat in the kitchen, having coffee while they waited for Cole. It was nearing nightfall when they heard footsteps on the gravel path. Cole swung the door open with a thud and stormed in. Garrett saw the look on Cole's face and stood.

Cole went straight up to him and shoved him up against a wall. "Why didn't you listen to me?" He shoved him harder. "I told you not to let her go. You should have tried harder." His voice dipped into a whisper. "I should have tried harder." Cole lifted his fist and punched the panel behind Garrett. "Dammit! Damn Iris. Why did she have to always put others needs before her own?" Cole shook his bleeding fist.

"It was my father's fault. I didn't put that in the letter." Isabelle sat straight up and hung on every word. How he had seen Iris, how their father had also seen her, and so on.

Isabelle went over to a table and grabbed an unopened letter. With a shaking hand, she gave it to Garrett to open. "It's from Father's lawyer. I couldn't open it. Not without you here."

Shock momentarily stunned him as he read the letter. "It seems that Father was murdered just after I left, but there will be no open investigation. We are to come and hear his will read and to sign papers at our earliest convince. Because of Father's physical state, they took the liberty to go ahead and bury him." He paused. "Iris warned him." With a sigh, he said, "If Iris hadn't gone when she did, we all would probably be dead right now. Iris had left the first time to keep us all safe. And now, she has run into the arms of Rune, all because of Father."

Isabelle sunk into a chair, looking dazed. Cole went over to her and hugged her from behind, whispering something into her ear. Whatever he said seemed to help. After a few moments, Cole straightened. "So, what is the plan? I would make a plan, but that was always…"

"Iris' job?" Isabelle looked up at him.

He swallowed. "Yeah."

Garrett took his seat again and hashed out a plan with Cole and Isabelle, who suggested getting Micah involved. Agreeing with her, Cole went to go get him. But before he left, Garrett told him to keep it hush. They didn't know who was one of Rune's men and they didn't want to ruin their plans before they even started.

Iris woke to her head pounding and the feeling of vertigo. Her stomach churned sickeningly, but she only ended up dry heaving. Blinking, she looked down and saw that her feet had been tied to the floor, meaning she had no movement whatsoever. Rune could do as he pleased. The thought made her dry heave again.

She had never felt so vulnerable or helpless. He had learned from his past mistakes with her, and this time, she could see no way out of the hell she was in. One of Rune's goons brought her some water and helped her drink, then fed her a small piece of bread, which only made her stomach beg for more. The man was clearly trying his hardest to not look at her. He kept his eyes trained on the wall behind her or on the floor.

Iris didn't know how long she hung there. She could no longer feel her arms or legs, yet everything hurt.

Rune was keeping his distance on purpose, to draw out her nerves and make them raw in sheer anticipation at what he'd do. He had upped his game. She had escaped him many times, but this time… This time was different. She had something to lose, and he knew it.

Later that night, she could see light from the setting sun. A window on the other end of the room had been uncovered. The door opened, and a figure entered; Iris then knew why the curtains were drawn. Rune had finally shown himself.

He wore his trademark smirk. He tugged on a rope Iris hadn't noticed. It lowered her to a few inches off the ground. Her legs were now free to move, but she couldn't move them from how numb they were. He clearly knew, and the knowledge only made him smile all the more.

"So, here we are. At last." He drew out his words, almost like a snake hissing. And in her mind, he reminded her of a snake. "How long has it been—four, five years—since our last encounter? Way too long, if you ask me. I admire tenacity. Every time I thought I was close to having you in my grasp, you slipped through my fingers. The chase, this long chase has made me want you all the more, Iris." He leaned in and kissed her neck. She tried to pull away, but her muscles refused to work.

"Tell me, how far did you and your doctor go?" He moved his lips to the top of her breasts. "Did he make you his own?" Rune looked up, searching for an answer. "You were always a hard one to read. But from what I can gather by what I know and what I see…" His eyes roamed the full length of her. "He must have. What man in his right mind could see you and not want you?"

Iris knew if she were to respond that would only add fuel to his flames. Rune wanted to provoke her, to know how far they've gone. Even the smallest remark would give him something to go on. And that would be too much. Sometimes, silence was better when the madman wanted to play.

Leaning in again, he took her lips in his, and she made no movement, showing she would not return his advances. He put one of his hands on the back of her head, grabbing her head and pulling her back. She bit her lip to hold in a groan of pain. "You will return my kisses, and on that day, you will realize you love me. I will make this happen. I have shown how patient I can be."

"You don't show love by hurting someone!" she snapped. No. Love made you want to be a better person.

Thinking back on how much Garrett wanted her to stay, he wanted to fight Rune with her. How many times he had saved her life? The thought of him made her heart ache, knowing she would never see him again. He had saved her life only to prolong her torture. If she had known then what she did now, would she have fought harder to die, or to love him more?

The thoughts that swam in her mind were cut off when Rune kissed her again, harder this time, putting his body against hers.

She wanted desperately to pull away but couldn't. Iris was thankful that he was fully clothed at least…

He put his thumb against the still healing cut, pressing. She gasped, which made her lips part. Taking this opportunity, he jammed his tongue into her mouth. She bit down hard. Hissing, he pulled away and slapped her with the back of his hand. The crack echoed through the small room.

"You bitch." He wiped his mouth. She had brought blood. But so had he. She felt her own blood drip from the split lip he had given her.

With swift movements, he stopped her swaying motion by gripping the back of her head, pulling her hair hard. She bit her swollen lip to hold in a groan, not wanting to give him the pleasure of hearing her in pain.

"Listen to me. I will break you. I always do, whether you know it or not. Deep in your mind, I am there. Always have been, always will be. I am that little voice in the back of your mind telling you that you are not good enough, that you don't deserve love. Because you don't, Iris…" He leaned toward her ear, his breath ghosting across her skin. "This world hates the likes of you. You don't belong out there. No one can fully love someone who has killed as many as you have. The blood that stains you is far too great."

As he backed away toward his table of tools, she glared at him. He laughed and turned back to her, holding a small jar of leeches. She swallowed hard, knowing all too well what he meant to do.

"I had meant to do this later on, but since you seem so eager, I think it's best we start sooner rather than later. Don't you?" Stepping near her, he opened the jar, and with small prongs placed the bloodsuckers onto her skin. "Don't look so worried. I won't use these for too long, just enough to make you compliant. I wouldn't want you to die on me, now would I? But I can't keep having you fight so aggressively. You've grown stronger than last time it seems."

"Damn you…" Iris spat when he pulled away from putting the last leech onto her.

But all he did was smile maliciously, telling her that this was only the beginning to the long game he had planned for her...

Rune played with her like this twice a day for several days. He knew doing this would not just weaken her with the loss of blood but also wear on her nerves because of the fear of what he would and could do next and when he might make that move nagged at her in the back of her mind. This was his game. He would play with her, find her weakness, and toy with it until she broke, revealing yet another weakness. Rune did this over and over again until a person was completely broken. He then remade them into what he needed or wanted at that time.

Iris had seen him do this. Most weren't as lucky. The lucky ones ended up dead at the end. He only bloodlet the ones he liked. For the ones he didn't, he used knives, making small incisions, letting them bleed out slowly and painfully. All the while, he made their end as torturous as possible. Iris remembered their screams from other rooms as she awaited her own torment.

With her, he took his time. Rune was almost delicate at times, loving in his own twisted way. And she knew he didn't act that way with others. Because no one that had escaped him had remained alive.

She'd experienced almost every torture firsthand. But she had always gotten away before he completely unmade her. Even though he had only started to unravel her each time, it still took a while for her to get back to her normal self. This time, this time was different. Iris had come to him already in a bad state of body and mind.

To Rune, she had always been his pet project because she was the one who consistently got away. Every time she would find a way to undermine him or his men and escape. At first, they just locked her in a room. She acted as if she were dead, making one man get really close to her. She grabbed him, pulled him to the floor, and somehow got atop him to bash his head on the floor. She was younger then and much more scared. Another time, she broke the leg off the bed they had mistakenly given her. During mealtime, as the man came to give her food, she charged him and beat him to death. Blood was everywhere. She remembered how warm it was, how red...

They figured out her tricks and changed how they handled her. She always found other ways, a loose nail to work her shackles free or to cut a rope. One time she even dislocated her own wrist to free herself. There was nothing she wouldn't do to escape him.

And now, here Iris was, in the worst position she had ever been in. He had learned from his many mistakes with her.

She thought back to how hard it was to fix what Rune had tried to destroy. It took great will and inner strength. It made her nervous about this time and that was exactly what he wanted. He wanted to make her worry and fret. He was very good at getting inside a person's head and preying on their emotions. Cruel though he might be, he was also intelligent and perceptive, and that was what made him so dangerous.

One night when the moon shone like a bright beacon in the sky, Rune came in. He closed and locked the door behind him. He had always closed the door, but this was the first time he had locked it. She eyed him under heavy lashes. The bloodletting along with very little bread and water was working to his advantage. Iris was so weak she could hardly breathe. To her anguish, he slowly undressed. His naked chest gleamed in the moonlight. Much to her great relief, he stopped there, leaving his pants on.

Rune knew full well that she was aware of his actions and intentions.

"I only want a taste. I won't have you fully until you love me," he whispered into her ear.

He usually waited longer until he played with her like this, using the threat of something worse as his weapon. Rune knew this was one true way to break her. He knew her past and used it against her. But he would not hurt her the same way others had. Rune wanted to break her, but he would use his own methods, not someone else's.

She'd seen him do worse to others, but he wouldn't do that to her, and in some way, that made everything worse. Because, in his own sick way, he might love her.

Iris had lost count of the days, no, weeks, she had hung there. Once in a while, Rune let her down and massaged her muscles, knowing she was too weak to try and escape. This was how he truly broke her, by keeping her weak, showing her she was truly frail and could be taken advantage of just like everyone else.

When he hung her back up, he whispered things like, "You aren't in control like you think you are. You will never be free. No one cares for you but me." He came in several times a day and whispered these things to her when her mind was hardly awake enough to register his words. But Rune knew it was reaching her subconscious and reveled in the knowledge. He used words as his tool because words cut deeper than any knife ever could.

Iris' mind repeated words that were not her own. *You are unloved. You are nothing. You are not strong. Let Rune take care of you.*

Deep down, she knew the words were untrue, but her heart ached as if it were being pulled in two. She wished he would just take a real knife and plunge it into her heart to stop the pain. One thing she was thankful for was that he kept her awake, even if it was in a half daze. At least that way she would not dream about Garrett. She didn't want him to see her like this. To her, that would be worse than death.

Days turned into weeks, which might have bled into mouths. Iris no longer had a hold on reality. The figures that entered the room were blurs. She could only make out Rune because he shook her. Her mind was just as heavy as her eyes were. The thoughts that sluggishly floated within were not her own.

You are weak. Give in to Rune… No one loves you… You are nothing. Rune is the only one. Give in…

But somewhere, deep down, past the darkness that had begun to fill her very being worse than it ever had before, another voice came to mind, a smaller, fainter voice. *Garrett loves you. He will come…* Then the louder voice would respond, *No he won't. He didn't come before. He won't come now.* Iris wanted to cry but had no energy to do so. She was too weak to do anything. All she could do was hope the darkness that crept closer would come take her away soon. Iris wanted the end to come, wanted the pain to have a release. Or was she to feel this agony forever? Her way of being punished for all she had done in her life? *For all the blood on your hands, you deserve more.*

On a day where all was a blur to her, she heard shouting and gunshots. Her body shook at the sound while her mind was confused, not fully understanding what she heard. Iris tried to wake up fully but couldn't. It was almost like molasses coated her mind, making it difficult to think clearly. Blinking, she saw Rune standing in front of her with a small knife. Was he finally there to kill her? Or, worse, harm her?

He leaned in and kissed her hard. "Seems like someone came for you," he whispered. "No matter. I will find you again. What I have started won't be undone. You are already mine."

She felt sharp pain on her hip, making her scream despite her parched mouth.

Rune took his leave. Her mind was so stressed and so tired that she couldn't comprehend what was happening. Several people she couldn't make out stormed into the room only moments after Rune left.

She felt a warm embrace lowering her to the floor and someone moving her arms. They pressed her arms down below her head, a normal position that only made her cry out in pain. Iris wanted to kick and hurt this person who was hurting her, but all she could do was moan pitifully.

As voices echoed around her, she gave in to the darkness, hoping that her death had finally come ...

It had taken Cole over a month to track down Rune's hideout. Even then he wasn't quite sure where Iris was being held. He rushed back to the homestead as fast as his horse could carry him, wanting to give the information he had found to Garrett and the others.

Jumping off his steed before it had even come to a full stop, he ran to the door where Isabelle met him, eager arms awaiting his embrace. Lifting her into his arms, he buried his face in her lovely blonde hair. He had forgotten how good she smelled, like flowers mixed with sugar and apples from baking.

Putting her down when Garrett entered the yard, he studied his face for answers. "I've found her. I've finally found her." They all let out a collective sigh of relief. "She's in an abandoned warehouse. A day and a half's ride from here, toward the coast. I'm surprised there weren't more of Runes men about..."

"Are you certain that it's the right spot? That Iris is truly there? Did you see her?" Garrett's eyes were filled with worry and a spark of hope.

"Yes, that is where Rune is, which means that's where Iris is. There's no other place she would be. I questioned some old buddies in the agency and it seems she had been on the hunt after she left us. She killed a lot of Rune's closest guys. That might explain why there's so little reinforcements there at the moment. But that's better for us. Iris helped us rescue her without even knowing it." He smiled, trying to ease the tension filling the air.

"That's Iris for you. She's our badass." Isabelle laughed.

"You're right. So, how many men did you see? What are we looking at? Tell me everything." Garrett now had a determined look about him. He was ready to take on Rune, to get Iris back, just as Cole was.

They made plans and Garrett was almost proud of his input into the strategy they all made. Micah, a few men he knew, Cole and himself would be in the party that would rescue Iris.

Garrett was thankful Iris had trained him on how to use a gun. He had a feeling he'd have to put those skills to use. He wanted Isabelle to stay behind, but she would not have it and pointed out that Cole had trained her with a pistol as well.

"I'm just as good with a gun as you are, Garrett, and you know that." She glared at him, hands on hip. He knew this look. She was daring him to defy her, to order her to stay behind.

Sighing in defeat, he said, "All right, but you stay behind the rest of us. If you see danger, protect..."

"Shoot them dead. Or kick them in the nuts. I know. Now let's go!" Garrett smiled when Cole busted out in loud laughter at her. He hoped that the two of them never lost their goodness, their shine.

But worry weighed him down. What had Rune done to Iris? Was she still alive? He knew what he had done to her in the past. He'd seen the trauma firsthand. Last time he saw her, Garrett knew she was on the brink of something. Her nightmare was so strong it took over both of their dreams. How pale she was in the dream before that. He hadn't stopped cursing himself for not going to her sooner. If he had, she wouldn't have gone to him. Garrett had long stopped blaming his father. He knew all of this was because he had not fought for the one he loved.

They moved in on the base, which was a big storehouse. It was easier than expected, as if it were meant to be that way. Like Cole had said, very few men guarded the place. Had Iris really taken that many of Rune's men? Garrett's heart raced so much that it almost blocked out Micah's words when he insisted that he and his men would go in first. Holding his gun, it almost slipped from his hands. They were drenched with sweat. Isabelle eyed him, not staying behind as she was told. He noticed she had a good grip on her own pistol, along with Cole, who was next to her. *They really do make a good pair.*

Garrett admired the two of them all the more. And Iris even more so. She went into places like this all the time, holding a gun in the face of danger without a moment of hesitation. His heart soared with pride. He was a nervous not for himself, but for the state he might find Iris in. What if she were beyond repair? Or dead? What if Rune had tortured her so much that he turned her mind into loving the monster? He's heard of that happening...

Everything flowed well, too well. He questioned if they had been tipped off and if this was all a trap. When they were entering the back toward the upper rooms, Garrett heard gunshots. Cole pushed him and Isabelle back.

Micah's voice rang clearly above the gunfire. "Aim true, men!"

Garrett could see the sheriff brandishing his own pistol, firing faster than the men on either side him and reloading at even faster speeds. When the all-clear was called, they moved forward. They made it to the upper rooms, having already searched the lower ones.

Cole was nearing the top of the stair when he came to an abrupt halt. Before he even knew what was happening, Cole had pushed Garrett down low on the stairs. Cole threw himself on the landing and fired a rapid shot at a lone gunman at the end of the hall. He smiled. *Iris would be proud, of him at this moment.*

When Garrett opened the far-left door, what he saw made him freeze as the others rushed into the room. Seconds later, they froze as well. No one moved, no one spoke, and everyone seemed to hold their breath.

Garrett slowly moved forward, his mind not understanding what he was seeing. A skeleton with skin hung limply from ropes that were tied to a pulley system. The hair atop the gaunt face was straight, but it seemed to be almost as dead as the body it was attached to.

He swallowed and lowered the ropes. She would not be able to move her arms for quite a while. He slowly eased her arms back to their normal position, and she screamed, unmoving with a blank stare. She was a shell. It seemed that nothing lived inside. Despite how frail she looked, she wasn't dirty. Rune had kept her clean. The smell filling the room reminded him of his clinic, which made his blood boil even more.

Scanning the room, he saw leeches, surgical tools, such as needle, thread, and scalpel. He also saw a bottle of chloroform, which made him cradle Iris all the more, not wanting to hurt her already delicate form. How could Rune use such a thing? Using that stuff on her with the state she was in could have easily killed her.

A few tears trickled down his cheeks, but he quickly wiped them away. Now was not the time. Now, he had to be strong for Iris. She needed him now more than ever. He couldn't let her down again.

Micah and the other men left Garrett, Cole and Isabelle to help Iris. Isabelle helped wrap her in a cloak, and Garrett gently picked her up. She soon blacked out, and for that, Garrett was thankful. Cole led the way back to the horses, gun drawn, ready for anything.

As Garrett rode with Iris securely nestled against him, he cursed himself at how long it had taken to find her. And more so on how he hadn't gone to find her before she had to give herself over to Rune, to save him and Isabelle. He didn't think he would ever forgive himself. It didn't help the fact that Iris had been weak and already thinning when he last saw her.

He couldn't believe it was really her that he held against him. He still couldn't wrap his mind around it all. How could she look like this? How could someone do this to her?

They set up camp for the night, starting a fire to warm Iris.

Stopping gave Garrett more of a chance to look at the wound on her hip. With the fading light of the winter evening, he saw the wound was shaped like an R. He muttered a curse. Never in his life had he hated another person as much as he hated Rune. He didn't know how or when, but the bastard was going to pay for what he did to Iris. Garrett promised then and there that Rune would never lay another finger on her, not if he had any say in the matter.

He cleaned and bandaged the area and then laid her on several blankets so the hard ground would not hurt her. Garrett looked at the gloomy faces that were cast with shadows from the firelight. Micah stared into his coffee mug. His men muttered to themselves, woeful expressions passing among them. Cole held Isabelle who cried softly into his shoulder; all the while he himself held back tears. Seeing the ever-strong Iris in such a state seemed to be hard on everyone. Garrett couldn't bring himself to talk to anyone, not a word.

Yes, they have her back. They rescued her. But why didn't he feel victorious?

Garrett, Isabelle, Cole and Iris arrived at their homestead midmorning. Micah had stayed back in town, saying he needed to do sheriff business, but the look in his eyes told Garrett it hurt too much to see Iris in such a state. He understood.

When the four of them arrived home, Garrett carried Iris to his room with Isabelle following close behind. "Will you help me wash her?" He didn't want to hurt her more than she was already hurting.

"Of course."

It took them a while, but once she was washed, they dressed her in a clean gown. Afterward, all three of them stared at the shell that no longer resembled what they had all come to know and love.

Cole was the first to break the silence. "I want to kill that bastard. She'll never be the same, mentally or physically. Damn him." He balled his fists so tightly, his knuckles turned white.

Garrett griped Cole's shoulder. "It's up to all of us to bring her back. To let her know that she is safe and loved."

Cole swallowed. "You're right."

Isabelle sighed. "I have no words..."

"That's a first," Garrett muttered.

Isabelle smiled slightly. "Be quiet."

At the sound of their voices, Iris's eyes shot open. Isabelle gasped. Garrett was hopeful. Had she come back to them so fast?

Leaning down to her, softly touching her arm, he whispered, "Iris. It's me, Garrett. You're safe. You're home. How do you feel?" He waited for an answer. But nothing, no blinking or looking toward him or anything. No sign that she heard him. She laid there, catatonic. Isabelle and Cole tried as well, speaking softly, sweetly. But none of their words seemed to reach her. It was as if she were in a deep dark world none of them could reach.

They all took turns, never leaving Iris alone, not even for a moment. They fed, bathed her and talked to her. She only stared off as if seeing something beyond them. Garrett slept next to her, hoping his dreams would intertwine with hers, but nothing had happened for weeks.

Gradually, her face filled out, and the deep dark circles under her eyes faded. Physically, her body was healing, but her mind didn't seem to be.

Iris hadn't spoken, had hardly moved, and didn't seem to even see them. Garrett knew she might be trapped in her own mind. He had seen it before in patients, which was why he desperately wanted to connect with her through their dreams. The people who he had seen like this never recovered, but they were different. They weren't as strong or as stubborn as Iris. He just had to figure out how to connect with her.

Two weeks after they rescued her, he laid next to her, holding her hand, and thought of what she must be feeling, how lonely she must be, how scared. His heart ached. He imagined someone had ahold of his heart, holding it tight, and wouldn't let go until he saw a glimpse of Iris' normal self.

When he finally fell asleep, he found himself in a dense dark fog. It wasn't like that one time, where it was water. This was actual fog, but it felt like hands, trying to grab at him, holding him back, stopping him from moving forward. The thickness of it almost choked him. He searched and searched, all the while fighting against unseen hands. He called her name, but there was no sign of Iris. Just darkness that teemed with pain.

Garrett woke from the dream, shaking. Looking around, he saw Iris staring blankly at the ceiling. He steadied his breathing, trying to calm himself. If what he felt was only a small measure of what she was feeling, then she must be in extreme pain.

He sat at the dinner table after trying to connect to her for several nights. He thought about how to connect with Iris. Knowing he needed to eat to keep up his strength, he poked at his food but had no appetite. He forced himself to eat a bite of whatever Isabelle cooked and wasn't even sure what it was, not paying attention to what he had put in his mouth.

"Garrett," Isabelle said, her voice stern. "You won't be able to help her heal if you are sick as well. You need rest as well. Don't push yourself. It will take time to reach her."

He knew she was right and decided to take a few nights off from the connection. But to leave her to the fog alone made the hold on his heart tighten.

Chapter 19

Iris was in a never-ending nightmare…

Her vision blurred between Rune and his torture to visions of Garrett, Cole and Isabelle. But this was no nightmare. She was fully awake, and this was now her life, one in which she knew she would never escape from, one she willingly walked into to save those she loved from certain death. But now she wished for her own death. Death would bring freedom from this pain. From this nightmare. But if she were to die, would that only bring an even worse outcome? Would she be sucked into the depths of hell to a torture far worse than this?

When she did drift into sleep, deep darkness surrounded her. Her thoughts were muddled, and Iris couldn't make sense of anything she felt physically or mentally. Why was she even asleep? Rune must be letting his guard down or was trying to treat her nice to make her fall for him. Iris screamed into the darkness, her pain overwhelming every part of her. She couldn't think clearly, and it seemed as if her own mind was trying to crush her. Was this her new normal? She laid in the darkness, hugging her knees, screaming in pain.

Iris couldn't tell how long she had been in this in-between, half-awake state with the illusions of her loved ones and this all-consuming darkness. Both were agony to her. Among the dark, she heard a voice.

"Iris," the voice called, so faint she almost didn't hear it. She squeezed her eyes shut. The near-inaudible sound sent her head pounding.

"Stop. Stop..." she whispered. As if the person heard her, the calling stopped. And again, Iris spiraled into mind-numbing darkness where her fears and nightmares surrounded her, nagging at her, repeating the words Rune used.

You are weak, no one loves you. I am the only one that can love your blood-stained hands.

Iris knew these words were not her own, but her mind would not accept this, no matter how many times she told herself.

Wrapping her arms around her head, she tried to block out the voices, trying not to hear, trying not to feel.

"Iris," she heard again in the same voice as before, but she tried to block it out, too. The voice felt like it stabbed her through the heart. Hearing it was painful and heartbreaking. Iris sobbed when the voice grew near, the pain increasing with every inch that it came closer.

"Stop... Stop," she repeated. "Don't, don't come." The voice that grew nearer was one she did not want. Did not want? *What don't I want?*

She felt like the fog had turned into a whirlwind out of her control. *I'm going insane...* she thought as the winds picked up. *I can't stand this. This has to end...*

After waiting several nights and getting some sleep, he dove back into the dark thick fog to search again. This time, the fog felt heavier. Garrett felt the weight on his chest and shoulders. An array of feelings rushed to him. Fear, hate, pain, confusion, and... it was barely there, but hope. He tried to reach out and grab ahold of that one strand that might be the key to lifting this fog.

Focusing, he tried to imagine it as a string of light to help lead him through this nightmare. He was surprised that it actually worked. In some way, Iris was reaching out for help. Looking down, he saw a small thread that held a faint light.

Garrett spun it in his hand as he moved forward. He didn't know how long he had been in this abyss. After what felt like days, the fog around him changed. The hands that used to grab at him disappeared. Now, a strong wind battered him mercilessly, making him lose grip of the string. But he could still see its faint glow. He crawled toward the center of this whirlwind, but the further he pushed, the harder the gusts got. Garrett lost count on how many times he got so close to the eye of the storm, only to be pushed back out.

"Dammit!" he screamed into the wind.

"Leave…" a voice immediately responded. "Leave now. You do not belong!" The voice didn't sound like Iris. It was deeper…

Rune… He made her inner voice his….

The realization instantly pissed Garrett off. "You are the one who does not belong! You have crept in like a parasite, trying to grow and feed. You are not welcome here!"

The voice laughed. "I beg to differ. I am in my true element. This is my world, and I have control!"

The winds picked up. Garrett laid flat and covered his head, trying not to give the gusts something to pick up. He reached out for Iris. She was the only one who could truly stop this, if he could only reach her.

"Iris! Listen to my voice! Only my voice!" The winds howled. "I am here for you! Cole and Isabelle are waiting for your return. You are safe now! You are with us! We love you." Astonishingly, the winds died down to a strong breeze. Seeing his chance, he lifted up and crawled toward the thin line of light.

"We will never leave you. We will always try our best to protect you. We are all family and that will never change!"

His breath caught in this throat at his next words, scared to speak them. But they needed to be heard, and he was ready to say it, now or never. "I want to marry you, Iris! I want you to be by my side every day and every night until we're old and gray. We will never be apart! Please, please, be my partner in life. I love everything about you, and I never want you to change. I want you to be you. Because you are the most amazing person I've ever met. I feel like I will go insane if I don't have you in my life. I love every part of you, past, present and future."

Garrett had come to the conclusion that Iris was the love of his life when she had first left. And then he met her again on the street in Smithington and he knew he had to have her for their lifetimes. He wanted and needed Iris to be his wife. These feelings would never wavier, and he had never been more confident about anything in his life.

"The girl... Fiancée... Well-dressed," another, softer voice murmured.

The image of Abelia ran across his mind. "Abelia is an old friend. She is engaged to another man. She is not mine, nor am I hers." He paused. "My heart belongs to you, Iris," he said with all the sincerity he could muster.

He waited for a reply, a sign, something, that his words had reached her. She didn't appear or reply, but the breeze vanished, and the fog lightened. Garrett walked over to where he could now see Iris lying, but before he could reach her, the dream shifted, pushing him out.

A gasp escaped him. He was lying in his bed next to Iris. Had he gotten through to her? He propped up on one elbow and leaned over, brushing her hair from her face. "Iris… Iris, I meant what I said. Please come back to me. I will wait forever if I have to." He saw no sign of movement, no fluttering of eyes, no opening of the mouth.

The waiting was unbearable. Did she hear him? Would she say yes? Would she marry him? He sighed, leaning his forehead against hers. "I love you, Iris. Every part of you. Be my wife." Kissing her cheek, he gazed at her, taking her in. And for the first time, his heart eased. Her fog had lifted. She was safe and back at home.

Several more days passed with no improvement. So, Cole suggested putting a gun next to her at all times to help her feel safer. After all, she was never without one. The doctor agreed and wherever she was, so was her pistol, right next to her. Iris had put on enough weight to be moved, so he took her outside. Garrett sat her in a chair against the house. Her view was of the large yard and stable to the left and the road leading to town to the right. It was a nice early spring afternoon. Winter had given way to spring as she laid inside, resting and recovering. But the air still had a chill to it.

But not for Garrett, Cole or Micah who had their sleeves rolled up as they played baseball in the front yard. Isabelle still wore a long-sleeved dress, laughing at Cole who chased her around the bases in the flattest part in front of the house, next to the road.

"Let's get on with the game!" Micah yelled, clearly irritated. "You two can play chase later on, without us!"

Cole burst into laughter. Isabelle giggled, her long blonde hair flowing behind her. Garrett looked from the playful couple to Iris who still stared blankly.

They were all about to head into the house for an early dinner when all the sudden, Iris stood straight up, her expression still vacant.

"Iris?" Garrett asked, his heart leaping in his chest. This was the first time she had moved on her own.

She held the gun in her hand. Before anyone could react, she fired. The bullets whizzed past Garrett. Seconds later, there came groans of pain, and then two men fell out of the bushes next to the road. The men were either dead or close to it.

"Get to the house!" Cole yelled and sprinted to the stable, quickly returning with the shotgun Micha had given them.

Garrett couldn't stop staring at Iris. She fired without blinking. She now moved forward as Garrett and Isabelle passed her, going the opposite direction. Them toward the house, her toward the road and the assailants. She continued to shoot along with Cole and Micah, moving slowly toward the men who had been coming out of the woods. The furthest anyone of them had made it was in the middle of the dirt road that lay next to the woods.

Still expressionless, Iris stopped when she reached the edge of the yard where it met the road. She stood there, waiting. The gunfire ceased, and a hush fell over the area. A lone man stepped out of the tree line, holding his hands high, the universal sign for surrender.

Garrett stepped closer to Iris who stepped back, holding her pistol at her side. She quickly turned her head from side to side and looked at each end of the house. Anger now coated her features. He followed her gaze and saw armed men at each side of the house, waiting. Garrett's heart raced at the sight of her more than the gunmen. Iris was back. She came back.

Iris stepped a few more feet backward, stopping in the middle of the grass-dirt mixed yard. She glared at the man who stood in front of her. "No one else has to get hurt. Just come back with us," one of the men yelled to Iris.

Garrett was about to step forward when Cole extended his arm, stopping him. He shook his head. Cole had placed

Isabelle behind him, shielding her from what might come their way.

After a few moments of no reply, the man opened his mouth to speak, but Iris held up her hand to stop him. "No." Her voice was raspy from disuse. She cleared her throat. "No."

"No? No you won't come with us?" the man questioned.

"Yes..." Iris smiled, clearly getting satisfaction out of his confusion.

"Come with us, or they die." He motioned for the others to move in on the four who stood near the door of the house.

Before any of the men took two steps, Iris held the pistol up to the side of her head. "I advise... to call them back. Your master won't like it if any harm comes to me. What would he do to all of you if that were to happen?"

"Iris!" Garrett started forward, only to be held back by Cole. Surely, she didn't mean that. He'd just gotten her back. He couldn't lose her all over again, and this would be permanent. His heart almost stopped at the sight in front of him. He fought against Cole, trying to get to Iris to stop her.

The man's eyes narrowed. "You wouldn't dare."

Iris cocked a defiant eyebrow. "Tell, Rune... I will come when I'm good and ready. And today is not that day, nor is tomorrow. If I see any of his goons near me or my four friends, I will not hesitate. Do you understand? If I even think one of you are near, I will blow my fucking brains out... Have I made myself clear?" She waited until he reluctantly nodded. "I will not hesitate and he will never see me again, ever. Because why? Say it!" she yelled, making Garrett flinch. She had been still and silent for so long and now, here she was yelling.

The man glared at Iris. "Because you will be dead by your own hands. I understand and will pass on the word."

"To your master." They both glared at each other. "Now, call your men back before my finger gets trigger happy." He hesitated. "Dammit! Call your dog's back before I put this bullet in my head! Do it *now!*" Garrett saw her finger tighten on the trigger.

Isabelle gasped. Cole clenched his fist. Garrett stood there, anger building. Iris didn't bluff, and they all knew it.

The man waved his hand for the others to fall back. "Let's pack it up, boys."

He bowed his head to Iris, eyeing her as he backed into the wood once more. Each man nodded to Iris in some kind of sign of respect or admiration as they passed. All the while Iris held the gun near her head until she was certain all the goons were gone.

The second all the men were out of eyesight, Garrett pushed past Cole. Iris turned and pointed the gun at the ground in front of Garrett. Her hand shook slightly. He stepped forward, holding out his hand for her.

She glared at him, almost daring him to move again. He put his arm back at his side and stared right back. "I can be just as stubborn as you, Iris. Push me away, and I'll push harder to be with you."

Garrett was so angry at her for pulling something like that but also knew her actions saved them all, and he loved her all the more for that. All he wanted to do now was hold her in his arms and make her feel safe. But his anger got the better of him.

"Why in the hell would you pull a stunt like that? To... To hold a gun to your own head." He choked on his own words. The image of her and the pistol at her temple still fresh in his mind. "Dammit, Iris. Let me help you. Please. Please..."

Iris, on the other hand, wanted nothing more than to gather her thoughts. They whirled in confusion, and she just needed to go through her mind, find any trace of Rune and expel it from her. She needed to be alone to do that.

But the sight of Garrett and the mix of emotions on his face set her body aflame. She had missed his touch, but wasn't there a well-dressed woman?

She shook her head and ran her fingers through her hair. Looking back up, she saw the look on his face and knew if she did not isolate herself right now, her body would move to him like a magnet.

Stepping back, she looked down. "I need time. I need to make sure whatever Rune did to my mind... is gone. I just need some time to..." She shook her head, her thoughts fuzzy. "To be alone. I won't go far. Just to the creek. That's all. Please..."

"All right," he said reluctantly after a moment. "But if you don't come back before nightfall, I will come look for you."

Iris left the four of them at the house and walked down the small trail to the creek in the woods. She thought back to the first time she had walked this trail. She'd been afraid her dreams gave Garrett too much insight into her inner thoughts and fears.

She sat next to the watering hole and stuck her bare feet in. Closing her eyes, she searched her memories, starting with the last thing she remembered before going to Rune, and worked from there. She moved rapidly through her thoughts until they started to get murky.

Lying back, Iris stared at the freshly budding leave and the pink sky, telling her sunset was nearing. She had only started. She needed more time.

Closing her eyes, Iris pushed through her mind and memories faster, only stopping if the thought felt like it held a sign of Rune or made her confused. As she dug deeper, her body shook, and her head hurt more and more.

Someone gasped. Was that her...? But why? She tried to open her eyes, to move...

Garrett followed Iris, making sure to stay back but close enough to intervene if trouble arose. She might not need his protection, but he was going to be there regardless. He sat, waiting, listening.

The sun was about to set, so he walked closer to the creek. When he got close enough, he heard labored breathing and picked up his pace. As he turned the corner, he saw Iris lying on her side, shaking, struggling to breathe. He fell to his knees by her side and took her in his arms, trying to get her to stop shaking.

"Iris. Iris. I'm here. You're safe. I'm here for you." He thought of the last time they were here together. He placed his lips over hers, forcing air into her mouth and lungs. He repeated this until her breathing normalized, and she stopped shaking.

When he was about to pull away, her lips moved under his, her tongue slipping into his mouth. He pulled away, confused and uncertain. She slowly opened her eyes. The light of sunset made her eyes purple eyes shine brighter than he had ever seen them. Her beauty took his breath away.

"Are you all right?" he asked breathlessly.

She nodded. "I... moved too fast. Trying to remember, so I can forget and heal."

"I see. Do you remember being in dark fog with a whirlwind surrounding you? Me calling out to you?" He tried to read her expression.

"I'm afraid I don't. I'm sorry. Reaching into each other's dreams again?" She smiled up at him.

He laughed. "Yeah, I tried to reach out to you so many times while you were away. And then when we found you, I tried hard to find you in your mind. It was so dark." His eyes drifted to her lips. It was all he could do to not kiss her senseless. It'd been far too long since he'd tasted her.

"Thank you, Garrett. You've saved me so many times. I will never be able to repay you."

"You don't repay someone who does it out of love..." He smiled back her.

She studied him. When she bit her lip for a split second, his body reacted. Before his mind could process what he was doing, he reached out and rubbed his thumb across her full bottom lip. He was about to pull his hand away when she let out a tiny sigh. *Fuck it,* he thought. He couldn't go a second longer without her.

With one swift move, he pulled her into his lap, hugging her tightly against him. Iris let out another soft sigh as he kissed her.

Their kisses grew longer, filled with passion and desire.

Garrett moved his hand down to her legs, lifting her skirts. Iris froze.

Garrett immediately pulled away. "What's wrong? Are you hurting?"

She shook her head slightly. "The lady you were with in the city was quite pretty. The ring was also very lovely." Iris stood up, not looking at Garrett. His body already yearned for hers.

Garrett swiftly moved to his feet, his erection making it difficult. He hugged Iris from behind, which only made his body yearn for hers all more. But her trembling body in his arms made him focus. "She is a childhood friend. She is engaged to another. I belong to you and no other." He whispered the words in her ear. She did not remember his words from the dream, which meant she did not hear his proposal.

Iris shook him off, stepping a few feet away from him, staring at the water.

When he turned her around, her eyes had become vacant. It was as if she had returned to her previous state. Almost shaking her, Garrett said, "Iris. Iris. Can you hear me?"

Garrett watched her, trying to see if she would respond in anyway. He tried to speak to her, shook her again, but there were no signs that she saw him or the world around her anymore. She had gone back into her daze, back to the thoughts that Rune had planted, back to the darkness.

"Please come back to me," he whispered, his heart breaking. "I want no other than you." He hugged Iris tightly, his body shaking this time. Had he once again lost her to the darkness?

Chapter 20

Iris felt her consciousness sink into darkness. She desperately tried to get out of the shadows' grasp, but no matter her actions, there seemed to be no escape. She felt as if Rune had control of her mind, her thoughts no longer her own.

Blinking, Iris found herself back in the room Rune had held her in; she knew this was not real. It was all in her mind. Someone moved behind her, and she turned to see who it was.

"I'm glad you're here. You scared me with that stunt of yours." Rune grinned, looking her up and down.

"You're not real…"

"But aren't I?"

She shook her head. "No… This is all in my mind."

He laughed. "Then why can't you control any of this? Try it. Try and change something." Rune walked over to his desk next to the window, right where she remembered it. He picked up a book and extended it to her. "Change this book into something. Anything." He eyed her, grinning all the while.

Iris stared at the book in his hand, and like she had in the dreams with Garrett, she tried to will the book to change; she thought of it changing into a piece of paper, cake, a gun.

It lay unchanged.

Rune put the book back on the desk and moved toward her. He swiped his hand to the right, and she found herself bound, almost like before. He gripped her chin, pulling her to him. "If I am not real, and this is all in your mind, then does that mean you can't control your own mind? I ask you, which is worse: me controlling you, or you not being able to control your own thoughts?"

He leaned down and kissed her lips.

Surely this is just my mind in a state of weakness. I have to push him out. I have to take control.

Garrett carried Iris back to his house where the others waited. They hoped to see the old Iris and were shocked when they saw him walking up from the side of the barn, an unconscious Iris in his arms. Isabelle rushed to his side.

"Is she all right? What happened?" She brushed hair out of Iris face and felt for a fever, all the while keeping pace with him. Once he laid her in his bed, he told the others what had happened over a cup of coffee in the kitchen. Micah had decided to do a sweep of the surrounding area before heading back to town, promising to let them know if he came across anything.

Micah seemed busy as of late, more than usual. But every time Garrett tried to ask, he replied that it was just sheriff business.

Sitting down, Garrett held a cup of coffee in between his hands, warming them. He sighed, unable to meet their gaze. "She was fine for a few moments, but something clicked in her mind. Her eyes glazed over, and her mind seemed to recede back into the darkness." He stared at the untouched coffee before him. Garrett imagined Iris back in the swirling storm of her mind. *Will I be able to reach her again? Will we ever get her back? Will she ever be free from this torture?*

As if reading his thoughts, Isabelle took Garrett's hands in hers, gently squeezing. He looked up from the cup of coffee to see her sweet smile. He returned a waning one. Cole put his hand on Garrett's shoulder.

"She will come back to us," Isabelle said in that confident voice of hers. "We just have to give her the time that's needed. She went through what no living being should ever experience."

Garrett nodded and opened his mouth to speak but swallowed the words, not wanting to speak them.

"I'm worried she won't come back to us, that Rune has truly taken her from us," Cole whispered, saying the words Garrett had swallowed down.

Isabelle giggled. Garrett frowned at her, not sure what there was to laugh about. She smiled at their puzzled expressions. "You forget who we're speaking of. This is Iris. Cole, you yourself said she had been fighting him off for a long time. I think it would take a lot more than this to make her Rune's puppet, don't you?"

Cole nodded. He went over and kissed the top of her head. "I think you might be the smartest one out of all of us."

"Stop it. You'll embarrass me," she teased.

"More like inflate your ego," Garrett grumbled.

Isabelle turned an icy glare his way, and he returned it. Cole raised his hands as if to push their stares away from each other. But after looking from one to the other, he started laughing, doubled over, grasping his side. "You two really are the perfect brother-sister duo. I could watch the pair of you go at it all day." This made Garrett smile and helped his stress ease.

After eating, Garrett went back into his room and sat with Iris, holding her hand in his. *How can I reach her, fully reach her? Is she past my grasp?* So many thoughts ran through his head. He thought he might go mad with the bombardment of them all.

It was nearing midnight when Garrett drifted off, his head lying next to Iris' sleeping form. The next thing he knew he was standing in a large room, like the one he had made long ago with Iris where she was dressed as a knight. This one was filled with people moving about their day. This was much different than the dreams he'd shared with her before.

Out of the corner of his eye, he caught a glimpse of her. Moving fast, he ran in her direction. Once Garrett reached the area, there was no sign of her. She had vanished. *Can she do that? This is her dream, isn't it?*

Someone grabbed his arm and roughly pulled him into a dark room. The person held a bright candle close to his face, making it hard for him to see who it was. He was about to speak, but they beat him to it.

"What are you doing here? You shouldn't have come. When you leave, make sure the dream catcher is under my pillow. I mean it. I don't want to see you in here again." She backed away, her face still shadowed. "Please, Garrett. I don't know what's going on. All I know is I'm trying to release him from my mind and to do that, I have to play his game." Iris blew out the candle, leaving them in darkness. She moved closer to him, her mouth near his ear. "When I do awaken, you will question my actions, my request and plans will seem farfetched, but I beg you to trust me. You might even think that I want to be with Rune, and if you do find yourself thinking that, then I must be a better actress than I realized. But no matter what I say, no matter what I ask for, or what actions I may take, you must trust me, Garrett." She pressed against him, hugging him tightly. "I'm trying my best to push what he has done out from my mind. I don't know how I'll act when I wake. Please know that I miss you. I hope to be with you soon."

He felt a warm sensation on his neck as he was pushed out of her dream.

Garrett woke with a start. Looking around the room, he found Iris still sleeping and the moon starting to give way to the morning sun. Sighing, he stood up and went to the window, looking up at the sky.

"Iris, if you're listening, I am waiting for you, and I will never give up on you." He turned, looking at her motionless body. Walking over, Garrett kissed her lips. When he placed his hand next to her pillow, he felt the dream catcher. It had been under her pillow all that time yet these dreams still reached her. She had made it before she left and put it under her pillow. He assumed to disconnect their dreams.

A dream catcher with a web design in the middle would catch the dreams, allowing only the good dreams to flow down the string, beads, and feathers. But she thought it would stop them from connecting. That was not what dream catchers were for. She also hadn't put it in the window, so the light from the rising sun would cleanse it. Walking over to the window, he tied it to the middle.

He thought back to his dream with the bear… Maybe his path was to help her through this. Their dreams had to be connected for some reason. Maybe this was the reason, to push Rune out. But Iris had told him not to return, that she was handling it in her own way. Garrett didn't know what to do. He felt like he was going mad with all the feelings and thoughts bottled up inside him. He turned and punched the wall, breathing hard.

Glancing at Iris once more, he left the room, taking in the fresh air of the morning dew, hoping it would ease the ever-building anger that seemed to increasingly grow within. Then there was torrent of guilt that fought for primary space in his mind. And Iris once again, pushing him away, not wanting his help.

Isabelle woke to a beam of morning light streaming into her room from an adjacent window. Sitting up, she stretched to work out the stiffness of the night. Her morning routine consisted of washing, dressing, and reading a few chapters in one of her many books she ordered every month. Her brother always got onto her about how much money she spent on books, but it was a hobby well worth the price; how else could she enter new lands and explore different worlds?

She went downstairs to start breakfast and saw the front door ajar. Walking closer, the figure of her brother caught her eye. He sat on a chair that leaned against the house, his face in his hands. Reaching out, Isabelle touched his shoulder. Sobs wracked his body. She hesitated for a split second, then she gripped his shoulder tighter. Kneeling, she took his hands from his face, holding them firmly in her own.

Smiling, she took in the sight of her brother. Isabelle could tell he had been crying for quite some time, which was unlike him. "The strongest of us know when and how to show our pure emotions. Working through the turbulence of our own minds, and accepting how we feel, is how we move forward." Squeezing his hands, making him look at her, she continued. "Iris is strong. She will work through this, and we will all be here waiting for her."

"I don't know how to help her. I've never felt so helpless..." His words drifted off.

"This is not that time, Garrett. This is Iris we're talking about, and she has all of us behind her to help her in any way possible. This..." Her words drifted as his had.

"This isn't my mother," Garrett finished, and they smiled at one another remorsefully.

"Nor are we our father." These words lightened both their hearts but also brought his death to the forefront. "Our father was really in business with this Rune?"

Garrett nodded. "It seems so. I had always known he was working with the illegal trade market. I didn't know how deep he was in until Iris talked about Rune and how our father had doomed us all by putting a hit out on her. She saved us by going to him." He looked out into the nearby woods, his thoughts seeming to drift to a much further place.

"This is a lot to take in." She sighed. Iris had done so much for them. Isabelle knew this. Leaving her love, Garrett, and running to that nightmare of a man, Rune. Seeing her in pain stabbed Isabelle in the heart. She wanted Iris to feel safe, to finally feel happiness. She deserved that and so much more. Iris was the strongest person she had ever laid eyes on, including Cole and Garrett. Iris was on a whole other badass level of her own. Isabelle smiled to herself.

Then there was Garrett. Her brother, who had always had a lock on his emotions, hardly showing how he felt, even to her. She had never thought he would fall in love. Not like this, so deep, so fast, so strong. But he had and to the best sister she could ask for. When something good came along, sometimes, you had to fight all the more for it. And fight he would have to. She knew her brother was strong, but if he continued to let this wall stay up, he could go crashing down along with it.

"But we have each other," Cole said, leaning against the doorframe with a smile, "and the four of us will be able to handle anything Rune can throw at us."

An almost mocking laugh came from inside the house, effectively ending their conversation. Cole turned and backed out of the house, revealing Iris. She leaned against the doorframe like Cole had done moments before.

"Iris?" Garrett asked, standing, taking a step forward.

"I only heard what Cole said, but am I really the only realist among us? You really think the four of us can take on Rune and his legion of madmen?" She folded her arms. "The reason you were able to find me and recuse me so easily was because I had worked for almost a whole year taking out Rune's forces one man at a time. Do any of you have any idea how difficult that was? Trust me." She looked down, her expression becoming ever darker. "All of you would have long been dead."

"Iris, none of us can begin to imagine the torment you went through…" Isabelle had begun but stopped when Iris started forward.

Stepping out of the doorway, she looked at each of them in turn. "If all of you are hellbent on taking down Rune and his goons, you are going to have to follow my every order, no matter how farfetched any of it may seem. That is the only way any of you will survive. I have been playing his game for quite some time. You think you know what hardship is? You think you know what pain is?" Iris laughed hollowly. Isabelle had never heard such a sound come from her. "None of you can imagine what terrible things he does. Rune would take great pleasure in torturing you all. Never, and I mean never, think otherwise; underestimating him will be your downfall." The three of them looked stone-faced at her words but that did not stop her from continuing. "I have a plan, and it will seem crazy and I'm sure one or all of you will be against it, but it is the only way to take down Rune."

She paused, gazing down once more. "I say again, if you do not trust me, my plan or you do not follow my every instruction to the smallest of detail, you will die." Iris looked up, her face showing she had never been more serious, that they would indeed die.

"All right, Iris. We'll listen," Isabelle said softly, grabbing Cole's arm. She had never seen this side of Iris and it almost scared her. It was like she was a different person, as if she were possessed. Cole placed his other hand on hers reassuringly.

"Let's hear this plan of yours." She looked up at Cole, who wore a worried expression. The feeling that passed between Iris and Cole didn't feel normal. Isabelle didn't like this at all.

As they walked inside, her eyes followed Garret. His stone wall was back up.

They all went into the kitchen and dining area as Isabelle and Cole fixed breakfast; Iris and Garrett sat across from one another, not a word passing between them. Iris could feel the chemistry between Cole and Isabelle. What she was feeling from Garrett was something much different. He held his stone expression, but animosity seem to seep from his very core. Was it toward her? From what she had told him in the dream last night? Was she losing him all over again? But she had never had him again in the first place. They hadn't really reunited. Her throat tightened. She took a sip of coffee, forgetting the last time she had had some. The warmth filled her throat, opening it up, easing it.

Garrett turned his gaze toward the dark coffee before him. She looked down at it as well, the darkness reminded her of the shadows that overtook her dream. She was about to speak when a plate of food was set in front of her. Iris couldn't remember the last time she had had a warm meal. She didn't remember any of the meals Garrett and the others had fed her, and Rune… Rune hardly fed her at all.

Sighing, she ate slowly, not wanting to upset her greedy stomach. Noticing how quiet it had become, Iris looked up to see all three of them staring at her. She turned her head to the side in question, and a dizzy spell made her set down her fork and close her eyes. Someone gripped her hand. Opening her eyes, she met Isabelle's concerned look.

Isabelle released her hand. "You shouldn't push yourself. You've been through a lot. We have time."

Iris looked away from her, staring at the blackness of her own coffee. "Time is not on our side, I fear. The longer we wait, the more Rune's forces grow. I haven't almost killed myself time and time again to let him take back his ranks. We have to hit him now while he lacks the numbers to defend himself. I know this isn't what anyone of you want to hear, but moving as soon as possible would be in all of our best interest. Like I said before, you will not like what I have planned and will probably think I've lost my mind." She sighed heavily. "And in some ways, I might have."

Cole took her hand this time, smiling at her when she met his gaze. "But you need to regain your strength, or you won't be able to fight him or his men."

She nodded. "Yes, but I won't be fighting."

Isabelle frowned. "What do you mean?"

"Not yet at least. Shall I explain my plan, or wait until your stomachs have settled?"

Cole cringed a little as if not liking where she was headed with her plan. He shook his head, then nodded for her to go on. She looked to Garrett who only nodded. He hadn't spoken a word since they came in. Isabelle smiled sweetly in approval for her to continue.

"Please listen to my plan before objections; I know there will be some." She took a drink of coffee and almost moaned. She hadn't had any in such a long time. "I will go back to Rune, along with someone else, someone he may not know. It can't be one of you."

She saw the look Garrett cut her. He might be remembering what she had told him last night in the dream. Cole and Isabelle's face showed concern as she went on.

"We can figure that out later. Once there, I will act like his plan truly worked, that I am indeed in love with him."

Garrett stood, his chair slamming to the floor in his haste, interrupting Iris. She flinched at his movements. His glare seared into her, his anger building. And this time, she knew it was directed toward her. "You can't be serious?"

Iris reached across the table toward him. "Please listen..."

"No. I can't, and I won't." He turned and strode out of the room.

Sighing, Iris eyed the others.

"Go ahead," Isabelle said, clearing her throat.

"I act like he wants me to, to get close to him. The other person, if we can find someone under his radar, will move up his ranks, earning his trust. Once that is done, you three will move in. As the two of us attack from within, you all will attack from the outside. This is just an overview of it. Once we have Micah and whoever this other person may be, I will explain further." She gripped the cup of coffee in between her hands, trying not to think of what all this would entail.

"You're really just going to go in and act as if you love him?" Isabelle questioned, her brows pinched together.

"It's what he wanted. I think it will catch him off guard, make him vulnerable. Open to attack."

"I see. But that's dangerous." Cole was concerned, as was Isabelle.

"I've been in worse. We'll talk more later…" Iris felt tears threatening to spill over, revealing how scared she truly was. To give herself to him again, to leave Garrett a third time.

Feigning a smile, Iris stood and went into the bedroom. Closing the door behind her, she leaned against it. Hot tears fell down her cheeks. She gripped her dress to hold back a scream of frustration. Breathing hard, she tried to calm herself and listened to see if Isabelle and Cole were still in the kitchen. After a while, Iris heard silence and slowly opened the bedroom door so it would not make a sound.

After seeing they were all out front speaking to Garrett, she made her way out the back and into the woods. When Iris reached the tree line, she ran as fast as her weakened body would carry her. She couldn't run nearly as fast or as long as she used to. She fell to her hands and knees, sobbing as all her fears and wishes came crashing to the forefront of her mind.

Fear that she would forever remain a puppet to Rune, that the ones she had learned to love would die or leave her in the madman's hands. Then wishes of being with Garrett, to be in his arms and never leave his side. To grow old with him and the others, to watch Cole and Isabelle marry and raise children. The fear of what her plan could bring to them hurt the worst. Crumbling to the ground, she curled into a ball, gasping for air.

The year she had been away, the year where she had to bury her feelings, her hopes, fears and wishes so that she could move forward to take down Rune's forces, so that the ones she cared for would not be a target—was all of that time for nothing? Would it all end with her loved ones dead all because of her?

She tried to curl into a tighter ball to push away all the emotions from the past year but there was no stopping them. Her floodgates were broken.

Garrett couldn't stand the thought of Rune with Iris. Images of them together kept coming to his mind, no matter how much he pushed them back. The food he had just eaten threatened to rise. He stumbled to the barn, leaning against its siding as his breakfast came back up. There had to be another way. He searched for some other way to take Rune down, so Iris would not have to be a victim to his madness once more. How could he let the woman he loved go back into the arms of her torturer? Punching the side of the barn, he heard footsteps approaching. Turning, he sharpened his gaze on Isabelle, who was followed by Cole.

Before he could speak, Isabelle glared at him. "I understand why you are upset and why you stormed out. I don't want her to do this either. It's all insane, and I hate to say it, but there are no safe options, Garrett. The way I see it, we either let her do it on her own and lose her, or we help her with her plan and we keep her. She knows him best and knows how to take him down. Those are the two options we have, like it or not."

Cole intertwined his hand with Isabelle's. "Iris has been trying to escape him ever since their first meeting. She's survived everything he's thrown at her, and that shows how strong she really is. This plot of hers will take time and will be hard for everyone, but no one more than Iris. She will have to act like she likes him all the while truly hating him. I know you are worried she will really love him and be lost to us, but I assure you that no matter how she might be acting when she is with him, it is all a front. None of it is real. What you and Iris share is real and that is what will pull you both through this. Without your help in this, she will truly be lost."

Garrett punched the barn wall again in frustration. "The barn did nothing wrong," Isabelle said, smiling at him when he turned to her.

"Yes, I know. You're both right. But to let Rune touch her..." He leaned his fist against the barn, shutting his eyes tight. "Dammit, how can I let the bastard..." The words trailed off. He couldn't bring himself to say it.

"I know, it makes my blood boil as well. Not as much as yours, and not in the same way. But I don't see any other way. All we can do right now is be here for Iris. Maybe this is her way of working through all that he has done to her. We have to be here for her no matter what, right?" Cole said.

"Right."

"Why not go and talk with her?" Isabelle suggested.

"Would you check to see if she wants a bath first?"

"Aye, aye, doctor."

After Garrett cooled down a little more, the three of them returned to the house. Isabelle went to check on Iris to ask if she wanted a bath, but she quickly returned. "Iris isn't in your room."

"Her guns?" Cole's face had become stone, and Garrett could read his thoughts.

"Her guns are still beside the bed where you put them. She is the only thing missing."

"Shoes?" Cole asked.

Isabelle went back into the room and came right back out. "Her shoes are gone."

As the last word left her lips, Garrett was out the back door, running to where? He didn't even know. All he knew was that he had to find her. Garrett ran where his body took him, following his mind, or was it his heart? His blood boiled as he ran. He couldn't tell if he was angry at Iris, himself, or Rune. He decided to direct his anger toward the bastard who kept hurting Iris.

It was mid-day when Garrett saw a figure huddled on the ground. It was indeed Iris curled up as much as she could be. Despite the warmth of the day, she was shivering. Taking her in his arms, he started back to his house.

Looking at her dirt-streaked face made his heart lighter and heavier at the same time. "I will protect you, Iris. I will do whatever it takes to free you from this darkness. I will not lose you. I will die before that happens. We will find our happy ending together. I will fight tooth and nail to make it happen."

Garrett laid Iris back into his bed and watched her sleep as he held her hand. Cole and Isabelle went into town for the day, leaving the house quiet. The stillness of it all made him drift into dreamland.

He found himself back in his room, sitting where he had been. *Is this a dream?* Looking to the bed, he saw no sign of Iris. Standing, Garrett went into the kitchen and saw no one. His heart raced when he couldn't find her, but then he heard a noise coming from the back. Stepping into the garden, he saw Iris digging in the dirt, planting seeds and pulling weeds.

"I guess this is my happy place," she said, standing and brushing her hands off on her dress.

Cutting her off, he hugged her tightly, not wanting to let go. Before she could speak again, he kissed her softly. Pulling back, he looked into her eyes; they showed the same passion he felt. He wrapped his arm around her waist, pulling her closer, kissing her harder. Iris wrapped her arms around him, hugging him tightly. She tangled her hand in his hair, making him moan.

He pulled back, gasping for air. "I love you, Iris," he whispered. "I won't give up on you. On us."

She smiled at him. "I love you as well. And I have no intention of releasing my love. No matter what the future has in store, I will always love you."

Garrett lifted Iris up against him, carrying her toward the house. He tried to find his way back to his room, fumbling several times, making them both laugh. He threw her on the bed. The look Iris gave him made his body heat up more than it already was. As he tugged off his shirt, she watched him hungrily, biting her lip when he undid his pants. Iris let out a sigh when he stood in front of her naked. When she was about to move to undress, Garrett swiftly stood over her.

He put his hands on the top seam of the spring dress she had been wearing that same day and yanked, ripping the top of the dress. Garrett pulled the rest of her clothes off, skirt, undergarments and all. She laid naked on the bed, and as he looked her over, Iris smiled, eyeing his growing erection with pleasure.

She moaned at the sight of him, and he grinned. He knelt and ran his hands up her legs, moving toward her inner thighs. Garrett nudged her legs apart. He traced the inner part of her knee with his tongue, slowly trailing up to where they both needed him to be.

Her moans grew as he continued to lick. One hand explored her body, cupping one lush breast and flicking her nipple as his other hand gripped her hip. She gripped the sheets as her body arched. A wave of satisfaction hit Garrett. *I did that*, he thought with pride.

"Garrett. Please. I want you, I need you," Iris whispered in between pants.

He lifted his head, watching her. She looked to him and a sly grin appeared on his face. He lifted himself toward her, but as he did, everything around them shifted then went black.

Chapter 21

Garrett awoke with a start. Iris still laid in bed. Getting up, he went to see if Isabelle and Cole had returned. They had not, thankfully. His body hurt with how much he wanted Iris. Taking a deep breath, he entered his room again. Iris now sat on the bed, staring at him. Before he knew it, she was up and had closed the door behind him. In the next instant, she was lifting his shirt.

He gave her a surprised look. Smiling, she frantically kissed him while trying to undo his pants. Laughing at her struggled attempt, he helped and then unhooked her dress rather than ripping it as in the dream.

"Garrett..." He kissed her softly and lifted her onto the bed. There was no need for words. They knew what the other wanted. As Garrett laid Iris down, he glided above her and as he entered her, Garrett could feel how much the dream had affected her.

She lifted her legs, hugging his waist, letting him penetrate further. Iris moaned loudly as he gripped her hands above her. Garrett's slowed his movements.

"Garrett... Garrett..." she whispered, her eyes closed in pleasure. He loved it when she said his name.

Everything about her drove him mad with pleasure. His body was too hot to continue the slow motions. He had to move faster, thrust harder. Iris' eyes opened wide, staring at him. He slowed and was about to pull out when she tightened her hold on him.

"No, keep going. Please. Harder."

"As you wish." He kissed her, biting her lip. She gasped. Garrett placed an arm under her, pulling her closer to him. She used her inner thighs to tighten her grip on his waist.

As Garrett's pleasure arched, Iris whispered in his ear, "I will always be yours, Garrett, no matter what happens. I am yours."

When they separated, he laid down next to her, still touching her body. He noticed she wasn't as plump as she had been their first time or even in the dream. Garrett studied the new scars, outlining each one with his finger.

"You really have been going through a lot. I can't even fathom what you've been through. I'm so sorry you had to do it all alone. I should have done more. I should have gone after you."

She placed her finger on his lips. "I did it for you, for us. I won't let the demons of my life become yours. I won't let what hurt me hurt you. Don't blame yourself. We would have both ended up hurt or dead if you had followed. You did the right thing."

Garrett raised up on one elbow. "But that's what partners do. They share the good and the bad. I want to help shoulder your burdens, Iris. Please let me. I won't let you face this alone. Not again."

Her face changed. It was strange how vulnerable she could be one moment and stern and unemotional the next. How easily she bottled up her feelings almost scared him. Garrett knew why she did it, to protect him and to protect her heart.

"I have to proceed with my plan so I can rid myself of Rune once and for all. I have to do this, Garrett, or he will chase us our entire lives. You can help me by finding someone to go with me to his hideout. And then you and the others will wait and practice your skills with Cole until I call upon you. I'm sorry it has to be this way." Her eyes showed a hint of sadness.

Garrett leaned in and kissed her. "I don't know Rune as you do, so I will follow your lead, despite how I may dislike it." He thought for a moment. "I think I might know someone who can go in with you. It will take a few days to get them here though. In the meantime…" Leaning in for another kiss, he heard the front door open. Within seconds, he was up on his feet getting dressed. Iris eyed him as he turned to stare at her. "Hurry. Get dressed," he whispered.

Iris laughed and put on her clothes as well.

"I'll bring you a warm bath, okay?" He kissed her forehead and left.

As she sat there, her body still tingling and throbbing, Iris was at war with herself. She wanted so much to be with Garrett and to have a life with him. To fall asleep each night in his arms and wake to his smiling face. Iris sniffed back tears as the thought of what she had to do came forefront in her mind and how her actions would hurt him.

She was somewhat relieved when Cole brought in her bath. "Garrett had to go see to a townsperson who is running a high fever." He paused and looked at her. Setting down the large tub, he came and sat on the bed next to her. "You're scared, aren't you? It's such a rare sight on you. I've only ever seen it in your expression for a split second. But this…" Cole grabbed her hand in his. "I'm scared for you as well, Iris. I wish there was another way. You going back to Rune makes my stomach turn."

She squeezed his hand. "It's not that I am scared for myself. I am scared of what this might mean for Garrett and you and Isabelle. I will have to act like I hate you all. My actions will end up hurting you all. And in the end, the three of you might believe that I have really turned to Rune."

"I know you, Iris. You keep your word, and I will be here to remind the others that your actions are to only to fool Rune." Cole stood up, smiling. "Garrett is going to bring Micah on his way back. It's all going to work out. Now, get into the bath before it gets cold."

Cole went and sat with Isabelle in the kitchen. He thought about how much strength it took Iris to willingly go back to that monster. She was trying to protect all of them the best way she knew how. He had always admired her courage, ever since she had come to his rescue that stormy night. It was as if she was brought in on the wind of the storm.

Two older boys had found his stash of food, and after raiding it, they beat him. He was a scrawny thing at the time and couldn't hold his own, unlike now. Now he was much broader, making sure to chop and carry fire wood every chance he got to strengthen his arms. That way, he could knock any man down that came his way.

The night Iris found him, she had come right before they had really hurt him. He was curled into a ball, covering his head with his hands as best as he could. Hearing screams, he peeked up, seeing what was making his attackers stop. That was when he saw Iris for the first time. Like a raging storm, the wind had caught her long black hair, whipping it behind her as she held the two boys by the throats, lifting them both off the ground, their leg kicking at her. Her glare made even him shutter in fright. And the way she held herself, proud and sure.

After that night, she had taken him under her wing, protecting him, showing him how the streets worked. She made him strong in body and mind. Cole owed everything to her, and he couldn't let her down, not now and not ever.

"You seem like the whole world is on your shoulders." Isabelle went over and rubbed them. "Want to talk about it?" she whispered. The feeling of her breath on his ear sent shivers down his spine. Clearing his throat, he was about to stand when Isabelle went around him and sat in his lap.

"Isabelle..."

She placed a finger on his lips. "Let me get your mind off things for a few moments." Leaning in, she kissed him lightly. His blood turned sweltering hot. Cole wrapped his arms around her, bringing her closer. As he returned her kiss harder than she had, Isabelle sighed, making him lose control.

"Izzy, please." Isabelle pulled away to look at him. "We can't. Not yet."

She stood, looking hurt. "And why not? Do you...?"

He grabbed her wrist, pulling her to him. He buried his face in her dress. Feeling the warmth of her stomach made him smile. "I want you more than anything. But with all that is going to happen, I don't want to bring a child into it. Not yet. Please understand, Isabelle. My thoughts are always with you and the many ways I want to have you." He swallowed hard. "But I wish to wait until all this is over."

Isabelle laughed lightly. "Even though we don't know when that will be? It could be years…"

"Then we will wait. I know I might sound prudish, so unlike a man… But I want our first time to be right, not rushed. I want to lay with you all day and all night, not leaving the bed. I want my full attention to be on you. And right now, it wouldn't be."

She nodded. "Thank you, Cole."

He stared at her in confusion. "What for?"

"For thinking of the future, for thinking of us and our life together, rather than just the moment."

He took her hands in his. "We will marry, Isabelle. We will have the best life and children running around that look just like us. That is the future I want." Isabelle's eyes filled with tears. Standing, he brought her in for a long, hard hug. "I love you," he whispered in her ear.

It was her turn to bury her face in his shirt. "And I love you, my outlaw."

The name made him laugh. After kissing the top of her head, Cole asked, "How shall I help with supper, my lady?" He backed away and made a show of bowing.

Laughing, she curtsied. "How noble of you, good sir. This way if you will."

After Iris bathed, she dressed in a thin dress Isabelle had given her. She still didn't like wearing dresses, and she wished she had the clothes she had made for herself. Thinking of those clothes brought back old memories. It felt like a lifetime ago that Garrett had come to the rescue when she was about to be thrown onto the fire. How so much had changed since then. It was almost a different world.

Stepping into the kitchen-dining area, Iris smelled a lovely blend of herbs. Looking to where the smell originated, she saw Cole and Isabelle laughing and talking over a large pot of stew. Grinning at the loving couple, she sat at the table and watched them. Cole turned to set the table and jumped when he saw Iris sitting there, quietly admiring them.

"What a lovely couple you two make," she said smiling. "I ordered you two a gift, but the location of it is now unknown to me."

"You being here is a gift enough to me, Iris." Cole went over to her and hugged her shoulders. "Are you sure there is no other way to do this?"

She sighed, looking down at her hands. "Sadly, I can't think of any other way. If I... We don't take him out, he will hunt us all until we're all dead. He is insane, and to defeat him, you have to think like him. You have to take risks where others wouldn't." Gazing up, her eyes locked with Isabelle's. "I'm sad to say that I'm mentally going to have to start pushing you all away. That means I will act distant and uncaring. I know I have time till I go to Rune, but to prepare, I have to delude myself and all of you." Iris took Cole's hand, locking eyes with him. "No matter what I say, how I act, or what I do, these will not be my true feelings. I will come off as if I am really brainwashed by Rune, but you know me; remember that." Standing, she hugged him and then went over and hugged Isabelle. "Please remind your brother of this."

Isabelle nodded. "I will and remind yourself as well. You are strong, Iris. We are with you." As they released their embrace, when the front door swung open.

Garrett stepped through, staring at Iris. The sight of him made her heart skip a beat and then race faster. Micah followed

Garrett with a furrowed brow. She gave him a smile and greeted him. As the others set the table, Iris took Garrett into his room. Iris looked down, taking his large hands in hers, taking in their smoothness. She fought back tears. This was going to be harder than she thought. Would this be what killed her? She was thinking about death an awful lot lately.

Garrett lifted her chin, and their eyes locked, which almost brought tears to hers. Leaning toward her, he gently kissed her. "I love you, Iris."

Those words cracked the dam. She rushed to hug him, sobbing onto his chest. He wrapped his arms around her, hugging her tightly. "This is a rare side of you. I know that it will all be an act, but I want you to promise me something." She nodded, rubbing her head against his shirt. "Promise that you will not fall for your own lie." He paused. Lifting her chin, he kissed her tears away. "Remember that I am here, that I am waiting for you, that my love is never-ending. No matter how you act or what you say, my love will not diminish." Garrett's voice grew soft. "Promise me that you will come back. That we will have our happy ending."

Iris leaned in and kissed him, wanting time to stop. She pushed back the thoughts of what lay ahead and the pain that would accompany it. Once Iris left this room, she would have to shut off her feelings and turn her heart to stone once again. Just as she had done so many times before, but this time would be the hardest, and Iris hoped she had the strength to face it, to push through the plan and to take down Rune once and for all.

Chapter 22

Several days passed. Iris did as she had set out to do. She pushed down her feelings and distanced herself from the others. They had filled in Micah on the plan and now they all waited for Garrett's secret allies to come. Iris busied herself by cleaning everyone's guns and knives and making sure Cole and Micah got better at aiming. Despite them already knowing how to shoot, she wanted them to be better. Iris would leave it to them to teach the others and prepare them when she no longer could.

She avoided the others as much as possible, often going out of her way. Iris would catch Garrett staring at her from across the room or table from time to time. She tried her hardest not to meet his gaze and when their dreams intertwined, she pushed him out, hurting even more as a result. After, the dreams turned into a nightmare, despite the dream catcher hanging at the window. Her inner fears were too strong, too deep.

Looking in the mirror, she saw dark circles under her eyes. She half grinned at her reflection. This look would suit her well and better sell the story she was to tell Rune. Iris just had to hold a little longer, meet this person who was going with her, train them for a short time, then leave.

After a few weeks of waiting, Garett and Micah left to meet the coach in town to pick up his long-awaited guest and bring them back to his homestead. Iris leaned against the side of the house, staring off into the nearby woods. When she heard the sound of approaching horses, she placed her hand on her pistol at her hip. She saw Garrett and Micah on one horse. The sight made her almost laugh, but the two on the other horse made her somber.

The two ladies jumped off the horse, once they arrived at the barn. One was dressed in a fine lace spring dress, the other in male attire meant to show off her figure. Unlike when Iris wore men's clothing, she liked to wear it loose and baggy, trying to look like a man as best as she could. Iris recognized the lovely lady in the spring dress as the one on Garrett's arm so long ago. One she thought to be his betrothed. *Had he done this to punish me for pushing him away? For going back to Rune? But he knows why I must do that…* Then she looked to the other woman again, the one in men's clothing. Iris' stomach turned and then sank when she locked eyes with this woman. Her gray eyes were piercing and eerily familiar.

Garrett and the others walked into the house. The woman Iris had been eyeing eyed her in return, giving her a wink. Iris scoffed, folding her arms. After a moment, she followed them all in. She didn't like this one bit, and this one lady, didn't she know her from somewhere?

She watched as Garrett made the introductions. He first pointed to the redhead, the one Iris thought he might have brought to spite her. "This is my good friend Abelia. We met when we went to medical school together and all of you met before."

Iris' stomach felt heavy. They all knew her? He had brought her here? She wanted to throw up...

Where Abelia had soft features and red hair, the other girl had a sharp bone structure almost like a bronze goddess she had seen at the worlds' bazaar a lifetime ago. Her hair was cut short, just above her shoulders but had a wave to it, making it almost bounce as she walked. The color was brown with a hint of gray showing through, as if her hair was aging thirty years before the rest of her. Then it hit Iris. She had met her before, a longtime ago.

But before Garrett could introduce the other girl, she smiled at everyone and introduced herself. "Nice to meet all of you. My name is Alvera, but you can call me Alvy for short."

Cole grinned from ear to ear. "Alvy and Aby. I like it!" Isabelle eyed him. "You seem familiar to me, Alvy. Have we met?"

She shook her head. "No, but I've heard of you. I'm sure Iris knows me, though."

Everyone turned their eyes to Iris, who stood to the side of the group, watching them exchange greetings. She sighed. "It seems she is from the same agency." Iris paused, thinking of the last time they crossed paths. "I do believe I've met you only in passing. Am I wrong to assume the agency had a hand in this?"

Alvera smiled slyly. "It seems they have caught wind of something to do with Rune, but no details were given."

The more people who know, the more likely Rune is to find out about the plan. This isn't good, Iris thought.

As if reading her mind, Alvy cleared her throat. "You know as well as I do that they keep no documents, and as for hearsay, you also know they would not share any intel unless it was a dire need. So, I assume this is indeed a grim situation, or I wouldn't be here."

Iris locked eyes with Alvera. The air filled with the tension between the two. Even though Iris knew she was sent by her captain, Alvera had always been his righthand woman, the closest agent to him. But something about Alvera had never set well with her.

Because she reminds you of yourself? Or someone else? a small voice in the back of her mind said.

She shuttered at the thought, trying to push them away.

"I brought something, Iris." Alvera reached into a large bag next to her. First, she pulled out several paper packages. "These are the dresses you ordered. I thought you might feel better wearing them." She flashed a grin at Iris. Alvera put a small square box on top of the other packages. "And this was waiting for you as well. I was told to give these to you."

Iris smiled slightly, still feeling a little perturbed. "Thank you. I appreciate it."

She reached for the items and held them close to her, thinking of where she had been when she had first ordered it all. At the time, she didn't think she would ever see Garrett or the others again, much less be on the road to either free her or bind her forever.

"I bet it would be interesting to see you and Iris spar," Cole said.

Iris and Isabelle glared at him. "I'm sure you would like to see that," Isabelle said, nudging him with her elbow. "Don't you think it's time better spent going over all of the plans and our parts within it?"

So, once again, they went over what each person's job was in this elaborate plan. Setting at the dining table, Iris stood, speaking clearly.

"Alvera will find a way into his ranks and start climbing to get into his closely knitted group of men he keeps close to him. I will brief you on how to do that later. Micah and Cole will train some trusted men on a mission they will not disclose to them, while I fool Rune into thinking he has brainwashed me. Once Alvera is closer to Rune, we all make are attack at once. Alvera and I from within, Micah and Cole from the outside."

"And the rest of us?" Garrett's voice was rough, cutting.

Iris didn't want anyone else involved. She didn't want anyone else to get hurt, not because of her. She wanted to take all the pain, to take all the danger alone.

Placing her fist on the table, trying to hide her trembling hand, she said, "Since you, Isabelle and Abelia have medical training, we will need you for when we return. Just in case there any among us who are injured." She hoped he didn't push the issue, that he wouldn't want to do more. Iris tightened her fist, digging her nails into her palm.

After going over it all in more detail, it was soon to be dinner.

While the others helped prepare dinner, Garrett took Abelia aside, out of earshot of the others. "Are you all right with all of this?"

When she looked up at him, he could tell she was hurting just as much as he was. "I think we're both in the same place at the moment. Sending the woman we love off to a monster. I despise it as much as you do. But we both know they are strong and if anyone can pull this off, it will be the two of them." She wrapped her arms around herself. "I know you're worried that I will resent you for bringing her into all of this. A part of me does..." Abelia looked away from him, staring off into the nearby garden. It lay barren much different than the last time she was here.

"Are you still pretending to be engaged to that man? That way your parents won't find out about Alvera?" He studied her, knowing it was hard to love someone as she did. It wasn't just frowned upon. It was dangerous. So, he understood why she did what she did.

"I had started the engagement before I met her. And she understands why I keep up the charade."

"And you only recently told me of Alvera through letters. But I've known..."

"That I don't like men in that way since we first met."

He smiled at her. "Yes. It seems within this madness we have both found the love of our lives and now fear for their safety."

"I trust Alvera and her ability to see this through. I just hope everyone else will be able to fulfill their duties. I have just found her. I don't intend to lose her."

Iris sat on a stool overlooking the garden, thinking of the past and dreading the future as she nibbled on her dinner. The others were inside, sitting around the table, chatting. Her mind held images of Garrett and their time together. His hands on her, his body filling her own with his warmth, only made the need for him rise all the more. She stood, putting her food on the stool she had been sitting on. How could she go through with all of this? How could she willing let them put all their lives on the line for her?

Grief gripped her lungs, making it hard to breath. Was there truly no way for her to defeat Rune without involving them? This was going to be hard on every single one of them, and Iris wished with every cell in her body that she could shoulder all of it alone. Walking over to the edge of the woods, Iris punched a nearby tree in frustration.

"What did the tree ever do to you?" Iris turned to see Alvera standing near her, eyeing the tree. She turned her gaze to Iris, looking at her from head to toe. "You've changed quite a bit since the last time our paths crossed. A lot more scars." Alvera went over and lightly touched Iris' cheek, then stepped back. "You've also grown a little scrawny. I hope I will be able to help you. If anyone deserves their happy ending, it's you, love." Alvy turned and walked back to the house without another word.

Iris looked past her and saw Abelia watching. She had seen the whole thing.

But as Alvera went out of sight, Iris had a flashback from the last time she had seen the gray-eyed beauty. *The shadows will be your downfall.* Iris felt the icy grip of death take hold...

Alvera smiled at Abelia as she approached the house, but her smile soon faded when Aby crossed her arms and frowned at her. "What's that face for?" Alvera reached out to her, but Abelia stepped back.

"I know you had a crush on her from afar, but now that you are up close, have you changed your mind?"

"What? Changed my mind? About you?" Alvy laughed lightly, trying to ease the own tension in her own body. "Come on, Abs. Out of everyone in this fucked up world, you are the only one who understands me. The only one I connect with. I would never do anything to jeopardize what we have."

Abelia wasn't giving in. "Then why touch her cheek?"

She looked down ashamed, still not used to this relationship thing, never having been in one. "I guess I wanted to see if she was real." Her voice dropped to a whisper. "In some way, I think I was hoping she wasn't real because that would mean none of us would have to do any of this, and she wouldn't have to put herself in a bad situation."

Abelia hugged her tightly, seemingly taking her by surprise. "If we're both being honest," she whispered, "I'm scared as well, but you signed up for this."

She hugged Abelia back just as tightly. "And you, dear one, signed up as well. You have been friends with this family for a long time. They are your family, and you can't turn your back on them. I can't turn my back and let you do this without me." Alvera backed away slightly, looking her in the eye. "We are in this together. Because we no longer do things alone, Abelia. We are partners in every sense of the word."

Smiling, she leaned down and kissed Abelia's lips. Moving one hand down to the small of her back, she pressed their bodies together.

Chapter 23

Days passed with training and planning. Iris distanced herself from everyone, none more so than Garrett. Abelia and Alvera spent every waking moment together, and Cole was rarely seen far from Isabelle's side. Garrett almost envied them. He would stare at everyone, taking it all in. He saw how much Iris was retreating into herself. He questioned if she could really come back from all of this.

Cole went over to Garrett and reassuringly put his hand on his shoulder. "She's only doing this because she has to be in the right mindset."

"But isn't that what we weren't wanting? The reason we went after her in the first place? And now she's willingly putting herself back into that." He lowered his voice. "Will she even be able to come back to us?"

"Like I've said before, she is strong and will get through this. But we have to be here waiting for her on this end." Cole turned to Garrett and smiled, squeezing his shoulder once more. He left him standing, staring at the others.

Cole found Iris in the back, staring up at the rising moon. "You wanted to see me?"

Iris turned to him. "Yes, I wanted to give you something."

"Before that, I have a question. The first time you met Alvera, there was a lot of tension. Where did that all come from? I don't remember her from anyone we've worked with."

Iris kicked the dirt with the toe of her shoe, watching it fly. "I worked with her a long time ago, prior to our missions together. When we first went into the agency, you were trained by others while I went off on assignments. Remember?"

"Yes, I don't miss those times."

"I went on a few jobs with her. On our last one, she told me a premonition of my future. She's what some call a seer or fortuneteller. After that day, I stayed my distance."

Cole stared at her. "What was it that she saw?"

She shook her head, not willing to tell him. "Cole, it…"

He interrupted her. "Tell me what she saw, dammit. Or I will go in there and ask her myself in front of everyone."

Iris looked at him wide-eyed. "I can't."

Cole put his arm against the panel of the house, then leaned in toward her. "Tell me, Iris." His voice held an aggressive tone to it. "I mean it, tell me now. What did she say?"

"Isabelle is coming," Iris whispered, pushing past his out stretched arm.

Cole grabbed her wrist. "I told you, you aren't getting away from telling me this, Iris."

Isabelle stepped out the back door, seeing the last interaction between the two of them. "What's going on? Telling what?"

Iris looked from one to the other; she rarely panicked, but this was one of those rare times. The others apparently heard and came to see what was going on. Iris had all eyes on her. Cole let her wrist go, and she immediately backed away. *Shit. This can't be happening. I should have stayed quiet. Shit. Shit.* Sheer utter terror raced through her.

Her mind was drained from pushing all her feelings down. If she couldn't guard herself against Cole, how would she face Rune?

"Tell me, Iris." Cole stared at her unrelentingly. "Or I'll ask Alvera."

"Tell what? Ask what?" Abelia chimed in, glancing at Alvera and then Iris.

Iris was screaming on the inside; how could she let that slip? Maybe it was best they know anyway. *No, they can't know. Shit!*

Just before Iris could speak, Alvera cleared her throat. "It's all my fault. I told Iris a long time ago that I could see people's future. I told Iris hers, but we were both young then. I thought of it as a game, but it seemed she took it to heart." She tried to laugh, but it sounded brittle.

"What did you tell her?" Abelia asked.

"I told her she would find her love in the darkness. Or something to that effect. I'm guessing she thinks this is the darkness. I'm not quite sure. It was all just fun and games. Really, nothing to worry over." Alvy looked down at Aby. "Truly."

"Come now, we've had a long day. Let's go get some rest, shall we?" Abelia took Isabelle's arm.

Cole and Garrett remained as Isabelle, Abelia and Micah went in. Clearly, neither of them bought it. Garrett grabbed Iris by her arm and pulled her to the edge of the woods, leaving Cole and Alvera in the back yard. Iris' heart raced.

"Garrett, really it…" Iris lightly pulled against him but didn't put much effort into it. She loved his touch and being so close to him.

He cut her off. "Look, Iris, you went sheet white. I know there's more. Alvera was just trying to play it off so we all wouldn't worry. But I believe in seers, so…" Garrett leaned her against a tree, blocking her movement by placing a hand on either side of her.

Iris looked up at him. The moon shone down, making his eyes look darker than they were. His jaw was set tight. Iris was fighting her own body, which was set aflame at his closeness. It took everything she had not to kiss him and rip off his shirt to see his caramelized skin set alight by the moon. She bit her lip, thinking of his toned body.

"Tell me, Iris. What did she see?"

Iris looked away from him, knowing he was not going to let this go. "She saw my death, Garrett. I had long forgotten about it. It's only when I saw her again that I was reminded of it."

"What about your death?" He lifted her chin, but she averted her eyes.

"She told me the shadow that followed me would be my downfall. That I would be swallowed by it, never to see the light of day again." Iris didn't dare look up at him.

He tensed. "And you think this shadow is Rune?" he asked roughly. She could only nod. "Yet you still want to go through with this?"

Iris' breath caught in her throat. "If I don't give into the shadow," she managed to whisper, "then all that I love will take my place in the darkness."

He grabbed her by the shoulders. "So, you're telling me that either you die, or we all do? Is that what you're saying?"

She looked up at him, tears in her eyes. "Garrett, I have to..."

"I've tried to understand all of this. Why you wanted to go back, to take down Rune. To find closure. How can I stand by and watch you throw yourself to your own death, Iris? Dammit, you're asking for too much."

Her stomach bottomed out. *His giving up on me? On us? Am I truly losing him this time? I can't breathe... Please, don't leave me alone in the darkness.* She fought back tears, her heart aching.

"You said you would wait." Iris searched his face, not wanting to believe his words.

"How can I stand by and let the woman I love go to her death? All of this just keeps getting darker and darker. I can't... I can't watch another person I love die in front of me. I can't do it. I *won't* do it. Dammit, Iris, tell me you won't go to Rune and I will stay. Say those words, and I am yours." He shook her as if trying to shake some sense into her.

"I have to finish Rune. I will never be free if I don't." Iris' eyes blurred with tears. She cursed them for it, not wanting her view of the man she loved to be blurred, not if this were to be the last time.

"Even if it means your own death? Then what will the use of freedom be when you're dead at the end of it? If you were going to be free of him that way, then there's no reason to go to him." He hugged her to him, his grip so tight it was almost painful. "Spend what time we have left and die with me. Don't go to him and die in the end."

"Garrett, you know," she put her face on his shoulder, "I love you." She felt him tense and then ease.

"I love you as well. That's why I'm asking you to not go through with this."

"If I do go, I will lose you either way." Iris hugged him tighter.

He swallowed. "I do love you, and that's why I can't stand and watch you die. You don't really even need me for your plan."

"Garrett, I do need you. Knowing you are waiting for me at the end of all this is what will keep me going through all the shit Rune will do."

"I told you, Iris," he whispered fiercely. "I can't stand by and watch you die. If you choose to go, know that I love you, but I will not support you in this endeavor."

Garrett released her and headed to the house, not looking back. She felt as if he had ripped out her heart and took it with him, leaving a gaping hole in her chest. She felt void and empty.

Iris followed after him, not to stop him but to see Cole who was waiting for her outside the house. She stopped a few feet away from him. "I wanted to give you something," Iris said, trying to feign a smile, wiping away the remaining tears.

"You should have just told me instead of having to hear it from Alvera. And now it seems Garett knows as well. We've all known it was a possibility but now it seems more so. I'm not going to stop you. I know you need to do this. I just hope you come out of it whole." He hugged her tightly. "I love you, Iris. You are my sister and all I want is your happiness."

She wrapped her arms around him as well. "And you are my brother, Cole. I'm sorry to ask so much of you, but let's not talk about this anymore. I have a gift for you." Pulling away, Iris reached into her dress pocket, pulled out a small box, and handed it to him.

Cole took the item and unwrapped the paper. He opened the box to reveal a small ring inside. It was made of yellow gold with an oval ruby in the center and two small diamonds on either side. "What is this for?"

Iris laughed. "What do you think it's for? It's for Isabelle, an engagement ring. The red stone is a ruby, the two on the side are diamonds."

"Wait… Why did you get this? This must have set you back." Cole looked up from examining the ring in surprise.

"It's my wedding gift to the both of you. I had enough saved up, and I wasn't going to spend it on anything anyway. I wanted to do this for you, Cole. We're family and I wish I could do more for you and Isabelle. I'm happy you found each other." She smiled sweetly at him as he became teary-eyed. "I want the two of you to live a long happy life."

He sniffed. "You sound like you won't be a part of that life."

"Let's not think of such things. But if I don't make it back in time for the wedding, know that my heart is with you."

She hugged him once more and then walked into the house and to the room she now shared with Isabelle. Thankfully, she wasn't there. Iris sat down on the bed, put her face in her hands and let herself cry. A really good cry. *Have I really lost Garrett? Is all of this for nothing? Am I destined to die?* To have felt this love, only lose it all, never truly knowing what it all could bring. *Maybe all of them would have been better off, never knowing me in the first place, none of them would be in danger now...* These thoughts only made her cry harder.

Lying down, she fell asleep as her tears dried. And found herself within a dream, one she did not want to find herself in. This dream was not like the others. She was floating above herself, watching from a bird's-eye view. Looking down, Iris saw herself kneeling, dark fog surrounding her. Then there was a light coming toward her, casting away the shadows.

"Though darkness may take you, there is a light that can bring you through, just like it has many times before," a faint voice said as the dream faded.

Iris woke with a start. Looking around, she saw Isabelle lying next to her still asleep. Slowly, she crawled from the bed, making sure not to wake her. She went outside to breathe the cool night air. There was a change to the air, from spring to summer. The cooler nights would soon give way to humid ones. The stars were bright above her, which somehow only made her feel even sadder. So many lights among the darkness...

Taking in deep breaths, she tried to push down the panic that kept trying to rise to the surface.

Footsteps sounded behind her. "There's another part of the vision I never told you." Alvera came to stand next to her. "It wasn't clear to me until I met the light in your life."

Iris turned to her in question. "Light? What else did you see?"

"After I saw you being taken by the darkness and you were on the verge of no return, I saw a faint light coming toward you. But when it comes to that light, there are two paths it can take, and their choice will seal your fate." Alvy averted her gaze.

"I'm guessing this light is a person and it depends on them to bring me out of this darkness I will be put into?"

"Yes," Alvera said simply.

"So, my fate lies in someone else's hands and not my own?"

"I'm afraid so." She gave Iris a sideways glance.

"I've always tried my best to make sure that my fate and my life was solely in my hands, but it seems destiny has its own plan." Sighing, she eyed Alvera. "Tell me, can you see which path this holder of the light will take?"

She shook her head, meeting Iris' gaze. "I'm afraid not. It seems it has yet to be decided."

"Let me ask this. If he doesn't go on the pathway to me, will they live a happy life?" Iris didn't want to say his name.

"Alas, his path is unclear, still yet to be decided, unlike yours. You have been set on this course before I met you. I am sad to say you are intertwined with Rune, and for that reason, I knew I needed to help you to escape him. Even if you find yourself in darkness, at least it will be of your own making."

Iris gazed into the dark woods in front of them, imagining shadowy claws reaching toward her. She hugged herself as her body involuntarily shuddered. "I wish I didn't have to bring all of you into this. The only good that has come from this is Cole and Isabelle meeting."

"You also found love that you wouldn't have known otherwise."

Iris nodded. "Yes, but I've ended up hurting the one I love in the end and may lose him despite how I feel."

"I wish all of this wasn't happening as well, but some things have to be done to move forward, and this is one of them. The agency wants you to succeed in taking Rune out. They all support you, Iris. No matter what happens, you have people who care and will be waiting for you at the end of all of this."

Iris wanted to say something about Garrett but decided against it. All words fell short of how she felt. "I hope I can do what is needed."

"You have been through more than most. You have the inner strength of an elephant. Remember that. And as for Garrett, remind him in some way of how you feel before you leave." Alvera patted Iris on top of the head before she turned to head back inside, leaving Iris with her thoughts.

Standing there, looking into the darkness of the woods, she was surrounded by the thoughts of how within the last few weeks she had tried her hardest to push down the feelings she had for Garrett, to ignore them. But no matter how much she tried, those feelings were always in the forefront of her mind. Iris decided to try a different tactic and hoped it wasn't too late.

Hopefully, she hadn't lost him completely.

Chapter 24

Garrett was furious Iris hadn't said anything about what Alvera had seen. The dream he had so long ago with the bear started to make sense to him. How could he support her on a mission that would ultimately end in her death? But then a small voice in the back of his mind murmured, *But she could be saved by the light of her life…*

He shook his head, not wanting to listen, not wanting to contemplate its meaning. He wanted to be left alone in his own brooding for a while, even if nothing would come of it. Trying to calm his racing thoughts, Garrett went and laid on his bed.

After tossing and turning for what seemed like hours, he finally drifted into dreamless sleep. But at some point, Garrett found himself in a dream. Looking around at his surroundings, he noticed he was in a beautiful field of lovely dark purple irises blooming all around him, the color so dark they looked almost black. The vast field extended as far as the eye could see in all directions; the breeze filled the air with the fragrance of the flowers, casting some of the petals in the air.

As Garrett rotated, he caught sight of a young woman in a long flowing dress in the same color of the irises around her. She walked toward him, and as she got closer, he could make out that it was his Iris approaching him. The dress she wore was off the shoulder, the material so light, it was almost see-through if it wasn't for the dark color. The breeze caught her hair, blowing it behind her.

His body went rigid when he caught himself calling her *his Iris*. Staring at her as she neared, Garrett asked, "Why are we here?" His breath caught in his throat as his feelings made their way to the surface, no matter how hard he tried to fight them down. He loved her with everything in him.

Her voice started off so soft, he could hardly hear her words. "I don't want to lose you. Do you know the meaning of these flowers?" She brushed her hand lightly across the tops of the blooms. He shook his head. "The meaning is before the storm. I am about to go into the biggest storm of my life. It seems my whole life has been one storm after another, but what I'm about to go do is by far the most dangerous thing I've done. Despite that, I have to do it. I will never be free otherwise." The wind picked up her words as if they were connected.

Pausing, she reached for him, looking into his eyes. "I know this is asking a lot from you, to wait for me to come back to you. But I don't think I can do this... No, I know I can't do this without knowing you are with me. That you will be here for me when my nightmare is finally over, and my dreams can start to come true. I also know this is a lot for you to bear, and you deserve far better than what I can offer you."

The look of her enticed him. How she had been avoiding him had only made his body want hers all the more. Garrett loved her, and there was no denying it. The anger raging inside him started to subside. Here Iris stood, asking for help, asking for him to bear this burden with her, something he had wanted from the beginning…

To her surprise, he took her hands, grasping them tightly in his own. Iris' eyes widened, and he smiled at her. "My heart aches to be near you. My body desperately wants your touch. No matter how I try to rid you from my mind, you are like a shadow that never leaves my side. Will you offer me your mind, body, heart and soul?"

His declaration took her aback. His words didn't just express his own feelings. It also mirrored her own. She had tried to prepare for him to run from her, so him reaching out to her was a pleasant surprise.

Clearing his throat, Garrett squeezed her hands, bringing her back to the moment. "Yes," she whispered. Heart racing, she looked away, feeling her cheeks heat up.

"Then I am in turn yours. My whole body." He leaned down, whispering in her ear, "My heart." Garrett kissed the top of her bare shoulder, slowly trailing kisses to the top of her chest.

"My mind." He raised up, taking her in his arms. "And my soul."

Finally, their lips met in a passionate kiss that stole her breath.

His words and touch released all the tension she had been feeling. She eased into him as he pulled her close. Placing his hands on the small of her back, then on her ass, he pushed her pelvis into his, letting her feel how much he wanted her. She moaned. Garrett glided his hands up the back of her dress to the top. With a swift motion, it pooled around her feet, leaving her bare to him.

He smiled as he stepped back, taking in all of her. His eyes started at the dark purple dress at her ankles, to her knees with a few small scars around them, to her hips, and then to the scar that made him freeze. The one shaped like an R.

"I didn't make myself have my scars in this dream, Garrett," she said softly. "I think you somehow changed how I look in here."

Nodding, he stepped closer to her, putting his hand on her hip. His other hand trailed up. Lightly cupping her breast, he rubbered her nipple with his thumb, watching her reaction all the while.

She bit her lip, a shudder wracking her body. A slight smile tugged at his lips. He moved his other hand to her inner thigh, up to the tuff of hair. She swallowed, her body throbbing with need and desire.

"If this is to be our last time for a while, I'd rather it not just be a dream," he whispered, the words a sensual caress.

Sighing, she nodded in agreement. "The house," she gasped as he cupped her other breast.

"Is full," he finished.

"Yes… Yes…"

He laughed lightly. "I know a place. Wake up, and meet me out front."

Garrett sat up, groaning at how his erection made him fully aware of his need, his desire. Rather than putting on a shirt and pants, he put on a long robe he rarely used. As quietly as he could, he moved down the stairs and out the front door, which he found already ajar. The knowledge made his heart race even more.

The night was cool despite the spring season. It was almost a full moon, which he was thankful for. He wanted to see every inch of Iris. As he looked away from the moon, he saw a dark figure in the shadow of the house.

She stepped out into the open. His breath caught in his throat at how the moonlight seemed to almost lovingly caress her fair skin. *How could a dream ever compare to reality?*

He reached for her, and without a word, he took her hand. Garrett led them to the top of the barn where a small loft that held hay for the winter season was located. Due to summer's approach, it was almost empty.

Walking to the end of the barn that overlooked the woods, he opened two large wood panels that helped with ventilation and bringing in hay. He went over to the loose stacks of hay and swiftly moved a pile to the center of the room where the moonlight was best.

Iris watched his movements and grinned at how fast he was moving and how apparent his need was. After the hay was moved, he laid a blanket over the top, which she hadn't seen him bring. Turning to her, he smiled, motioning her to come closer.

She took a light hold of the tie that held his robe closed and pulled, letting it fall to the floor just as her dress had in the dream. It was her turn now to study him. Iris intended to start at his ankles and go up from there, but it was hard to get past the hardness of his erection.

The moonlight set his skin aglow, highlighting his muscular body as if he were a bronze god that had come to earth for her. He lifted her up and placed her on the bed of hay he had made. All she could do was watch him as he kissed her leg, moving up to her inner thigh, lifting her nightdress. Tugging it slowly above her head. He then brushed her cheek with the back of his hand.

"I love you, Iris," he whispered in between kisses. Garrett gave her pleasure she never knew existed until he had touched her, setting her body ablaze.

He reached where he had left off in the dream. Kissing, licking, teasing. She couldn't wait any longer. She reached down and guided him in, yearning to have him in her, to have them connected.

They moaned in unison when they joined together. Iris raked her nails across his back, making him grind harder. She grabbed him tight and wrapped her legs around him, pushing him further.

Iris arched and desperately held back the scream that tried to escape. No longer able to hold back, they came together, panting and sweating.

They lay in each other's arms. The moon shifted out of view, casting dark shadows around them. Neither of them spoke, not wanting this night to end.

Tomorrow, Iris would head straight to her nightmare, and Garrett would have to willingly let her go. She was scared of losing him and everyone she loved. If this didn't work, Rune would kill them all.

The day finally arrived for the plan to be set in action. For Iris to be thrown into the eye of the storm. She packed up the dresses Alvera brought her, knowing Rune would provide anything else she needed. If he believed her, that is. Iris didn't want to say farewell to everyone, so she ended up hugging them and handing a letter to each in turn.

Garrett walked her to the horse she would use while the others watched from afar. Cole held Isabelle while she cried, both watching on. Micah stood stiff and tightlipped. Aby and Alvy talked in hush tones, glancing over at Iris.

Before she could speak, Garrett hugged her tightly. "While you're there, know that I am always here for you. No matter what happens, no matter what you do or what is done to you, we are connected, and that connection will never break. I love you, Iris." He leaned in and kissed her softly.

Kissing him back, they had to tame their passion as it built. "I love you, too, Garrett. I will put an end to all of this soon." She swiftly hugged him back and then just as quick, she jumped on her horse and headed down the road, not looking back at what she left behind. She hoped there was truly an end to all of this, and a happy one at that.

Chapter 25

Iris rode out of town and down a long-abandoned road. Several days passed with her stopping only at night to rest. She did not dream and her mind had time to wander. *Has Rune been watching me? Does he know the plan? Did his men warn him of what I set out to do? Would all of this be for naught? Would he kill all the ones I love, despite my efforts?*

Gloom shrouded her like a heavy cloak. Iris had known where Rune was for a while, solely to be able to avoid the area. It took her nearly four days to reach a summit that overlooked an old plantation. Those were four very long days where her mind was filled with dread and thoughts of what torture he had laid in store for her.

To the untrained eye, the area looked uninhibited. But Iris saw signs of Rune's goons busy at work receiving and distributing illegal goods. Three lines of large magnolia trees hid a lot of their movements. Two large barns stood to one side and a larger building sat on the other end of the trees. In the middle stood a two-story house with a wraparound porch. It had once been white but had been stained over time. Men dressed in the same color as the house stood guard at each corner. She watched their movements, noticing how often they changed positions and how far each one patrolled.

Iris hardened herself, pushing down the gentleness Garrett and the others brought out in her. She would have to turn back into the person she was before. The one who killed without a second thought. She would become the Iris Rune had been wanting for so long.

She made her way down the narrow winding road to the plantation. The men soon saw her, and as she expected, they knew her. Their leader had a pocket-sized portrait of her that he pointed out to each of them so they would be on the lookout for her everywhere they went. She wondered if he had a larger version in his house. She imagined it hanging above a fireplace and cringed.

The men pointed their guns at her, but no finger was on the trigger. None of them had any intention of hurting her. That privilege belonged to Rune, which made her stomach churn. Two goons took her toward the house while others took her bags to be searched and her horse to be put in the stables.

Will this be the beginning of my end? she thought as they neared. Iris had never felt so sick in her life, not even the other times she had faced him. Because she went willingly this time, she had to act like he wanted and had everything to lose.

Stepping forward, she saw a familiar figure standing on the stairs leading from the yard to the porch. He wore a large grin as if he had just won a long war, which meant her deception had already begun to work. His dusty brown hair and gray eyes brought back buried memories she wished would remain repressed. The heat of the day made her realize it was hotter here, reminding her it was days from turning summer.

Rune's features and muscular physique made him handsome to a lot of ladies. But he had little time to play with any woman who might have any interest and would much rather spend his hours finding ways to find her or expand his holdings.

He cleared his throat. "I see you have come to me. I must say, I am a little surprised it took you so long. My men told me how you threated them, and I thought you may be close to breaking. So, I ordered them to stay their distance. It seemed my plans for you have worked for once. But there's only one true way to find out." He stepped down and held his hand out to her. She took it lightly, sheepishly. Rune's smile widened in smug satisfaction.

All she could do now was hope the deception would work and she might have her happy ending soon.

Rune came to her early in the morning. He crawled into her bed, waking her from her fitful sleep. Iris stiffened at the awareness, and even more so as his cold hands that touched her.

"Why so stiff?" His gray stormy eyes studied her, watching to see if she was really his.

Trying to loosen her ever cringing body, she sighed. "Your hands are so cold, despite the warmth of the day." *Remember why you're here, you like him. You are in love with Rune...* Swallowing hard, she gave him a sweet smile, which seemed to ease the oncoming storm that had begun to rise within him.

"Why do you think I came in here? For you to warm me." Rune lifted her nightgown, wrapping his arms around her waist and resting his head on her breasts. "Your heart is racing."

That was true, but not for the reasons he thought. "I haven't been this close to you in so long. I'm nervous and..."

"Excited," he finished, lifting his head to rest his chin on her sternum, applying pressure, making her wince in pain. He liked that, the monster...

Moving his arms out from around her, he grabbed her wrists, placing them above her head. He then straddled her, grabbed her chin with the other hand while the other held her hands tight. She knew he wanted to leave bruises to look at later on.

"I'm still skeptical." Rune leaned down, kissing her roughly, but she did not push away. She let him and tried to kiss him back. Without warning, he lifted and hit her across the face with the back of the hand.

And for some reason, she couldn't stop the tears that sprang to her eyes and hoped the waterworks would work to her advantage in some way. Iris hated his touch and wanted more than anything for it to be Garrett and only him. She wanted to chop off his hands, right here, right now. And why couldn't she? Why in all creation did she have to come up with such a long drawn out plan? How was she supposed to make it through the next few weeks and months if she couldn't even last the first day?

Eyeing her tearful face, he leaned down and kissed her even harder than before. She let out a moan, hoping he would like it. She hated herself in that moment, hated that this was happening. But to her surprise, he stopped, and she felt his breath against her ear.

"I will take us a little further each day... I love the buildup... The wait... The enticement. I want you as hungry as I am. And there's also something I want you to go through before we completely become one." He licked her ear, then kissed her neck.

So, Rune intended to do this to her every day, increasing his advancements. For how long? How long would she have to endure yet another type of torture? She tried her best to crawl in the depths of her mind, to hide from reality. All of this was too much, too close, too personal.

The next few days, Rune had seamstresses come to make a whole new wardrobe for her. He liked the skirt with pants she wore, but for him, it didn't show enough skin. Rune also sent off for jewelry and hairpins. It seemed he was true to his word. Once she came to him and gave in, he would treat her like a princess. But for how long?

Thankfully, much to her relief, Rune visited her room every other day, and not every day. He said he hoped it would make her want him more...

About two weeks after first stepping onto the plantation, Rune requested a walk around the grounds with her. The maids set out an outfit he had picked for the occasion. An off-the-shoulder spring dress. The maids pulled her hair into loose ringlets atop her head, a couple pieces left to delicately brush her bare shoulders.

"You must be excited to get out of this room, miss," the maid said sweetly.

"Yes, some fresh air will be nice." Iris felt sorry for the poor girl and didn't want to think about what she might be going through.

"It has been quite stuffy in here, with all the doors to the porch closed. And you have such lovely views of the magnolias." The maid was right. There were three doors that could be opened to the second level porch that overlooked the lands. But guards were placed at each one, and she was locked in. Rune had kept her in tight ever since she had arrived.

After the final touches, Iris stepped out onto the porch and saw Rune in a dark brown suit that matched his hair. He wordlessly extended his arm, and she took it. He led her around the estate. She tried her best to act shy and infatuated by him.

"So, now that you have settled in, I wanted to ask you a question. Well, several questions." She nodded for him to go on. "Why is it that you went and killed so many of my men? And some of my best men at that." That's right. When he came to her room, he hardly talked to her...

She shrugged, but that wasn't the response he wanted. Rune turned and tightly grabbed her arm, pulling her close to him. His glare sent flashes of past torture sessions racing through her mind. He wanted answers, and when she didn't give him any, he took her by the shoulders and shook her.

Iris looked away, tearing up. "Because I felt as if I were going mad," she whispered. "I couldn't kill you. I wouldn't..." She paused, trying to show emotions that were mostly true. She did want to kill him and couldn't. So, Iris did the next best thing. She had killed his men. Faking a sob, Iris said, "But something in me snapped. I knew these men were near you when I wasn't. It wasn't until later that I realized why." Iris then shyly looked away, waiting to see what he would do.

"What was the reasoning?" he asked lowly, obviously fighting back a smile. She wanted to smack him for it.

"That I was jealous of them being close to you. They were receiving orders and talking to you where I was not." Iris fought down ever urge to plunge a knife into his chest, and she hated knives.

"Yet you stayed away for quite some time and have only recently returned to me." Rune eyed her. "Did you stay so long because of the doctor?"

"I realized how I really felt when I saw him again. I was confused after leaving you. It took a while to figure things out." Even though the words were true, would Rune see through her act? She needed to push all other things out of her mind and believe the lie herself. That was the only way this would work. There was no turning back from here. She had to go all in.

Putting her hand on Rune's chest, she sighed. "I haven't felt at peace in a long time. For some reason, being here…" *Makes me want to crawl into a deep hole, even if it means being buried alive. Just to get away from you…*

Rune lifted her chin, making her look at him. "Being here does what?" He leaned close to her.

Iris sweetly smiled. "Being here brings me clarity. I can finally be with you. We can be together. We can be a normal couple." She locked eyes with him unflinchingly. "I think fighting back all these feelings for so long has made coming to you that much more bittersweet."

He laughed, his eyes lighting up. "We're anything but normal, my dear." Leaning in, he softly kissed her.

But this kiss was different. He had never kissed her like this before. It was kind. As Rune pulled away, she nodded. "True, we've never been the normal type."

"What is even normal? The meaning changes within each person's mind. So, there really is no such thing as normal." Wrapping his arms around her, hugging her tight, he sighed. "I feel like I'm dreaming. I didn't think this would ever happen. I thought this game we play would be played until one of us died."

But as she hugged him lightly back, she felt the icy layers within. Despite his smile and warm hug, there was no true emotion behind it, at least not any loving emotion.

Their embrace was cut short when one of the goons came up to him and bowed his head. "I'm sorry to interrupt, sir," he said tentatively.

"Get on with it," Rune growled, eyeing his man.

"The package you've been awaiting has arrived."

"And two days late at that." He clenched his fists, but then a bright smile came to his face. "Come."

She took his outstretched hand; he took her to an old building she hadn't seen when she surveyed the area because it was tucked into a patch of trees. A pungent smell came from the building, and Iris instantly knew what was going to be inside. This was a test for her. She'd have to prove herself.

Stepping through the door into a dark, dank one-room building, flashes of the past crashed into Iris, not only of her own torment but of what she had done to others without regret or a second thought. As the sight in front of her came into view, she knew her past would come back to haunt her.

Rune went up to a man who was hanging from a rafter, much like she had been when Garrett had found her. This man was older, and by the looks of him a fisherman, his upper body muscles giving it away. He had a full beard that was as white as the hair on his head, but despite the whitening of hair, he didn't look much older than Micah. The man was bloody, but his injuries were not so severe that he would die.

Several men stood around the fisherman. One man held a bat embedded with nails. Rune took it from him. He looked to his men. Pointing the bat at each one of them, his eyes shifted. His expression darkened. The Rune she knew, the one who made her life a living hell, was now in the room, and he was angry.

"Tell me why it took five of you almost a month to find this old man." He tapped the bat against the ground. One of the men flinched at the sound.

That man had just made the biggest mistake of his life. Right after the man cringed, he was down on the ground, head bloody from where Rune had hit him with the bat. "I've told you all time and time again, do not show your weakness to anyone, including me, because I will take advantage of it each and every time." He turned to the man hanging nearby, lifting his chin with the end of the bat, now stained with blood. "Everyone out! All but Iris." The men hesitated. "I said leave!" Rune yelled in a deep tone, making them scurry away.

He looked at the helpless man then back to Iris with an evil smile that sent shivers down her spine, but she knew better than to show it. After a few moments, Rune laughed. "I have to say, the two of you look nothing alike."

Iris' blood turned cold, and her mouth went dry, but before she could speak, the old man rasped, "I've told your men I don't have a daughter. Never have."

"Come, come. I've been watching you almost as long as I have your daughter. When I became fond of her, I wanted to know about her past. And all trails lead to you."

The old man laughed roughly. "I would know if I had a kid. I'm telling you again, I don't have a daughter."

Rune jabbed the man in the stomach. The man flinched, but he tried hard not to show his pain, not wanting to give Rune the satisfaction or ammunition. "You think you are the only man who fathered a child and doesn't know it? But no... You knew it, you know it. From the information I gathered, you took care of her until she was two. But when her mother died, you couldn't take care of a child yourself, so you dropped her off at the nearest orphanage you could, thinking she was young and cute and would get adopted. But you were wrong."

Rune's grip tightened on the bat, his eyes narrowing dangerously. He sank into the deepest darkest version of himself. Her eyes widened as she thought, *He is mad I was abandoned? No... He's mad I have the life I do. Could he also be angry that I met him?*

He hit the man in the side with the bat and yanked the man's head back, making him look at him. The fisherman's white hair was now red with his own blood. "As I was saying, you were wrong. She was never adopted and had to fend for herself. Think clearly now... Do you really not have a daughter?" he said, elongating his words.

"I don't...." the man grunted.

"Wrong answer!" Rune lifted the bat, hitting the man in the stomach. He then turned to Iris who had been standing by quietly watching, knowing that was what Rune would want. "Come, Iris. Meet your father. The one who left you in that hole called an orphanage home." He extended his hand for her to take. "Here is the father that left you all alone, abandoned."

Rune was wanting a reaction. But to play this game, she had to be as honest as she could be. Instead of taking his hand, she lightly touched Rune's shoulder, softly saying, "I admit, I was sad when I was younger, but as I grew, I learned that all I really needed was myself. Yes, it would have been nice to have a family. But to me..."

Rune eyed her. "But to you, anyone close to you only became a distraction from your own goals."

She beamed a smile at him. "Quite right. A father wasn't something I ever really missed, and I hope I became a better person without him."

Laughter filled the room as Rune wrapped his arm around her. "I think you turned out perfect." He turned to the old man once again. "Any last words?"

The man glared at him and spat in Rune's face. "You're insane."

Smiling deviously, wiping his face, Rune whispered, "Why, yes... Yes, I am. Thank you for noticing. Now, Iris, would you like to join in on the fun?" He extended the bat for her to take, which she didn't. "Or would you rather wait until the last course and serve your just deserts?"

Iris put on her best smile. "Dessert is my favorite part of the meal. Should I stay and watch the feast?"

Runes eye's widened at her play on words. Dropping the bat, he grabbed her in his arms and kissing her face and lips repeatedly then came in for one long kiss, exploring her mouth with his tongue. Coming up for air, he whispered in her ear, "You have no idea how happy I am that you finally came to me." She pushed away the feelings that crept forward, the ones that wanted to scream out in protest. Iris had to be who she was before, someone who only cared about the next kill, the hunter.

Touching his cheek, Iris found it easy to smile at him. "We don't have to be alone anymore. We understand one another. So, what is it that you wish for me to do?"

"I have to admit, I do like to have an audience. And it would only be right to watch the man who was the cause of your suffering to suffer in return." Rune looked around, quickly finding a chair. He sat it several feet away from her father. "I don't want to ruin that nice new dress of yours. It fits you quite perfectly."

The dress hugged her in all the right places. A tight corset pushed up her breasts, putting them on full display. The middle hugged her tight, flowing around her hips and bringing out her hourglass figure.

He bit his lip hungrily. "I think I might have another idea for dessert." Smiling, Rune led her to the chair.

A nearby table held an assortment of tools laid out. Rune skimmed the tools, and Iris came to a realization. He had been doing all of this to her not just to break her but to make her like him. Rune had been wanting someone like himself, so he would no longer feel alone. *Why hadn't I seen this before? It's so obvious now. He wanted a true partner, someone just like himself, someone who understands him.* But the terrifying truth was, she did understand him. She had killed needlessly and had become her own judge, jury and executioner.

Iris had turned into what she hunted. *I've become an outlaw.* That thought made her blood run cold. But the thought that came next froze her to the core and made all other thoughts retreat into the depths of her mind. *I've become the monster Rune had always wanted... I am no better than him. And I must meet the same fate as him.*

Chapter 26

Alvera made her way into a small town called Wrackterville, the closest one to where Rune's hideout was located. She thought the name was fitting since it lay so close to that madman. Sitting in the darkest corner she could find, she eyed the door, waiting for her target. Soon, a cloaked man came in and walked toward her. Swiftly sitting down, he tilted his hat so no one could see his face.

"Do you have information for me?"

She slid a parchment to him. "Things are set in motion. What we have been working for will soon come to pass."

"No one knows of our involvement?" The man asked in a gruff voice.

"No one. As long as things go as planned, everything will end. Shortly, we will all be free."

The cloaked man left. She sat there finishing her coffee, a smile on her face.

The plans were set in place, more than one plan if she were honest. Now all she had to do was wait. She stood and went over to a table tucked into another dark corner. One reason she picked this place, lots of shady places to hide. Sitting down, Alvera whispered, "It's in motion, Father."

"Good job, my dear. Hopefully, this will shift the attention of the marshals onto Iris and Rune. I suggest you prepare to disappear." He slid a small packet to her. "This should set you up with a new life."

"What of the agency?" She took the packet, holding it tightly in her hands as if it were her lifeline.

"They shouldn't be a threat when they're all six feet under."

Iris just sat there, listing to the screams of the man Rune said was her father. She stared at Rune as he mangled this innocent man in front of her. But Iris did not see. Her eyes were vacant, looking past everything in front of her.

She knew that if this man truly was her father, she should feel something. Maybe remorse. Maybe try to save him or at the very least end him quickly. Nevertheless, in that moment, she felt nothing. She even tried to think of Garrett, his golden eyes, the sun touching his skin on a warm summer day, but those thoughts brought nothing to the surface. And that in itself scared her.

Rune's voice brought her back to the dark damp room that now smelled of fresh blood and piss. "Iris…. Iris!" He stepped toward her, blood dripping from his hands and arms.

She shook her head, bringing herself out of the daze she had put herself in. "How may I help?" The smile on her face came too effortlessly.

"Would you like to finish up?" He held a knife for her to take.

Flashes of what choices she had entered her mind. One, take the knife and plunge it into Rune's chest just like she had wanted to earlier. Two, put the man out of his misery. Three, turn it on herself.

But as she took the knife from Rune, she remembered why she hated the things so much. It made killing too personal, too intimate.

As Iris cut the man's stomach open in one smooth swipe of the blade, she knew she was past saving. She cut more and even used her hands, severing skin and muscle and tendons. The man's, her father's, entrails hit the floor with a wet splat, blood spattering on her shoes and dress.

She wondered if Rune had any idea of the monster he had just made, and that monsters often turned on their masters.

Iris and Rune watched as the life left the man's body. Just as he took his last breath, Rune took her in his arms and kissed her. He fisted her hair, yanking her closer. She smelled blood on him. He smeared it everywhere he touched, in her hair, on her skin. His erection jutted against her stomach, further proving how sick he was. If she didn't stop him, it would go past the point she wanted. But Iris didn't care anymore.

She knew how this was all going to end: with both of them dead. It had to.

But the thought of betraying Garrett on such a deep level hurt. Tears dripped down her cheeks. Noticing, Rune pulled away and studied her.

She wiped at her face, streaking blood down her cheeks. "I... I don't understand..." Her words were true. The intense feelings she had moments before were gone within a split second. And now, she stood there feeling nothing, blankly staring at Rune.

What came next surprised her. He smiled, genuinely smiled. "Those are tears of happiness, aren't they?" He cupped her cheeks. "You have your revenge." Rune hugged her tightly.

Revenge on a man she never knew? No... the one she wanted revenge on was the one with his arms wrapped around her.

Lying in a red-tinted bathwater, Iris mulled over the events of earlier. Had she really just killed her own father? It's not that she hadn't killed before… But this time, it was different, more personal. Most of the time, when she had taken a life, her life or someone else's was in danger. He couldn't even defend himself and fight back. This time, this was murder, plain and simple.

She sank into the water, covering her head. *I can never face Garrett or the others again. I need to send a message somehow to tell them that the mission is to be abandoned. That I am to be abandoned.*

After she washed up, Iris found a lovely red lace gown laying out for her. A maid helped her with her hair, putting her hair in ringlets atop her head with pins adorned with roses. Iris was in such a daze that when the maid spoke, she only responded with nods or grunts, not even hearing what the poor girl said. Not even caring she was in a dress made of all lace, which she hated.

Walking into the dining room, a lovely scene sat before her. Candles were lit, and light purple iris adorned the room, creating a pit in her stomach. The air was filled with their sweet scent, which made her cringe all the more. It all reminded her of the dream she shared with Garrett, and that was the last thing she wanted to remember right now. *At least the flowers are a different color...* A lighter hue of purple.

Rune pulled out a chair for Iris to take. Sitting down, she looked at the meal before her. It looked like something she had never seen before. Was that rice? Something she had only had once, long ago. And the sauce on top was orange with hints of red. *What is this?*

"It's a meal I learned on one of my excursions across the ocean to the far east." Rune motioned for her to try it. "I did change some of the ingredients to fit my own wants and needs. I warn you, it's spicy. It's nothing you can't handle, I'm sure."

Iris remembered a time she had eaten with him many years ago. If you did not eat what he provided, he forced it down your throat. So, no matter how bad something tasted, how hot something was, you ate it or choked trying.

The meal Rune had made was extremely spicy, so much so it made her sweat. But by the intense look he gave her from across the table, she knew she had to eat it all. Iris tried to figure out the ingredients, but soon, incoherent thoughts took over.

Looking around, Iris tried to focus on something, anything, but lines blurred. Iris tried to stand but sat back down when she saw movement from the corner of her eye.

Rune came into view, kneeling in front of her. "I've given you my own concoction. It will make you face your past fears head-on. It will feel real. You will feel like you're going insane."

"You shit..." Iris glared at him best as she could, sweat still running down her face. Her mouth was dry and hot from the food.

Rune laughed. "Let me know your thoughts after you get through this night. Trust me when I say it's worth it. Our past makes us what we are. But we must face our fears and let them guide us. You burying yours as you do will only drag us both down." He stood and looked to his men. "Take her to the barn. Keep an eye on her. Make sure she doesn't hurt herself."

The form of Rune stood on the pouch, watching. She reached out to him as his men dragged her through the yard. Her head swam as she was shuffled into a vacant barn. Light from the late afternoon sun gave little light, so a few oil lamps gave the barn more of an eerie look and cast more shadows than light. Iris sank to her knees and took in her surroundings, the heat from the meal still lingering.

"What was in that stuff?" Iris asked no one in particular. *What was he talking about? Face fears?* But as she said the word fear, the shadows around her seemed to grow. She hugged herself, eyes darting, unable to focus on one spot.

"Seems to have had several ingredients." Iris twisted around, looking at all the dark corners and lighted circles.

"Who's there?" She stumbled back, leaning on her elbows.

A figure stepped out from the shadows, a ragged older man who was dragging his left leg. Iris' eyes widened at the sight of her first kill.

"Oh, don't give me that look." He watched her. "You've grown so much since I last saw you."

"You're dead... Long dead..."

"Don't I know it. I can still feel that knife plunge into my chest. Isn't that why you hate knives so much?" The man moved closer to Iris.

She instinctively crawled backward. "Don't act like you know me. You preyed on children."

"And for that you killed me."

"I feel no regret for that. I'm not the evil one here."

"Yet, here I am. And there you are, crawling on the ground."

Iris stood up, still unsteady on her feet. Before she could say anything else, the figure rushed at her. It hit her body, and she fell to the floor with a thud.

In the next heartbeat, she was twelve again, back in the orphanage. She was walking the dirty dark halls when she heard soft whimpering. Following the sound led Iris to a closet. Hesitantly opening the door, she found an eight-year-old girl. Iris didn't know her very well, but she tried to look after all the younger ones.

Squatting down to the girl's level, Iris squeezed in next to her. "Mary, right?" The girl nodded. "Do you want to talk about what's got you upset? You can tell me."

"You're Iris, right?" The girl sniffed, rubbing her snot onto her sleeve. "I've heard about you. You've helped others." She sniffed again.

"Yes, yes I have. Would you like to tell me?" Iris smiled sweetly at Mary.

Mary told Iris of what the new groundskeeper had done when he had found her during a game of hide-and-seek. "He… He kept me behind the bushes… Put his hand on my mouth…" She sobbed as Iris held her. "Ripped my new dress… Hurt me… Between legs…" The poor girl probably didn't even know what had happened to her, which made her angry beyond reason.

Iris knew she had to do something before anyone else got hurt. After taking Mary to the older girls who could help her, Iris let her rage lead her to the kitchen. They were closed for the night, but Iris knew where the knives were locked up at and how to get them. For once, she was glad of the caretaker's shitty job. Her hand shook as she reached for the carving knife, the largest one she could find. She shook not from fear but from the anger building inside her.

The night was quiet and still. Even the crickets were weary that night. The moon was high in the sky when Iris started toward the shed the gardener slept in. It leaned against a tree, the only reason the shack was still standing. Iris quietly made her way across the yard and knelt next to the shed with the side of the tree. There were two loose boards, making for easy entry; she knew the door would have made too much noise.

Moving the panels, she made her way in. It was dark and hard to see. The air was rank with the smell of liquor. Eyeing the bed, Iris made her way closer and caught sight of the man's sleeping form. Not on the bed but on the mat next to it. He had apparently passed out right before he had made it to the bed. His chest rhythmically rose and fell with each breath.

Thinking of how easy he could sleep made her move forward to stand over the man's sleeping form. If she did this, there was no turning back. Her life would change forever. But she couldn't leave this man here to do as he pleased. Authorities and people never cared about any of them at the orphanage. No, she had to do this to at least save them from one predator. No one else cared, no one else would stand up against people like him. She had to do this to save them all or remain a victim herself.

Raising the knife, she swiftly plugged it into the man's chest several times in quick succession. He jerked upright with a gurgle, coughing up blood, kicking, grabbing at her. His hands desperately tried to fend her off, but the damage had already been done.

As she stood over him, his blood dripping from her hands, she decided to do more than just be a bully to the bullies. She would seek out those who hurt others, those who killed and split apart people's lives. She would take control of her own life, her own destiny. Iris would become her own hero.

Iris' vision faded and reality came crashing back to her. Frantically looking around, she saw empty stables, hay mounds, and lanterns. She was still in Rune's barn. Standing, her head throbbed, and the room blurred. Then figures once again closed in on her. Hands reached forward, bloody, rotten flesh peeling away from bone. As the faces of all the people she'd killed came into focus, her heart pounded in her chest so hard it hurt. But just as everything was closing in on her, the figures parted, making way for a new form.

This new face came into view, and her tension eased slightly. Was she safe? Garrett took her in his arms. "You are safe now, it's all over. I am here now," he whispered.

"Are you real?" She couldn't believe her eyes. Why did he come?

"I am real. You're safe." He leaned down, taking her lips with his.

But when he straightened, Iris' heart dropped to her feet. Rune, not Garrett, stood before her.

This nightmare was far from over.

Chapter 27

Iris had hardly dreamed since arriving at Rune's and had not connected with Garrett. But with help of a sleeping potion Rune had given her after her hallucinations, she fell into a deep sleep. One usually didn't dream when this deeply unconsciousness, but there she sat, in the kitchen of Garrett's house.

Her thoughts still felt heavy, which meant this must be his dream. She couldn't face him like this, not in the state she had just been in. Despite this being a dream, and Garrett's at that, she felt reality seeping into it. Her body felt heavy, her brain muddled. Iris hoped she looked better than she felt, but then Garrett walked down the stairs, and the look on his face let her know she looked as bad as she felt.

Before she could stand to greet him, he was standing in front of her, staring, clearly at a loss for words. Her eyes glided down to see his clenched fist. Iris wanted to say something, anything, but what could she say? That all of the planning wasn't going to end the way he had hoped? That she wouldn't be coming back to him?

Iris lowered her head in defeat, not wanting to meet his gaze. He knelt in front of her. "What happened? What did he do?" He lifted her chin, trying to get her to look at him.

All the thoughts and visions came rushing back to her, making her want to vomit. "I will end it all soon," was all she could say.

He glared at her. "You... You will end it? He's your stalker and he has done unspeakable things to you in the past, but Iris, you are no longer alone in this fight. Cole, Micah and I are only a day and a half's ride from Rune's compound. Micah overheard Alvera plotting to have the marshals come in and kill not just Rune and his goons but you as well. We don't have the manpower to take all of them on, but we will get you out of there, hopefully before the marshals or anyone else shows up."

Iris cut him off. "Alvera has turned against us?" *Something isn't right...* It hurt to think. "Don't come, Garrett. Let the marshal's men come. They might be able to take out the rest of Rune's men and even Rune himself. With the state I'm in, I can't do anything." She hated to admit it.

"How can you say that? They'll kill you as well, Iris. Don't you understand that?" He grabbed her hands in his, trying to get her to look at him.

She finally locked eyes with him and let him see the inner turmoil tearing her apart. "I know, Garrett. That's what I want. I've killed so many people in what I thought was the name of justice. But I never truly had the right. I'm just as bad as Rune. I'm a murder."

"Don't say that."

"I am... You don't know all the things I've done. Garrett, listen to me. Whatever he gave me, I don't know what I'll see when I wake up. I can't tell the difference between what's real or a hallucination. I don't know if it will wear off or if it's permanent. Coming here will only get us all killed."

Garrett stood up in frustration. "That bastard, I'm going to kill him."

"Listen. Don't come, it's suicide." Iris felt herself being pulled away. Someone was trying to wake her. "Garrett, I love you."

And with that, she felt someone shaking her in real life. Opening her eyes, bright light flooded in, making her retch up what little was in her stomach. Her body felt heavy and her head pounded. Someone was trying to talk to her, but all she could hear was muffled voices. When she tried to look around and make out the faces surrounding her, it only made her head worse.

She had never felt that kind of pain before. It pierced right through her and blocked out all else, making pain the only thing present. Someone tried to move her, and sharp agony set every nerve aflame. The darkness that swept over her was her only relief.

Garrett jerked upright, eyes wide, heart racing. Images of Iris flooded his mind. Dark circles under sunken eyes. Pale skin with a tinge of purple. He gritted his teeth in anger. Rune had driven Iris to the edge of madness again, as if once wasn't enough. He stood quickly and woke the others in the makeshift camp.

"Hurry, we must get to Rune's compound. Iris is in more trouble than we thought." He immediately went about packing up his stuff.

Cole yawned, only half hearing what Garrett said. "What?"

"What kind of trouble?" Micah asked, his voice gruff with sleep.

Grunting in frustration, he kicked the ground. "Rune has messed with Iris' mind again. She doesn't have a hold on reality."

"How do you know?" Cole asked, rubbing the sleep from his eyes, moving slowly, not yet grasping the full situation.

"We don't have time to talk about that now." Garrett packed his horse and then helped the others.

"Come, now. How can you know?"

Garrett glared at Cole. "I'll tell you along the way if you move faster."

Once they were on the road, Garrett explained to Cole and Micah that Iris and his dreams had somehow connected, "After Iris was stabbed, we found out that our dreams connected. We can't connect to each other if we're too far apart and can push each other out if we try. We've never really found out why we're connected. I've heard old tales of my mother's people being able to walk into other's dreams, but it was quite rare. I'm certain this is the same thing."

"Am I hearing you correctly? When you and Iris dream, each of yours intertwin with the other?" Micah stared at him wide-eyed, as if he had found out fool's gold was actual real gold the whole time.

"Yes, but we can't control when we step into the other's dreams. We don't even know how or why. Neither of us has had anything like this happen before."

"And in these dreams of yours, can you control your actions and words?" Cole asked, just as giddy as Micah, if not more. "Isabelle is going to love this."

"Yes, and sometimes the surroundings as well."

Cole laughed. "I can only imagine. I wonder if Isabelle and I can connect in such a way. Oh, what fun we would have." His gaze went distant, as if he were pondering all the things he could do in such dreams. But he also moved his horse faster, showing he wanted to reach Iris just as soon as the others did.

Micah moved his horse closer to Garrett. "What did Rune do to Iris? How bad off is she?"

Garrett sighed heavily, his shoulders slumping at the thought of Iris and what she could be going through at that moment. "It seems Rune has made it so that she can't tell what's real or what's in her mind. She told me to not come, that it would be suicide." He sat up straight, resolved to his mission. "I want Iris to see she is no longer alone. That she doesn't have to do everything by herself."

Micah reached out and patted Garrett on the shoulder. "I agree. She is no longer alone. And who best to show her than her friends?"

Opening her eyes to the fading light of the day, her head pounded as she stood. Iris made her way downstairs. Everything was a blur, and what was in focus scared her.

The people she had killed in the past came in and out of view as she made her way from her room to the porch downstairs. Looking out onto the yard, she saw what looked like

Rune's figure at the edge. Iris didn't know why she made her way to him, but she found herself walking to him regardless.

But when she got to Rune's side, he was not alone. The other person made Iris question if what she was seeing was real or remnants of what Rune gave her. The girl in front of her watched her with gray eyes similar to Rune's.

"Rune! What did you give her? Don't tell me." The lady glared at him then turned a sympathetic gaze on her. "You should have known not to give her your concoction. Giving that to someone who has been through what she has is never a good idea."

"Why are you even here, sister?" Rune folded his arms. It was the first time Iris had seen Rune act like a normal person. This must all be in her mind.

"I came to tell you that our father has sent..." The woman's eyes went wide.

Iris' vision blurred even more, only picking up fragments of what was going on around her.

"Rune, you selfish ass." Someone picked Iris up. "It's a good thing I came when I did."

"Will you be able to help, Alvera?" Rune's voice was hushed.

"Yes, but it's not going to be pleasant for anyone. And if you backstab me." Alvera's voice was sharp as it faded. Iris felt her body settle on a hard surface.

"Why is it that you're here anyway? I haven't seen you in years. And now, of all days, you appear. You've always shown up before something major happens in my life. It's as if fate follows you to me," Rune hissed.

"Fate will do what it will to you, with or without me. The reason I came is to warn you that our father has sent his head assassins to kill you and Iris. Anyone who can be used against him, which is the whole agency, is to be killed before the marshals can round them up."

"But that won't be happening, will it?" Rune's voice held a hint of excitement to it.

"Correct, bother. Despite me being near our father, I used his plans against him. He sent the marshals here, but instead, they are in route to him. When he found out, he sent his assassins. I knew he would do this and warned everyone."

"I thought you loved him... I used him for my own means. But I thought you were different." Iris had trouble making out Rune's voice. Other muffled voices filled her mind, each voice feeling as if it were clawing at her mind, trying to break free.

413

Alvera laughed. "After all he did to you? I might love him in some form, but I couldn't stand by and let him kill innocent people. Good people. I turned a blind eye to him, working with you. I will no longer do so. After I help Iris, I wash my hands of you both. I wish our lives could have turned out differently, but fate had other plans. Now, hold her down. This is going to be rough. To bring her back from the edge of insanity, I must first push her off the ledge."

Alvera placed her hands on Iris' head, and within seconds, searing pain coursed through Iris.

"And brother, dear, there's someone you might want to worry about more than assassins."

Garrett, Cole and Micah rode throughout the day, only stopping for a few moments to let the horses rest and for them to stretch their own legs. Their plan was to ride past sunset if the moon was bright enough. The three men road toward the setting sun, which was giving its last rays of light to the clouds.

Just as day shifted into night, Garrett gasped, clutching his chest in pain. His head felt heavy all of the sudden. Everything around him blurred, then turned black; pain radiated throughout his body. After the pain eased, he opened his eyes to find himself in a raging storm. He was no longer in the real world. But a dream world? How? He didn't fall asleep.

Taking in his surrounding, he could not place where he was. The land was unfamiliar. He found himself in a field of grass, looking to his left, he saw a creek flowing through the valley below. Beyond that were mountain ranges, where the center of a storm raged. The winds started to pick up where he stood. How did he get here, and what happened to him moments before? As he asked himself these questions, a noise came from behind. Turning swiftly, dark gray eyes met his gaze.

"Alvera. How? Where?" he asked, frowning.

She stared at him intently. "Where has a simple answer, Iris' mind…" Garrett was about to ask another question when she raised her hand, halting him. "As to how, that is more complicated. I am not just a seer, I can also dream-walk. But what I am doing now is quite dangerous and may kill all three of us."

"Then why in the hell do it?" Garrett had to yell over the blustering winds.

"Because now is the time for your light to bring Iris back from the deepest darkness she has yet to face. Rune gave her something that has made her mad. I'm having trouble maintaining my connection. If that happens, you may lose yours as well. I brought you here. That is why it hurt. Most of the time you two connect on your own. But before Iris sinks into madness even more, I had to do this."

"Why should I trust you? You sent the marshals to kill not just Rune but Iris as well and now here you are, saying you're here to help." Garrett clenched his fists, his anger building, not at her betrayal of them but at her betrayal of Abelia.

"I don't expect you to believe me," she said shortly. "And to tell you the truth, I don't really give a shit. Right now, we have to help Iris. Priorities, Garrett."

He grabbed her forearm, squeezing it hard. "I don't trust you," he said lowly.

"And you shouldn't. I don't blame you. So, here's the deal." Alvera breathed in deeply. "I actually sent the marshals to the agency that hired Iris and Cole. The agency had been working with Rune. The captain found out my alternate plan and is now sending his secret force to kill all those with ties to the agency and himself, including Rune, Iris, and Cole. I went to Rune's compound to warn Iris and found her like this. I am now risking my life trying to bring her back from the edge of insanity. Again, I don't give a shit if you believe a fucking word I just said because right now, we need to move to the center of the storm and save the love of your life or die trying. If that's all right with you." She glared at him, daring him to disagree.

Garrett stared into her dark gray eyes, which were nearing the color of the storm. The depths of them held a sense of otherworldly knowledge. Letting go of her arm, he breathed in deeply. Even if she was lying, he couldn't take the gamble, not when Iris' life might be on the line.

"Right, let's move." Alvera started up the steep mountain range.

They headed up a ravine, toward the darkest part of the storm. The winds picked up even more, so much so they could hardly stand.

"You need to know, this dream is different than the others," Alvera yelled over the rushing wind. "Because of what was given to her and all that she has been through, her mind is weak, and she has very little control over it. This is the time where you have to be the light in her darkness. If you aren't able to pull her from this, she will die just as I foresaw. No pressure!"

The two of them moved forward. Their surroundings grew darker as the wind blew without clemency. Garrett had helped Iris through her own darkness several times, but this time was different. And what she had said only made him worry more. If she had given up, this would be harder than ever before. Iris had called herself a murderer. Did she really believe that? He had to reach her, to show her that she was wrong. She was a protector. Fear would not stop him.

He thought about the love he had for Iris, her smile, how she risked her life time and time again, even for strangers. Without a second thought, she put her life on the line for others. No murderer would do that, and he had to remind her.

Reaching the peak of the precipice, a small clearing stood at the highest point. In the center was a horde of people. When Garrett and Alvera got closer, he saw various wounds covering most of the people. One man had a hole in his head, another had an arm missing, and one held his own guts as he walked in a circle. They all seemed to take turns, going in and out of the center. *Is Iris in the middle of that swarm?*

"These must be the people she's killed. Or at least the ones she feels guilty about," Alvera said into Garrett's ear, the winds still whirling around them. But just when she opened her mouth to say more, a vortex picked Alvera up, separating her from Garrett, throwing her down the mountain and out of sight.

The throng of people scattered at the appearance of the vortex, giving Garrett an opportunity to surge toward the center where a lone figure sat, hugging their knees to their chest. The sight of her made his heart ache and his stomach churn. Iris looked much like she had in his dream. She wore a thin nightgown that showed the ever-paling skin underneath. Iris seemed to be trying to sink into herself, her face buried in her knees. She was crying judging by the shaking of her shoulders. If he didn't know better, he would have sworn he was looking at a scared, lost child.

But something changed. She moved, and before Garrett could even blink, the swarm pounced, surrounding her like locusts on a field of wheat.

Chapter 28

Darkness surrounded her. So dark. After what felt like an eternity, the darkness gave way to figures that haunted her dreams. She had long laid them to rest in the recesses of her mind, but they had crept forward when she'd started killing more often to take down Rune's empire. They had only worsened after he gave her his brew. The guilt and pain made her want to crawl out of her own skin.

Iris had no right taking those lives. She should have stayed with Garrett and protected her loved ones, but she had done the opposite. Iris had sought out anyone with a tie to Rune, anyone who had murdered in cold blood, and took their lives in turn.

In the end, she was no better than the people she had killed. She had no right to be happy with Garrett. Iris deserved the same fate as Rune. *You are a murderer, after all,* a small voice told her. *You don't deserve a happy ending. No one could love you, not with all the blood that stains you. It seeps through your very pores.*

Every choice she had made led her here, big or small. She had finally found something good in her life, but the path she was supposed to walk had long been laid out for her. No matter how she tried to divert from this path, it pulled her back every time. The bombardment of her past was endless.

The pain made it hard to breathe in between sobs, making her gasp. Without warning, the shadowy figures attacked, clawing at her, tearing her skin. She laid there, motionless, as they kicked and tore at her. Iris stopped trying to curl up, stopped trying to protect her head. Just laid there, staring at the dark storm clouds above her. Giving in to the attacks, the agony.

I finally had a family. Cole, Micah, Isabelle, Garrett.

Garrett… I was never meant to have that kind of love. I know that now. I was always meant to be right where I am, right now. The only thing I wish I could change is them ever meeting me. I am better knowing them. They were only ever in danger knowing me. I'm sorry I hurt them. They deserve more. They deserve better…

Iris closed her eyes, ready to let go, when she felt weight on top of her. Confused, she opened her eyes to see Garrett staring back at her. He had placed himself on top of her, the mob now thrashing him instead of her. Iris moved her mouth, trying to form words to ask what he was doing, to see if it was even really him, but all she could do was stare in astonishment.

"You don't deserve this, Iris. Yes, you killed people, but you never killed an innocent," what he said was with so much resolve, her stomach churned.

She shook her head. "You don't know that. You can't say such things."

"I do know," he stressed, wincing, "because I know you. Yes, you became your own law, but it was to protect me. All that you did before we met was to defend those who could not do it themselves. To help those who got hurt and could not pick up and fight." He flinched and groaned, then focused his gaze back on Iris. "Then when we met and all of us came together, you wanted to guard us and make sure no harm came to us because that is what you have always done for all the innocent people you meet, Iris."

Garrett cringed, hissing in pain. She tried to push him off, but he wouldn't move. Her heart ached at the sight. "Please. Please, Garrett. You're getting hurt. Don't do this. Don't get hurt for me." His pain was intensifying. She saw it in the way his shoulders tensed, his teeth clenching. "Don't die for me! It's not worth it. I'm not worth it!" she screamed, tears running down her cheeks.

A smile crossed his face, even though the pain still showed. "Iris, I love you. We look out for each other. That's what families do, no matter what. We're a family, Iris. You and me. Cole, Isabelle and Micah. When you first left, I should have gone after you. Never again. No matter where you go, I will follow you, even if it's to the ends of the earth. There is only one person in the world I want, and it will always be you, Iris Evergreen." He leaned down and kissed her.

Her eyes searched his. "How did you know my last name?"

The pain that had been written on his face began to lessen, bringing out a bright smile. "The last name you gave yourself so long ago because you didn't have one?"

"How?" His eyes sparkled all the more in this moment. The storm that had been overhead gave way to the sun. At first, Iris thought the beam of light was from the sun then realized it was actual Garrett shining so brightly.

"It came to my mind, like a memory. And Evergreen is the name I will take when I take you as my wife." He lightly caressed her lips with his, the bright light enveloping them both.

The pain that had consumed Iris faded like it had been nothing more than a dream. When she woke, she was in the room Rune had set up for her. The sun streaming in through the open doors told her that it was midday, making her dress in a hurry.

While dressing, she realized how weak she had grown. The last meal she remembered eating was Rune's brew. Had she eaten anything in the two days since then? Had it been two days? More? Less? Her hands shook as she donned men's pants and a shirt. The shaking only worsened when she reached the buttons.

Just as she laced up her boots, Iris heard gunfire and loud bangs. By the location of the thunder-like booms, she knew it was Rune's hidden bombs that had been triggered. Before she could gather her thoughts, more noises came from outside. Shouts, thuds, then heavy steps ascending the stairs.

In the next instant, her bedroom door swung open. Rune stormed in and grabbed her arms. For a split second, she saw fear. Fear of the assassins or her?

"Good, you're finally awake. We need to leave now. My men should be able to hold them off while we make our escape. I am glad to see you are feeling better, but we must leave now, or we will miss our chance."

The conversation between Rune and Alvera during her delirium came back to her. Her captain had sent assassins to kill not just Rune but her as well. Not marshals as Garrett had said. Alvera and Rune were siblings, and Alvera had come to warn them. What had happened to Alvera? Did she betray them? Was she in league with Rune? Iris' head spun at all the questions.

Rune shook her, bringing her back to reality. "Iris, we're leaving now." He grabbed her wrist and dragged her toward the door.

The sounds of battle only grew. She refused to play into this madness of his anymore. This game of Rune's was going to end now. Iris wrenched her arm from his grasp, making her even more aware of her weakened state.

Rune saw and reached for her other wrist. He pulled her in close, holding her tight. "Do you really think, after all these years, that you will escape me that easily? Your mind may be stronger now, but your body is weaker. You haven't eaten in two days and have been given very little water. I can feel your legs wanting to give way as we stand here." Rune smiled, the twist of his lips pure evil.

"I'm stronger than you know." She stared back into his piercing gaze, and Iris knew no soul lay in the depths of his gray eyes.

His laugh cut through the air. "Quite right. One reason I picked you. I knew I could go toe to toe with you. Well, at least to a point. We have reached that point. Now, will I have to throw you over my shoulder, or will you come willingly?"

"I'm not coming." He still held her against him, but she stood defiant, no matter how weak her body was.

"Now is not the time to be your usual self; both our lives are on the line. We can go around in circles later." Rune huffed and then said through gritted teeth, "You come with me now on your own two feet, or I will knock you unconscious and carry you out."

His eyes dared her to choose the latter. But it seemed like she wouldn't have to choose. Despite her mind finally being free of his potion and dark memories of the past, the lack of food affected her in more than one way.

Iris' vision blackened around the edges. *No, not now... Any time but now...*

Iris heard muffled voices and felt her body being carried. Her eyes fluttered open seconds before her body hit the ground. She groaned at the abrupt awakening. Looking around at the scene before her, things became clear rather quickly.

Assassins had come across Rune as he carried her out. He had dropped her to focus on the assassins. Fighting the men off, he reached for his own gun, still in its holster. The attackers' guns were on the ground, unclear on how or why.

With her body still weak, she looked around for something to protect herself but soon found herself with two assassins of her own, their barrels pointed right at her. As she was about to stand and face them, two shots rang out and the men's bodies fell to the ground.

The sun glimmered behind him, nearly blinding her, but Iris could tell by the scruff on his chin and white hair that it was Micah who had saved her life. The sight of him eased her heart. She did truly have a family. Just as she was about to stand and greet him, another bang filled the air, and Micah's smile left his face.

Time slowed down in that instant, almost as if she were seeing things outside of her body.

Red stained Micah's shirt in a growing bloom. He fell to his knees, then to his back and moved no more, his eyes going vacant. Rune stood behind him holding a gun, a smirk plastered across his face.

Hate radiated through her as she saw his smile and Micah's bloody body lying before him. She stood slowly while Rune just watched as if pleased by her suffering.

"Are you no longer in hurry to leave? You were in such a rush to leave. Now you only seem eager to see me grieve," Iris hissed, trying to distract him while she looked around for anything to be used as a weapon. She didn't care if he still held a gun.

I'm going to rip his fucking eyes out if I have to. This ends here and now.

"But grief is so becoming on you." He winked at her.

She couldn't believe the bastard just winked at her. Rune had just killed her friend, and he had the gall to wink at her. Iris clenched her fist and glared at him, finally eyeing what she had been looking for. She walked toward him to get herself closer to the end goal.

"You have been my tormentor, torturer, the dark shadow that was never far behind. The voice in the back of my mind. I will now be the raging storm that turns the tide. You will no longer be by my side or in my mind. Today is the day you die!" Iris dove for a nearby dagger an assassin had dropped earlier in the fight with Rune.

Rune laughed and aimed the gun at her, but he didn't move fast enough.

Iris picked up the dagger and used her momentum to flip, kicking her legs toward Rune and knocking the gun out of his hands. She wouldn't let him get a breath in, not this time. Before he could recover and regain his footing, she landed on her feet, dagger in hand.

Rune looked down just as the blade dug into his flesh. Iris hit her mark, sliding the blade in between his ribs, right in his heart, stopping it cold. She pushed his body to the ground and yanked the knife out. Needing to make sure he was truly dead, she straddled him and plunged the blade into his heart once more, twisting for good measure.

Despite having his lifeless body underneath her, she did not feel like she thought she would. He'd brought her years of endless torture, the endless shadow that followed her. And now, he had taken someone she had grown to care for like a father. Yet, she felt no relief at his death. When he took his last breath, no wave of ease washed over her, taking all he had done to her with it. Iris still felt bound by invisible shackles. She looked back down at his unmoving form. His eyes stared vacantly at the sky, their colors strikingly similar.

Did she even have a soul?

She felt nothing at his death. Anger only brought more questions, which, in turn, brought more anger. Not wanting to look at Rune any longer, Iris turned to Micah, who had saved her life. He twitched, barely noticeable, and she immediately rushed to his side.

He was barely conscious. She took his hand and leaned down to hear him speak. "Iris. Don't… Let this weigh on you…" He coughed roughly.

"Shh. Don't talk," she said, swallowing a painful lump in her throat.

"My death… I am ready. I am glad. I will watch over you. Do me proud. Let go of the past now. Live for the future." Micah smiled up at her, making sure she was listening. Reaching up, he brushed a stray tear from Iris' cheek. "You deserve happiness now. Remember, I'll be watching."

His hand fell from her cheek, hitting the ground with a slight thud. All Iris wanted to do was lean over Micah's body and cry, not caring who came to kill her, but his death would be meaningless. After closing his eyes, she stood, her legs threatening to give way as she did.

All that had happened within the last few moments alone, not even the last few days, had made her mind and body weak. Iris highly doubted that she could take more than one man just then, but she caught sight of the two men who meant the most to her, and adrenaline surged through her body, rekindling her sense of purpose.

Chapter 29

Somehow when Cole and Garrett got to Rune's plantation, they were surrounded on both sides. One side with assassins on top of a hill, the other side with Rune's men who seemed to be far back near a line of large trees. Too far for Garrett and Cole to reach without being shot in the process. To the right and left of them were lines of small trees but not enough for cover. A barn in one direction, another building in the other. Too far to make a run for it. But thankfully, neither side seemed to care too much about the two of them stuck in the middle of it all. So, they ducked behind barriers Rune's men had made.

"How did we end up on this side of things?" Cole asked, almost shouting to be heard over the barrage of gunfire. They were outnumbered and outgunned. Before they went into the thick of things, Micah had gone off in another direction in search of Iris. He had said Alvera had told him to go a certain way, and Garrett didn't like where it was going to lead him.

"How are we supposed to get out of this now?" He looked at Cole to see an equally anxious expression on his face. Thankfully, Rune's men had been taken care of or had retreated, but they had been holding off about a dozen assassins for a while and were now out of ammo.

"I guess we could throw our shoes at them." Cole smirked at his own wit.

"I hope you never lose that humor, brother." Garrett patted Cole's shoulder, giving him a warm smile. "I'll make sure you make it back to my sister. No matter what." Garrett was trying to reassure himself as well as Cole and hoped his anxiety wasn't showing on his face as bullets flew around them once more. Bullets pierced the stone and crate barrier, creating holes. There were other barricades like it a few yards behind them, but if they were to move out from the shadow of this one, they would be shot. The assassins knew they had the advantage on top of the hill.

"We're both going to get out of this! Lay down flat!" Cole yelled over the barrage of gunfire.

The barrier had started to weaken and in a split second, Garrett felt a sharp pain in his hip. Cole reached out, putting his hand over Garrett's wound.

"Don't worry about me. It's just a graze."

"Shit!" Cole yelled, dropping to his stomach. "Why haven't they moved closer to us?"

"Maybe they see something we don't?" Garrett yelled back, putting pressure on his bleeding wound.

Shots came from their side, bullets now flying in all directions. But he couldn't see where it came from. After a few moments, the firing on their side stopped. In an instant, the ground shook, and dirt filled the air around them. To the right, what looked to be a line of explosions ignited one right after the other, all around them, following the line of small trees on either side.

Cole peeked over the small barricade. "That's why they weren't moving!" Garrett sat up and glanced over to see for himself. "Rune must have set traps! But who set them off and why weren't they used before?"

The hill where the assassins once stood was gone. Completely flattened. *That's why the ground shook.*

"Because very few people knew how to trigger them," a voice behind them said. "It was set up like a puzzle, so the enemy couldn't use it against him."

They turned simultaneously. Iris stood before them, covered in blood. Garrett tried to stand on his own, but Cole was soon by his side, helping him to his feet.

His heart sank at the sight of Iris. "Are you hurt?" The doctor in him could tell she was weak and tired, drained. Something had happened, not just the potion Rune had given her. Something much worse. He wouldn't push it, though. He would wait until Iris was willing to let her walls down. *She's gone through a lot. I will be here for her, always.*

"I'm fine, but you're not. Come, let us get you in the house. Rune's men have fled, and the assassin's last stronghold is gone. But once you are patched up, we should leave." They followed her into the parlor where Cole helped Garrett onto the sofa.

Iris was all business and had a stern look on her face as she asked Cole to help her with something around back. But before she could leave Garrett reached for her, lightly touching her bruised wrist.

"I'm here, Iris. I'm not going anywhere. No matter what." He let her go as she nodded, not looking at him. And he knew Micah was dead.

When Cole was tying up the horses, Micah had taken Garrett aside. "You know Alvera is a seer. Right?"

"Yes, but…"

"No, listen. I've been working with Alvera trying to bring down the agency Iris and Cole worked for. It's a long story… She found out I knew some bigwigs in the government and came to me with information to show the marshals. Proof that the captain was working with Rune. Alvera needed help to bring it down but couldn't go to the government without putting herself at risk of being exposed."

"And didn't tell any of us this, or Iris? She let Iris go back to Rune, to be tortured..."

Micah cut him off. "That's all for another time, another story, doc. You know how I feel about Iris. Seeing her hurt, hurts me like nothing else." His hands balled into fists. "But I also knew Iris had to face her own demons her way. Now. Back to Alvera being a seer. I believe in her ability. You have experienced it firsthand now." Sighing, taking Garrett's shoulders, he looked at him lovingly, like a father would. "She saw my death, son. No, listen. I've accepted it long ago. What more can I ask for than saving her life?"

Micah had gotten his wish. He had saved the daughter he had always wished for.

As they reached Micah, Cole sank to the ground, hugging him and sobbing. Iris knelt next to him and wrapped her arms around Cole, grieving with him.

"He saved my life..." Iris whispered, regret filling her very being.

Cole sniffed. "I'll see to him. You go help Garrett."

She squeezed him once more and then went back inside. Iris gathered suture tools she knew Rune had stored. She then gathered some clean cloth and water.

How was she going to face Garrett? Micah had died because of her. Walking back into the sitting area where the doctor lay outstretched on the sofa, so many emotions filled her, the guilt she felt over Micah's death at the forefront. Would he blame her or, worse, hate her?

Iris knelt next to him and cut away the fabric around his wound. After, she handed Garrett a bottle of whiskey she thought to bring from the kitchen. Once he took a few swallows, she motioned for him to give it back. She cleaned the area, making Garrett groan in pain. She hated seeing him in pain. This was the first time she had to stitch him up. Even though she loved touching him, she didn't like this. Iris felt his gaze on her as she stitched up the wound. He simply watched her, not once looking away from her, almost as if he were afraid she would disappear if he did.

"Why are you so quiet? What's happened?"

"What can I say, Garrett? All of this is my fault. If I hadn't pulled you and everyone else into this blasted game Rune had set up, none of this would have happened. You would have all be safe..." Hot tears trickled down her cheeks, and she let them, not wiping them away. "How can I ever forgive myself for all that has happened?" She remembered what he had said in their last dream. *We look out for each other. That's what families do, no matter what. We're a family, Iris. No matter where you go, I will follow. It will always be you.* But what had just occurred had pushed all that away.

Despite his injury, he swung his legs around and grabbed Iris by the shoulder. "We helped you because we love you, because we want you to live a happy life."

"I would have been happy if none of you got hurt or…" She didn't dare look at him. All she felt was guilt. He was shot, and Micah… Micah was dead…

Garrett sighed. "Micah knew the risks coming into this. He loved you like a daughter, Iris. He wouldn't have changed the outcome. He wouldn't have traded your life for his."

"And that makes it so much worse… How did you know?" Iris couldn't stop the tears or the ache deep in her heart, making her very soul seethe with pain.

He knelt in front of her, bringing her in for a tight hug.

Sighing, Garrett said softly, "We have to live on, for those we've lost. Live the life they would have wanted for us. If we don't, their sacrifice would have been for nothing. Remember what I said in the last dream? The one where all your past demons were attacking you?" She nodded. "We're family. Family looks out for one another. Micah looked out for you and considered you family. The last thing he would want is for you to carry the guilt of his death for the rest of your life. What he would want is for you to carry his memory. The happy times we all shared. Can you do that?"

Iris was at a loss for words. "I..." Her heart too heavy with guilt. Outside, horses and a cart pulled up out front. Iris heard the sound of their hooves and the quiet crunch of rocks and twigs.

"That must be Cole. I need to help him with something out back. I'll be back. Stay here and rest."

She stood and started to leave the room but he followed, grabbing her wrist and twisting her toward him. Garrett hugged her tightly once more. "You're not in this alone, Iris. Let me help. What is it that you need?"

"I need to bury Rune. Despite who he is, I can't just leave him there for the dogs. I'll go get shovels and then we can dig the bastard a hole." She said the last part through clenched teeth, still unable to let go of the anger she held.

Cole had wrapped Micah in a sheet and had laid him out on the cart to be taken back to his hometown of Valden where Isabelle waited for them all to return. Afterward, he helped carry Rune to a spot near a tree. Garrett followed, trying not to limp, and used the shovels as a makeshift cane.

Iris and Cole got to work digging, wanting to leave this place before sundown. Once Rune was put in the ground, the three of them stood there, staring at the mound of dirt. The anger that still raged inside her made her want to dig the body back up just to stab it more. Iris worried she would never feel at ease. Rune's death brought nothing she had longed for all the years he had haunted her. *Am I always going to feel this anger and guilt?* Staring at the mound brought no solace. The knowledge that she would no longer be tortured by those madman's hands didn't ease the pain in her heart. How could Iris ever feel at peace when a good person was gone from this world?

Chapter 30

When they arrived in Valden, Garrett went into town to tell the townspeople of Micah's death and to make preparations for his funeral.

Iris watched as Cole hugged Isabelle tightly. "I love you, Isabelle. I'm never leaving your side again." She wrapped her around his neck.

Catching Iris' eye, Isabelle rushed over to her, hugging her tightly. Seeing the tears of this sweet fairy girl caused her own to flow down her cheeks.

Iris bathed, dressed, and cleaned what guns she could find. She thought about recent events, the agency, the assassins. Her loved ones would not be safe until she was away from them completely. The marshals would now be after her. After all, she was truly an outlaw now.

The agency had been working with Rune all along, her torturer. She couldn't believe it. Had she been doing his bidding all along, or Rune the agency? Iris hated not knowing.

Several men in suits showed up as she was about to mount her horse. She placed her hand on her pistol, ready for a quick draw. Judging from how they were dressed, they were marshals. They had come for her already. All she could do was hope they didn't bring Garrett, Cole, or Isabelle into it. But then she a sickening feeling. *Did they get to Garrett already?* Holding her hands at the ready, she watched them dismount and walk toward her.

"We mean no harm," the oldest of the three said preemptively. "Are you Iris Evergreen?"

She studied each man in turn. "Yes," she said shortly, not in the mood. "Who are you?" Iris asked, despite knowing, trying to throw them off guard.

He pulled out his badge and gave it to her. "We are government marshals."

It looked legitimate, so had they come for her? "How can I help you, gentlemen?" she asked cautiously.

"The agency you worked for has been dissolved, which means you no longer work for the government. We suggest you cease all activity associated with them."

The agency had been dissolved...? Surprise washed over her. Whatever she was expecting, that wasn't it. "I assure you, our ties have already been severed." She thought they would think she was tied up with Rune somehow.

The man gave her a tentative smile. "Good. Your boss was found guilty of treason. He used his power to kill whomever he wanted, along with many other accusations. When he found out we were coming for him, he set up a plan to kill anyone and everyone we may use against him. That list included yourself. As we were trying to detain him, the building he was in exploded. We have yet to find his body."

The news rocked her. As much as she detested the man now, he had been a big part of her life for a long time. "The captain is dead?"

"Yes."

She considered that. "So, what happens now? Are you going to try to bring me in?" Try, of course, was the keyword. They were welcome to try all they wanted. Iris would never let them.

The man cleared his throat. "We have gone over your file and would like to offer you a pardon. Despite your connection to the agency, it seems you had no hand in what was happening behind the scenes. We suggest you find a more stable job. As we were coming through town, we heard they're in need of a sheriff. If I may be so bold, I think you would be a good fit. I would also suggest never speaking of this to anyone. Leave the past in the past, Miss Evergreen." The three of them walked toward their horses. "I think Micah would have wanted that." He tilted his hat toward her and then mounted his horses.

Before she could even ask a question, they were headed back toward town. Iris stood there in a daze, not sure what had just happened or what it all meant.

Cole came out of the house moments later and handed her a letter. "Micah left this for you…"

Swallowing, she accepted the letter and opened it with shaking hands.

Dear Iris,

If you are reading this, that means I was not able to tell you everything in person. Know that I don't leave this world with a heavy heart because I know you are in it. The town and its people that I leave behind will need someone to protect them, and I don't know a better person than you to take my place. This is my wish for you. To live with your newfound family, to have a home and to no longer roam as you have done.

Know that I will always be by your side watching you. So, make me proud, and don't go off and get hurt. The good doctor has patched you up one too many times. I don't think his heart can take much more. I have left you all of my worldly possessions. All of you had become my family.

Please know that I loved you all, but do not mourn me. I have gone to a better place, I believe that. I had been doing my own research while you were away and have set things in motion, which I hope will help you in your endeavors. It's too long of a story to write in this letter, but one day, everything will become known to you. Don't go hunting for trouble, Iris, but always be on your guard. Let others into your world. Don't wait till you're old and gray like I was.

I have included my will and testament. I have also enclosed some documents that will help explain what might have already occurred. Do not mourn me, but always remember me.

Sending you all my love,

Micah.

Tears rolled down Iris' face as she read the will and looked through the documents. It seemed Micah owned a house on the outskirts of town that he had never used, as well as several buildings in the town that were rented out by shopkeepers. A large amount of money was held in the bank. The documents detailed information about the agency and how her boss had used his power to overstep many laws. Apparently, Micah's evidence had caused the other heads of government to step in. There would be no record of the agency. Probably one reason they had never given it a name. That way, it would be harder to trace. They also had ties with Rune, who was the captain's son and Alvera's brother. She kept close to the captain and had given Micah these documents. It didn't say where she or Abelia were, but Iris had a feeling there was more to their story.

Her body was still weak, and her mind was still trying to comprehend everything that had happened the last few days, but Iris wouldn't let herself rest and set off into the house to tell Cole and Isabelle about the letter and the papers Micah had left behind.

"I can't believe Micah was doing all that. He was trying to set you free his own way, Iris." Isabelle's words washed over her like a cooling wave. It was true. He was trying to set her free. Micah had found out the captain was corrupt and could use it to take down Rune in a way.

"He had been looking out for you, Iris. For all of us..." Cole wanted to say more but choked on the words.

"He really was a noble man," Iris said, almost in a whisper. Isabelle hugged Cole, who was almost crying as much as she was. The two of them warmed her heart, as much as it could be warmed at the moment. The three of them continued to talk over the realization and the loss of such a great man.

Now that Iris was able to sit and run through things in her mind, her heart ached for Garrett, what he must have gone through while she was away, how he was dealing with his own loss. Iris left Cole and Isabelle to talk and walked to the pool of water down in the woods near the house. She and Garrett had been there several times. It was surrounded by large trees that provided shade in the mid-summer heat.

She pulled off her shoes and plunged her feet into the cool water. So much had happened since she had first come to this sleepy town. Her life had changed in so many ways. Would she really be able to settle down now? Iris had come to town on a hunt but had found something she wasn't looking for in the least. Love and family. During her absence from them, she had turned into what she hated, a monster. And that monster had brought those she loved into the darkness with her. Garrett had gotten hurt, and Micah...

But you are free from the shadows. You are in the light and the darkness can no longer follow, a small voice said, bringing tears to her eyes and a smile to her face.

"Micah," she whispered and sat, taking in the calm day as afternoon gave way to evening.

The sun had begun to set when leaves rustled behind her. Turning around, she saw the tall form of Garrett staring down at her. Just as her eyes locked with his golden ones, her body felt as if it had burst into flames. Her heart longed to touch him, to feel him against her.

Before she could pull herself to her feet, Garrett was behind her, lifting her up into his arms. They held each other for several long moments, taking in the warmth of one another. The two of them had barely spoken since their reuniting. So much to say and so few words to do so.

"How do I move on from all of this?" Iris asked quietly, the tension in her body slowly easing by his mere presence.

"By putting one foot in front of the other. By taking each day as a new beginning." He hugged her tighter, breathing her in.

He pulled away, only to capture her mouth with his. She groaned at the feelings of his lips on hers. She had wondered if she'd ever kiss him again. It seemed he had been wondering the same thing. He kissed her with a passion she'd never seen in him before, stealing her breath. In the next instant, they were pawing at each other's clothes, desperate to feel skin against skin. She needed his flesh against her own, to feel as close to him as she possibly could.

Garrett pulled down her dress, revealing her body to him. For a split second, she was worried about how she looked and what he'd think. She'd gained a few more scars since last time as well as lost a significant amount of weight. She wasn't as curvy as before, with her ribs now noticeable. And then Garrett met her eyes, and she saw nothing but desire. Just like that, all her worry vanished.

Garrett pulled her flush against him, cupping her ass in his large hand. Iris moaned, feeling the evidence of his desire against her pelvis. Breath hitching in her throat, she took him between her legs, teasing them both, loving the feeling of his warmth between her thighs.

He gasped. "I love you, Iris. We will never part, not after today. You are mine and only mine, forever." Leaning down, he kissed her neck and shoulders.

"I am only yours, Garrett. Mind, body and soul."

Kissing her, Garrett laid her on the soft ground at the edge of the water.

"I've missed you." His breath tickled her ear as he leaned over her. He then leaned up, his fingers at play with her.

She gasped, her need too great. Eyeing him, she smiled. She ran her hand down his bronze skin, down to his erection, lightly touching it. He shivered, making her smile in delight.

Leaning up on one elbow, she guided him toward her. "I need you. I have to have you, now." She drew out the last word, eyeing him.

Garrett smiled and placed his legs between her. She bit her lip in anticipation. Rising above her, he watched her face as he entered. The wave of pleasure that rushed over her was incredible. Iris bit her lip to hold in a scream of pleasure threatened to erupt from her.

Garrett leaned further down, tightening his hold on her. "Don't hold it in. No one is here but us. Let me hear you."

Wrapping her legs around him, she did scream, and it only made his thrust more intensive. She had never felt him so hard or so warm inside her. Waves of pleasure crashed into her one after the other. Iris knew she would never get enough of him, of what he did to her, mind, body and soul.

The fire for one another felt as if it would burn for a lifetime. Coming together, their moans and gasps intensified as their movements became ever rapid. It felt like their first time, not able to get enough of the other, always wanting more.

Iris watched the moon rise above them, her body intertwined with Garrett's. The tension, the grief and hate she had felt slowly melted away. She had found a home, a safe place within his arms. The shadows that had chased her no longer came, but the scars remained. With the help of her family, every day would bring a new dawn.

Several weeks passed, and along with them Micah's funeral, and preparations for Isabelle's and Cole's wedding. Iris had taken Isabelle to a boutique in the Smithington while Cole went with Garrett to finish up some business he had there with his father's estate. It would be quite a while until he let Iris out of his sight for more than a few hours. So, he entrusted her to Isabelle while they shopped for her wedding dress.

When they entered the shop, the seamstress greeted them cheerfully. "Welcome! How can I help you on this fine day... Oh my... It's you..." The lady's loose curls seemed to tighten just at the sight of Iris, her cheerfulness gone out the window.

Isabelle looked at the dressmaker then at Iris who seemed quite interested in lace doilies. Iris hated doilies and lace even more. A clear sign something was amiss. Stepping forward to soothe the lady, she gave her the sweetest smile while Iris still feigned fascination with the doilies.

"Ma'am." The lady harrumphed and turned her back to them, irritating Isabelle.

"Isabelle, perhaps we should spend our money elsewhere?" Iris watched the seamstress. "A wedding dress is something important and shouldn't be taken lightly."

The lady turned right back around, taking Isabelle's hands. "Well! Congratulations are in order! When's the big day? Tell me all about it!"

Isabelle looked to Iris who just shook her head. She then turned back to the dressmaker. "In about a month..."

The lady cut her off before she could tell her more about the wedding. "What kind of dress do you have in mind, my dear?"

"I'm looking for a light pink..." Again, she was cut off.

"I hope it's not something ghastly like she wears. A woman shouldn't wear such things. A horrid girl..." The lady turned her nose up at Iris who only shook her head again. Isabelle knew Iris had gotten this all her life, but she had enough of this rude seamstress. Cutting her off twice and now being rude to Iris. That was something Isabelle would not stand for. Iris had been through enough and didn't need the likes of her to put her down even more.

"Now, you listen here. I've had enough of your deplorable rudeness. We only came to give you some business, which I see you are in no need of. Because if you were, you would not talk to a customer in such a way. I try to be nice, especially to shopkeepers. Having to deal with so many people throughout the day must be difficult, but I will not have my friend spoken about in such a way. You don't even know her, yet you speak as if you do. I beg you to think before you speak. My father was judge Clarkson and I will make sure his lady friends know of this..."

She hated her father, but at least he came to good use, even if it was after death. She stared down the dressmaker, daring her to kick her out of the store before she stormed out on her own.

But before she knew it, Isabelle was getting fitted for her dress, and the lady had changed completely, saying that the dress would be free. The judge had been a good customer of hers and so on. Another thing her father had come to use for.

When Iris and herself walked down the street, she interlocked arms. "You know, Iris, I love how you dress. It's bold, and beautiful. Quite like you. And that is why I ordered five new dresses for you from that mean ol' lady. All free because my father was such a loyal customer and all." Isabelle laughed. "That poor seamstress. I'll make sure to send her a nice thank-you basket after the wedding to ease some of her suffering." She poked Iris' nose. "Some."

Both girls laughed as they continued walking down the cobblestone streets to meet both of their betrothed.

The wedding was held in front of Micah's log cabin. Some flowers still had a few buds left over from summer despite autumn now starting to set in.

The bride was a sight to behold in a light pink lace gown that hugged in the middle, lifted at the top, then flowed like a waterfall toward her feet. It ebbed and flowed in all the right places. The groom was just as handsome in a dark blue suit that fit to a tee, showing off his broad shoulders. After the ceremony, the reception was held in the saloon, which had been decorated with countless flowers.

As everyone gave their speeches, Iris went over to give the couple their gift. It was train tickets and hotel reservations to a cape town called Riverdan, where the ocean water was as clear as the pond near their house. Garrett gifted the house him and his sister had shared for so long, knowing his sister wanted a big family. It would suit them more than it would him. Garrett and Iris would live in Micah's log cabin, about half the size of Garrett's old place. It would fit them well, being closer to town. After all, the good doctor and the new sheriff would need to be on beck and call.

Time continued to pass in the small town. Day turned into night and winter turned into spring. Many changes accrued over the years. Cole and Isabelle's family grew. First with a daughter who was as mischievous as her father, then a son who was energetic as his mother. And years later, twin girls who both ended up with red hair like Isabelle's mother and after another boy who became the bookworm of their family. Their house was full of life and neither of them would have it any other way.

Iris took a great deal of the money that had been left to her by Micah to build onto the town to help bring in new revenue and business. When the railroad grew near, they helped build better roads, a standalone school and a church that wasn't falling down, and two restaurants that could fit more than twenty people at a time.

Even though Garrett proposed in more or less a dream state, he took Iris to meet his mother's tribe. They stood in a clearing with the full moon above and snow-peaked mountains off in the distances. Garrett asked again to take her last name of Evergreen, thinking it suited their new start nicely.

After several years of marriage, they ended up having three children of their own. One girl and two boys. Garrett continued with his practice, and Iris took up the role of sheriff. Both rarely spoke of their past but told many stories filled about Micah, keeping his memory alive in the next generation. They even built a park in his name and named their youngest after him. He acted much like they thought Micah would at a young age, jumping in to help whenever someone needed it, even before they asked. He hated injustice and bullying of any kind. Sheriff Micah would be proud of his namesake.

Their connection through dreams stopped after Rune's death, but they told their children stories of how people with a deep connection could visit each other's dreams and of the dream-walker and seer who helped save her life with the help of the light and love of her life. And about the one who had guided Iris' out of the darkness, the one who shined so intensely no shadows had come near her since. And when she needed him to be at his brightest, he was there. Never to leave her side hereafter.

Thank you for reading.

For those who suffer from depression, it can feel like a shadow, never leaving your side. A torturer that lives within your own body that you can't escape from.

Know that you are not alone, that you are strong and there is help out there. Keep fighting towards the light, no matter how dark it may get. Because, one day, the storm clouds will clear, and a new day will dawn.

To those who may know someone that suffers from the pain of depression. Know that it's not something easily dealt with. It takes time, days, even years, for some, like Iris a life time. Many suffer in silence. Be there for that person. Be the light in their darkness, help them see the sun, the moon and stars. Because they are worth the fight.

Let us all speak and hear, to heal.

S. L. Vaden

www.ingramcontent.com/pod-product-compliance
Lightning Source LLC
Chambersburg PA
CBHW051509250626
47156CB00001B/19